YOU[...]
TO A PA[...]
HOLIDAY SEASON!

If you want to get away from it all this Christmas,
escape to these three exotic destinations!
Here you'll discover the steamy heat of

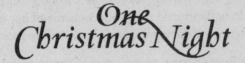

Christmas Night

ABOUT THE AUTHORS

Michelle Reid grew up on the southern edges of Manchester, the youngest in a family of five lively children. But now she lives in the beautiful county of Cheshire with her busy executive husband and two grown-up daughters. She loves reading, the ballet and playing tennis when she gets the chance. She hates cooking and cleaning, and despises ironing! Sleep she can do without, and she produces some of her best written work during the early hours of the morning.

Jane Porter grew up on a diet of romance books, reading late night under the covers so her mother wouldn't see! She wrote her first book at age eight and spent many of her high school and college years living abroad, immersing herself in other cultures and continuing to read voraciously. Now Jane has settled down in Seattle, Washington with her two sons.

When **Susan Stephens** graduated from the Royal College of Music, she enjoyed a wonderful and varied career as a professional singer. Through this she met her husband. They now have three children and live in a beautiful old converted cottage in the Cheshire countryside. A turn of fate at a charity auction allowed Susan to spend a day with one of her favorite authors, Penny Jordan. It was Penny who encouraged her to write romance.

One Christmas Night

Michelle Reid ❆ Jane Porter
Susan Stephens

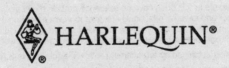

HARLEQUIN®

TORONTO • NEW YORK • LONDON
AMSTERDAM • PARIS • SYDNEY • HAMBURG
STOCKHOLM • ATHENS • TOKYO • MILAN • MADRID
PRAGUE • WARSAW • BUDAPEST • AUCKLAND

ISBN-13: 978-0-373-83738-0
ISBN-10:   0-373-83738-0

ONE CHRISTMAS NIGHT

Copyright © 2004 by Harlequin Books S.A.

The publisher acknowledges the copyright holders of the individual works as follows:

A SICILIAN MARRIAGE
Copyright © 2004 by Michelle Reid

THE ITALIAN'S BLACKMAILED BRIDE
Copyright © 2004 by Jane Porter

THE SULTAN'S SEDUCTION
Copyright © 2004 by Susan Stephens

www.eHarlequin.com

Printed in U.S.A.

CONTENTS

A SICILIAN MARRIAGE

Michelle Reid

CHAPTER ONE

NINA did not want to listen to this. In fact she was so sure she didn't that if she hadn't been sitting in her own home she would have seriously contemplated getting up from the lunch table and walking out.

As it was, all she could do was stare glassy-eyed at her mother and silently wish her a million miles away.

'Don't look at me like that,' Louisa said impatiently. 'You may like to think that the state of your marriage is none of my business, but when it is I who has to listen to ugly speculation and gossip about it then it becomes my business!'

'Does it?' Her daughter's cool tone said otherwise. 'I don't recall ever questioning you about the many reports on your various lovers throughout the years.'

Her mother's narrow shoulders tensed inside the fitted white jacket she was wearing, which did so much for her fabulous dark looks. At fifty-one years old, Louisa St James could still pass for thirty. Born in Sicily, the youngest of five Guardino children, Louisa had taken the lion's share in the beauty stakes, along with her twin sister Lucia. As small girls they'd wowed everyone with their black-haired, black-eyed enchantment, and when they'd grown into stunning young women besotted young men had beaten paths to the Guardino door. Now in her middle years, and with her twin sadly gone, Louisa could still grab male attention like a magnet. But a lifetime spent being admired had made Louisa so very conceited that Nina could sometimes see by her expression that she was bewildered as to how her womb had dared to produce a child that bore no resemblance to her at all.

Nina was tall and fair, and quiet and introverted. She looked out on the world through her English father's cool blue eyes, and when trouble loomed she locked herself away behind a wall of ice where no one could reach her. In her mother's Sicilian eyes the burning fires of all the passions were alien to her daughter, and she tended to treat Nina as if she did not know what they were.

'Your father made me a widow ten years ago, which means I am allowed to take as many lovers as I choose without raising eyebrows,' Louisa defended, completely ignoring the way she'd been taking lovers for most of Nina's life. 'Whereas your marriage is barely out of the honeymoon stage and already gossip about it is hot!'

Hot? Nina almost choked on the word, because the last thing she would have called her marriage was— *hot*. Cold, more like. A soulless waste of space. A mistake so huge it should be logged as an official disaster!

'If it's just gossip you're concerned about then you're talking to the wrong person,' she responded. 'Rafael is your culprit—go and talk to him.'

With that she got up, not quite finding the courage to walk out of the room but doing the next best thing by going to stand in front of the closed glass doors that led out onto the terrace.

Behind her the thin silence feathered her slender backbone. Her cold indifference to whatever her husband was doing had managed to shock her mother into stillness—for a moment or two.

'You are a fool, Nina,' she then announced bluntly.

Oh, yes, Nina agreed, and she stared out towards the glistening blue waters of the Mediterranean and wished she was on the little sailboat she could see gliding across the calm crystal sea.

'Because it is not only gossip. I saw them together for myself, *cara* and even a blind woman could not mistake the chemistry they were generating it was so—'

Hot, Nina supplied the word because it seemed much more suitable now than it had earlier.

Her mother used a sigh. 'You should keep him on a much tighter leash,' she went on. 'The man is just too gorgeous and sexy to be left to his own devices— and you know what he's like! Women fall over themselves to get closer to him, and he doesn't bother to push them away. He could charm a nun out of her chastity if he put his mind to it, yet how often are you seen at his side? Instead of isolating yourself up here on your hilltop you should be out there with him, making your presence felt—then *she* would not be trying to get her claws back into him and *I* would not be sitting here having to tell you things that no mother wants to—'

'Where?' Nina inserted.

'Hmm?'

Turning around, Nina was in time to watch her mother blink her lovely long black eyelashes, having lost the main plot of her exposé because she'd been so much more comfortable lecturing her daughter on things she knew very little about.

'Where did you see them?' She extended her question.

'Oh.' Understanding returned, sending those slender shoulders into an unhappy shrug. 'In London, of course...'

Of course, Nina echoed—London being the place Rafael spent most of his time these days, which was pretty ironic when she was the Londoner and he was the Sicilian.

'I was eating out with friends when I spotted them across the restaurant. Someone's mobile was ringing. When it just kept on, I looked up, and that is when I saw them. I was so shocked at first I just stared! I watched him pick his ringing cellphone up off the table, and without taking his eyes off her face he switched it off and put it in his pocket!' Louisa took a tight breath. 'I had this horrible feeling that it was you calling him, so to watch him do that made me—'

'It wasn't me,' Nina said, though she had a good idea who the caller had been.

'I am so relieved to hear you say that. I cannot tell you how it felt to think that you might need him and he—'

'Did they see you?' she cut in.

Her mother's smile was dry, to say the least. 'Darling, they were being so intense across that candlelit table for two that they didn't see anyone,' she said. 'I thought about going over there to confront them—but, well… It was just a bit embarrassing to witness my son-in-law getting it on with my niece in public.'

'So you left them to it?'

'It could have been innocent.'

But it wasn't, Nina thought—and how did she know that? Because this particular woman was more than *just* her mother's niece.

'And that is not all of it,' Louisa pushed on. 'I saw them again later on, going—going into your apartment building.'

'How unfortunate for them,' Nina drawled. 'Did you follow them there, by any chance?'

Dark eyes gave a flash of defiance. 'Yes, if you must know. I did not like what I was seeing, so I thought I would keep an eye on them! *She* should not even be in London,' she tagged on stiffly. 'New York is her hunting ground, and it would have been better for all of us if she'd just stayed there.'

'So you spied on them going into our apartment building…?' Nina prompted.

Louisa looked pained suddenly. 'I could see them through the glass doors, Nina! They were standing there, waiting for the lift to come. He—he was touching her face while she gazed up at him. It was all so…'

Oh, my… Nina thought, and had to turn away again so that her mother wouldn't see what was happening to her face.

Another thick silence crawled around them while her mother brooded over what she'd said and Nina stared at the view. The little sailboat had gone, she saw, disappearing round the headland to her right, where the ancient city of Syracuse clustered around the tiny island of Ortigia.

When her gaze drifted to the left she could just make out Mount Etna in the distance, shrouded in one of her hazy mists. The volcano had been very active lately, spewing out the most spectacular paratactic displays throughout the long hot summer. Now winter was here, and although the days were quite warm for December, the gentle plume of smoke she could see rising from Etna's peak said the volcano had cooled her ardour to suit the cooler temperature—for now, at least.

'How does she look?' she asked after a minute.

'The same,' came the flat reply. 'As beautiful as ever, if not—' *More so*, was the observation left hanging in the air. 'She reminded me of her mother,' Louisa added huskily.

Nina smiled a bleak little smile. The beautiful dark-haired Lucia had produced a beautiful dark-haired daughter and oh, how Louisa had always envied her twin for doing that.

'What are you going to do?' her mother asked after another of those heavy silences.

Do—? Nina turned to face the room again, wearing a smile that was so paper-dry it actually hurt her lips as they stretched. 'Rafael paid a high price for my loyalty and he'll have it, whatever *he* decides to do. I've already told you that you're talking to the wrong person about this.'

'Oh Nina…' The pained sigh matched her mother's expression as she watched Nina cross back to the table. 'How did you and Rafael ever get yourselves into this state?'

'Money, darling,' Nina drawled in her very best boarding school English as she sat down again. 'Our appalling lack of it and his abominable excess.'

'Rubbish,' Louisa dismissed. 'You adored each other. Rafael was besotted with you from the first moment he looked at you, and you were so in love with him that even that—that prissy manner your father insisted on breeding into you used to melt for him.'

A game, Nina cynically named that little deception. It had all been just a very clever game they'd played out for the sake of anyone who happened to be interested. Rafael had set the rules by which their marriage would run and Nina had agreed to keep to them—for a price. They were to show a loving front to the world, and in return he would keep the great Guardino name clear of bankruptcy.

Some price for him to pay for what had only been a face-saving exercise, Nina conceded, recalling just how much it had cost him to bail her grandfather out. But then saving face had always been of paramount importance to Rafael. The monumental size of his pride demanded it.

That and some deeply hidden hang-ups he never spoke about but which ruled his life far more than he realised.

'It was the sole reason why she went away in the first place,' Louisa insisted. 'Once she realised what was happening between the two of you she really had no other option but to step back and leave the field clear.'

And there, Nina thought, was *the* deception. 'Yes,' she agreed.

Rafael had been hovering on the brink of asking her beautiful cousin to marry him when Marisia had discovered something about him she couldn't accept and walked out. She'd walked out on his love, his fabulous wealth and, most important of all, she'd walked all over his precious pride as she went.

'You used to be so happy together.'

'Delirious.'

'Rafael used to eat you with his eyes and he did not care who saw him doing it.'

Nina found a wry smile for that observation—wry because in an odd way her mother was right. Rafael *had* eaten her with his eyes.

With his eyes, his lips, his tongue, his…

But that had only been for the first few wild months of their marriage, when they'd set out to fool the world and had done it so successfully that they'd actually managed to fool themselves at the same time.

And the special ingredient to aid and abet this deception?

Sex. She named it grimly. They'd been so bowled over by the discovery of a wildly passionate and very mutual sexual attraction to each other that it had shocked them stupid for a time. Blinded them to the reality of what they really felt for each other.

Blinded her anyway, Nina amended as something worryingly close to despair began to swell up inside her. Blinded her enough to let her believe that they were actually in love.

Love. She could scoff at the very word now. As far

as Rafael was concerned he had simply played the game, as any man would play the game, and taken what was on offer because it had been there to take, whereas she…

Well, blinded as she had been, she had committed the ultimate sin in his eyes, by taking their relationship one step further—unwittingly crossing into forbidden territory—and in doing so had forced Rafael to open her eyes to the size of her mistake.

Since then—nothing.

Nothing, she repeated, feeling the desolation of that nothing echoing in the deep, dark void of her now empty heart.

Louisa must have seen it, because she reached across the table to cover one of Nina's hands. 'I know you have been through a bad time recently, darling,' she murmured very gently. 'God knows, we all suffered the loss with you, believe me…'

Nina stared at their two hands, resting against pristine white linen, and wished her mother would just shut up.

'Your grandfather still blames himself.'

'It was no one's fault.' Her reply was quiet and stilted, her thoughts even more so—cold and bleak.

'Have you told him that?'

'Of course I have. Countless times.'

'Have you told Rafael the same thing…?'

Suddenly she wanted to run from the room again. 'What is this?' She sighed. 'An inquisition?'

'He worries me—*you* worry me— No, don't get angry…' Louisa begged as Nina reclaimed her hand and shot back to her feet. Louisa stood too, her tone suddenly anxious. 'It's been six months since you lost the baby…'

Six months, two weeks and eight hours, to be precise, Nina thought.

'Before that the two of you were never seen apart and now you are never seen together! You just shut everyone out, Nina—Rafael more than anyone! And—OK,' Louisa said, 'I understand that you needed time to recover, but after what I've just told you, surely you must see that it is time for you to put that tragic loss aside if you don't want your marriage to end in tragedy too!'

For an answer Nina spun on her heels and walked away, hating everything—everyone—and despising herself. She didn't want to think about her poor lost baby; she didn't want to think about Rafael!

Her heart ached, her bones ached. She caught a glimpse of herself reflected in the mirror hanging on the wall and was shocked into stillness by what she saw. Her skin was pale by nature, but it had now taken on the consistency of paste. Her eyes looked bruised, her mouth small and tight. Tension was gnawing at the fine layer of flesh covering her cheekbones, making her look gaunt and wretched—and she was not going to cry! she told herself furiously. She just was not going—

'He is not a man to neglect like this, *cara*,' her mother persisted. '*She* wants him back. And you have just got to face it!'

I won't faint if you say her name, you know,' she drawled.

It was like a red rag to a bull. Her mother's response

was incensed. 'Sometimes I find it difficult to believe that you're my child at all! Do you have *any* of my Sicilian blood? Marisia—yes—that is her name, and you did not faint! Your cousin *Marisia* was in love with your husband long before you came on the scene, and by the way she is behaving I would say that she is still in love with him—yet you stand here looking as if you could not care less that they are conducting a very public affair!'

'So you want me to do—what?' Nina swung round, blue eyes offering up their first flash of real emotion since this whole horrible scene began. 'Am I supposed to jump on the next flight to London and face them with what you've told me? Then what?' she challenged, moving back to the table to glare at her mother across it. 'You tell me, Mamma, how my half-Sicilian blood is supposed to respond once I've dragged it all out in the open—do I draw out my dagger and plunge it into both their chests with true Sicilian vendetta passion?'

'Now you are being fanciful just to annoy me,' Louisa said crossly. 'But, having asked me the question—*si*!' she retorted. 'Some drama from you would be a lot healthier than looking as if you don't give a damn!'

CHAPTER TWO

MAYBE I don't give a damn, Nina thought later, when she was alone in her bedroom. She didn't know if she cared one way or another what Rafael was doing.

And that was her problem—not knowing how she felt about anything.

A sigh slipped from her. Her mother's final volley before she'd left in a huff was still ringing in her ears.

'I suppose you will manage to drag yourself down from the hilltop to be present at your grandfather's birthday party tonight?'

Her weary, 'Of course I'll be there,' had made Louisa's lovely mouth pinch.

'There is no *of course* about it. You are in danger of becoming a hermit, Nina. For goodness' sake, snap out of it!'

'I had lunch three days ago in Syracuse with Fredo,' she'd retaliated. 'Hermits don't do that!'

'Hmph.' Louisa hadn't been impressed. 'That man is about as much use to you as the plethora of kind words and sympathy he will have dished out. You need to be pulled out of it, not encouraged to sink further in your wretched misery!'

Stopping what she was doing, Nina stood for a moment, blue eyes lost in a bleak little world of their own. Inside she could feel her heart beating normally.

She breathed when she needed to and blinked her eyes. Her brain was functioning, feeding in information, and she was able to get information out, but when it came to her emotions, everything was just blank—nothing there, nothing happening. It was like living in a vacuum, with a defence space around her as big as a field.

'Oh, what's happened to me?' she breathed, looking around at the bedroom she'd used to share but now had to herself. Even in here the only sign that life was still going on was the black dress hanging up, which she was going to wear tonight.

Snap out of it, her mother had said, and Nina truly agreed with her. But—into what?

The sound of a car coming up the driveway stopped her thoughts and sent her over to the bedroom window. The prospect of yet another unexpected visitor dragged a groan from her throat that was cut short when she recognised the sleek, dark limousine.

It was Rafael.

Her heart gave a sudden tight little flutter—not with pleasure, but with a sinking sense of dismay. He wasn't due back from London for days, so what had brought him back here sooner than he'd intended?

Had someone told him about her mother's visit? Could he know what that visit had been about?

No, don't be stupid, she told the second sharp flutter that now had her freezing to the spot. He might be equipped to throw power around like thunderbolts, but even Rafael couldn't get from London to Sicily in the space of two short hours.

The car slowed to take a sweep around the circular

courtyard, then came to a stop at the bottom of the shallow steps that led up to the house. Rafael didn't wait for Gino, his personal bodyguard and chauffeur, to climb out and open his door for him. With a brisk impatience that was his nature he pushed open the door and uncoiled his long frame from the back of the car. The top of his dark head caught the light from a golden sunset, then slid down to enrich the warm olive skin of his face as he paused to look at the house.

He was tall, he was dark, he was arrestingly handsome—a perfect example of a man in his prime. Black hair, golden skin, hard, chiselled features, straight, thin nose, and a firm and unsmiling and yet deeply, deeply sensual mouth.

Nina traced each detail as she stood there, despising herself for doing it yet unable to stop. Everything about him was so physically striking—the way he looked, the way he moved, the way he frowned with a restless impatience that was inherent in him. His dark silk suit was a statement in design architecture, tailored to a body built to carry clothes well—the wide shoulders, long arms and legs made up of steely muscle, wide chest and tight torso behind a white shirt.

But the really important things about Rafael had nothing to do with his physical appearance. He was frighteningly intelligent, razor-sharp, and ruthless to the core. The kind of man who had come from nothing and made himself into something in spite of all the odds stacked against him, amassing his wealth with a gritty determination that came from his fear of having nothing—again.

He was, Nina thought as she watched him turn to speak to Gino, a very suave, very sophisticated—mongrel. And she used the word quite deliberately. Rafael did not know where he had come from, so he'd spent most of his adult life hiding what he feared he might be by surrounding himself with status symbols of the kind of person he wanted to be.

Rejected by his mother before she had even bothered to register his birth, he had lived his childhood in a Sicilian state orphanage. The only thing that faceless creature had given him to cling to when she'd dumped his helpless newly born body on some unsuspecting stranger's doorstep had been a note pinned to the blanket he had been wrapped in.

'His name is Rafael,' the note had said, and he had gone through the latter stages of his childhood fighting to hell and back for the right to use that name.

The orphanage had called him Marco Smith, or Jones, or some Sicilian equivalent. For the first ten years of his life he had truly believed it to be his name, until the day something—an inbuilt instinct to be *someone*, probably—had sent him sneaking into the principal's office to steal a look at his personal file.

From that day on he had answered only to Rafael. Sheer guts and determination had brought him fighting and clawing to the age of sixteen, with his name legally changed to Rafael Monteleone—the Monteleone stolen from the man on whose doorstep he had been dumped.

But tenacity should be Rafael's middle name—or the one Nina would add in if she could. From the minute he'd left state care he had set out like a man with a single mission in life—which was to trace the mother who had abandoned him.

To finance his search he'd worked hard and long at anything, and for anyone who had paid a fair wage, until he had accumulated enough money to risk some of it on a little speculation—thereby discovering his true mission in life: to make money—pots of it—bank vaults of it—Etna-sized mountains of it in fact.

Strangely, though, as the money mountain had grown so his need to know his roots had diminished. Rafael had succeeded in becoming his own man. If you did not count some deeply buried fears that lurked beneath the surface of his iron-hard shell, which forced him to struggle with the most incredible inferiority complex.

'The mongrel syndrome'. Rafael's term, not Nina's. 'I could come from the loins of anything.'

Rafael lived with the awful fear that the blood running in his veins might be rotten. It didn't seem to help that the man he had built himself to be was so morally upright, honest and true that any suspicion of him being rotten inside was actually laughable. He could never know that for sure, so he dared not let his guard on himself drop for a moment—just in case something dreadful crept out.

How did Nina know all of this? The man himself had told her, during one of those long rare nights when they lay still closely entwined after the kind of loving that had always seemed to blend them into one. They'd swapped secret hopes and fears in the darkness because it had seemed so right, sharing—sharing everything. Bed to bodies, souls to minds.

That was the same night that she'd foolishly let herself believe he loved her, Nina recalled. To hear that soft, deep, slightly rasping voice reveal all its darkest secrets had, to her at least, been confirmation of something very special growing between them. She had discovered later that it was just another aspect of his complicated make-up that Rafael could bare his soul to her whilst keeping his heart well and truly shut.

It wasn't long after that night when she'd discovered they were going to have a baby. She'd been ecstatic; to her way of thinking a child of their very own would only bond them closer together. What it had actually done was drive them wide apart. And she would never forgive him for the brutality he had used in forming that gulf.

They had barely communicated since. From that moment on their lives had reverted to the original plan—she being the beautiful well-bred trophy wife Rafael had bought to shore up his bruised ego, and he the man she had sold herself to so he could keep her family in the luxury they were used to.

The only blot on this otherwise squeaky-clean landscape Rafael had made for himself was Marisia—his first-choice bride. The Guardino granddaughter with the pure Sicilian pedigree who'd walked out on him the moment she'd discovered his mongrel beginnings, leaving his pride in tatters at his feet.

'I will not marry a man who can't say who his mother is, never mind his father!' Marisia's harsh words to Nina echoed through the years. 'If you are so concerned about his feelings then you marry him. Trust me, *cara*, he will take you—just to leech onto your half-Guardino blood.'

He had done too—taken her—and it was pretty lowering to remember how eagerly she'd jumped at the chance. But then, she'd already been in love with him, though thankfully no one else knew that—including Rafael. He'd put his case in practical business terms, pointing out the financial advantages in marrying him and, because he was ruthless enough to use any persuasion, he had made her aware of other advantages by more physical means.

Oh, where had her pride been—her self-respect? How was it that she'd only had to look into his eyes to convince herself that she could see something burning there that made her cling to hope?

The sound of his laughter floated up to the window. Looking down, she saw his mouth had stretched into a grin. He had not done much of that recently, she mused.

Was that Marisia's doing? Had her cousin put the laughter back into Rafael?

Were they sleeping together?

Had it gone that far?

Did she care?

Nina turned away from the window, tense fingers coiling around her upper arms to bite hard. She wasn't ready to answer that question. She wasn't ready to face Rafael.

Oh, why did he have to come back here today of all days, when she needed time to think—to *feel* something, for God's sake?

The moment Rafael Monteleone stepped through the front door he felt the lingering residue of laughter he'd just shared with Gino die from his lips as a chill washed right over him.

It was the chill of cold silence.

He paused to stare at the perfectly symmetrical black and white floor that spread out in front of him like a chequered ocean—flat, cold, and as uninviting as the black wrought-iron work forming the curving staircase and the pale blue paint that coloured the walls.

Home, he mused, and thought about sighing—only to tamp down on the urge. Instead tension grabbed at his shoulders, then slid up the back of his neck before linking like steel fingers beneath his chin. He employed an army of staff to help keep this miserable if aesthetically stunning house running smoothly, yet but for the sound of Gino moving the car round to the garages he could be entirely alone here.

The sigh escaped—because he allowed it—because he needed to ease away some of his tension before he went looking for his wife.

Wife, he repeated. There was yet another word that had become a term of mockery—within the privacy of his mind, at least. He did not mock Nina—did not mock her at all. He mocked only himself, for daring to use the word in reference to the ghost-like image of that once beautiful person which now haunted this house.

He knew exactly where she was, of course. He'd felt the chill of her regard via her bedroom window from the moment he had stepped out of the car. If he closed his eyes he could even picture her standing there, slender and still, observing his arrival through beautiful blue eyes turned to glass.

'Good afternoon, sir,'

Ah, a real human being, Rafael thought dryly, then had to laugh privately at that when he lifted his eyes to the ancient silver-haired pole-faced butler, who'd come with the house and all of its other soulless fixtures and fittings.

'Good afternoon, Parsons,' he returned, and felt himself grimace at the very English sound of his own voice.

But then, this house was English—a small piece of England placed upon Sicilian soil like a defiance. Nina's father had had it built as a summer home for his wife and daughter to use when they visited. When Richard St James had died, leaving his wife and daughter virtually penniless, they'd been forced to sell up their fourteen-thousand-acre family estate in Hampshire and come to live here, bringing their faithful butler with them. The house belonged to Nina now, left to her in her father's will, along with a trust fund aimed to ensure that she completed her education in England.

And if all of that did not add up to a man with an axe to grind on his beautiful Sicilian wife's faithless hide, then he could not read character as well as he'd thought.

'There are several telephone messages for you.' Parsons' smooth voice intruded. 'I placed them in your study. One, from a—lady, sounded particularly urgent...'

Ignoring the slight hesitation before the word *lady*, Rafael offered a nod of his head in acknowledgment to the rest, but made no move towards his study. Instead he turned and headed for the stairs. Urgent messages or not, he had a chore to do that must take precedence.

Knowing and respecting this small ritual, Parsons melted away as silently as he had arrived, leaving Rafael to make the journey up the curving staircase to the upper landing, and from there through an archway which would take him to the bedroom apartments of a house he had agreed to live in only to please his wife.

A mistake? Yes, it had been a mistake, one of many he had made with the beautiful Nina, and all of which he intended to rectify—soon.

On that grim thought he arrived outside the bedroom suite, paused for a moment to brace his shoulders inside the smooth cut of his dark silk jacket, then gripped the handle and opened the door.

He never knocked. He found it beneath his dignity to knock before entering what he still considered to be their bedroom, even though they had not shared it for months.

Serenity prevailed—that was his first observation as

he stepped into the room, closing the door behind him. She was wearing a blue satin wrap that covered her from throat to ankle and she was sitting at her dressing table, quietly filing her nails. Her hair was up, scraped back into an unflattering ponytail, and her face looked paler than usual—though that could be a trick of the fading light.

When she turned her head to look at him he met with a wall of blue glass.

'*Ciao,*' he murmured, keeping his voice pleasant, even though pleasure was not what he was feeling inside.

'Oh, hello,' she returned, 'I wasn't expecting to see you today.' With that excruciatingly indifferent comment, the blue glass dropped away again.

Irritation snapping at the back of his clenched teeth, Rafael let the hit to his ego pass. He crossed the room to an antique writing desk on which sat a silver tray complete with crystal decanter and glasses. The ever-discreet Parsons had begun this small piece of thoughtfulness at the beginning of their marriage, when they'd used to spend more time in the bedroom than out of it, and had determinedly continued the habit though he must know that their marriage was now in tatters.

The decanter held his favourite cognac. Lifting off the smooth crystal stopper, he placed it aside, then turned to look at Nina.

'You?' he invited.

She gave a shake of her lowered head. 'No, thanks.'

It was like talking to a dead person. Turning back to the tray, he poured himself a small measure, took it with him over to the window, then unclenched his jaw and drank.

Ritual rules, he mused as he stared out at the deepening sunset. Give her a minute or two and she was going to find an excuse to get up and leave the room.

Only this time he was going to stop her. This time he was going to stop the rot taking place in this room by bringing her—screaming and kicking if necessary—out of hiding and into reality.

His stomach warmed as the cognac reached it, and somewhere else inside him a different sensation gathered pace. The call to battle. He had wrecked this beautiful creature once, and now it was time to put her back together again.

With a bit of luck she would give him a chance to fortify himself with brandy before battle commenced, he mused wryly, unaware that the subject of his thoughts was already struggling to stay where she was.

CHAPTER THREE

TIMING was everything, Nina was reminding herself as she sat there fighting the urge to get up and go.

It was part of the ritual Rafael had developed, aimed to hide the true sickness in their relationship from the servants. He always came directly to her room when he arrived home, and stayed long enough to consume a measure of cognac. He always asked her if she wanted to join him in a glass and she always refused. After a suitable length of time one of them—usually her—would make up an excuse to leave.

But today was different. Today he had come in here wearing the shadow of another woman's kiss on his lips, and there was no way she could sit here playing this the way it usually played out. She either said something, or left. It came down to those two options, she told herself tautly.

Rafael turned. 'Nina, we need to talk—'

'Sorry.' She stood up. 'I'm going for a shower.'

'Later,' he frowned. 'This is important. I want to—'

'So is my shower,' she cut in. 'Y-you should have warned me you were coming home, then I could have told you that I am out tonight.'

'Your grandfather's birthday—I know.' He nodded. 'That is what I want to talk to you about.'

Not Marisia? 'Why? What has he done now?' she

asked, in the wary voice of one who knew her devious grandparent well.

'Nothing,' Rafael said. 'I have not heard from him in several weeks. He is not the reason why I—'

'Then he's up to something.' Nina cut in on him yet again. A sigh escaped her. 'I suppose I had better try and find out what so I can—'

'I would prefer that you didn't...'

Just the way he said that was enough to put her nerve-ends on edge. Her chin came up. 'What is that supposed to mean?' she demanded, finding herself suddenly in danger of almost—almost making contact with his eyes. She looked away again—quickly.

If he noticed her avoiding gesture he kept it to himself. 'It means,' he murmured levelly, 'that I already know what he's up to, so you don't need to get involved.'

'He's *my* grandfather, Rafael. I have a right to know what he's doing if it means—'

'Not when it involves money, you don't,' he responded. 'That is my territory.'

The implication in that certainly hit where it hurt. 'Then I won't,' she answered stiffly. 'Taking care of my family is why I married you, after all. Thank you for reminding me.'

'I did not mean it like that.' He uttered a short sigh. 'I simply meant that I am able to handle him better if you don't interfere!'

Well, there you go, Nina thought. You are an interfering wife, as well as a useless, faithless, traitorous one. Things are on the move—hence the reintroduction of Marisia into his life, she supposed.

'I did not come home early to fight with you over your grandfather. I have something I need to tell you before—'

Time to leave, she decided. 'Tell me later.' Spinning away, she began walking quickly towards the bathroom, her spine tingling out a mocking challenge to the cowardly way she was retreating from this.

'Take a very healthy piece of advice, *mi amore* and don't do it...'

It was the silken edge to his voice that brought her to a wary standstill, with her fingers already gripping the handle to the bathroom door. Past experience with that tone warned her to beware—because the silkier Rafael's voice became the more dangerous he became. If she dared to open this door now then he would not hesitate to react.

'OK.' She turned, slender shoulders pressing back against the door. 'Say what you have to say,' she invited.

He was still standing by the window, so his face was shadowed by the sunset coming from behind him. But she could see the tension in his jawline; could *feel* his anger and frustration reaching out to her across the width of the room.

He held it all in check—he *always* held it in check! It was part of what they had now—Rafael taking what she dished out to him because his guilty conscience demanded it of him, and she dishing it out because—

She didn't want to finish that—did not want to think about them as a *them* at all!

He moved at last, taking a few short steps so he

could put his glass back down on the tray. When he turned to look at her his face was no longer shadowed, but right there in full focus.

Nothing showed on those hard aquiline features—nothing. But she suddenly felt as if the sky had darkened and a loud thunderclap followed by a lightning strike was piercing directly into her.

It was the way of the man—a force to be reckoned with. Love him or hate him, it was impossible to look at him and pretend she didn't feel a thing. In fact she hated him—she was sure that she did—but he could still hold her transfixed.

He was going to come close; she could actually sense him making that decision. Her nerve-ends began to scream, her fingers and palms beginning to sweat where she'd flattened them against the door behind her as he took that first deliberate step. They didn't do close any more, so it had to be a conscious decision. And he might possess good looks any woman would die to stake her claim to—a body any woman would kill to experience—but as those long legs brought him ever closer she felt like a tortoise contracting into its shell.

He came to a halt a couple of feet away, the telltale scent of him invading her private space first. He was big and lean, and stood head and shoulders over her with all the power of a smothering black cloud.

She had to close her eyes. 'Don't touch me,' she whispered.

'Then don't challenge me to,' he threw back in husky response.

The husky voice hurt her heart somehow; she

tugged in an anxious breath. Her stomach muscles were coiling into agonising knots.

'Look at me,' he urged. Her eyelids remained closed over vulnerable blue eyes and he released a sigh. 'We cannot go on like this, you know,' he murmured grimly.

Yes, we can, Nina thought, feeling the sudden burn of tears at the back of her eyes. We can go on for ever like this. I *like* it like this!

'We have to move on. *You* have to move on.'

Her lashes flicked up. 'You want a divorce?'

The words were out before she could stop them. His response shook her to the core. His hands came up and slammed against the door at either side of her trembling shoulders, and even as a shocked gasp shot from her chest in a frightened flurry he was shifting his stance. The next thing she knew his lean face was exactly level with hers.

Eyes as dark as a deep, deep ocean clashed with her eyes. It was not supposed to happen. She *never* let herself make eye contact, and now she could not break away! Her throat had locked, with tiny breaths of panic fighting to escape and heaving at her breasts.

He didn't speak, didn't even move again, and still nothing of what he was thinking showed in those hard features as he held her trapped there like a mesmerised cat.

Was he sleeping with Marisia?

Did she care? *Did* she care?

Confusion ran like quick fire in a dizzying circle inside her head.

Ask him, she told herself. Tell him what you know and just get it over with! She parted her trembling lips.

He covered them. It was that quick—that shocking.

Her first response was to pull away from him. The second was to freeze. The third was to feel that kiss in so many places she had believed could no longer feel anything. Now an incandescence was sweeping over her in a tingling, shining shimmer of heat.

It was the shock, she told herself. She just had not expected him do this. They hadn't kissed in months— hadn't touched unless it was in the company of others, when keeping up appearances made it necessary.

Which was why she rarely went anywhere with him—why she was standing here now, feeling everything as if it were their first ever kiss.

The tip of his tongue made a slow pass over the tip of her tongue, and a shaken whimper lodged in her throat.

He did it again—and again. No! she cried inside when she felt herself tremble and begin to respond.

That first tiny tremor was all it took to bring the ordeal to an end. He lifted his dark head, studied her for a few wretched moments, then said smoothly, 'Go for your shower. We don't want to be late.'

Rafael turned away from the sight of her white-face and shaken composure, his eyes glittering angrily now that she could not see them doing it. She looked like some child's broken and discarded doll, left leaning against the door.

Had that been his intention when he'd started this? To break her up some more?

No, was the answer. But that had been before she'd

looked so damn vulnerable when she asked him if he wanted a divorce.

The rest of that brandy called to him. He was crossing the room to where he had left his glass when a sound from behind told him she was beginning to pull herself together again.

'We?' she murmured shakily. 'Y-You said *we* don't w-want to be late. *You* aren't coming.'

'Are you saying I'm not invited?' He picked up the brandy glass, noticed that his fingers were shaking and grimaced.

'I don't want you there.'

Well, that was blunt and to the point, he thought, and grimaced again. 'I am sure your grandfather will be delighted to see me.'

'If this has something to do with whatever he's up to then I don't want you spoiling his birthday!'

'Still his fiercest champion, *cara*?' he mocked.

'Just leave him alone,' she said shakily.

'I will be coming with you tonight,' he repeated. 'Resign yourself to it while you take your shower.'

The quiet and level quality of his tone did it, as he had known that it would. He heard her stifled sigh of defeat and turned in time to watch her disappear into the bathroom on a whisper of blue satin and quivering frustration.

The door closed with a slam. Rafael winced, then allowed himself a thin smile. She had not slammed anything in a long time. Maybe the kissing tactic had not been such a bad one after all...

CHAPTER FOUR

THE plain black silk jersey dress still hung ready on its hanger. Nina sent it an indifferent glance as she passed it on her way to select underwear from her lingerie drawer.

Black was not a colour that particularly flattered her, but her grandfather thought it did. He claimed the colour added drama to what he insensitively called her insipidness.

Nonno was an insensitive brute all round, she mused as she slipped a sheer black silk teddy on over her lightly perfumed skin. It never occurred to him that his opinion might hurt someone who had spent most of her life feeling thoroughly outshone by her vibrant Sicilian cousin.

'I only tell it as it is,' was one of his favourite statements.

Still, she loved him, and he loved her in his own unique way. So what if he was a reckless rogue who thought nothing of throwing away a million he didn't have on some no-hope business opportunity? Or, worse, gambled it away in a single night playing backgammon with his friends? He had been her tower of strength when her father had died and her mother had been too wrapped up in playing the merry widow to notice that her fifteen-year-old daughter needed her support. If Rafael thought she was going to let him challenge the old man tonight of all nights, then—

Rafael...

Just thinking his name was enough to cause the tension knot in her stomach to tighten as she drew black silk stockings up her long, slender legs.

Was he sleeping with Marisia?

She had just spent the last hour in the bathroom trying to work out why she had not just come out with it and asked him that question.

A desire not to know, maybe because confirmation would mean she would have to face the answer, crucified dignity and all?

But—no, there was more to it than that. They might not have a real marriage any more, but she still found it difficult to believe Rafael would be unfaithful to his marriage vows—and where would it put his precious pride if he did let Marisia back into his life after what she'd done to him?

Now you're calling your own mother a liar, she thought. Are you that desperate to hang on to the status quo—useless, empty thing that it is?

She wished she could answer that question too, but she couldn't. Each time she approached it she met with a brick wall in her head.

Self-preservation. She'd been living with it as her best friend for months, so she recognised it when it threw up one of its walls.

Just stay there while I get through this evening, she begged it. Grandpa deserved that much consideration, even if it did mean enduring Rafael's company and all that role-playing togetherness.

That kiss had been...

Oh, don't go there. She groaned silently as her blood sped through her heart in an accelerated rush and her lips began to heat.

She was beginning to feel things, she realised starkly. Some walls might still be shooting up, but others were beginning to fall.

The black dress dropped into place over the teddy. Slipping her feet into high-heeled patent leather shoes, she turned to look at herself in the mirror and saw exactly what she had expected to see—a blonde with blue eyes and pink lips wearing a short black dinner dress. Nothing more, nothing less.

The dress relied on its expensive designer cut for its classic styling, and on her slender figure for the rest. She'd left her freshly washed and blow-dried hair to float around her shoulders and her make-up appeared to come down to only a flick of mascara to darken her eyelashes and a coating of lipstick. In reality, it had taken some careful work to disguise how pale and bruised she was really looking beneath.

With a flick of her fingers through her silk-fine hair, followed by a nervous smoothing of them down the sides of the dress, she turned to gather up her clutch purse from the bed and headed for the door, pausing long enough to heave in a deep, steadying breath.

I'll get through this, she told herself determinedly. Then opened the door and went out to face an evening which promised to be an ordeal.

She could hear Rafael talking in his study as she came down the stairs. The door was open, and her first glimpse of him showed a man in a dinner suit who was completely at ease with himself. Lean hips rested against the edge of the desk, long legs were stretched out and crossed, one hand lost in his jacket pocket while the other held his cellphone to his ear.

He looked up, the deep, Italian tones of his voice going silent as their gazes held for a few seconds like two guarded adversaries, trying to read the other's thoughts. She looked away first, and he returned to his conversation. As she continued down the stairs she noticed Parsons standing by the front door, with her black winter coat draped over his arm.

Her first warm smile of the day arrived as she crossed the black and white chequered floor towards him. 'Is it very cold out there?' she asked lightly.

'It is the price we pay for the clear blue skies we enjoyed today,' the butler replied. He was about to hold out the coat for her when Rafael stopped him.

'I'll do that.' The sound of his loose-limbed stride coming towards them lost Nina her smile. He came to a stop directly behind her.

'Of course, sir,' the ever-correct Parsons conceded, falling back a few discreet steps to stand ready to open the door.

Reaching round, Rafael took her purse from her. 'Transformed and on time,' he said lightly. 'You never fail to impress me, *mia cara*.'

With the urge to tense up tugging on muscles she had to fight to keep relaxed, Nina said nothing as she slid her arms into the coat sleeves. Silk-lined wool settled gently across her slender shoulders, and the light touch of his hands brought her round to face him. She stood staring at the front of his white dress shirt while he spent a few seconds releasing her hair from the coat's fake fur collar, then her purse arrived back in her hand.

'Thank you,' she murmured politely.

'My pleasure,' he answered, then shook her self-control by placing cool fingers beneath her chin and lifting it.

Their eyes clashed again—his filled with the glinting challenge of what was to come next. He was going to kiss her again, and she didn't think she could bear it.

Please don't, she wanted to say, but knew that she couldn't—because Parsons was standing there and Rafael would be angry if she rejected him in front of him. It was one of the rules by which they lived.

'You can treat me how you like when we are alone, but in front of others you maintain the status quo,' he'd said once, icy with anger because she'd flinched away from his touch at a dinner party. She remembered the punishing kiss which had followed so clearly that she had never dared to challenge that anger again—hence yet another reason why she rarely went anywhere with him.

She dragged in an unsteady breath. Her eyes dropped to his mouth, watching as it began to lower towards her own.

Parsons opened the front door and a blast of cold

air hit them. She sucked in a shocked breath. Rafael tensed and tossed a slicing glance at the butler, then changed his expression with a rueful tilt to his upper lip.

Taking her arm, he walked her out of the house with a very dry, *'Grazie,'* to Nina's saviour.

Gino was standing by the rear door of the limousine. He waited until they were almost upon him before he swung it open so that Nina could sink inside. The door closed, surrounding her in warmth and luxury leather. Rafael strode around the car to get in from the other side, and in seconds they were sweeping around the circular courtyard and onto the driveway, with Gino's familiar dark bulk dimmed by the screen of tinted glass that separated the front of the car from the rear.

A mingling of scents teased her nostrils—one light and subtle, the other spicy and dark. There were butterflies taking up residence low down in her stomach, and nervous tension sent the tip of her tongue on a slow tasting of her upper lip.

'Now we talk,' Rafael said, suddenly turning to look at her and catching her in the nervy little act. His eyes blackened. Her tongue-tip stilled. Tension cracked like a whip in the space between them and—

She felt his kiss again. Maybe Rafael did too. Because there was a single tight second when his own lips parted and she thought he was going to touch his lip with the tip of his tongue.

Erotic, it would have been—suggestive, inviting. They'd used to play games like that, so she knew exactly how it went.

Then an electronic beep hit the silence. Her tongue-tip disappeared and he was digging a hand into his jacket pocket. A second after that he was holding his cellphone to his ear.

'Ah, Fredo—*ciao*,' he greeted, and Nina's mouth changed shape into a very wry smile.

Rafael saw it and his eyes narrowed. His manner with Fredo altered to become short as he conducted a brief conversation in the Sicilian dialect that came naturally to both men.

'Why the wry smile?' he demanded, the moment the call had finished.

'Fredo must be counting himself fortunate to have caught you with your phone switched on for a change.' Maybe she did have a desire to use knives, Nina thought, as the slicing cut of her tone narrowed those dark eyes some more.

'Fredo knows I cannot always be at the end of a telephone,' he responded levelly. 'He's called you, looking for me?'

'Several times.' Nina nodded. 'It sounded—urgent.'

'He should control the urge to panic.'

'I would call it concern.'

'I would call it an imposition I don't much care for.'

She frowned, puzzled. 'I don't mind if he—'

'*I* mind, *cara*,' he inserted grimly. 'If Fredo needs a sympathetic shoulder to cry on let him use someone else's.'

'He did not cry on my shoulder,' she denied. 'He simply asked if I knew where you were because he needed to contact you and your phone was switched off. And how can you speak about him like that when he's supposed to be your closest friend?' she demanded. 'He's going through a really rough time at the moment. You should feel—'

'Sorry for him?' he put in. 'Trust me, it is dangerous to feel sorry for Fredo, and I advise you to heed that—for your own good.'

Suddenly it was Nina sensing knives being drawn. She stared at him as undercurrents of old issues began to ripple through the tension. He might be sitting there looking beautifully relaxed, but there was nothing relaxed about those hard features or the glint in those eyes he had fixed on her.

'This is a ridiculous conversation,' she said in the end, withdrawing from battle by sinking back into her seat.

'You think so?' he drawled. 'Fredo is a sucker for lost souls. That makes you and him a dangerous combination. Therefore he stays away from you or I will make sure that he does.'

'I suppose you're *not* a sucker for those same lost souls?' Nina countered, too stung by his implication that she was a lost soul not to retaliate. 'The Monteleone Trust was set up merely for its tax concessions, and the lost souls it gathers in don't really count?'

A frown lashed his brow. 'My name is listed on hundreds of charities.'

'But it heads only one. Why dismiss it as nothing special?'

He shifted tensely, turning his head away, but not

before Nina had seen the vulnerable glint shoot across his eyes. He might hate to talk about it, but the Monteleone Trust was Rafael's big acknowledgement to his past.

It was a string of projects set up and designed to give troubled young men and women from a similar background to his own the opportunity to do something constructive with their lives. He employed only the very best to guide and encourage them, and Fredo was the best of the best. He too had known the same childhood as Rafael. His ideals were in complete sympathy with Rafael's ideals. And Rafael might prefer to sit here mocking Fredo's passion for *lost souls*, as he put it, but they were his lost souls too.

A sigh hissed from him. 'We were talking about you and Fredo.'

'You were. I was trying to change the subject.'

'You had lunch with him three days ago—'

Nina stared at him. 'Are you accusing me of something—again?' she dared to demand.

It was like teasing old issues to come out and show themselves. His lips thinned out, and his teeth, she suspected, were clenching behind them in an effort to keep those issues locked in. But they were there now, rattling away at her and reminding her why she hated him. And reminding him of things about her that he much preferred to forget.

'He is already halfway to falling in love with you. I would prefer it if he was not encouraged to make it more than that.'

She wanted to laugh because it was such a joke.

'We had lunch in Syracuse. We shared a bowl of pasta, not an interlude of untrammelled lust!'

The word *lust* turned those glinting eyes into lasers. If she could, this would be the point where Nina would get up and walk away from him.

'I don't know how you can sit there talking about Fredo like this when he has never been anything but loyal to you.'

'Men in love do strange things…'

'Is that so?' Her laugh escaped. It was short and derisive. 'That explains it, then.'

'Explains what?' he asked, and then, while she fought with the answer she knew was bubbling up inside her, 'Has he already made his feelings clear to you? Is that it?' he shot at her.

'You are such a hypocrite, Rafael,' she informed him coldly. 'I wonder sometimes how you manage to justify it to yourself.'

The car came to a stop then. Nina had never been more relieved about anything. Without waiting to listen to what else he had to say, she opened her door and stepped out into the crisp, cold night.

She was trembling all over, but she told herself they were shivers of cold and huddled into her coat.

Her grandfather's house was a tall, thin *palazzo* situated in one of the tiny squares in Syracuse. Lights blazed from the windows; cars lined the square. Nina had never felt less like going to a party, but the alternative was to finish what she had just started and she would not ruin her grandfather's birthday!

Rafael was striding around the car towards her. Gino had not even bothered to get out. The chauffeur could sense a heated row when it was taking place feet away from him, and was wisely keeping out of it.

Nina made for the house. As she reached the front door it swung open, flooding her with light, and she walked in with her head high and her legs trembling dangerously. A servant murmured polite greetings as he waited to take her coat. She could feel Rafael's anger as he waited for the servant to move away from her again.

Another door came open on the floor above, and the sounds of a party already in full flow poured out. As the servant moved away with her coat Nina turned towards the stairs which led up to the main salon, defiance running like fire in her veins—only to suddenly feel chilled to her very bones as one particular sound separated itself from all the rest.

Laughter.

It had always been able to do that, she was thinking dizzily. Had always managed to shine brighter than anyone else's laughter could.

Rafael arrived beside her, big and dark and angry because she'd spoken to him the way that she had. He caught hold of her arm again.

As he swung her to face him her eyes had already glazed, her skin prickling with rising nausea, her face turned so pale it took on a whole new dimension of paste.

He saw the change, and whatever angry retort was about to shoot from his lips altered. 'What's the matter?' he asked sharply.

'You bastard,' she whispered, and the fact that she was using that word to him of all people made it all the more potent.

CHAPTER FIVE

SHOCK rendered Rafael still for a second. Nina began to shake. It came again then, as clear as a lightly toned bell chiming out its presence—and Rafael heard it too.

A curse ripped from him. That curse said more to Nina than if he'd tossed out a full confession to her.

'You knew she was here and you didn't bother to tell me. How could you do this to me?' she breathed.

'She has as much right to be here as you do, Nina,' he returned grimly. 'A two-year exile from her home and family is long enough. Show a little compassion, for goodness' sake.'

Nina would have smiled at that if she was able—but she was incapable of doing anything right now.

Another sound from upstairs separated itself from the others. It was her grandfather's voice, calling her name. Looking up, Nina saw him standing looking down at her over the first floor balustrade. Rafael uttered another thick curse.

With her stomach churning out dire warnings and the rest of her clutched in bands of steel, Nina dredged up a smile from somewhere.

'Happy birthday, Nonno,' she called up to him, and began walking on legs that didn't feel real.

'*Grazie piccola.*' He beamed a smile back down to her. 'I do not feel like the seventy-year-old man people insist I am. But come up—come up,' he added impatiently. 'You are late. I was about to telephone your house to find out where you were. Good evening, Rafael, I am happy that you could make it…'

Rafael said nothing. He was tracking behind her up the long staircase and she could feel his anger and frustration hitting her rigid spine. Her grandfather didn't notice the missing answer; he didn't notice Nina's sickly pallor or her tension or tremors as he welcomed her into his arms.

He was too excited, his eyes flashing with it. 'Has Rafael told you about the surprise he delivered to me on his way home this afternoon?'

Rafael delivered—? Nina froze yet again.

'Have I put my big foot in it?' her grandfather responded sharply. 'Did he not tell you?'

Brazen it out, she told herself. Pretend you're ecstatic. 'Of course he told me,' Nina assured him—and smiled.

'Good—good.' Relief fluttered momentarily behind his excitement. Then he was fitting her slender frame beneath the crook of his arm. 'Then let us go in!'

The first person she saw when she stepped into the salon was her mother, her face looking whiter than the silk gown she wore. Louisa hurried forward, ostensibly to embrace her daughter, but the real reason was the hurried words she whispered. 'I knew nothing about this until I arrived here five minutes ago or I would have told you.'

'I know,' Nina said. It was all she could manage,

because her eyes had already found the real star of the show.

She was standing not far away, wearing purple for passion, beautiful, exotic, her dark hair floating around her exquisitely perfect but apprehensive face.

The first thing Nina felt was a rush of warm tenderness for this cousin who had once been her closest friend—until she reminded herself that the face which had spent the last two years fronting one of the biggest beauty campaigns did not do apprehensive. And the way Marisia lifted those anxious eyes up over Nina's shoulder to where Rafael stood, grim and silent, told her why she was playing the vulnerable one.

If he offered any reassurance then it did not alter Marisia's expression. She dropped those incredible dark eyes back to Nina's face. And what made the whole charade all the more sickening was that everyone present here believed that Nina had stolen Rafael from Marisia in the first place.

She was the original sinner in this room, and Marisia the one to be pitied.

Well, I can deal with that, Nina told herself. I prefer to be the sinner than the sinned upon.

And on that thought she drew on every bit of her strict English upbringing and put her mother to one side. 'Marisia,' she greeted her warmly. 'How very nice to see you here…' And she smiled.

How very nice indeed, Rafael thought grimly as he watched his wife run the gauntlet of everyone's curiosity to substantiate her greeting with the expected kisses on her cousin's cheeks.

Hypocrite.

That word was still sticking its sharp point into him. Nina had not used the word just for effect. Did she know? Could she know?

His attention switched to his mother-in-law, who was standing beside him wearing an expression that was more anxious than Marisia's as she watched the two cousins embrace. He hadn't thought much about Louisa's presence here; it would be expected that she attend her father's birthday party, but a week ago she had been in London, being wined and dined by a rich banker who'd been recently widowed.

Had Louisa seen—heard—something and passed that information on to Nina?

Sensing his eyes on her, Louisa glanced up, her dark eyes instantly growing cold. Her lips parted impulsively, then she had second thoughts about whatever it was she had been about to say and closed them again.

'Got something you want to tell me, Louisa?' he prompted smoothly.

'No,' was all that came out, and she returned her eyes to the embracing cousins.

'Good,' he said. 'For a moment there I really thought you were going to say something to me that you might regret later, when you'd had time to think about it.'

He was making subtle reference to the healthy

amount of money he paid into her account each month, which kept Louisa's privileged lifestyle afloat.

She glanced back at him. 'You have eyes like a killer hawk,' she told him.

Rafael smiled, because he hadn't expected that comment. 'Windows to my soul, *cara*,' he confided.

Louisa shivered and looked away, again having received the message.

Her father turned towards them then—and beamed out a delighted grin. 'This must be the perfect birthday gift for an old man, to see those two together again like this,' he declared, as insensitive as ever to what was really going on around him. Then almost immediately he lost interest in his 'gift'. 'Rafael, if you have a few minutes I have a little something interesting I would like to—'

'Another time, Alessandro,' he cut in. 'I promised my wife I would not spoil your birthday, you see...'

With that said, Rafael left father and daughter standing there, knowing that Alessandro had received his message too. The old man now aware that Rafael knew what he was up to, and was not pleased about it. So he would keep out of his way for the rest of the evening.

Which was exactly what Rafael wanted him to do.

Nina's smile held without faltering throughout the next hour. She'd smiled when she greeted the beautiful Marisia like the prodigal come home again, and she shone over everyone else's curiosity and made them smile too. She talked and she laughed and she greeted each individual as if they all were warmly welcome prodigals. Uncles, aunts, her many other cousins—and friends of her grandfather who beamed beneath the warmth of her smile.

And she drank champagne by the gallon.

By the time they were called into dinner she was amazed she could still walk in a straight line.

Everyone took their places at the long table. Nina found herself seated next to Rafael—with Marisia sitting directly opposite.

Oh, great, she thought—and smiled.

The first course arrived. Wine bottles chinked against slender-stemmed glasses. One of her male cousins was sitting on her other side, and she engrossed herself in conversation with him about—goodness knows what, until the poor guy was exhausted.

There was noise and fun and talking over talking—a meal enjoyed Sicilian-style.

Marisia wowed everyone with stories about her celebrity lifestyle, and Nonno inserted eager prompts that showed how closely he had been following Marisia's career.

Louisa was quiet.

So was Rafael.

'More wine please, darling,' Nina requested, holding out her empty glass to him for its third refill.

He had spent most of the awful dinner dividing his time between watching her from under brooding dark eyelashes and sending coded little messages across the table to Marisia. As his eyes fixed her with a steady look she knew he was going to refuse.

Try it, her own flashing blue invited him. Because I hate you and I am really warming up to causing a good scene by telling you how much I hate you—and she smiled.

His gaze flicked across the table to Marisia, and another one of those infuriating messages passed between the two of them.

Nina gave an impatient shake of her glass to regain his attention.

'Fill Nina's glass for her, someone,' her grandfather said.

Mouth pinned flat to his teeth, Rafael obliged, taking a wine bottle from its bed of ice and stretching out to pour some into her glass. The crisp dry white barely splashed the bottom. Nina stared ruefully into it—then at him. It was his turn to send a warning with his eyes telling her not to dare push it.

So she didn't. She turned her attention on Marisia instead. 'How long do you have with us before you need to go back to New York?'

It was intriguing to watch the little start she gave at being asked such an ordinary question. 'I will not be going back,' she said with a tense smile, and for the life of her could not hold Nina's deeply interested blue gaze.

Guilty conscience, Nina named it. And was impressed that Marisia had managed *not* to look at Rafael before she spoke.

'She is staying here with me over the Christmas period,' their grandfather put in. 'We mean to enjoy ourselves—heh, *cara*?'

'Yes.' Another tense smile was flicked his way. 'It feels so good to be home. I've missed you all so much...'

A flurry of 'we missed you too' rippled round the table. But for some reason the wave of assurance did not ease Marisia's unease. Her lovely olive-toned skin had gone pale, and her mouth was actually trembling. Nina even thought she could detect genuine apprehension in her cousin's dark eyes when she could not hold out any longer and threw yet another of those glances at Rafael.

Rafael in his turn did not move a muscle. When Nina allowed herself a quick glance at him she saw he was sitting there with his eyes carefully lowered, his glossy black eyelashes curling against his chiselled cheeks. It was as if he'd withdrawn his support, or whatever it was that Marisia looked for each time she looked at him.

Or maybe he was thinking of other things. Maybe he was hiding his eyes like that because he was seeing Marisia in his arms, in his bed.

Were they sleeping with each other?

Did she care?

Marisia uttered a strained little laugh. 'You might all change your minds about that in a minute,' she said tensely.

Silence followed—a hint of a warning that feathered itself down Nina's spine when she saw one of Rafael's hands curl into a fist. She looked back at her cousin and, like everyone else, waited for her to go on.

'I h-have something I need to tell you,' she continued unsteadily. 'I w-was going to leave it until after Christmas, but I don't think I can...' She paused yet again, to pull in a stifled breath. 'I've come home because I'm going to have a baby!' she finished with a defiant rush.

Shock threw itself around the table. Nina froze. Rafael straightened in his seat.

Alessandro Guardino was the first to recover, his eyes beetling a look down the table towards Marisia. 'And where is the father of this child while you sit here announcing this?' he demanded. 'Where is your wedding ring?'

'Th-there won't be a w-wedding,' Marisia informed him. 'H-he already has a wife, so I—'

Nina came to her feet with a jerk.

'Nina—' Louisa followed suit, her cry pained and anxious.

'Excuse me,' Nina whispered, and turned, almost staggering around her chair in her need to get away.

More chairs moved as others came to their feet. Pandemonium broke out. But she just kept on going, weaving an unsteady line towards the door and escape. Everything was moving in and out of focus. She had a horrible feeling she was going to faint.

'Stay where you are, Louisa,' Rafael's grim voice commanded.

'How could you be so cruel as to set her up for this?' she heard her mother whip back at him, and she almost sobbed in her need to get out before it all blew up.

She managed to get the door open, then headed like

a dizzy drunk for the stairs. Her mind was sloshing about on a sea of champagne bubbles. It kept trying to toss up hard truths at her, but she blocked them out. She just needed to get out of there, she told herself frantically—away from those angry voices she could hear raising hell, away from those angry feet she could feel vibrating on the oak floor as they came after her.

She was halfway down the stairs when Rafael came to a stop at the head of them, and she knew why he'd pulled to a halt there. If he came after her she might stumble. It had happened to tragic effect once before. They'd rowed, she'd walked away, and he'd come after her to apologise.

The next thing she'd known she'd been falling—falling...

No. She pushed the rest of that memory away, along with every other one trying to batter a hole in her head. Her feet made it to the ground floor and kept on going. She'd reached the front door before Rafael dared to let himself move at all.

Outside, the cold night air rushed into her lungs and she gulped at it. Instantly those champagne bubbles began fizzing and popping, flooding her bloodstream with pure alcohol, and she staggered.

A pair of hands grabbed her by the shoulders and grimly steadied her. 'I h-hate you,' she choked.

He said nothing. He just held her upright while she shivered and shook.

Gino had been parked across the square, but the moment he'd seen her step out of the house he had started up the engine and was already purring to a halt by her side. Rafael opened the rear door and bundled her into it, with no finesse, no striding round the car to get in from the other side. He simply followed her, forcing her to scramble out of his way.

Her coat landed on top of her. How he'd found time to get it, Nina had no idea, but she huddled into it as the car moved off.

Rafael sat beside her with a profile like granite.

'You knew that was coming, didn't you?' she bit out accusingly.

There was a pause, a rasp of a sigh, followed by a teeth-gritting 'Yes…'

CHAPTER SIX

NINA wondered if she was ever going to breathe again without hurting. 'So you set me up.'

Rafael turned his head. 'Your mother said something similar—as if it is a sin for someone else to have a baby while you are still grieving the loss of your own! Did it not occur to either of you that Marisia's present situation deserves your understanding and sympathy, not some dramatic exit staged to swing the sympathy all your way!'

He was angry on Marisia's behalf? Nina stared at him as if he had just crawled out from beneath a stone. 'You really are,' she breathed tautly, 'the most absolute bastard—to dare to expect understanding and sympathy from me when your mistress announces that she is having your baby!'

'Mistress?' The single word shot from his lips in stunned astonishment. 'I don't keep a mistress!'

'What do you call her then—your true love?'

He met that piece of flaying sarcasm with silence. Nina looked away, hating—*hating* him! How could he *do* this to her?

Her mouth began to tremble, her eyes to fill with hot tears. She clutched her coat to her with icy fingers and stared fixedly out of the car window, seeing through the layer of tears that they'd already left the lights of Syracuse behind them and were climbing the hill towards home.

Home. No place had ever felt less like home to her. She hated the house—hated the life she had been living there in a marriage that had never been anything but a huge pretence.

'I think you had better explain what the hell it is you are talking about,' he said finally.

'I know about you and Marisia,' she obliged, and wished that she'd said it the moment he'd stepped into her bedroom this afternoon. Then she would not have been exposed to the horror of tonight! Her head swung round, blue eyes stabbing into his taut profile. 'Did you think you could swan around London with her *without* someone I know seeing you together there?'

His first response was to turn his head to look at her, the next was to draw himself in. Danger suddenly lurked in those lean, hard features. The kind of danger that arrived when a man like him found himself backed into a tight corner he knew he was not going to get out of.

'Who was it?' he rapped out.

He wasn't even going to lie and deny it! Stomach-churning distress joined in with the rest of the mayhem taking place inside her.

'You know what, Rafael?' she said. 'It doesn't matter who told me, or even if I did know about the two of you before that staged scene you put me through tonight. The fact that she was there at all says that you must have given her your blessing, or my grandfather would not have dared let her in the house!'

It was all to do with priorities. Her grandfather might love Marisia, but he loved Rafael's money more.

A frown broke his rigid expression. 'What does that have to do with anything?'

'It has everything to do with me!' Nina cried. 'She is the woman you were in love with—the one you would have married if she had not walked out on you! To have given your consent for her to come back here means you have to have had contact with her. To have had contact with her means you broke a promise you made to me on our wedding day! To have broken that promise means that my feelings matter less to you than hers do—which you well and truly proved tonight.'

'You're crazy,' he breathed.

Maybe she was, Nina allowed. Maybe she had been out of her head for the last two years!

The car came to a stop. Reaching for the door, Nina pushed it open and scrambled out. As she ran up the shallow stairwell Parsons opened the front door.

'Good evening,' he greeted her. 'I did not expect you back so—'

'Close the door,' she instructed as she ran past him. 'I don't want him in here!'

With that she kept on going, dropping the coat in a black puddle on the floor at the foot of the stairs. She was trembling and shaking and the champagne was still fizzing.

The door did close, but it wasn't Parsons who did it. 'Nina!' Rafael roared after her. 'Go up those stairs the way you came down your grandfather's and I will kill you—if you don't do it to yourself first!'

She stopped two steps up and twisted to glare at him across the length of chequered flooring. He was standing there in his black dinner suit and bow tie looking as handsome as hell, yet so pale she knew what he was envisaging.

Maybe it was the look on his face that made her bend to take her shoes off. Then again maybe it wasn't, because the next thing she did was launch the damn shoes towards his still frame.

'Just get out of my house!' she yelled at the top of her trembling voice as the black patent leather shoes landed just short of their target.

Then she turned and ran up the curving staircase in a heaving, stumbling mess of anger and tears.

Rafael tried telling himself he should be pleased to see that she'd turned on all her emotions again. But pleasure was not the emotion he was feeling as he watched her fly up that damn staircase while her coat lay at the bottom like a grim reminder of how she had looked that day she had landed in a final heartbreaking twist of slender limbs.

He hated this house. He hated that damn staircase!

As soon as she had safely reached the top, one gut-wrenching set of feelings were swapped for a different set, and it broke him free of his grim stasis.

Marisia—his mistress?

The child she was carrying was—his?

He began striding after her, stepping over the shoes

and the discarded coat, leaving the butler standing by the door trying his best to appear as if he had not witnessed that little scene.

But Parsons *had* witnessed it, which only infuriated Rafael all the more. He took the stairs two at a time, arriving on the upper landing as her bedroom door slammed. With dire intent burning like a blister on his pride, he strode through the archway, feeling as if his face had been carved from stone it was so rigid with anger.

His fingers grasped the handle; he threw open the door and stepped inside. She was standing in the middle of the room with her arms wrapped tightly around her. He slammed the door.

'Right, let us get a few facts straight,' he gritted. 'Marisia is *not* my mistress. She is *not* having my child!'

Nina responded by turning for the bathroom. Bright balls of pain and anger were propelling themselves to the backs of her eyes.

She took just one step before a pair of strong arms came around her and scooped her off her feet.

Her shrill cry of protest earned her nothing. 'Oh, no, you don't,' he gritted. 'Not this time.'

With a lithe twist of his body followed by two strides he tossed her onto the bed, then followed her down there, a solid package of lean, hard, long-limbed masculinity pinning her to the bed.

She gasped at the shock of it, and found herself staring into black holes for eyes and a tensely parted mouth that was so close she could actually taste it.

Awareness rushed through her like a raging torrent, every sense she possessed leaping to life at the return of a physical contact they had been denied for months. She tingled and pulsed—and despised herself for letting it happen.

'Get off me, you brute,' she choked out thickly.

'I will when you promise to stay still and listen,' he said huskily, but she knew he wasn't going anywhere.

Like her, he was aware that this was the closest they'd been in months—and she could see by the look in his eyes that he liked it. She could feel every tensing, flexing, sensational muscle he possessed, and the worst part about it was that he could feel every one of hers.

His jacket lay spread open on either side of her; his long fingers were buried in her hair as they cupped her head. Her skirt had rucked up around her hips and the heels of her hands were braced against his shirtfront, to stop him coming any closer, her tense fingers fighting to relax into contact with the familiar warm firmness they knew waited a tantalisingly small inch away.

She sucked in some air and her breasts made that contact. A panic of pleasuring frissons set her fighting him for all she was worth.

She pushed at his chest and bucked her hips in an effort to dislodge him. She gasped and choked and spat out words she had never used in her life. When nothing made him move she hit out at him with her fists, then tried using her nails—until he denied them the chance to do any damage by capturing both wrists and pinning them to the bed above her head.

Her eyes flashed blue lightning at him and her lips quivered. 'You are a faithless, cheating liar and I hate you,' she hissed.

'The only liar I know is the one who told you I'm sleeping with your cousin!'

'So you took her to our apartment for a chat, did you?' she flashed up at him. 'After you seduced her across a candlelit dinner table for two!'

The sarcasm clicked. He went still, his eyes hooded over.

Nina began to struggle free with new impetus.

'Stop it while I think.' His strength subdued her.

'You're crushing me.'

'No, I'm not,' he denied, making her aware of the way he was evenly distributing his weight between two key points, his bent arms and his legs placed on either side of her own.

'Louisa,' he murmured in the end. 'She saw us together and rushed straight back here to tell you what she'd seen. What a pleasure it must be to have such a caring mother,' he mocked cynically. 'I think I would rather have an indifferent one, like my own.'

At last he moved away, rolling onto his back beside her to stare grimly at absolutely nothing.

Nina sat up then, and surprised herself by doing nothing either. 'She's her father's daughter,' she said.

'Ah, si,' he drawled, as if that explained everything.

Which it did. Louisa had not come chasing up here to surprise her daughter with the pleasure of her com-

pany for lunch. She hadn't even come bearing grim
warnings about what Rafael was doing in London for
Nina's benefit. She'd done it because she'd seen her
allowance at risk and had wanted to jolt Nina out of
her apathy and get her to fight for her ailing marriage
before they all lost their only income source.

'What it is to be a billionaire,' Rafael murmured
bitterly, making Nina aware that he was thinking more
or less the same thing. 'It makes you so popular your
head could swell if you so allowed it.'

'You're as guilty as everyone else of using your
money to get what you want,' she threw back.

His hand came out, long fingers trailing lightly
down her arm. 'I had to buy you, *cara*,' he murmured
huskily. 'It was the only way you would have me.'

Nina pulled her arm away, then rubbed where his
fingers had been. 'Stop trying to divert the subject.'

'This is the subject,' he argued. 'I never wanted
Marisia. I *always* wanted you.'

'Gosh, it showed,' she responded bitterly. 'Especially when you told me you did not want children—
having told her that you did.'

She got up then, feeling sick again, restless and—
hurt.

'I never said that.' He sat up. 'Why would I say that
to Marisia when I knew it wasn't possible?'

He had a—point to which Nina had no answer.
'Well, you didn't bother to tell *me* that you thought
you couldn't have children. Maybe you told her that
you could because you thought it was what she wanted
to hear.'

'If I did then I made a lousy error of judgement,' he denounced, 'because Marisia does not want children. She cannot bear the thought of them. She does not even want the child she carries!'

Nina swung round. 'What do you mean?' she demanded.

'Exactly what I say.' He got to his feet, angry fingers dragging the bow tie loose. 'Marisia does not want the baby.' His shirt button was loosened next. 'I spent the last few days talking her out of aborting it. She agreed in the end—hence tonight's announcement.' The jacket came next and was dropped onto the bed.

Nina stared at him, looking at what he had just said from a completely different perspective. 'And how long have you been in such close contact with her that she felt she could confide all of this in you?'

'Ah,' he sighed. 'I think am digging myself a hole here.'

'You're so right you are,' Nina agreed.

He strode across the room towards the drinks tray. 'I have never been out of contact with her—OK?'

The defensive *OK* ripped her heart in two. Did he love Marisia so much that he had not been able to keep away from her?

'She was struggling in New York. Homesick—miserable,' he pushed on as he uncapped a decanter. 'She got into an affair with this wealthy businessman, then found out too late that he had a wife and children tucked out of way somewhere. She decided that London was the best place to have an abortion. We—

bumped into each other. She told me what she was about to do.'

'Bumped into each other?' Nina repeated. 'As in— by accident?'

He grimaced. 'She called me,' he added with a shrug. 'Said she was in trouble and needed help.' Cognac splashed into a glass. 'We arranged to meet for dinner and she told me about the baby then. You know my past,' he added grimly. 'What right has any woman to deny a child its right to survive?'

'What right does any man have to deny his own child?'

'Marisia's baby is not mine,' he repeated angrily.

'I was talking about my—*our* baby!' Nina shrilled. 'You denied responsibility for that!'

'And you know why!' he thrust back at her.

'Because you had a vasectomy ten years ago, therefore I had to be the faithless one who'd taken a lover?' she lashed back. 'I know what you prefer to believe, Rafael.'

'I was still prepared to love it as my own.'

'And hate me all you could.'

'Daniel Fraser was in your life before I came into it. He had an emotional grip on you that I could not break.'

'Oh, you broke it,' she assured him. 'You bought out his company and had me dismissed!'

'After he seduced you into bed to get his revenge on you for marrying me!'

'Revenge?' she repeated. 'Well, thanks for letting

me know that I'm only good for a quick lay in the name of revenge!'

'I did not mean it like that.' He sighed.

'You married me to get your revenge on Marisia. Daniel seduced me in revenge for marrying you!' She laughed because it was so ridiculous to hear it said. 'I suppose I am seducing Fredo to get revenge on you for turning me into a cheap little tramp!'

He put the glass to his lips again and drank, his taut profile ripping her to shreds because she could see from it that was exactly what he did think!

'Very Sicilian,' she derided shakily. Then, because she just could not stand here listening to this any longer, 'Get out of here, Rafael,' she said, 'before I really say something you won't like to listen to.'

'Say it,' he invited. 'At least we are talking, which is infinitely better than the silence we've enjoyed for the last six months!'

Without warning the lid came flying off her temper. Before she knew what she was going to do she'd closed the gap between them and had snatched the glass from his hand. It landed with a crash back on the tray.

'OK, you asked for it.' She looked up at him, blue eyes full of burning contempt. 'Revenge is a fine word to fall from the lips of the man who took revenge on his own body by denying it the right to reproduce!'

He went pale as the hard accusation hit home. 'Only a fool would want to pass on my genetic fingerprint.' He turned his back to her.

'You don't *know* your genetic fingerprint!' Nina

lashed at that rigidly set back. 'You only fear what it might be!'

'Is this leading somewhere?' he bit out tautly.

'Yes!' she cried. 'Because you fear it so much that you could not even bring yourself to look it in the face when I got pregnant! If you had then you would have started to ask questions about yourself! It's common knowledge that a vasectomy can reverse itself—that's the power of our instinct to reproduce! But did you check that out? No.' she said, and began to shiver. 'You preferred to believe I could sleep around like a whore.'

'I did check it out...'

'What?' he'd spoken so low in his chest that she thought she'd misheard him. Then he flexed his shoulders and she knew she had not misheard a thing. 'When?' she said, and because she needed to look at him when he answered she stepped round in front of him. What she saw written on his face dragged the breath from her throat. 'You know, don't you?' she heaved out breathlessly. 'You *know* the baby I lost was your baby!' She began to tremble all over her. 'Do you feel bad about that, Rafael, or are you all the more relieved that it's gone?'

'Don't say that!' he rasped. 'I never wished it any harm!'

She hit him so hard it rocked him on his feet.

CHAPTER SEVEN

TEARS flashed like blue lightning across her eyes as she watched her fingerprints stand out on his cheek. She did not regret hitting him, but she did not want to look at that arrogant face wearing her mark of contempt so she turned away.

'Get out of my house,' she said thickly. 'I never want to see you again so long as I live.'

It took every bit of withered strength she had left in her shaking limbs to turn and walk away from him.

'No.' He sounded gruff and harsh. She was not surprised to find herself caught by the shoulders again. 'I want you to listen,' he rasped, then let free with a string of thick, tight curses when his touch turned her to stone.

It was his turn to step around her so he could look her full in her icy white face. 'I am not going to let you shut me out now you have managed to remember that I do exist—faults and all,' he warned.

It was the *faults and all* part that made her unbend a little. The knowledge that he knew he had some deep personal issues that made him impossible to live with.

'All right, say what you want to say,' she invited stiffly, folding her arms beneath her breasts and locking her eyes on the floor.

His second string of soft curses turned all women

from victims into ruthless tormentors. 'How you can think that a man like me would want to involve myself with two women at the same time is beyond me— No, don't cry, *cara*,' he said gruffly. 'If you let those tears fall then I will not be responsible for what I—'

'Just talk!' she cut in thickly.

He sucked in some air, his fingers tightening their grip on her arms. 'I took the test twice,' he said. 'The first time the result was inconclusive, and because it came only a couple of weeks after you told me you were pregnant I was happy to hang on to my version of the truth. I was scared that I might have made the biggest mistake in my life, so it suited me to push all the blame onto you.'

'My hero,' she mocked him.

He let go of her, swung away tensely, then immediately swung back again. 'Do you want the truth or some dressed-up version that makes me appear bigger than I am?' he lashed at her. 'You went away with Daniel Fraser for the weekend!'

'It was a business convention he was my boss and the whole firm was there!'

'The whole firm did not stop him from getting into your room!'

'He came to collect my suitcase!'

'I came to collect you!' he thrust back at her. 'And found myself having to break up a bloody clinch! He said, 'Nice having you, Nina,' before my fist was in his face!'

'I told you—he tried it on but that was all. Nothing else happened!'

'And I did not believe it!'

'Did not *want* to believe it.'

'Did I suggest the dressed-up version would sound better for me? My apologies.' He bowed stiffly. 'I was wrong. I still come out of it looking like the fool. And watch those tears,' he tagged on when he saw them fill her eyes again. 'Because I'm still hovering on the brink of saying to hell with this and throwing you back on the bed!'

Nina heaved in a deep breath, feeling her breasts quiver against her crossed arms—as if they preferred the bed option too!

'So you took the test and it was inconclusive?' she prompted, in an effort to get this back on track.

He nodded, then pushed his hands into his trouser pockets and drew himself in. 'We left London and came here to live. You walked around this house like a wounded animal and I hated it,' he went on thickly. 'We did not look at each other; we did not even speak!'

For weeks it had gone on, Nina recalled bleakly. Weeks and weeks of feeling like a stranger to herself. He'd told her he'd had a vasectomy. And then he'd told her why. 'I don't want children. I never want children!'

'Well, tough luck, Rafael,' she'd said. 'Because I am having your baby, whatever you think or want or believe...'

'In the end I could stand it no longer,' he continued. 'I took a hard look at what we were doing to each other and decided that if I wanted our marriage to survive I was going to have to swallow my pride and tell you I could forgive and forget, that I wanted to put the past aside and try again...'

And he'd told her with enough stiff-necked coldness to put an icy chill on her flesh, Nina recalled.

'You flew at me in a rage, then rushed out of this room vowing you were going to leave me. I went after you, knowing I had made a mess of it. You were already on the stairs. I said something—I don't know what...'

'*I'm sorry,*' he'd said. '*I did not mean that the way it came out...*'

'You turned to respond, but the front door flew open and your grandfather walked in,' he went on. 'As you spun back to look at him you stumbled off the top step—'

Nina put a hand up to cover her eyes. 'Please— don't say any more,' she begged.

'But I have to say it,' he insisted. 'It was my fault! I moved too late to stop you from falling. You lost the baby. Now I watch you take that fall every night in my sleep!'

'And you think that I don't?' Her hand dropped away again. He was standing in front of her, big and tense, with the agony of guilt carving grooves in his face. 'Do you think you are the only one to carry blame around?' she questioned. 'I was the careless one! I was the one who didn't watch my step! I was the stupid one who let you get to me the way that you did!'

'That is the whole point.' He reached for her again,

long fingers curling over her slender arms. 'You might pretend to be the cool English rose, but you have so much Sicilian passion running riot inside you that you are a danger to yourself! I knew that. I should have backed off when you started shouting, then the fall would not have happened.'

'Well, don't worry about it. You backed off afterwards,' she said bitterly. 'So far back that you hardly came home—and you took a lover to keep you company at the same time!'

Dio,' he rasped. 'I did not take a lover—have you heard anything I've said? I stayed away because you coped better when I was not here to remind you. I— Oh, don't, dammit,' he groaned, when he saw the tears arriving yet again.

Then it came—the muttered, 'What the hell?' And the next thing she knew she was lifted up hard against him, with his arms wrapped around her and his mouth taking driving possession of the first sob as it broke on her lips.

It was a hellish kind of heaven. She hated him so much, yet her arms hooked around his neck and clung so tightly there was no way he could break free. She sobbed and she whimpered and she kissed him back with a passion that sang like a shrill tune in her head. When he managed to drag his mouth away she buried her face in his shoulder and sobbed like a baby.

He didn't like it. She could tell that by the way he stood so tense and silent while she sobbed.

'You know what you need?' he rasped out then.

Nina kept her face buried in his shoulder and shook her head.

'You need me,' he told her. 'All of me. Wrapped around you, inside you, naked flesh, naked passion—how else are you going to get rid of all this grief?'

'I want to hate you,' she mumbled on another sob.

'And you hate to want me. I know,' he grated, then he turned and did what he'd been threatening to do—returned them both to the bed. He covered her mouth again, taking her sobs as his own while she clung and let him.

She let him stroke her body and remove her dress. She let him kiss her where he wanted, let him suck gently on her breasts through the sheer black teddy and let him slide long fingers between her legs. And he did it all so carefully and sombrely that the tears began running down her cheeks again.

'Do you want me to stop?' His voice, like the finger he trailed across her wet cheek, was gentle and grim.

She shook her head, her hand still clutching his nape because the rest of her was beginning to float. 'Take me away with you,' she whispered.

There wasn't a moment when he questioned where she wanted to be taken to. The breath feathered from him as with a solemn gentleness he drew the teddy from her body and whispered it down her legs. Her knees came up, her toes curling inside her silk stockings as she curved herself into him. Her mouth hunted his, lips soft and trembling and desperately needy, touching and tasting while he dealt with the stockings too.

It felt good to be naked. It felt good to feel his hand moulding her breasts. When he moved away so he could take off his own clothes she watched him through big blue sombre eyes that kept his own eyes sombre and his movements tense.

No man had a body like Rafael. The broad shoulders, the wide chest, the light covering of hair that arrowed down his long golden torso to the flat plain between his narrow hips. When aroused, as he was now, he was magnificent, and when he eased himself on top of her it was the most wonderful feeling on earth. All hard muscle and living warmth, and a breathtakingly seductive and overpowering strength.

She looked into his face and saw the man of her dreams there. Loving or hating him, that dream never changed. I still love you, she thought, and hoped she did not say the words out loud.

He kissed her so gently that she thought maybe she had. He kissed and touched and stroked her where she needed him to, and eventually encouraged her to do the same to him. It was so long since she'd tracked her fingers over his flesh and watched him shudder in response, watched his eyes close with pleasure when her fingers closed around his sex....

The tears had long gone—driven away by the first probe of a sensual finger that arched her spine and then allowed it to relax again. He captured one of her breasts, rolling the tight rosebud nipple around his tongue then sucking gently until she groaned out a breathless protest, then he moved to the other breast.

Then it all suddenly changed. And it happened so

fast that she didn't see it coming. His mouth came up to fuse with hers in a fierce, deep hunger, and at the same moment he located her G spot and turned the rolling waves of gentle passion into a driving, racing, turbulent storm.

She groaned and gasped and arched and panted. She scored her nails down his back and he took her, ruthlessly and without mercy, to the peak—only to stop and let her drop down again. When she opened her eyes to accuse him of teasing she met with raw desire, lashing his skin to his facial bones, and she knew what was coming just before he made that first deep silken thrust.

It was the difference between slow, sensual foreplay and hot, physical sex. He could indulge her for hours, but when he flipped over the edge he went without warning.

He needed it now, needed it all, and he needed it voraciously.

Each powerful thrust was deeper than the preceding one, and her muscles grabbed and held on, then quivered each time he withdrew to begin the next stroke. When she cried out with pleasure he shuddered; when she quivered he shuddered. When she shouted at the top of her voice, *'Please—!'* he strapped her to him with his arms and increased the pace. And he kept on increasing until he felt the familiar sensation building through her. Quickly the feeling overtook the thrusts, and she became lost in that electric world of pure sensation.

Coming down afterwards was like trying to swim

against the flow of a river. Her heart wouldn't stop racing, and her blood was rushing so fast through her veins that she thought she could hear it. She tingled and shook and felt him still pulsating inside her. Her dry mouth and throat ached, because she still could not control her breathing.

'And that,' Rafael murmured huskily, 'is having all of me—wrapped around you and inside you.'

While they still lay in a tangle of trembling limbs, recovering from their most intense experience yet, Nina could not argue with his husky-voiced comment.

His warm mouth moved against her shoulder. She shrugged it away. 'Tell me about the second test you had,' she prompted.

He went still, then uttered a sigh and carefully withdrew so he could ease himself away. Then he rolled onto his back beside her on the bed.

'Last week,' he said abruptly. 'When the desire to exonerate you of everything grew strong enough to make me want an excuse to crawl to you on my knees and beg your forgiveness.'

'It took you six months to get there?'

His eyes flashed darkly. 'Do you want to hear this or not?'

'Yes,' she said.

He took a deep breath. 'As soon as I found out the result I was coming straight back here to tell you— then Marisia called with her news and told me what she intended to do.'

'I still can't stand to think of you seeing her behind my back.'

'Ditto you and Fredo,' he countered grimly. 'He is fresh out of a serious relationship. The last thing he needs is to see a door open to your broken heart, giving him ideas about two broken hearts making a whole one.'

'It isn't like that,' she protested. 'He's nice—he's your friend. We had lunch a couple of times and we talked about anything but broken hearts!'

'He told me to my face that I do not deserve you,' Rafael told her. 'He said that if I had any feelings for you at all I would let you go, so someone else could give you what I obviously could not. Who do you suppose he was thinking about when he offered that advice?'

'When did he say that?' she gasped, lifting her head to stare at him.

His face was like rock again. 'A couple of weeks ago,' he added with a shrug.

Curiosity had Nina levering herself up a bit further so she could capture his guarded eyes. 'He worried you,' she murmured silkily. His mouth flattened into a straight line. 'He planted the idea that I might actually give up on you altogether. You didn't like it, so you forced yourself to retake the test!'

'It was time.'

'You were scared and jealous!'

'I thought we were talking about Marisia!' he rasped.

'Oh, yes,' Nina murmured, and subsided again.

He heaved in yet another deep breath. 'She was frightened of what the family would think of her and saw abortion as her only way out,' he continued. 'You know what it's like here, Nina. There is still a heavy stigma attached to unmarried mothers. I delayed my trip by a few days so I could try and talk her out of it. It was not easy, and I did not dare leave her behind in London while I came here to you because I could not be sure she wouldn't change her mind. So I brought her with me—made her promise she would think about it over Christmas before she decided what she was going to do. She wasn't supposed to blurt it out tonight.'

'Then why did she?'

'Because she's a crazy woman—I don't know!' He sighed. 'I did not hang around long enough to find out!'

'Or because she wanted you tied down while she had the rest of us there as witnesses. If I knew about your affair with her then how many other people at that table knew?'

'This is going in circles.'

'Because I am still not convinced that her child is not your child?' She sat up. 'One mistake can easily become two mistakes, *caro*,' she said deridingly. 'Especially if you took so long to have your precious test! That makes the rest of this just—wallpaper!'

'If you want proof, *cara*—' he threw the same tone back at her. '—then you are going to have wait seven months. But I *will* prove it! I do not sleep around!'

'Neither do I!'

'All right—' He held up his hands. 'So I deserve all of this.'

The sound of a car coming up the drive caught their attention. Nina snaked off the bed and went to the window, tugging back the edge of the curtain, then releasing a sigh.

'I think you are going to have to prove it sooner than you thought,' she murmured, and turned to look at him. 'My grandfather is here,' she explained.

CHAPTER EIGHT

IT WAS like watching a light switch off, then come back on again to reveal a completely different man. 'She set me up.'

Realization was finally beginning to hit him.

'She's very good at it.'

'Her motive?' He climbed off the bed.

Nina could only offer an empty shrug. 'Regret for walking out on you? Or that good old motive revenge—on me this time, for jumping into her place?'

'She did not walk out on me.' Rafael frowned as he reached for his trousers. 'We did not have the kind of relationship either could walk away from. But I did tell her I was in love with you.'

'Me—?' Nina stared at him. 'Why would you tell her a lie like that?'

'It was not a lie.' Her huff of scorn made him grimace as he closed his trouser zip.

'I don't recall the word *love* coming into anything you said when you suggested we marry.'

'It would have seemed less of a blow to my pride if you'd turned down a simple business deal than if you'd turned me down. You're so...' A hand came out, long fingers making a helpless gesture. 'Special,' he finished huskily.

It was like being hit by one too many revelations.

Nina sank down on to her dressing stool and then just stared. Did she believe him?

He was standing there looking like a man who'd recently enjoyed a woman inside and out. His hair was ruffled, his mouth was wearing that sexy glow of too many hot kisses—but did that collate with a man in love?

'I think you're pulling rabbits out of a hat now,' she said.

'Meaning what?' He sent her a curious look.

She shifted restlessly, because she wasn't exactly sure what she meant—only that... 'I have this horrible feeling that I am being manipulated,' she said in the end.

Car doors slammed then—several of them—bringing Nina back to her feet.

'No,' Rafael said gruffly. 'You stay here.'

'But he's—'

'Sicilian. I know,' he nodded grimly. 'Well, so am I—I think,' he added with a wry smile.

It was the first time she had ever heard him actually mock himself like that. It brought tears to her eyes, which was silly—but it did.

'What if he—?'

Grabbing up his shirt, he walked over to her and settled it across her shoulders. 'Just think about this while I'm down there,' he suggested huskily. 'We all use manipulation in one form or another. At the moment I am fighting for my marriage, and I am prepared to do anything to save it. But lying to you is not one of those things. There has already been enough of that.

So I am telling you, *cara*, I have been in love with you since I first set eyes on you, and if you can bring yourself to believe that then we can deal with whatever else comes at us.'

'That is supposing I love you back.'

His eyes took on a glow. 'You are a tough lady when you want to be.' He sighed. Then he grinned and kissed her—once—briefly and was gone, leaving her with the itchy feeling that he *knew* she loved him—had always known...

The sound of knocking on the front door echoed through the hallway. Rafael was striding down the stairs just as Parsons was opening the door. The butler was barely given time to step to the side before Alessandro Guardino and his two sons were shouldering their way inside.

'Good evening again, Alessandro,' Rafael greeted him. 'What brings you away from your own birthday celebrations?'

All three Guardino men came to a stop when they saw him. Bare-chested and shoeless, and with his trousers resting low on his waist, he should have cast a vulnerable figure—but he didn't. Whoever his parents had been, they had endowed him with the kind of physique that intimidated other men.

It took the old man several seconds to deal with that before he took a threatening step forward. 'I want a word with you,' he gritted. 'You have been playing my granddaughters for fools.'

Parsons was about to do his usual and melt away,

but Rafael stopped him with the lift of a hand. 'Wait,' he said quietly. 'Our—guests will not be staying long.'

Without a word the butler stayed perfectly still by the open door. The three Guardino men moved forward, their expressions pouring scorn on Rafael's idea of back-up in a fist fight.

'If you think *he* is going to stop us from killing you, then you are a fool,' Alessandro jeered.

'You have a point,' Rafael conceded. 'But I think Gino could sway the odds my way.' And he lifted his eyes as his bodyguard stepped in through the front door. Built as wide as he was tall, Gino walked across the hall and went to stand beside Rafael.

All three Guardino men went very still.

'Now,' Rafael said, 'I think you had better explain why you feel the need to kill me.'

'You know why, you bastard.'

Strange, Rafael thought, but being called a bastard by this man was nothing like being called one by his wife. It must be the English accent that made the difference. Nina made the word sound so—sexy.

He smiled.

'This is not a joke!' Alessandro shouted.

'Too damn right, it isn't,' Rafael agreed, his face suddenly hardening. 'You had better explain what it is I am being accused of before I get Gino to throw you all out.'

Alessandro's sons were eyeing up the bodyguard and wondering if the two of them could take him. Don't try it, Rafael silently advised them. Gino had been known to wrestle five angry men to the ground.

'You are the one who made Marisia pregnant!'

'And you believe that?'

'She has brought shame on the family—you are her cousin's bastard husband!'

There was that word again. Rafael did not like it. He frowned. Beside him Gino flexed his muscles. He did not like the word either, since he wore the same label himself.

'Your penchant for backing the wrong horse is showing again, Alessandro, so take care what you say to me or you may alienate the source which usually bails you out!'

The old man stiffened at the reminder—and the threat. But this was a matter of honour, and in any Sicilian household family honour had to come before everything else.

'My own daughter confirms that she has seen you together! How do you explain that?'

'Louisa, like the rest of you, should learn to think before leaping to conclusions. I have no desire to touch Marisia. She turned me cold two years ago and she turns me cold now.'

'That's a lie. You were going to marry her.'

'You offered her, Alessandro, as a bargaining chip in lieu of the money you owed me. I politely declined.'

The old man went red. 'Only because you saw Nina and decided you wanted her instead.'

'Well, I can't argue with that.'

'Nina knows that you are the father of Marisia's child! It is the reason the poor girl ran from my house!'

Rafael said nothing. The truth was the truth after all.

The old man read that silence as a crack in his argument. 'She must be deeply hurt.'

'It is understandable.'

'You have been playing her for a fool—you have dishonoured her and the Guardino family. We have come to take her home with us.'

'Nina is already home,' Rafael pointed out.

'We demand to see her!' Angry frustration was beginning to set in. 'For all we know you might have hurt her again, like you did the last time when you threw her down the stairs!'

Danger raised its head suddenly, and everyone sensed it, even Rafael himself. 'I am going to give you a very good piece of advice now, Allesandro, and I suggest that you heed it.' He began walking forward, his steps slow and measured across the chequered floor. 'Leave this house now, while I still have some respect for you. You are, after all, my wife's grandfather, and you do care for her—which is the part I still respect. But if you say one more word I will probably hit you, and then we will both lose respect—for ourselves.'

As he moved closer all three men started backing, and the fact that they were doing it while Gino remained where he was, made a point that hammered itself home. There wasn't one of them witnessing this who didn't see that Rafael in this mood was strong enough for all three Guardino men.

'I'm an old man,' Alessandro blustered. 'My granddaughter would never forgive you if you laid a hand on me.'

'Precisely,' Rafael agreed. 'Which is why I am asking you to leave.'

'She deserves better than you.'

Another point Rafael had no argument with.

'Don't kid yourself that this is the end of it.' The door opening was now between them and him. 'We will be back tomorrow—with more of us.'

'I will look forward to it,' Rafael said. Then quietly and calmly closed the door.

When he turned round to face his two companions he discovered both had not moved at all. It was interesting, he mused, how danger emanated from within. He could feel it himself as he stood here. Was he pale? He felt pale, as if danger had leeched all the warmth from his blood.

He looked at the stairs. The stairs Nina had fallen down. He saw it happen again—watched her slip on her spindly heels then stumble, listened to her cries and his own as she rolled.

He flicked a glance at Gino. 'Make sure they leave,' he said.

With a nod the bodyguard eased out of the stasis holding him and disappeared towards the back of the house, meaning to carry out the task by stealth.

Parsons still had not moved a muscle, yet in some odd way Rafael knew he was not standing there like that because he was afraid to move. Too undignified, he thought, and would have smiled if he were able.

When he began walking towards the stairs again

Parsons spoke. 'I will lock up now, sir, if you don't mind,' he said.

Rafael nodded, then paused with one foot on the first stair. 'Do you like living in this house, Parsons?' he asked curiously.

For the first time since he'd known him Rafael saw the butler's eyes give an anxious flash, as if sensing a trap. 'I am content to live where Mrs Monteleone lives, sir,' the butler replied.

Which did not answer the question. 'But would you care if we all left here and never came back?'

The *we all* eased some tension out of Parsons's shoulders. 'No, sir,' he said.

Rafael nodded, looked around him for a few seconds, then came to a decision. 'How long will it take you to make the house safe to leave?'

'No time at all, sir. Will an hour be too soon?'

'An hour sounds about perfect,' Rafael approved.

The butler was turning away, but he paused. 'If you don't mind me saying so, sir, it will do Mrs Monteleone good to get away from here.'

All I have to do is convince *her* of that, Rafael thought, and he continued up the stairs feeling every nerve-end he possessed cringe, as they always did when he walked these stairs.

When he stepped into her room she was standing by the window, watching the red taillights of her grandfather's car make their way down the hill towards Syracuse.

But she was still wearing his shirt.

'They will come back,' she said, without turning.

'I know.' Crossing the room to stand behind her, he slid his hands around her waist and gently drew her back against him. 'How much did you overhear?' he asked.

'Most of it,' she said. 'I don't want you to hurt them,' she added, and he smiled, because it was good to know that she realised he could do so if he wanted to.

'I like your grandfather,' he admitted. 'He might be a reckless rogue with my money, and he uses his connections with me to his own advantage, but he loves his family. When the chips were down he came here willing to sacrifice my money for your honour.'

'He believes what Marisia has said.'

'The point is, Nina—do you believe her?'

Her reply was to turn and snake her arms around his neck. 'I just want all of this to go away—now.'

It was not the answer he had wanted, and it showed in the way he frowned. 'I'm going to give you two choices,' he said. 'You can get dressed and I will have Gino drive you back to your grandfather's house. Or you can get dressed and come with me, and we will retreat to a safer place until the fuss has—'

'I go where you go!' Her arms tightened their hold on him.

She sounded like the butler, he thought. But that was all it was—a brief thought—because his attention was shifting to other, more seductive things. She had the warm, supple feel of a recently loved woman, and the bloom of that loving still lay soft on her lips and in the darkened blue of her eyes.

His senses stirred, and Nina saw it happen. The frown softened out of his hard features and his eyes took on that dark, sensual look as he studied her mouth. Her lips parted and her fingernails curled into his nape. She moved that bit closer, drawn by the heat of his body and the promise of what it could make her feel.

'We leave for London in an hour,' he murmured.

'OK,' she agreed.

His fingers moved on her waist, crushing fine cotton as he pressed her close. 'That means we don't have time for this.'

'OK,' she said again, not really believing him. He would *make* time. That was what Rafael did; he turned the world on its head to suit his requirements. 'I'll go and get dressed, then…'

Like hell you will, those black eyes said, and his mouth took her mouth by storm.

CHAPTER NINE

Two hours later they were boarding a helicopter. It was midnight, and the clear night sky was alive with stars. As the helicopter lifted into the air Nina glanced back at the house, all shrouded in darkness now.

'Will you miss it?' Rafael asked quietly.

'The house? No,' she replied without hesitation, and turned away from it.

An hour after that they were seated on a chartered private jet.

Nina slept for most of the flight to London, curled up on a banquette with her head resting in Rafael's lap and her face pressed up against his waist while he worked on a laptop computer placed on the seat beside him. He was frowning in concentration, but was still aware of the way a set of her slender fingers had crept around his back and eased his shirt out of his trousers so she could have contact with his skin.

They were still making love. It had been like this for them from the first time he had dared to approach her with intimacy, days after they'd married. They'd been lying on a Caribbean beach, supposedly soaking up the sun, but the sensual vibrations flowing between them had reached such a pitch by then that it was either make a move or go back to their villa and take yet another long cold shower.

He had made the move, rolling onto his side, then over her. 'I want you,' he'd murmured, and kissed her before she'd had a chance to protest.

She hadn't protested, he recalled, giving up on trying to work and closing his eyes instead. They'd kissed themselves into a steamy stupor, then he'd gathered up enough sense to move location. He'd carried her back to the villa and she'd clung to him, blue eyes big and dark and driving him crazy—because they'd told him how much she wanted him.

A sigh threaded from him. Her cheek moved on his lap. It took some teeth-gritting control to stop his body from responding beneath that resting cheek.

They'd made love for the first time in the heat of the afternoon, and he'd never been so enchanted or so aware of his own prowess. She'd given him all of herself and he'd given the same back. He had never been the same man since. His cool English bride with her cool English reserve was not cool or reserved when it came to making love with him. And after the loving came this—the need to maintain contact with his skin, no matter where they were or how large the crowd they were in. She made him feel like the only man alive worthy of what she was giving him.

It had become like a drug. The more she'd made him feel the more he'd wanted her close—this close— all the time. When it had all exploded in his face it had been like having a vital part of him ripped out.

He'd become jealous and possessive, and moody with it. If he'd seen her look at another man and it had set his teeth on edge. She had worked for Daniel

Fraser. They'd been an item before she'd arrived in Sicily to visit her grandfather. He'd heard about her— had known of her existence because Alessandro and Marisia talked about Louisa's half-English daughter who owned the big house on the hill.

Seeing her for the first time had been like being hit by a runaway truck. He had never expected to come up against love in any of its forms, never mind the kind that pinned him to the spot. He could not even say it was her fair-skinned beauty that had done it. He'd always preferred dark-haired women, who wore their desires on their warm golden faces, not blonde-haired blue-eyed creatures who wore their reserve like a wall of glass.

'What are you thinking about?' a sleepy voice murmured.

'You,' he replied.

'Thought so,' she said, and rubbed her cheek against his hardening shaft, before levering herself upward until her face came level with his. 'You have a one-track mind.'

'Mmm,' he agreed, waiting for the hand she had just removed from his back to find some other place to latch on. It found his nape, then clearly was not satisfied with that, and slid beneath the neck of his black tee shirt to curl into the tight satin muscle between his shoulder and neck.

Then she kissed him. It was a slow and sensual invitation, made all the more potent because they were hidden from view of everyone else by the bulkhead.

Did he want to make love here? All it would take

was a few strategic moves and she could be straddling him. She liked it like that. She liked to pin him down and ride him slowly. She liked having control of his hungry mouth. She was wearing a skirt, and his trouser zip was no real barrier. He could sit here and let her put him on another planet without having to do very much.

'You're thinking about it,' she murmured softly, reading his thoughts as if they belonged to her. 'Are you worried that we might get caught in the act?'

'No,' he said. 'And you are a tease.'

It was her turn to offer a sensuous little, 'Mmm.'

She kissed him again, holding his face between both hands now, and flexing her body with pleasure when his hands arrived at her waist. It was now or not at all, he told himself ruefully. She wanted him and he wanted her, so what was holding him back?

He frowned at the question. She sensed the frown and pulled back so she could look at him. 'I don't want to be a nuisance,' she drawled, ever so politely, and went to pull right back.

Which just about finished him.

His hand snaked up beneath her skirt and located her panties. He stripped them away without losing contact with her darkening, promising, beautiful eyes. Next he dealt with his fly zip, then picked her up and repositioned her across his lap.

The feel of him sliding into her dragged the air from her throat. She quivered, then settled on him for the few seconds it took for those first sensual tugs of her muscles to mould themselves around him. After that she rode him, slow and deep, his hands encasing her smooth behind, hers still framing his face. Eyes locked, breathing warm and heavy, she brought him to the edge.

'I love you,' she whispered, and tightened her muscles around him as he shattered, taking her with him as he did.

Afterwards she lay against him, shocked, he suspected, at what she'd encouraged them to do. 'You think I'm a hussy.' She confirmed his suspicions.

'I think you are amazingly, naturally generous, the way you give yourself to me.' He lifted a hand to her hair so he could use it to bring them face to face. 'I'm sorry I messed it up for us,' he said deeply. 'I mean to do better this time, I promise you.

'I just want you to love me,' she confided, and it was so vulnerable it made his heart clench.

'I do—believe me.' He kissed her gently, then added lightly, 'I am also fertile. Has it occurred to you yet that we have made love three times without using protection?'

Then, while she stared at him in shock at his revelation, he stood up with her still closed around him and made the few strides it took to take them to the tiny bathroom...

Christmas had already come to London. Festive lights hung across the streets and decorated shop windows.

Gino was driving them, with Parsons seated at his side and the usual glass partition separating the front of the car from the rear.

Nina sat quietly beside Rafael. She had not spoken much in the last hour and neither had he. She was still shocked by what he'd said to her on the plane—even more shocked at the casual way he had said it. Why he wasn't talking was less easy to explain.

She turned an anxious look on his smooth profile and instantly felt a warm feeling pool in the pit of her stomach. She had barely seen him as a living, breathing human being twelve short hours ago, and now he had become the very centre of her universe—again.

How had he managed to do that?

How had he turned this marriage of theirs around without seeming to do anything much at all other than argue a lot and—?

She tried shutting the next thought off before it got started, but she seemed to have lost the ability to do that. The walls had tumbled, leaving her open and exposed and feeling so very vulnerable that she wasn't at all certain she wanted to feel like this.

Warm and alive and fizzing with feeling. The champagne bubbles of earlier had nothing on what was circulating in her blood right now.

Awareness—sexual awareness—spiced up with words of love...

He still had her panties. He'd refused to give them back to her, and now here she was, fizzing away in the knowledge that she was sitting here primly beside him with no underwear on because it was stuffed in his jacket pocket.

And could you tell that from that smooth, lean, too-handsome-to-be-true profile? No, you could not. The chin was level, the mouth flat, there wasn't a hair out of place on his dark silk head or a single crease in his dark suit that might hint he had been doing anything other than travelling from A to B in the trouble-free ease with which sophisticated and wealthy business-men expected to travel.

Rafael had walls of his own that kept people out when he wanted it that way. He'd allowed her a glimpse of the vulnerable man earlier, the needy man—both emotionally and physically—the man with weaknesses and fears like everyone else. But he'd let her see that man once before, only to slam the walls up when she'd dared to step too far over the line.

Where was the line going to be this time? Where were they about to go from here? How could he be so calm about them having unprotected sex when only six months ago the very idea that he could be sowing fertile seed had horrified him?

'You're sure you don't mind about—?'

'Yes,' he responded. That was all. After hours of silence between them he'd anticipated what she had been about to ask him and given his answer, neat and precise.

Nina pressed her lips together and looked to the front again. What was that reply supposed to repre-sent? Don't speak about it because I might change my mind? Or why bother to ask when the deed has been done?

A fatalist. Was he a fatalist? Was she being a com-plete fool to let him close again when he'd proved time after time that he could let her down badly when she needed him most?

The car turned into one of those streets that made Mayfair the exclusive district it was. As Gino guided it into its reserved off-road parking space Nina looked up at the elegant building which housed elegant apartments for elegant people.

Her father had used to own an apartment like this. Her mother had it now, left to her as her only bequest from Richard St James, along with a cold comment: The only part of my life that gave my wife pleasure. He'd been referring to the apartment's position within the high society life Louisa loved to live. Her father had been a cold man, and very bitter by the end. He'd loved Nina in a fashion—but not enough to let her warm his heart.

Rafael was like that. A man whose needs were tempered by the amount of feeling he was prepared to give out.

The car engine went silent. Parsons got out and opened Nina's door for her. Nobody spoke as all four of them walked towards the glass doors through which Louisa had spied Rafael and Marisia waiting for the lift to come.

Marisia... A sudden cold little draft feathered Nina's skin. They still had not finished with the Marisia thing, and Rafael *had* brought her here, and they *had* stood together in this very foyer, touching and gazing at each other intimately.

The lift was there waiting for them, instead of the other way round, so they rode it together—the man and his wife, the butler and the chauffeur-cum-bodyguard.

An odd bunch, Nina thought wryly.

Beside her, Rafael shifted his stance and she glanced up, met with a pair of half-hidden glinting black eyes. He wasn't hiding, he was waiting, she realised. Biding his time until he got her alone and begin the whole sensual experience all over again.

Had he ridden in this lift wearing the same look for Marisia?

Stop it, she told herself crossly. This is just being silly.

But even as they emptied out of the lift tension was beginning to creep up her spine. What if she found something inside the apartment—proof that there had been more to Rafael and Marisia's night together than just—?

His hand came to rest at the base of her spine as they waited for Gino to use his key to open the apartment door. Maybe he could feel her tension, because she felt his fingers begin to knead.

It was better to move away—easy to do it when she could follow Gino through the door.

'Go and get some sleep,' Rafael told Parsons and Gino as soon as they were all inside.

'You don't want me to make something warm to drink before I—?'

'No—thank you,' he murmured politely to the butler. '*Grazie,* Gino.'

The chauffeur was wiser than Parsons. He knew when they were not wanted. With a nod he ushered the butler towards the back of the apartment, where their private rooms were situated.

And then they were alone.

'Shall we do the same?' he invited softly, and Nina jerked into movement, walking forward down the spacious hallway, bypassing the elegant reception rooms on either side of her and only pausing when she found herself standing in the centre of the bedroom they'd used to share.

Removing her coat as she looked around her, she was aware of Rafael standing in the doorway, watching her familiarise herself with the straw-coloured walls, the dark furniture and the soft furnishings in subtle shades of copper and bronze.

She was looking for signs of female occupation. She knew it; he knew it.

'Found anything?' he asked.

She made no answer. Instead she dropped her coat across the back of one of the soft-cushioned chairs that flanked the white marble fireplace, then turned to head for the connecting bathroom.

'Don't try it, *cara*,' his smooth voice advised her. 'If something is bothering you then say so, but do not walk away.'

'All right.' She spun round to face him.

He was propping up the doorway with a broad shoulder, arms casually folded across his chest and everything about him as relaxed as a man could get. But it was all just a front, because there was nothing relaxed about his narrow-eyed, flat-lipped expression. He was ready for this.

'Where did she sleep?' she demanded.

'In the small guest room at the end of the hall,' he supplied.

'No diversions along the way?' she challenged. 'No deep and meaningful talks over a pot of coffee followed by some comforting hugs and kisses to reassure her? You just marched her down the hall to the small guest room and shut her inside it, then shut yourself in here?'

'You asked me where she slept, not what came beforehand,' he answered smoothly. 'I've told you nothing happened. Why are you fixating on this?'

'Because I have an issue about the two of you maintaining contact throughout our marriage,' she said. 'It's all a bit too cosy, very clandestine—and if I catch a whiff of her scent in any corner of this suite I will never believe another word you say to me!'

With that she turned towards the bathroom.

'She did not come in here.'

'Good,' she said, and kept on going.

'And what you call being clandestine I call being sensitive to your feelings and sympathetic to hers. I all but dumped her for you—does that count for nothing?'

'No,' she replied. 'It sounds like one big cover-up to me.'

'Cover-up of what?'

Nina twisted back. He still hadn't moved from the door, but his arms had unfolded and now he was angry. 'A few nights ago you had another woman sleeping in this apartment.' She spelled it out for him.

'Twelve hours ago our marriage was nothing but a very bad joke. Since then I've been humiliated in front of my family, thoroughly seduced by you, and up-rooted from Sicily and replanted here. My panties now reside in one of your pockets, like some kind of trophy—'

'Due to your seduction of me,' he put in.

Cheeks flushing, she ignored that. 'You've been leading me around by the nose and I don't know why I'm letting you do it!'

'Because you want to?'

'Oh!' she exclaimed, because he was so right. She almost stamped her foot in angry frustration. She retreated to the bathroom instead.

When she came out again, wearing one of the soft bathrobes that always hung behind the door, she found him waiting for her—dangling her flimsy white lace panties from his fingers like a taunt.

'I kept these,' he said, 'because you knowing I had them added an excruciating kind of tension to the rest of our journey. And I wanted to keep us both up there on a sexual high until I could get you alone.'

Nina snatched them away from him, so full of tumbling conflicts she didn't know whether to laugh at his audacity or just break down and cry.

'A few days ago you were still the only woman I wanted near me,' he continued. 'Twelve hours ago our marriage was in a mess, but salvageable—thank God. I had no wish to humiliate you and I did not seduce you. We made love,' he declared, 'because we both badly needed to, and I uprooted you from Sicily to offset a fight with your grandfather until he learns the truth, and because you were in danger of being swallowed up by that cold, empty shell of a house!'

Her sharp gasp at that last part had him muttering something, but did not stop him from going on. 'Marisia is not and never has been my lover. I did not break any code of marital ethics by bringing her to stay here for the night.'

'So if I brought Fredo to stay here overnight you would have no problem with it? Is that what you're saying?'

'No I am not saying that.' His mouth snapped together and he frowned.

'Then stop expecting more of me than you can give back,' she denounced. 'Now, I'm tired, so I'm going to bed—to sleep,' she added as a warning afterthought.

With that she stalked around him, walked up to the huge, deeply sprung divan bed, dropped her robe to the carpet like a defiance, then lifted a corner of the featherlight duvet and slipped between it and the cool cotton sheet.

If she'd expected a response then she did not get one. As she lay there shivering—the bed was cold and she was wearing nothing because her hastily packed suitcase still languished in the boot of the car—that other part of her—the part trembling with expectancy—withered when she heard the bathroom door quietly close.

He was taking his turn in the bathroom. Nina curled onto her side, closed her eyes, and grimly willed herself to fall asleep before he returned.

Surprisingly, it happened. One second she was deciding how she was going to freeze him out when he joined her in the bed, and the next moment she'd simply dropped like a stone into a deep sleep.

CHAPTER TEN

BY THE time Rafael approached the bed she was so deeply asleep that he found himself smiling ruefully as he slid in beside her. With a stealth aimed not to awaken her he drew her naked body into the curve of his, whispered, 'Shh,' when she murmured something, then reached out to touch a switch by the bed, plunging the room into darkness. Then he settled his head on the pillow beside her, closed his eyes, and at last dared to let himself relax.

Two hours later a grey winter dawn seeped slowly into the bedroom. Two hours after that neither of them had moved. Two hours on again the familiar feel of his hand gently stroking between her thighs plus the wet heat of his mouth tugging gently on one of her breasts brought her awake.

She opened her eyes to find harsh daylight softened by the curtains still drawn across the window. She was still for a few seconds, absorbing the sultry hush that lay over everything. Then blue eyes drifted down to where his head covered her breast. Dark hair tumbled like springy silk, and tanned shoulders were glossed by those natural oils which came during sleep to lubricate skin like stretched leather.

Lifting a hand, she let her fingers gently trail through his hair, making him raise his head, lips still parted and moist, eyes dark with desire as they clashed with hers.

'*Ciao,*' he greeted softly.

'*Ciao.*' She smiled.

The smile had its effect. 'You still love me,' he declared.

Why deny it? Nina thought. So, 'Yes,' she sighed, and received her reward in the warm crush of his mouth on hers.

Making love with Rafael in the morning had always been special. Nina thought it had something to do with him not yet having had the chance to pull on his sophisticated garb, so she got the real man—raw passions and all.

He liked to watch her melt; he liked to make her cling to him and plead and beg in a breathlessly sensuous voice. And when he came inside her he liked to make sure every inch of flesh possible enjoyed the experience at the same time. Arms wrapped around her and long legs tangled with hers, their bodies in touch from breast to hip and their mouths bonded as if they would never be able to break them apart.

He was everything her heart desired when he was like this—giving yet demanding, darkly passionate yet unbelievably willing to let her know how deeply she affected him.

At some point while he was stroking them towards the waiting turbulent climax the doorbell rang. If either heard it they dismissed it, because what was happening here was so much more important than anything else.

The first ripples of release began to shake her body,

and his tongue caught her gasps of pleasure as he increased his stroke. Slow and deep, harder with each thrust. She clung with her hands to his neck and his back—to his solid calf muscles with the bare soles of her feet and curling toes. Then came the blinding rush of orgasm, the tight, tingling shots of electric pleasure, which flowed between them in the kind of fusing that turned two into a whole.

It was no use trying to move afterwards. No part of either of them was fit to move. He was heavy on her, yet she felt as if she was floating, and she never wanted to come down to earth again.

A light rap on the bedroom door warned of Parsons's imminent arrival. With a muttered curse Rafael responded like lightning, by reaching out with a hand to grab hold of the duvet. The next thing Nina knew they were buried beneath it, and Rafael was still cursing as he covered her shocked face with kisses.

The door opened. A short silence prevailed. Nina felt the nervous urge to giggle, but that urge quickly died when the butler announced, 'Mrs St James and Miss Marisia have arrived and are asking to see you, sir—madam…'

The door closed again. Another short silence arrived. Then Rafael was pushing back the all-enveloping duvet and launching himself off the bed. Nina shivered at the loss—not of the duvet but the man.

'Stay here,' he instructed angrily. 'I will deal with this.'

'Not this time.' Nina was off the bed and stooping

to pick up the bathrobe from the floor. 'If Marisia is here to cause trouble then she will do it to my face.'

He paused on his way to the wardrobes, turned to utter a protest, then saw the stubborn look on her face. 'You're going out there looking like that?' he asked as he watched her cinch the robe's belt around her waist.

'Why not?' Her chin came up, her face still wearing the flush of loving but her eyes like blue glass again. 'Does it bother you that she will guess what we've been doing in here?'

'Dio,' he rasped. 'You still don't believe me about her!'

'You should not have brought her to this apartment,' she said, turning away from the sheer beauty of this naked man, still aroused and angry with it.

'If you wish to play it this way then so be it,' he said, and diverted from the wardrobes to the bathroom. A second later he was pulling on a matching bathrobe and striding across the room in the other direction, to open the bedroom door.

His mocking bow invited her to precede him. Nina sailed past him with her chin in the air—only to find herself captured by a strong arm that curved her into his body.

'One day,' he murmured, 'you are going to have to concede you are wrong about me, and when that day comes I will expect a full apology—on my own very particular terms.' Then he swept the two of them down the hall and into the sitting room.

The first thing to hit Nina was the delicious smell

of freshly made coffee; the next was the sight of her mother, standing staring out of the window, holding a cup and saucer in her hand. Louisa was wearing black today. Black wool suit and black silk shirt that looked very dramatic against the tense paleness showing on her face as she turned to look at them.

Marisia was sitting in one of the soft leather easy chairs. She was wearing black too, and also looked pale. She managed a brief glance upwards, then flushed and quickly looked down again.

'This is an unexpected surprise,' Rafael said lightly as he drew Nina forward. 'The two of you must have been up with the birds to get here so early.'

'We are sorry to have disturbed you,' Louisa responded, with a contemptuous glance at the way they were dressed. 'But it is one-thirty in the afternoon.'

'So late?' he quizzed. 'We had not noticed. Did Gino frisk you for lethal weapons, by the way?

The taunt went home like its own lethal weapon. Louisa suddenly looked uncomfortable, and Marisia shot upright, seeming to only just notice their hastily donned bathrobes, dishevelled hair and bare feet. She blanched, then sent a pained, pale and pleading look towards Rafael.

'We have intruded. I apologise,' she said anxiously. 'We should not have come—'

'Speak for yourself, Marisia,' Louisa said coolly. 'And sit down again, before you fall down.'

It was a surprise to watch Marisia do exactly that, but it was the way she put a trembling hand to her lips that struck a chord in Nina that sent her forward to squat down in front of her cousin.

'You're feeling unwell, aren't you?' she said, recognising the signs, having experienced them for herself.

'It was the sudden movement.' Marisia wafted a hand over her mouth, then tried swallowing. 'I will be all right in moment. I just need—'

'To wait for the nausea to recede. I know,' Nina put in. 'Can we get you anything? A glass of water? Or would you like to lie down or—?'

'Oh, please don't be nice to me, Nina!' Marisia protested painfully. 'I did a terrible thing to you last night. I forgot about the baby you lost when I spoke out as I did. Rafael told me not to do it, but I thought—'

'She thought she would be saved from my father's wrath with all of us there,' Louisa finished for her. 'And ended up causing more trouble than she is actually worth—did you not, *cara*?'

'You are a hard woman, Zia Louisa!' Marisia cried.

'If your mother was alive you would be confined to your room by now and not allowed to leave again for the next seven months!'

'What do you know about being a mother?' Nina snapped, shocking everyone by coming down on her cousin's side. 'You were never there for me!'

'Well, I am here now,' Louisa said, completely unfazed by the criticism. 'Tell Nina the name of the man whose baby it is you are carrying, and let us get this over with.'

Rafael stiffened in readiness. Nina's heart lodged like a brick in her throat.

Marisia swallowed thickly, 'H-his name is not important,' she said. 'But I can tell you it is not Rafael.'

Nina sat back on her haunches. 'But you said—'

'I offered no name,' Marisia insisted.

'No.' Louisa sighed suddenly. 'I am afraid, *cara*, that was me.'

Bewildered, Nina stared from one face to the other. 'I'm not following this…'

'Then let me explain,' her mother said, and came to put down her cup and saucer, then released another sigh and sat down herself.

'You know I had seen them being very intense over a dinner table,' she reminded Nina. 'You also know that I followed them back here, and what I saw then.'

Rafael made himself comfortable on the arm of a chair and waited with interest for this to play itself out.

'When Marisia said what she did last night I put two and two together and came up with—Rafael. You ran from the room and I wanted to kill someone. Rafael went after you and I told everyone that he was the father of Marisia's child.'

'I should have corrected her,' Marisia put in. 'But everyone was so busy shouting at each other that they seemed to have forgotten I was there, and I—preferred to keep it that way.'

'Lovely child,' Louisa derided her twin sister's daughter. 'What she means is that she took the coward's way out and let Rafael take the heat.'

'I did not think that Nonno would chase off to kill Rafael!' Marisia said defensively. 'We are supposed to live in the twenty-first century, for goodness' sake!'

'He was defending your honour.'

'He was defending Nina's honour,' Marisia threw back. 'He's always preferred her to me—'

'No, he hasn't,' Nina denied. 'He adores you. You are his beautiful dark-haired princess while I am—'

'His golden-haired angel sent from heaven for him to cherish...'

The two cousins looked at each other, then actually laughed—because it was so typical of him to play one off against the other.

'Glad you find all of this amusing, but I am still the man on his hit list,' Rafael put in.

The three women turned to look at him, their expressions telling him that they'd completely forgotten he was even there.

'My apologies,' he mocked, 'for butting in with my problems.'

Then he sent Nina the kind of smile that told her how much he was going to enjoy his apology later.

She looked away quickly, her cheeks growing warm. 'I hope you haven't come to London without telling Nonno the truth,' she said sharply.

'Of course not,' her mother snapped. 'To give Marisia her due, she told the truth as soon as the lynch mob arrived back without Rafael's head on a stick.'

'Better late than too late, I suppose,' Rafael murmured dryly.

'If I thought that you could not hold your own

against a seventy-year-old man and his two middle-aged sons I would say you were not worth saving,' his mother-in-law said. 'And don't think that because I was wrong about what I saw that I have forgiven you for the way you have been neglecting my daughter when she needed—'

'All right—let's not start another war,' Nina cut in quickly. 'I told you yesterday, Mother, that my marriage is none of your business.'

'*Grazie, cara,*' Rafael said.

'I did not mean to imply that what she said was wrong!' she flashed at him.

'You have come alive again,' Louisa observed.

'I was not dead, just grieving.' Nina came to her feet. 'How is Nonno feeling now that he knows the truth?' She brought this discussion firmly back on track.

'Devastated,' Louisa said. 'He has convinced himself that he has forfeited your love.'

'But that's silly.' Nina frowned.

'Tell *him* that, not me. You left Sicily, darling. He has translated that into you leaving him.'

'Rafael...' Nina spun anxiously to look at him. 'I don't want him to feel...'

He had straightened and taken her in his arms before she had a chance to finish the sentence. 'We can deal with him later,' he assured her, then a pair of warm lips brushed hers, and for a few glistening seconds Nina was not in the room.

'Time for us to go, I think,' Louisa said dryly, getting to her feet. Then she turned a wary look on her daughter. 'I hope you don't mind, Nina, but Marisia is coming to live with me here in London for a while—until she decides what it is she wants to do.'

'With the baby?' Nina turned her anxious look on her cousin next.

'No,' Marisia said, and the way her hands spread a protective cover over her abdomen said everything that needed to be said. 'You were right, Rafael.' She glanced at him. 'I have learned to love this baby. I just needed the extra time to realise it. I will bring it up alone, no matter what my family think or what sacrifices I will have to make.'

'My offer still stands,' he told her quietly.

What offer? Nina frowned at him. He ignored her questioning frown.

'Thank you,' Marisia murmured. 'I will keep it in mind.'

'What offer did you make to her?' Nina demanded the moment they were alone again.

'Marisia has discovered that she has a gift for picking out photogenic faces, so I offered to set her up with her own agency,' he explained.

'Right here in London?'

'Or Paris—Milan.' He shrugged.

'Make it Milan,' Nina said decisively. 'It isn't a city you visit that much.'

'You really are a jealous witch,' he drawled lazily.

'She's still in love with you—and don't tell me I don't know what I'm talking about,' she warned when he opened his mouth to speak. 'Even sitting in that chair, feeling sick and worried for herself, she still had to keep throwing those coded glances at you!'

He laughed. It was infuriating.

The next thing she knew she was being scooped off her feet. A minute later she was naked and back in the tumbled bed, with an equally naked Rafael on top of her. What followed next was his idea of how she should apologise for not believing him...

Later—much later—he was in a lazy, playful mood, pressing light kisses in rows across the flat of her abdomen, 'What do you think?' he said. 'Have we managed to make a baby yet, or do we need to try again?'

'I don't understand why you've changed you mind about children.' Nina frowned. 'I don't mind, you know, if the idea really upsets you. I only needed you to explain it to me before I got pregnant. Not—'

'Cruelly and heartlessly afterwards.'

'You were punishing me because you thought the baby wasn't yours.'

'You are very charitable, *cara*, but I don't need excuses made for me. I was a—bastard to you.' That was the first time he had ever used the word, and it surprised him as much as it did Nina to hear it fall from his lips. He slid up the bed to come and lie beside her. 'I will make it up to you,' he vowed huskily.

He was referring to the lost baby, Nina knew that, but...

She turned to face him on the pillow. 'Do you love me, Rafael?'

'More than I can deal with sometimes,' he admitted,

and touched her cheek with a tenderness that almost brought tears.

'You know I love you the same way, so we don't need—'

'No.' The fingers on her cheek moved to cover her mouth. 'It's you who does not understand, *amore*, that I wanted the baby to be mine so badly that every one of my foolish objections just paled into insignificance on the strength of that need. I've grown up, Nina. I've shed my past. I will never know who my parents are, but that's OK. Our children *will* know their parents. They will be loved and cared for and protected, and they will grow into good, strong people because that is what we will teach them to be. And,' he added on a lighter note, aimed to lift the serious mood, 'finding out I have a very healthy sperm count has placed a spectacular new edge on making love with you. Kind of—lusty and macho,' he said, with a lusty groan as he tipped her onto her back so he could lean over her.

'Oh, no, you don't,' she said, pushing him away. 'I'm hungry and thirsty. Have you any idea when we last ate anything? Because I haven't. And I have to call Nonno,' she reminded him.

'Do you want to go back?' he asked.

'To Sicily? No.' She snuggled into to him. 'I'm happy right where I am.'

'Then go and call him up—invite him for Christmas. Hell, invite them all if you want!' he said. 'If it makes him feel better about coming then I will even go against my better instincts and finance his latest disaster for him!'

A knock sounded at the bedroom door.

Parsons did not let himself in this time, but waited for Nina to scramble off the bed and pull on a bathrobe before she opened it. 'Your grandfather has arrived,' he informed her. 'Gino has checked him out and he seems—safe. What would you like us to do with him?'

Nina turned to look at Rafael. 'Oh, dear,' she said solemnly.

Oh, dear just about said it, Rafael thought as he made a reluctant shift from the bed. One old man with his dignity in tatters was going to take a lot of soothing.

'This is going to cost me,' he muttered ruefully.

'You can afford it,' his wife said. 'Just think about the payback when I show you my gratitude and you will be fine...'

THE ITALIAN'S
BLACKMAILED BRIDE

Jane Porter

CHAPTER ONE

"You can't arrest me." Emily Pelosi's voice betrayed none of the icy cold she felt on the inside. "I've done nothing wrong."

"Step aside, *mademoiselle*," the uniformed customs agent repeated tonelessly, destroying the effect of his lilting Caribbean accent.

Emily worked to keep her irritation from showing. She wasn't easily intimidated, had never been timid, and after five years of fighting fire with fire she held her ground now, hanging on to what had been written up once in the *Times* as "her remarkable cool." "Can you legally detain me?"

The customs agent looked at her as if she were stupid. "Yes."

Emily's brain raced, trying to absorb facts. Clearly she was in trouble, and clearly it wouldn't do to alienate the customs agent further. "I understand. But if someone could just get my friend…she's outside, waiting?"

"She'll just have to wait."

Emily looked away, swallowed, the long veil of her chestnut hair half hiding her face, cloaking her frustration. *Be cool, stay calm. Annelise will eventually return to the terminal and we'll get this whole thing straightened out.*

Head throbbing, eyes dry and gritty after the red-eye flight from Heathrow, she scanned the small island terminal. The squat cement building was virtually deserted, leaving just her and the customs agent alone.

She wished for the first time she'd taken something to make her sleep, like Annelise had, instead of working. But Emily had made herself work through the night. Just as she always worked these days. Emily Pelosi. Workaholic.

For a moment Emily had a strange view of her life—a life lived in international airport terminals and foreign hotels, with business meetings conducted over pots of green tea.

She didn't live, she thought wearily, she existed. To attack. To plunder. To destroy. But now she had to focus on more practical matters—like that of Annelise outside, waiting. "I understand you're not interested in my friend, but if someone could just let her know what's happening?"

"Your friend has already been advised that she can't return to the terminal." The customs agent crossed his arms over his chest. "And you must wait until the detectives arrive."

Detectives? Detectives from where? Emily had been flying into Anguilla for years, *en route* to St. Matt's, and she'd never been stopped before, never been hassled about anything. "You have a warrant, then?" she asked, feeling as if she were piecing together a puzzle in the dark.

"Yes, *mademoiselle*. We have a warrant issued by a member of the EU." The uniformed officer spoke with the heavily accented English of the Eastern Caribbean. Most of the islands close to South America were multi-lingual—French, Dutch, English, Spanish— and many of the smaller islands, like St. Matt's, were privately owned.

"But this isn't part of the European Union."

"We're working more closely with US and EU Customs to control piracy."

Piracy. International smuggling. And suddenly Emily suddenly understood. "Which member of the EU?"

"Italy. More specifically, a group called the Altagamma."

The Altagamma. Her lips nearly curved in a small, bitter, brutal smile. Of course. It was all beginning to make sense.

The Altagamma was an association that represented quality Italian goods for national and international markets. Some forty brands comprised the Altagamma, with sales in excess of eleven billion dollars—most of which came from exports. And Tristano Ferre was the new president of the Altagamma.

Tristano Ferre.

Emily felt a shaft of ice pierce through her chest. *Tristano Ferre.* This was his doing.

For a moment her head buzzed with white noise, the kind of empty static that drowned out other sound. There were few people she knew as well as Tristano. Few people she hated as much. Tristano had taken over from his father, Briano, a number of years ago, and if Briano had been hard, tough, ruthless, Tristano was a thousand times worse.

"Ah." The guard exhaled with relief. "They've arrived. The detectives are coming now."

She heard a metallic clang, and when she turned around Emily saw the doors at the far end of the small terminal part. Three men entered the building—two uniformed, one in plain clothes—and Emily realized her war on Ferre Design was just about to get interesting.

Two hours later the detectives had gone, and for a moment Emily sat alone in a small room that had probably never served any purpose in all the years the little island terminal had existed. She'd flown in and out of Anguilla so many times, and had never known about the little room before.

Tired, hungry—she'd been offered nothing to eat or drink—she glanced down at her hands, flexed her fingers. As always, her fingers were bare, her nails unpolished, filed smooth and short. She had practical hands, and yet it was an impractical life.

Her trips to China, her meetings with manufacturers. What had once been merely a stab at Ferre had become a deep-rooted commitment to Asia itself. She'd learned that many of the Chinese were great capitalists—creative, driven, dedicated to perfecting technology—and she'd respected that drive to succeed, admired the fact that everyone she'd met in China wanted the opportunity to work for himself, everyone had a dream of being an entrepreneur.

The door opened quietly, and yet Emily heard it. Her head lifted.

Tristano stood in the doorway. His thick dark brown hair was neatly combed, and yet even dressed in elegant clothes there was still something fiercely masculine about him. He was very tall, and very broad-shouldered. Rugged. Like a Tuscan farmer instead of one of the richest design manufacturers in Italy.

"*Buongiorno*, Emily." His voice, so deep, whispered across her skin.

Her jaw clenched, and for the first time she actually felt sick.

She'd wondered when he'd appear, had expected to see him once the customs agent had said the Altagamma was involved, but somehow seeing him here, face to face, was worse than she'd expected. She hated Tristano. Hated him so much she wanted blood.

"You can't escape me this time," he continued genially, as if they were two friends meeting in the middle of a sunny public square.

But of course he hadn't given up. He'd never give up. Not until he'd removed her as a threat to his company. It might have been two years since his last lawsuit, but he had kept going. And that second one should have been a clear warning.

"Really?"

He entered the room, gently closed the door behind him, and yet she flinched at the click of metal on metal.

Tristano approached and she longed to look away,

avert her head, but she wouldn't let him have the upper hand.

"More interrogation?" she mocked, calmly crossing her leg above her knee, hands folded in her lap.

His eyes, the darkest blue, held hers. "This is serious, Emily."

She felt a sizzle of alarm as he continued to approach, the fabric of his slacks hugging his thighs, the muscles taut, honed, visible. "I'm sure it is." He was bigger than she remembered. Harder. But she was stronger, harder, too. Her lips curved in a cool challenge. "You're losing money."

"I have lost money, yes, but the association is losing, too. You're not just hurting me. You're hurting many, many Italians."

"I'm only reproducing Pelosi designs."

"Ferre designs," he corrected.

"But they're not your designs. They're mine. Emily Pelosi Designs."

He stood over her, the table between them, his eyes narrowed as he gazed down at her. "So why are your handbags and luggage lines exact replicas of ours?"

She shrugged. "It's as I told the detectives. The bags are generic lookalikes, which is legal."

"Not generic. Your luxury line infringes on our company trademarks, and when you sell the bags they're marketed as Ferre & Pelosi, like our original line."

Another cool shift of her shoulders. "I label nothing. If retailers choose to market a bag as such, how can I stop them? I'm in London, not Chicago or San Francisco.''

He leaned across the table, looked her in the eye. His voice dropped low, so low she had to strain to hear. "What you're doing, *cara*, is illegal.''

Cara. Cara. She'd once been his *cara*, but she'd been young and innocent. Trusting. He'd taken that trust, along with everything else. So she said nothing, just held his gaze, staring up at him furiously, defiantly, grateful in some respects that their battle was finally taking place face to face.

Her silence succeeded in provoking him. His features tightened. "Where are your ethics?" he snapped, leaning further across the table, moving so close she could smell a whiff of the spice of his subtle fragrance, see the grooves paralleling his mouth.

"Where are yours?" she countered.

"Everything I do is legal. While you…you're a pirate.''

A pirate? She nearly smiled. He was right. She felt like a pirate, a buccaneer, one of the many outlaws that settled in the Caribbean in the middle of the 1600s.

"You weren't raised like this," he continued tersely.

"Leave my education out of this. I'm doing what needs to be done.''

"Despite the consequences?''

"I'm not afraid.''

"Just foolish," he concluded, with a faint shake of his head, watching her, seeing how her blue-green eyes flashed fire, seeing how determined she was to bring him down.

Everything in her was bent on destruction. Specifically, destroying him. But she hadn't been reckless, she'd been smart. Very smart, and remarkably careful. Only he'd been just as smart, and even more careful, because this time he was going to make sure the charges stuck.

This time Emily Pelosi would be held accountable.

"The detectives have a plane waiting," he said, sitting down on the corner of the table, close to her, invading her space, making his presence known.

He saw her lips compress. She didn't like to be crowded, especially not by him. Too bad. This time Emily wasn't going to get what she wanted. This time it was his way.

Her head tipped back, long hair spilling down her back. "Put me on it."

Tristano had to admire her. She had guts, he thought, enjoying the hot spark in her eyes. But then, she'd never been afraid of a fight. He wouldn't call her a tomboy, but she'd always believed so fiercely in things, had loved her family passionately, loved her friends, too. Growing up, he'd never thought of her as English...British...but Italian through and through. And yet now she wasn't a girl but a woman, and she was the epitome of tough. Cool.

"The detectives will take you to Puerto Rico, where the investigation is based."

"Fine."

"They will toss you in jail." His lips curved,

firmed, and there was bite in his words. "With all the other thieves, smugglers and criminals waiting prosecution."

She shifted, one leg crossed high above the other knee, without putting a single wrinkle in her impeccably white pinstriped linen trousers. She'd paired the expensive trousers with a black halter-top which revealed her slim pale gold shoulders, and the pale gold column of her throat. "Great. Let them know I'm ready."

"You don't mind going to jail?"

"No."

"You'll be locked up with dangerous people—people without any regard for human life—"

"Fine," she interrupted. Her chin lifted. "You've no regard for human life either, and, frankly, I'd rather be there than here with you."

Maledizione. She *was* a pirate. A rogue beauty—brave, foolish, swaggering, cunning, vain. If she'd lived during the seventeenth Century he was certain she would have followed in the footsteps of famous women pirates, like Grace O'Malley, Anne Bonny and Mary Read.

Instead she was here, alone with him, beautiful, proud, intelligent, fierce.

And he wanted her. He felt like a bounty-hunter, because he'd been working for a long time to rein her in, bring some control back to his life and Ferre Design. But, unlike a bounty-hunter, he didn't want her shackled in jail. He wanted her shackled in his bed. He wasn't about to turn her over to the authorities.

But he wasn't going to tell her that. Let her think she'd be handed over to the detectives and customs officers. Let her think she had a choice when really she had none.

It was time Emily Pelosi faced facts, and this time she was going to face them. Alone with him.

"So what happens now?" she asked, and she sounded almost bored. Definitely complacent.

"After deportation, or after time in jail?"

Her expression didn't change. "I was thinking more in terms of my friend Annelise. What happens to her?"

"She's already taken a plane back to London."

Tristano saw a flicker of emotion cross Emily's flawless face. Worry? Dread? Regret? And then the expression disappeared, leaving her perfect oval-shaped face serene again.

"Going to jail doesn't scare you?" he asked, trying to understand her, wanting to understand how she'd changed so much in the years since they'd been close friends. Although friends wasn't an adequate description. They'd been more than friends, they'd been lovers, too, and for a couple of weeks one August they'd been together every moment possible.

He tried to remember the last time he'd seen her. It couldn't have been all that long ago. She'd once moved in similar circles. They both came from affluent Italian families, had both grown up in the same inner circle, with big houses in Milan and rambling estates in the Tuscan hills, estates where vines covered acres and orchards of olive trees covered more. But the problems with her father had resulted in a deep break between the families, and the Pelosis had left Italy to return to England, where Emily's mother was from.

And even with half of Europe stretching between them he had bumped into Emily more often than one would have thought. They had both attended a party in Sienna a year or two ago, and then there'd been the passing at the airport. Her flight had just landed and his had been about to depart. They hadn't spoken either time. They'd simply looked at each other and moved on.

It had been clear to him then she had nothing to say, and he hadn't been sure what he wanted to say to her.

Well, that wasn't entirely true. He'd wanted to tell her to stop with the counterfeiting, tell her he was cracking down, that he had to get serious. But he couldn't breach the divide, couldn't reason with her when she looked at him with so much ice and hatred in her eyes.

Emily.

He was only four years older, but right now he felt vastly her senior, knowing that the charges leveled against her this time would stick, that his director of security had gathered enough evidence, enough samples, enough of everything to cost her…everything.

"You don't want to go to jail," he said roughly, knowing she wasn't going to listen. If a week alone with him couldn't persuade her to change course, then he'd go the legal route. Punish her to the fullest extent of the law. But he wanted a week first. Christmas together.

"There's a lot of things I don't want to happen that do," she answered, and she glanced at her wristwatch, as if she had some pressing engagement to go to. Again he marveled at her cool, at her incredible calm.

"You do have other choices," he said.

Emily drew a slow breath and exhaled just as slowly. She was tired. She knew she couldn't fight forever. But she also knew she wouldn't go down until she'd brought him to ruin, too. "I'm not giving up."

The corner of his mouth tugged, but his dark blue eyes were hard, void of all compassion. "I don't expect you to."

"So what are my choices? How do I avoid arrest?"

"You don't avoid arrest—that's happened—but it's up to you where you spend your Christmas holiday." He paused and she stared at him, waiting for him to finish. "You can," he continued tonelessly, "get on that plane to Puerto Rico, or you can come home with me."

"Home with you?"

"St. Matt's."

"St. Matt's isn't your home."

His eyebrows lifted and Emily bit down on the inside of her lip hard. *What the hell?* A dozen questions welled up inside her but she wouldn't ask one. She had to stay cool, collected, had to hang on to whatever dignity remained. There was no way she'd let Tristano see how much he disturbed her. And he did disturb her. Not as an adversary, but as a man.

And that made him the most dangerous adversary of all.

"Let me see if I understand you correctly," she said rising from the table, sidestepping Tristano's powerful frame.

In the past five years she'd been confronted by tremendous difficulties—more problems and controversy than she'd ever imagined—and yet she'd survived every crisis by staying cool, keeping her wits about her. But right now her wits felt scattered. Lost. Instead of thinking her way out of the problem, she kept thinking about *him.* "I'm still under arrest, but I won't be deported if I agree to accompany you to your house on St. Matt's?"

Tristano nodded his confirmation.

"How convenient for you," she drawled coolly, shooting him an icy look.

"I'd say inconvenient—but why mince words?"

"Indeed." Her voice dripped sarcasm and she stared at him a long moment, then looked away, her lips curving in a hard smile. If this was war—and it had been war for several years now—he had just won a major battle. But he hadn't won the game yet. He hadn't stopped her.

Still smiling that small, faint smile, she glanced back at him. "Maybe I'd rather go to Puerto Rico."

"I wouldn't be surprised, dearest Em. You've always preferred doing everything the hard way."

She bit down, working her teeth, her jaw tight.

"Can you please use Emily, not Em?" She hated being called Em. Her father was the only other person who'd ever called her Em, and to have Tristano use the same intimate form of her name hurt.

Tristano had helped destroy her father. He'd taken her father's strength...stripped him of his power, his pride, that inherent male dignity...leaving him empty. Dead.

"Whatever makes you happy, *cara.*"

"What do you want, Tristano?"

He stood up, approached her, towering over her. "You know what I want. The question is, are you ready to work with me?"

"But you don't mean work with you. What you intend to do is shut down my company—"

"Your company isn't a company!" His voice rose, his anger palpable. "Your entire company is based on undercutting mine."

"I'm merely offering consumers a comparable product at a lower cost, and that's called commerce. Capitalism. Something even *you* should understand."

His eyes narrowed, creases forming at the corners, and his frustration became tangible. He was losing patience. "It would be fair commerce if you were truly offering a comparable product. But you're not. You're offering our line, reproducing virtually our entire line, flooding the market with counterfeit leather goods, destroying market value."

"How terrible." But she thought it anything but terrible.

If he'd been there Christmas morning, struggling to

revive her father, struggling to save him before Mother saw. If he'd been there, stretched out over someone he loved dearly, trying to force air into his lungs, trying to bring him back to life, he'd know what she felt and he'd know this wasn't about leather goods. It was about justice. It was about fairness.

It was about revenge.

She'd have her revenge, too. She'd find a way to bring peace to her poor father's soul.

And maybe, somehow, peace to her own.

"As I said earlier, this is serious, Em."

Her eyes burned, her heart just as hot, and the pain washed through her. The picture of her father sprawled on the bathroom floor was too vivid still, the picture forever burnt into her memory. "Yes, it is."

"I'll prosecute."

"I'm sure you will." And then she smiled, if only to keep the tears from forming, to shift her muscles, the tension, the need, the loss. "You see, the only reason you're going after me is because I'm successful. I've hurt your business. I'm doing something well—so well that it's forcing you to stop me, try to recoup your losses."

He said nothing, but she saw from his expression, the fixedness at his mouth, the hardness in his eyes, that she was right. She'd been good. Her business model—much to Ferre's consternation—was very good. But of course it would be. She'd taken Tristano's principles of commerce, taken everything he'd done well, and applied it to her own company.

Tristano's business model was brilliant. He'd make

her a very wealthy woman. A year ago she'd made her first million. This year she looked to make two.

"It'll get ugly when this goes to court," he said now.

"It won't hold up in court."

"It will. I'm pressing charges in the United States first, and the US courts will recognize your designs as the legal property of Ferre Design."

"Even though the Ferres haven't a designing bone in their greedy, manipulative bodies?"

"Article I of the US Constitution gives inventors exclusive rights to their discoveries."

"*Father's* discoveries."

He crossed his arms. "The legal fees alone will ruin you."

She thought back on her hard-won financial security, thought back on the years when she and her mother had struggled, especially right after her father's suicide. "I'm prepared."

"*Emily.*"

"You know the truth," she said bitterly, stepping toward him, fury sweeping through her. Did he think she was afraid of him? Did he think he could do anything to her that hadn't already been done? "You destroyed us, Tristano. You and your father. So don't think I have it in my heart to forgive. Because I'm not that big. I'm not. I can't forgive, and I can't forget. So here we are."

Tristano sucked in air, held his breath, his lungs hot, explosive. She pushed his control, tested his willpower. He wanted to touch her, wanted to take her in

his arms, cover her lips, plunder her mouth the way
she'd plundered his company, but he held himself still.

"You're the one who doesn't know the truth," he
said softly, staring at her mouth, at her lips, wide, full,
incredibly lush. She had the mouth of an Italian film
star, and yet her eyes were the stunning blue-green of
great English beauties. "And if this goes to court
you'll hear the truth. Along with thousands of strang-
ers."

Dusky pink color suffused her cheeks. "I can handle it."

Emily, Emily. He shook his head. "I don't think
you can."

"You don't know—"

"No," he interrupted curtly, his deep voice crackling with anger and impatience. *"You* don't know.
And if you think you can handle this on the front page
of the paper, or on the evening news, then think about
your mother. Can she? Is this what she needs? Is this
what's best for her?"

Emily stared up at him, onyx flecks in the blue-
green of her eyes. He could see her hatred there, could
see the violence of her emotion, but she turned her
head away, averting her face. "She'll be fine," she
said hoarsely. "She's been through a lot."

Tristano laughed hollowly. "Then bring it on, *cara.*
Let her suffer some more."

He moved to the door and knocked once, indicating
he was through. The door opened. The green-uniformed
customs agent appeared. "Is she ready?" the agent
asked, nodding at Emily.

Tristano shot her a glance through narrowed eyes. "She's ready. She's looking forward to Christmas in San Juan. Right, Em?"

Emily felt too hot, too alive, and with a wretched sinking in her stomach she found herself turning to Tristano and smiling a preternaturally calm smile. "Right."

He stood there a moment, staring at her. "You kill me, *carissima*."

Sometimes she killed herself.

Somehow she'd become this fierce.

Suddenly Emily didn't want to be so tough, so strong, but she couldn't let go of the past, couldn't forgive or forget. Not when her family had been crushed, reduced to bits of agony. "This is about Ferre Designs," she said, her voice breaking, her bitterness slicing through the room. "Not about me."

He looked at her. A muscle pulled in his jaw. "Are you sure?" When she didn't answer, he shrugged. "She's all yours," Tristano said to the agent, and then to Emily, "Have a good Christmas, Emily. See you in court."

"And when will that be?"

"January? February? Depends on the hearing date." He hesitated. "I'll call your mother—let her know the name and number of the prison in San Juan—"

"Don't, Tristano."

"She'd want to know."

"Tristano—"

"She's your mother, Em. She deserves the truth."

And he walked out, leaving her alone with the customs agent.

The truth? Emily silently repeated. But it wasn't the truth! The truth was that Briano and Tristano Ferre had destroyed her father and grown rich at his expense! *That* was the truth.

"If you'll put your hands out, *mademoiselle*."

The custom agent's voice brought her back to the moment, and the small dismal room where she'd been interrogated.

She blinked, eyes focusing, and felt her blood drain as she saw him draw out handcuffs. "You're going to handcuff me?"

"If you'll put your hands out?"

She really was going to be deported, sent to San Juan to who knew what kind of conditions. And while she wasn't afraid for herself, she was very afraid for her mother. She wasn't well, hadn't been well in years, and Emily knew she couldn't handle this—not now...definitely not after the last six months of agonizing pain. Her mother's arthritis had become so bad, completely debilitating. She didn't need anything else to hurt her.

"Get him," Emily said tersely, coming to a swift decision. "Get Tristano Ferre before he leaves."

CHAPTER TWO

TRISTANO had known the mother card would work with Emily—because he knew Emily.

She might think he didn't understand her, but he understood more than he let on. And maybe it hadn't been fair to dangle her mother like bait on a hook, but what was fair in love and war?

He watched now as she was escorted from the terminal into the bright afternoon light. She'd been inside the terminal for nearly three and a half hours. He knew she hadn't eaten since arriving, knew she hadn't been offered anything to drink, and her flight had been an all-nighter.

Yet as Emily walked toward him she looked stunning, her white pinstriped suit jacket still crisp as it dangled casually over one bare shoulder, long hair gleaming in the sunlight, high heels emphasizing her confident stride.

She could have modeled professionally, had been sought after late in her teens by several big Italian agencies, but she'd passed, devoted to school and apprenticing at the company.

For a moment his gut burned. Not guilt, he told himself, but a rare flicker of remorse.

She'd loved the company.

She'd loved Ferre & Pelosi as much as he had, but

she'd been cut out when her father had been written off. It must have hurt her. He suppressed the thought, knowing her father had nearly ruined the company, robbed the company blind. His father, Briano, hadn't had a choice.

"Changed your mind?" he said as Emily reached his side.

Her jaw compressed, eyes sparking defiance. "Do you really own a house on St. Matt's?"

"Yes."

She stared at him disbelievingly. "The Flemmings sold to you?"

"Five years ago."

"I can't believe they'd do that."

"Why not?"

"They…the Flemmings…promised they wouldn't."

"Did you ever meet them? The Flemmings?"

Emily's eyes narrowed as she studied Tristano's hard but handsome face. His dark blue eyes were almost too perfect with his thick dark hair and dark brown eyebrows. "No. But I talked to them on the phone many times."

"Mmm," Tristano said, his expression bland.

Emily battled her temper. For twenty years her family had owned St. Matt's; for twenty years it had been her second home… Every Christmas holiday had been spent on the tiny island, and when her father had been forced to sell St. Matt's he'd sold to John Flemming, a wealthy American.

John Flemming had been wonderful about keeping

in touch, letting them know when the island house would be free in the event that the Pelosis wanted to visit.

But they hadn't visited. Not after Father's death. Even though it had been tradition to escape London's chilly dampness for the Caribbean sunshine. It would have been too painful returning to St. Matt's, too painful facing what they'd all loved and lost.

Tristano held the door open to the waiting limousine. "Maybe you should have done a little more research."

Emily shot him a dark look as she slid into the back of the limo. "What does that mean?"

He climbed in after her. "It means there are no Flemmings." He shut the door and the car set off, heading for the water, where an anchored yacht would take them to St. Matt's. "Let me clarify myself. There *is* a John Flemming, but he doesn't own the island. He never did."

Confused, Emily stared at Tristano blankly. "I don't understand."

"John Flemming worked for me," Tristano continued blithely. "Represented me during the purchase of St. Matt's."

A wave of nausea swept Emily and blindly she reached for the door handle, as if to throw herself out of the moving car.

Tristano reached over her lap, covered her hand with his and held tight. "Don't do it. You'd break a leg...or worse...and then you'd be dependent on me for far more than you'd like."

His hand felt hard, warm, and far too personal. She flashed back to that summer years ago, when all she'd wanted was his hands on her body, covering her breasts, clasping her face, and him kissing her until she couldn't breathe or think.

Disgusted, Emily jerked her hand out from beneath his. He arched an eyebrow at her reaction and she shuddered, pulling as far from him as possible. "Don't touch me."

"You're scared of me."

"I'm not." She fought panic, realizing how she'd put herself in his care, handed herself into his keeping. Not good, she thought, glancing nervously out the tinted car window. Not good for body or mind.

"So why do you flinch whenever I get near you?"

She laughed, low and harsh. "Because I hate you."

"Hate?"

She laughed again, and the sound felt as raw in her chest as it sounded. Her insides were hot with emotion, bubbling with the acid pain that never went away. "Hate." Her gaze met his and she let him look into her eyes, let him see what she felt, let him see the anger burning there. "I will never forgive you for what you've done."

"You hate me because I let you believe the Flemmings owned St. Matt's?"

"No. I hate you because of what you did to Father. What you did to the company. What you did to my family."

"I'll take the blame for the purchase of the island, but the rest of it—" He shrugged, leaned forward to retrieve a chilled bottle of water from the limousine's mini refrigerator. "That was your father's doing."

She closed her eyes, held the pain in, holding tightly to what was left of her control.

But it was worse with her eyes closed. With her eyes closed her senses were sharper, more acute, and she felt even more aware of Tristano sitting so close. She could feel his warmth, his immovable presence, could feel his smug arrogance, too.

He was awful. Despicable. And she'd bring him down. All the way down. She'd fight to destroy him and his father, just the way they'd destroyed the Pelosis.

She heard Tristano twist the plastic cap off the bottle and swallow.

"Want a drink?" he offered.

She opened her eyes, saw he was holding the bottle out to her. "No."

"Are you certain? You're looking quite pale, *cara*."

"It's just the sound of your voice making me ill, Tristano." And she closed her eyes again, tipped her head back and prayed for deliverance. But even with her eyes closed she could feel his gaze on her, feel *him*—his size, his strength, the heat from his impossibly solid, muscular body. And now St. Matt's was just one more thing Tristano Ferre had taken from her family.

The car rolled to a stop, and as Tristano opened the back door Emily avoided his hand. She reached into the trunk of the car to retrieve her own luggage and walked quickly toward the waiting yacht.

They boarded the yacht in tense silence. The trip from Anguilla to St. Matt's would take less than ninety minutes. Fifteen if they'd flown.

As the yacht left Anguilla's harbor Tristano sprawled on a padded lounger, basking in the golden sunlight, while Emily stood stiffly at the railing, staring out across the endlessly blue water.

"Why did you buy the island?" she asked as they reached open water.

He folded his arms behind his head, sunglasses shielding his eyes. "I wanted it."

"Why?" she persisted, turning to face him, the warm wind lifting her hair.

"Memories."

She couldn't imagine how he could have such good memories of a place that had nearly broken her. Emily looked away and bit the inside of her cheek, feeling far more alone than she liked. She'd only felt able to make this trip this year because Annelise had offered to accompany her. Otherwise there was no way she'd have been able to return, much less for Christmas. She hadn't been back since Father's death, and yet she knew it was time.

Father wasn't coming back.

He was gone. His name wiped first from the famous Italian leather design company, Ferre & Pelosi, and now his memory wiped away by pain.

She couldn't bear to think of him. Couldn't bear to

think what had been done to him. Couldn't bear to think what he'd done to himself.

Emily swallowed the raw grief, her sorrow rising like a strong tide, threatening to engulf her.

"It was your choice to sell," Tristano said, and she steeled herself, resisting him, his voice, his reasonable tone. "We never came to you," he continued. "Never asked, encouraged or pushed. You chose to sell."

"To the *Flemmings*." She turned her head, eyes hot, furious, and shook her head. "You knew I'd never sell to you. You knew you'd be the last person I'd want to own it."

"I did." And he smiled, white teeth bared. With his strong jaw shadowed with the hint of a day's beard and the warm wind blowing through his hair he looked as if he could have been a privateer. "I kept wondering when you'd discover that we'd actually bought the island, that the Flemmings were just a cover, but it seems you were too busy…" he hesitated, considering his next words "…trying to stay one step ahead of the law."

"The *law*?" She spat the words back at him. "Just because you hold a law degree doesn't mean you know anything about justice."

"Someday you'll know the truth and you'll apologize."

"*Assolutamente no!* No way. Never."

He studied her a long moment, his dark blue eyes creasing at the corners and deep grooves forming next to his mouth. "You've always been welcome to return. I know Mr. Flemming always let you know the main house was available to you anytime you wanted to visit.''

She shook her head, still stunned. ''All those talks I had with him...all those things I shared...?''

''You didn't share that much, but, yes, whatever you told him, he told me.''

Emily couldn't believe it. She'd liked John Flemming—had found him so open, so friendly, so...American. And all this time he'd been just a front, a cover for Tristano.

Wearily, Emily rubbed her temples, her head pounding. The sleepless night was catching her up, as well as the realization that all these years her house, her beloved plantation, had been Tristano's. It was laughable. Horrible. Tristano just kept on winning, didn't he?

The rocking motion of the yacht should have lulled her, relaxed her. Instead the surging sea rocked her, maddened her, each crashing wave seeming to chant *Tristano Ferre, Tristano Ferre* as it broke against the ship's hull.

A half-hour into their voyage the steward appeared with lightly toasted Club sandwiches and wedges of fresh fruit. Emily was too hungry to refuse food. She was proud, but not completely stupid. Hunger was hunger. She needed to eat. But that didn't mean she had to share a table with Tristano.

When Tristano sat down at the table she moved to the padded lounge chairs and balanced her plate on her lap. When Tristano silently rose, leaving his place at the table to sit next to her on a lounger, she tried to rise to return to the table. But Tristano put an arm out, clasped her wrist and pulled her back down on the chair next to him.

"Stay put, *cara*, or I'll pull you onto my lap and hand-feed you."

Color flared in her cheeks. "I'd bite your fingers."

"What about your tongue?"

Her cheeks darkened to a crimson red. "What about it?"

He shrugged. "Just asking."

She ducked her head, her toasted sandwich clasped tightly in her fingers. Suddenly her appetite was gone. How could he do this to her? How could he make her feel so…unhinged? Like a derailed train?

She heard the soft pop of a cork and moments later Tristano was placing a glass of wine at her feet. "Drink it," he said dryly. "You need it. You're so uptight you're about to explode."

That was it. She'd had enough. More than enough. Flinging back her head, she opened her mouth to give him hell—and discovered Tristano's mocking smile. He was just waiting for it. He wanted her upset.

What was happening to her? Her famous calm was deserting her right when she needed it most. Emily drew a slow, deep breath and lifted her sandwich to her mouth, forced herself to eat. One bite, and then another. He wanted a fight? Fine. She'd give it to him.

She'd fight him to the end.

Fight him until she had no air left to breathe.

Swallowing the sandwich with difficulty, Emily reached for her wine glass and downed half the wine in one gulp. Courage, she reminded herself. Courage and control.

She was glad now she'd decided to go with him to St. Matt's. In jail on San Juan she could have accomplished nothing, but alone with Tristano she could make him feel, make him aware, make him know what it was like to be obsessed. Possessed. Alive with pain, and anger, and the burning need for revenge.

Revenge. She savored the word, watched Tristano refill her wine glass. She'd get even. She'd make him pay if it was the last thing she did.

Halfway through lunch St. Matt's appeared on the horizon, just a speck of green.

Riveted, Emily's gaze clung to the distant island. Slowly she set her wine glass down, her heart leaping to her throat as her right hand clenched and unclenched the linen napkin spread across her lap. St. Matt's. St. Matthew's. Her home away from home.

After a few minutes she was aware of Tristano's gaze resting on her, his expression closed but watchful. He said nothing, but she was certain he knew what she was thinking. She might hate him, but it wouldn't change the shared history between them.

Emily forced herself to turn her head and look at Tristano, who still sat far too close to her. "Exactly how does house arrest work, Tristano?"

"Like this. I stay close. I keep you under constant watch."

"No guards?"

"Just myself."

They were speeding along the water, growing ever

closer to the island. Little by little the steep green sloping hillsides took color and shape, rugged with buttonwood, coconut and sea grape. The island had been landscaped years ago, a mutual project between a prominent English landscaper and her father—her father who'd loved the island terrain nearly as much as he'd loved the Tuscan landscape.

"And that will be enough?"

"You want more?"

"No. I'm just surprised you don't feel the need for stronger measures."

"Like handcuffs?" he asked, his dark blue eyes the color of the deepest part of the ocean. "Because I'm sure I could get some. If you prefer."

"I don't prefer."

"Well, if you change your mind…" He let his voice drift off, and his speculative gaze slowly, leisurely swept over her, from the top of her head to the tips of her high leather heels.

Emily made a rude sound in the back of her throat. "You probably prefer your women locked up."

"Just how many women do I have?"

"Hundreds."

He smiled lazily and slipped his sunglasses back on, hiding his eyes. The sun glinted off the dark sunglasses. "That's right. I'd hate to forget."

"You are a playboy."

"Whatever you want to believe, *cara*." He stood up, pushed his chair back and left her to finish her lunch on her own.

The yacht was able to pull directly up to a long pier

built from an island cove. No car was necessary to transport them to the house, as it was just a short walk up from the beach.

From the water the plantation house had looked the same, but as Emily climbed the old stone stairs she heard the grunt and whine of big machinery. As she rounded the side of the house, its façade came into view, the entry hidden behind new lumber and extensive scaffolding.

Her house was being destroyed.

She stood frozen, her horrified gaze fixed to what had once been elegant weathered stone. "What... what's happening?"

A massive concrete mixer pulled out just then, lumbering over what was left of the green lawn and the neatly bordered hibiscus beds.

Hot tears spiked her eyes and she turned her head, briefly closing her lids.

This couldn't be.

It was cruel—bringing her to this, confronting her with this. She and her father had both loved the house, the gardens, the island history. How could Tristano destroy so much so thoughtlessly?

As staff dealt with their luggage Tristano headed up the front steps, the stone arch above the front door now invisible beneath the scaffolding.

"Hurricane Francis," Tristano said, gesturing for her to follow. But she couldn't move. "Once we'd started renovations, one thing led to another."

Literally, she thought, and discovered that the former sugar plantation had been enlarged, with new guest wings built on either end of the main house. From the front porch she glimpsed a new terrace fronting the ocean.

Emily felt a catch in her chest. "It's not the same house."

"It'll be beautiful when it's done."

"It won't be the same," she repeated.

"More people will visit now."

Who? His mother? His father? His incredibly stylish sisters? Impossible. They'd never leave their ritzy Mediterranean resorts, preferring their chic condos in Monte Carlo or larger, posher villas on the Italian Riviera.

"How many bedrooms did you add?" she asked, fighting to keep the bitterness from her voice.

She'd loved the house the way it was—loved the old hardwood floors with their scratches and nicks, loved the weathered floor-to-ceiling wooden shutters that had framed the five French doors facing the ocean. The house had felt so permanent to her in a sea of impermanence.

Now it was all new paint, new trim, new gloss.

"Seven. Three bedroom suites in the new right wing; four on the left."

She moved through the hall to the great room, and even here the ceiling was different, its beams refinished to the line of French doors overlooking the small protected cove.

At least the beach was the same. The water still the same dazzling azure blue, the strip of sand soft, powdery, an inviting white.

"I thought it'd be good for the family," Tristano said, and she laughed—because he had to know he'd never get his sisters here.

The house was lovely—new fixtures, new furniture, new everything—but it wasn't Cannes or St. Tropez. There were no beautiful people here, no parties, no glamour, no excitement. Just the warm sun, the dazzling sea, and the fragile coral reef just beyond the mouth of the cove.

She turned, looked back at Tristano, anger building inside of her. "Has the new house wooed them?"

"Not yet."

"So they're not spending Christmas here?"

"No. They're remaining in Italy."

"Of course."

He shot her a narrowed glance before setting off, leaving the great room with its cathedral ceiling to head to one of the new guest wings. Emily followed, hating that the house was so different, that it wasn't her house anymore but his.

Tristano stopped outside a bedroom near the end of the long hall. "You'll sleep here," he said, indicating a lavish bedroom. "I'm here—across the hall."

"So how are you going to watch me from across the hall?" Her hands were on her hips. "Or do you have hidden cameras recording me?"

"Sorry, Em. I've nothing hidden here. No cameras, no listening devices. Just you. Just me."

"And your staff of…?"

"Six." He entered her room and pushed open one of the massive plantation shutters, flooding the lime-

stone tiled room with warm light. The walls were
glazed the palest blue, the silk bed coverlet a darker
blue, with plump pillows covered in fine white linen,
edged with white lace. "Before I forget—I'm expecting visitors later. I'm not sure how many will be coming. Pay them no attention."

"Are you having a party?"

"No. It's business. An estate agent is coming with
clients. They've been pre-qualified. Apparently they're
serious buyers, or I wouldn't have them visiting now,
so close to Christmas."

His words were like a hammer in her head, and she
flinched as she realized what he was saying. "You're
selling the island?"

"I've been approached by a British hotelier with
visions of turning St. Matt's into the next St. Bart's."
Tristano paused, rubbed the back of his neck. "I
thought that before I made a decision I should find out
what the island's value would be in today's market—
who else might be interested in buying."

Emily heard him talking, heard the words, but she
couldn't move past the word "hotel". She couldn't
believe he'd just said that he was thinking of selling
St. Matt's—and to a hotelier. A *hotelier*. Her heart
constricted. Did he really mean it? Would he really do
it? Turn the island into a tourist spot? A place for
pampered, self-indulged playboys and It Girls?

"And the house?" she whispered, dry-mouthed.

"Mr. Viders has promised to contain the traffic. Try
to preserve the island's character."

Viders. Tony Viders. She knew the name well. Tony

Viders was Mr. London himself. He owned numerous chic hotels all over the world—places that catered exclusively to the rich and beautiful—and even if he promised to preserve the island's character, the plantation house would quickly become nothing but a pit-stop for those with more money than common sense.

"Sell to me," she said desperately, unable to contemplate the lovely old house littered with sandy high heels, half-empty bottles of suntan lotion and dirty cocktail glasses.

"You couldn't afford it."

"I could get a loan."

"Not for that much money."

"How much, Tristano?"

He walked out, heading for his room, but paused in the corridor. "I've poured cash—a couple million—into the renovations alone. I've been told the island would sell for twenty, maybe thirty million today."

"Tristano." Her voice came out strangled. "Please."

"No."

"But—"

"You can't afford it, so forget it. And why would I sell to you, Emily," he persisted coolly, unkindly, "when you've declared me the enemy?"

He waited, silent, knowing full well that he'd made a salient point and she had no defense—nothing she could say.

He was right.

She'd declared war on him for the past five years—had challenged him, mocked him, virtually humiliated him with her flood of knock-offs. Why would he give her what she wanted? Why should he care?

In her room, Emily opened her gorgeous luggage— a matched set of her own Pelosi design, of course— locating her shampoo and bath gel. She showered and changed into a long black chiffon skirt and a sheer black top over her white bikini.

Her head was pounding—jet lag—but she'd learned early on in her travels to shift time zones immediately, to fight fatigue and to push through. And that was what she'd do now. Dressed, she gathered her business papers, left her room and wandered through the house, eventually bumping into a housemaid who told her that Signor Ferre had gone down to the sea for a swim, and did the *Signorina* know her way to the beach?

It was all Emily could do to smile politely. Yes, she knew. It had once been her beach. And, no, she didn't wish to join him.

Instead Emily carried her briefcase outside to the terrace, where she sat beneath an umbrella reading charts and graphs until she thought her eyes would fall out.

Business was good. Profits were high. The forecast for the next year was brilliant. But even making good money—big money—didn't answer the horrendous anger burning inside her.

Mum was still sick. Father was still gone. And Tristano was still CEO at Ferre Design.

Ferre Design. Just thinking of the name ''Ferre'' without ''Pelosi'' made her see red. It wasn't ever supposed to be just Ferre. The Ferres had never designed

anything—much less come up with an original idea.
Her father had been the creative genius, and it was her
father's brilliant leather goods—handbags, suitcases,
belts, shoes—that she faithfully reproduced today,
manufacturing and selling them for a fraction of what
the Ferre Design charged.

Call it counterfeit if you want. She called it fair.

Emily heard car doors slam and the distant murmur
of voices—female voices. Tristano's visitors had arrived.

Disgusted, she slouched deeper in her chair, drew
her papers higher, and forced herself to focus on the
numbers in front of her. But the voices were loud, and
they carried.

"The view is worth thirty million alone."

"I'm not that crazy about the house, though."

The voices soon reached Emily where she sat.

"Darling, you can always replace the house."

"Bulldoze it down?"

"Of course. Everybody does it these days."

There was a pause, and Emily squeezed her eyes
shut. It was torture being here, torture hearing this. She
wished now she had gone down to the beach. Sitting
next to Tristano would be painful, but it would be
better than this.

"How much do you think it'd cost to knock it
down?" The women were still discussing demolishing
the plantation house—a house that had stood on St.
Matt's for hundreds of years, a house that had history...mystery...secrets.

"Fifty thousand? A hundred? No more than a hundred thousand, not even with all these stone walls. Bulldozers are amazing. One day here, the next gone. Whoosh. And think what you'd gain—all-new construction, the best of everything, top-line technology. You could even put in your media room here.''

Abruptly Emily sat up, anxious to flee. But her haste sent her paperwork flying. On her knees, she scrambled to gather the graphs and reports even as the women's voices echoed in her head. *The view is worth thirty million alone…you can always replace the house…bulldoze it down…no more than one hundred thousand…you could even put in your media room here…*

Two sleek, well-preserved blondes, with shiny gold hair and expensive jewelry, appeared in the doorway overlooking the terrace. ''Oh!'' one exclaimed. ''I didn't know anyone was here.''

Hands shaking, Emily shoved the crumpled pages into her open briefcase. ''Yes—I'm here.''

The woman marched over to Emily, hand outstretched. ''Di Perkins, Lux Estates. I'm showing the property to my client.''

Emily awkwardly rose. ''I'm not the owner.''

''Oh.'' The women looked disappointed.

''I used to be,'' Emily added, thinking that maybe she could say something about the house, and its history, that would give it value…respect. ''St. Matt's is a wonderful island—it has a fantastic history—''

''I'm not really into history.'' The second woman's nose wrinkled. ''I just want a great beach, a bay deep enough for my husband's yacht, and privacy. We don't get enough of that in the States.''

"It is private. You don't get visitors here. Not unless they're invited." Emily fought to hide her irritation. "It's said that Blackbeard hid here for a month one December—"

"Blackbeard? Ugh." The second woman shuddered. "Didn't he kill a lot of people?"

Not enough, Emily thought, smiling so hard her eyes watered. "Excuse me." She nodded and, leaving her briefcase on the table, practically ran down the stone steps heading for the beach.

She found him stretched out on a lounge chair on the sand, his arms extended over his head, his eyes closed, his long nearly black hair combed back from his face.

Either he hadn't heard her approach or he was ignoring her.

"You can't sell the island," she said flatly, not bothering with pleasantries. "Not like this—not to these kinds of people. The island's special. Beautiful. You can't let people without taste destroy it."

His eyes slowly opened. He looked up at her, his arms folded behind his head. Deep blue eyes met her own. *"Ciao, bella."*

"Did you hear me?"

He held her gaze.

"Did you hear me?"

Damn him.

He still thought he ruled the universe. Things hadn't changed. But then in the Ferre world why should anything change? The gods divided up the pie and gave the Ferres everything, leaving everyone else with crumbs.

"Those people want to tear down the house. Just bulldoze it." She held his gaze. She wasn't afraid of him, didn't need him, didn't give a flying fig what he thought of her. But the house, the island, the history—that she loved.

"It's their prerogative if they buy it," he answered, stretching a little, lifting his face higher to the sun. "That's the privilege of ownership. Something you lost when you sold."

"You know we didn't want to sell. You know we sold only because we had to."

"I'm sorry."

"You're not." It crossed her mind that the estate agent's visit wasn't coincidence, but rather something Tristano had arranged. He'd wanted Emily to see the future of St. Matt's. He'd meant for her to meet the prospective buyers. "You set me up," she said softly.

"Set you up?" He grinned, and his teeth flashed white. A small dimple appeared briefly in his carved cheek. "Intriguing deduction."

"And a correct one. You planned all this. The Flemmings...the arrest. You intended for me to come here, remain here. You've spent a great deal of time orchestrating this."

"I did hunt you down, yes." His smile had faded and his dark blue eyes burned intensely. "And, yes, I've deliberately brought us together. You're stranded here on St. Matt's, alone with me. And you're going to listen—work—co-operate with me."

"Never."

"Careful, *cara*. Never is a very long time."

CHAPTER THREE

"WHY are you doing this?" she demanded, her head spinning a little. She'd flown all night, hadn't slept. This had become a day that seemed as if it would never end.

"You know the answer, Em. Just look inside your heart—or your bank account—and you'll see the answer there."

She shook her head. "You could call them off, you know." She fought to keep the fury from her voice, fought for the control she so desperately needed. "Since you arranged this whole thing you can end it, too."

"Yes, I know." He'd closed his eyes again, and, exhaling, relaxed his tanned upper body into the chair. "But I won't." The warm sun gleamed on his bronzed skin, on one burnished highlights in his dark hair. "*Cara*, could you just move over a foot or two? You're blocking my sun."

Blocking his sun? She felt a bubble of hysteria form in her chest. She was standing here, pleading for her freedom, and he was worried about his *sun*?

"Sorry about that." Her voice dripped venom.

"No problem."

For a moment she remained rooted to the spot, frozen in anger and indecision, and then she moved. But not in the direction he expected. Emily knelt down and buried her hands in the sand, grabbing great handfuls of the fine warm grains, and before she could think twice she stood up again and poured the sand on top of his head.

Tristano sputtered, coughed, then gave his head a sharp shake, sending sand flying.

Emily planted her feet, hands on her hip. "How's that? Better?"

"Oh, yes." But Tristano clasped her by the forearm and with a tidy twist flipped her down on her back in the sand. He left his lounge chair and straddled her hips. "How's that?"

The sun shone in her eyes, blinding her. Tristano's body was heavy, hard and warm—very warm—and Emily felt stunningly aware of the size of him, the fierceness of him, the sensual nature he'd never tried to conceal.

"Off," she demanded hoarsely, her voice nearly breaking, betraying her rising anxiety. Maybe for Tristano this was nothing, but she was incredibly uncomfortable, almost paralyzed by the intimate contact.

Tristano Ferre had had more girlfriends than twenty Italian playboys put together. For him it had always been new week, new woman. It had galled her back then, when she had still been part of his life, and it galled her now. She shouldn't care who he was with, or what he did with whom, but somehow she did. She told herself it was anger, hatred, but the intensity of her feelings made her wonder.

"Not until we get a few things squared away," he

answered, and suddenly he was stretched out over her, his hands still wrapped snugly around her wrists, his body extended over hers until his chest pressed to her breast, his hip rested on hers, his thigh parted her thighs. And even though she was wearing the silky skirt and shirt, the sheer chiffon fabric allowed her to feel all of him.

"What do you think you're doing?" she breathed, ineffectively pushing up against his grasp.

"What you've been dying for me to do ever since last time."

"Screw you!"

"We already did that, *carissima*, or do you not remember?"

Her body grew tellingly warm, and blood rushed to her cheeks. Embarrassed, Emily struggled to drive her knee up, straight into his groin, but he knew, because he knew her, and he shifted, immobilizing her legs, his hips gouging into her.

Emily drew a short breath. Tristano lay heavily on her, pinning her down, pinning her legs, and the friction of skin on skin made her conscious of the hardness of his hips, the hair on his legs, the heat of his chest.

"I hate you," she choked, emotion filling her, sweeping through her, hot, so hot, and full of anger.

"You lie, *cara*." His head dipped, his lips traveling over hers in a brief tortuous caress. "You love me."

And his head dropped again. But this time his lips covered hers, completely, firmly, and he kissed her the way she'd remembered all these years. His lips slowly moved across hers, parting so slowly that she wondered if it was her encouraging him or the other way around.

This was the kiss that had driven her mad all those years ago, when she'd thought she'd tasted real life, real love, real passion.

And then she'd discovered it wasn't anything. It was just Tristano practicing his craft. Tristano the expert. The seducer. Tristano the Ferre sinner.

Eyes burning, she tried to hold back, pull back, tried to forget that his lips were making her shiver, that the flick of his tongue made her want to open herself up to him, that the feel of his hands against her neck made her want those hands everywhere, against everything.

This was how she'd given herself to him last time. Innocently. Naively. Sweetly.

She'd never be so stupid again.

Fighting tears, Emily sank her teeth into Tristano's lower lip and he cursed, rolled partially away, to gaze down at her.

Her heart was racing and she struggled to catch her breath, struggled to get a grip on the emotions that were flying all over the place.

He was right. She had loved him once.

And he'd broken her heart into a thousand pieces—broken her heart along with her trust.

Then his father had done the unthinkable—sold her father out, seized the company—and the Pelosis had suddenly become cast offs.

And Tristano hadn't just watched it all happen. He'd helped. He'd stood at his father's side and made sure with his fancy law degree that the Pelosis were stripped of everything.

"I never loved you," she said now, her voice deep, husky with the hunger she hadn't quite contained. "It was lust. You had the goods, and I wanted them."

His eyebrow arched. "Is that so?"

"Yes."

"And is that how you explain yourself this time?" He touched her soft lip with the tip of his finger. "Your mouth quivered. It wanted my kiss. It welcomed my kiss."

"Lust is lust."

"So I still have the goods?"

She thought of the company he'd helped seize, the company he'd torn apart, and the island she'd loved and lost. Her throat ached. "In more ways than one."

His smile grew, and yet it was the smile of a pirate, the smile of one taking exactly what he chose without fear, without worry, without conscience. She had to leave, had to escape before she did something criminal.

She fled back to the house, running up the steep steps, the stones weathered and worn smooth, and into the cool semi-dark house. She heard Tristano following close behind and ran faster, through the great room, where the big dark plantation shutters had been closed against the brightness of the afternoon sun, down the corridor toward her room. But before she could slam her door shut Tristano caught her, trapping her against the wall.

"I have the goods," he said, his voice deep, his hand closing around her wrist.

"And you love that, don't you?"

"Is that what you're thinking?"

"I don't know." She couldn't focus, too aware of the warmth of his skin against hers, his bare chest against her chiffon top, the salty spiced fragrance of him, the pulse pounding in her own veins.

"What *do* you know?"

Emily drew a shaky breath. "Don't ask. You don't want that kind of honesty."

"I wouldn't have brought you here if I didn't."

She stared up at him, her emotions barely contained, her pulse pounding wildly. It was all she could do not to faint. Everything about Tristano was huge. Significant. Like his treachery. His ability to detach and destroy.

"I trusted you." The words were torn from her, flung in his face. She hadn't meant to say them, hadn't even known she was going to say them, and she felt as if she were sailing straight into the eye of a storm. This was bad, so very bad, and there was no one—again—to help her.

Tristano leaned closer, his chest hard against hers, his knee brushing the inside of her thigh. "You know why you're in trouble now? You've confused objectivity with subjectivity—taken something that had nothing to do with us—"

"Nothing to do with us?" she interrupted roughly. "*Tristano.* We *were* them. We were—are—what they made."

"But that was your mistake, *cara*. We have always been different. We are different people, a different generation. We've always had different dreams. After your father left—"

"Left?" She laughed, feeling hysterical. "He didn't *leave*. You shoved him out. Tied him to a speedboat and dragged him out to sea."

Tristano abruptly reached for her, touched her cheek with the back of his fingers. "Is this the story you tell yourself? No wonder you hang on to such hate—"

"Don't touch me." Flinching, she closed her eyes, steeling herself against all response. The enemy, she whispered silently, reminding herself. He is and always will be…

Drawing a quick breath, she opened her eyes, his expression clear, cool again. "This isn't a story, Tristano. You know what you did—you and your father."

"Yes, I know what we did. But do you know what *he* did? Your father?" The cool shadows of the hall made his voice sound deeper, his accent warmer.

They were both fluent in English and Italian, and they switched back and forth between the two, comfortably, easily, neither noticing when the language changed.

She wanted to escape, but she couldn't move, squashed between Tristano and the wall. "He did nothing."

His head dropped, his voice lowering. *"Em."*

She heard the warning in his voice, and it sent a ripple of fear through her. He'd never hurt her. Not physically. But emotionally...he was as dangerous as hell.

"Unlike you, Tristano, Father was a good man—a principled man. He didn't do anything wrong. I'd have known it if he had. Mother would have told me. Father would have told me. But there was nothing for him to confess—" Emily broke off at the sound of voices echoing down the hall.

Tristano heard the voices, too. The realtor and the buyer. They were discussing the buyer's dream house. Pool pavilion here. Sculpture garden there.

Tristano saw Emily pale, one smooth line of her jaw tightening. He straightened, giving her a little space— but not much. He wasn't going to let her go. There was no escaping him this time. The course they were on was nothing short of madness. It would lead to nowhere good. He had to put a stop to the insanity before it destroyed her—him—all of them.

The two women disappeared into a bedroom and Tristano turned his attention back on Em. They were still standing close but he felt her resistance, saw the mutinous set of her mouth. She wasn't ready or willing to learn the truth. Her family had done her a disservice, keeping the truth from her, letting her father's flaws and weakness poison her life like that.

She was so different from the Emily he'd once known, the Emily he'd made his lover all those years ago.

That Emily had been so warm, so sunny, so open. She'd been passionate, earnest, hopeful, strong.

This Emily was strong, too. But it was strength born of bitterness. Hatred.

"What would it take to get you to cease and desist?" he asked, surprising even himself with the question.

But she wasn't ready to talk. There was still no negotiation. "Nothing."

"Nothing?" His eyebrows lifted. "Not even this…island?"

He saw her eyes widen, heard the soft catch in her breath. For a moment she looked hopeful, endearingly young as she stared up at him, torn between wonder and worry. He realized then how vulnerable she was—how vulnerable she'd been. And then the hope died in her eyes and her features hardened, freezing into the cool don't-touch-me mask she always wore these days.

"Nothing," she repeated, her voice low, brittle.

Emily squashed the rise and fall of emotion in her chest, squashed that flicker of hope—because really her only hope was removing Tristano from Ferre Design, taking Ferre Design apart, bit by bit, just the way they'd dismantled her father.

And remembering her father made her stronger, fiercer. Hurt was replaced by old rage. She wanted to take Tristano down, take him to the mat like the Greco-Roman wrestlers had, and beat him mercilessly. Show him what the Pelosis were really about. Show Tristano that he and his father had gotten it all wrong.

Integrity, she told herself. Truth. Determination. This was everything.

"I won't be bought," she said, her spine pressed

flat against the wall, her whole body rigid with years of heartbreak and hatred. "There's only one thing I want from you." She paused, held her breath a moment, lungs bursting, and then she exhaled. "I want you to fail."

Emily looked up into his eyes, such a dark blue, a lovely blue, if you loved sapphire and the sky close to midnight.

"I want you to fail so badly you lose everything."

She saw a small muscle jump in his jaw, but his voice was gentle when he spoke. "Everything?"

She didn't know why she wanted to cry—she who didn't cry, she who didn't feel anything, was feeling far too much. "Everything. Your house, your cars, your wealth, this island—all of it. I want you to know what it was like being me."

The women emerged from one of the guest bedrooms and Emily used the opportunity to duck beneath his arm and escape into her room, locking the door behind her. And as the women stopped outside her door to speak to Tristano Emily heard the strangest noise—a muffled cry somewhere between a mouse's squeak and the scream of a bird. She sat down on the foot of her bed and realized the agonized sound had come from her. She was crying. Huge tears, hot wet tears. Even though she hadn't cried in years.

Later, a knock on her door roused her. She'd fallen asleep fully dressed on her bed, and groggily she pushed herself into a sitting position. "Yes?"

It was one of the young Caribbean housemaids outside her door. "Dinner in an hour, *mademoiselle*. Drinks in a half-hour."

Emily didn't want dinner—not if it meant joining Tristano—but she wasn't the type to sulk and hide. All her life she'd been a fighter, and she'd continue fighting now.

Washing her face, Emily pulled herself together. She combed her long hair smooth, adding a little concealer to hide her under-eye circles, and a little blush to give color to her pale cheeks. She wasn't beaten. Not by a long shot.

Dressed in a white Spandex cap-sleeve top and a long black sequin-beaded skirt, Emily headed toward the great room—only to be told that dinner was being served outside, by the pool. Indeed, she could hear the faint strains of calypso—odd here, on the quiet, remote St. Matt's.

Turning a corner, she caught a glimpse of a slender, fashionably chic woman with long chestnut hair, wide somber eyes. Emily paused, puzzled by the woman's lonely expression, and then realized with a discomforting flash that it was her—her reflection in a mirror. She was seeing herself, seeing her own unhappiness, and it unnerved her.

She didn't even recognize herself anymore.

Emily started to move on, and then glanced back over her shoulder into the mirror one last time. The same face looked back at her.

Funny—she saw her father in her, her mother as well, and for a moment she saw a timeline to the past. She saw her father dressing for dinner—he'd always dressed, he'd been Italian and gorgeous: a Latin Cary Grant, her mother used to say. She saw her mother, too—her mother's blue eyes, her mother's porcelain rose complexion, a hint of her mother's sweetness.

Her parents had met when her father had been in London on business. Mum had worked as a receptionist for a London textile exporter and her father had stopped by to meet one of the owners. They'd met and, despite Father being nearly fifteen years older than Mum, they'd fallen in love. They'd married and had soon moved to Milan. They'd had a good life together, too, until Mum's illness had progressed and Father...

She suppressed the rest of the thought, knowing she didn't need to go there. She knew the history too well. She'd been tortured by it for years.

Reaching the pool, Emily stopped in the courtyard doorway, greeted not by the simple old pool but an entirely new landscape. The new pool was surrounded by buff limestone pavers, softly lit and lined by young native palms. A splashing fountain shot up from the middle of the illuminated pool and dozens of candles shone around the perimeter of the courtyard. More candles gleamed on the staircase leading to the new guest wing.

As she stood there, taking it all in, she gradually became aware of being watched intently.

Turning her head slightly, she scanned the exterior until she saw him—Tristano—standing in the shadows, too.

He was wearing pressed green linen slacks and an

off-white linen long-sleeve shirt, cuffs rolled back. He looked elegant, distant, a stranger.

Here they were, Ferre and Pelosi, together as they'd once been. Lives so entwined that in nearly every good memory Emily had—like the shiny new bike or the white Vespa scooter—Tristano was also there, riding alongside her, racing her to who knows where. And yet even though they were together, they were poles apart.

Tristano stepped out of the shadows. "You look beautiful," he said, moving slowly toward her.

She didn't feel beautiful, and suddenly she couldn't leave the security of one door, overwhelmed by all the changes on the island. This visit had been about coming home…making peace with her past…but nothing felt peaceful. In fact, she felt even less settled than before.

"I've noticed you only wear black and white," he said, his gaze roaming leisurely over her slim-fitting beaded skirt and the snug Spandex top that hugged her breasts and emphasized her small waist.

"It's easy to co-ordinate pieces for travel."

"As well as being stark. Hard. Controlled." Hands in his pockets, he crossed close behind her—so close she felt energy ripple between them, heat and awareness, and her lower back tingled, suddenly unbearably sensitive.

Her stomach clenched in a knot of anxiety, trepidation. "Is that how you see me?"

"Isn't that how you see yourself?" He stood behind

her, still—too still—and Emily's skin prickled, her muscles coiling.

She had to turn her head slightly to see him, and looking at him over her shoulder she felt very vulnerable, her throat, breasts and body open, exposed.

"What—?" And then her voice failed her, the air blocked in her throat as Tristano suddenly touched her low on her back, his fingers trailing across the small dip in her spine.

His touch felt like fire and ice, and she couldn't move, frozen in place. Eyes closed, hands knotted, she nearly cried out when he trailed his hand lightly up the length of her spine. How could she feel so much? How could she feel like this? Because it was huge, hot, sharp—it was as if life had expanded, so powerful, so sensual that it stopped the air in her lungs.

"Breathe," he murmured from behind her, and she shivered, feeling him, feeling him everywhere, even though he only touched her back. She felt his strength, and the shape of his chest and thighs, knowing he was hard, knowing he was responding to her just as much as she to him.

"Breathe," he repeated, fingers sliding up from her shoulderblades to the back of her neck.

And she did—only because black spots had fluttered before her eyes and she couldn't think, couldn't see.

His hand moved beneath her hair, his fingertips brushing the skin at her neck, circling her nape and then up into her hair so that she felt weak. Helpless. Boneless.

"You're killing me," she whispered, her voice faint as air.

"You're killing yourself," he answered, and his hand slid up, against her scalp, before clasping a handful of her hair, twisting the silky length around his hand. "Emily...my own little freebooter," he said, his voice dropping as he leaned forward to place a kiss on her nape.

She shivered, and balled her hands more tightly into fists, digging her nails hard into her palms. "You're not playing fair."

"No," he answered with mock gravity, turning her around to face him. "But when have you?"

Slowly she looked up, dragging her gaze first to his mouth—he had gorgeous lips—and then to his eyes. The intensity in his gaze stole her breath. His words were light, almost teasing, but she saw the fire in his eyes, saw the strength of his will.

His intensity touched her, teased her senses, stroked her nerves awake until she felt heat rise and shimmer between them. She was hot, too hot beneath her skin, hot and molten, like chocolate melted down to the warmest, sweetest, darkest liquid.

Her lips moved, tried to shape words. But nothing came to her—no sound, no thought. Instead she just *felt*. Emotion. Passion. Desire. All the things she shouldn't feel, all the things she didn't want to feel.

"No." The word slipped from her in soft, low protest.

"No what?" he asked, reaching out to touch her earlobe, and then the hollow beneath her ear. And all the while he touched her she looked up at him, fascinated, appalled.

If there was hell on earth, she'd found it. What he stirred within her was so strong, so raw and carnal, that the sensation threatened to pull her down—pull her under. It was, she thought, staring into his midnight-blue eyes, an agony being here. An agony feeling so much.

It crossed her mind as his palm cupped her collarbone, fingers lightly stroking her skin, that this was how it had always been between them. This was how she'd fallen so hard, so fast for him. This was how friendship—close, familial ties—had turned into wild, fierce emotion. His touch turned her inside out. His touch blew her mind.

There could never be anything platonic between them. Could never be anything but the fiercest love and the fiercest hate.

And she hated him. Didn't she?

Her heart seemed to slow, pounding harder, yet less steadily as she searched his eyes and then his face.

He'd aged in the past five years, but it was the kind of maturity that suited his hard, strong face, carving beauty into his jaw, whittling the broad cheekbones, putting the finest lines at his eyes and near his mouth. His dark hair was as thick as ever, and yet there was caution, wisdom in his eyes

Yes, he was a little older, but she was older too, and somehow the chemistry was so much stronger. Or was this how all women felt when Tristano touched them? Looked at them?

The thought knifed her, a cut in the chest, between the ribs, and she drew in a short breath, trying to discount the pain. She didn't care, she told herself. His life, his women…they meant nothing to her. Not after what he'd done to her father.

The reminder of his role in her father's humiliation should have chilled her, frozen her in place, but she wasn't frozen—just confused. His touch felt good. Right. And yet he represented everything wrong with the world, everything selfish and hurtful in human beings.

"You're torturing me, you know." Emily tried to smile, to make it a joke, but she couldn't pull it off.

"If only it were that simple." He leaned forward to pluck a tendril of hair that clung to her lashes, lifting the tendril and smoothing it behind her ear. His lips curved but he wasn't smiling. He looked piratical. "Torture isn't to be taken lightly. Proper torture requires effort. Planning. It's an art form."

"Father died here."

"I know."

"Christmas morning."

"I heard."

Tears scalded the backs of her eyes but she didn't let them fall. "Did you hear how?"

"A tragic fall."

"No." And the word whispered out—soft, stealthy, speaking of a heartbreak that few people would ever know about. "It was tragic, but it wasn't a fall."

Tristano said nothing, asking no questions, and Emily offered no more information. There were some things, she thought, too cruel, too ugly, too unbelievable to ever reveal.

Dinner was beautiful, the meal cooked perfectly. Tristano's chefs had trained on the Continent, and had prepared fresh seafood in the best French and Mediterranean styles.

Sitting at the table, with candlelight flickering and the torches around the pool burning, Emily saw light everywhere—the pale ivory taper candles, the stainless steel torches, and the nearly full moon reflected whitely in the pool. She didn't remember the island this way, didn't know the house like this, either, and she felt off-balance all over again, felt the strangeness of everything, the strangeness of her own emotions. She'd been so determined for so long, and yet she wasn't sure of anything right now—certainly wasn't sure of herself.

As coffee was served she turned to examine the pool courtyard again, dazzled by the perfectly matched palm trees and sophisticated lighting. It was all so pretty, but almost too perfect—like a designer set waiting to be photographed.

"Is this for your hotelier?" she said, and she'd meant to sound tough. Instead her voice had cracked.

"The new pool? No. It's for me. The family."

"So why sell?"

"To get your attention."

Emily sat very still, her hands resting in her lap, aware of the steam rising from her coffee cup but unable to reach for it. "You're selling something I desperately love to get my attention?

"Yes, *carissima*. And it's working, isn't it?"

CHAPTER FOUR

SHE stared at him, disgusted, appalled.

They were older. But no wiser. Everything with Tristano boiled down to a deal. Sell. Buy. Bargain. He was all about money. Power. He'd had it. She'd wanted it. Amazing how little had changed in five years.

And suddenly the source of her real hurt surged through her—a scorching memory. Their families had been as one.

"We were a family business," she said, forgetting the island, the house and the history in the Caribbean and returning to Italy, where it had all begun. "And I thought family business was about pooling strengths, everyone helping one another." She sat very still, and yet her voice blistered with fury. "Obviously I was wrong."

"The difficulty was between them, not us."

"No, we were like a family. We were always together. Your family, my family—we were what I thought a real family felt like. But I was wrong. Your father wanted more, and he cut us out. Not just Father. He cut me, Mum—"

"It was a business decision. You're making it personal."

"And it's *not* personal? It's not about giving everything to the Ferres and taking everything from the Pelosis?''

"Our fathers had differences in opinion.''

"So how did your father get everything and mine get nothing?''

"My father always was the practical one. He knew the business—''

"While my father was just the genius, the creative mind, and therefore dispensable?''

"Emily.''

"No, Tristano. I shall never forgive your father, and I shall never forget how you've allowed—encouraged—this injustice to continue. You yourself have grown rich from my father's designs. You have built your own empire on his back.''

His dark blue eyes looked nearly black in the candlelight and his expression was taut. "And it's my empire you hate most. Not my father's. But mine. That which I've done.''

"Yes! You're perpetuating a sin.''

"A sin?'' he demanded, rising.

She left her own chair, moved toward him, conscious of the height difference between them, conscious of the fact that he would always be bigger, larger, more dominant. At least physically.

Mentally she was his equal, though.

Emotionally she'd hold her own.

Maybe her father had cracked in the face of such ostracism, maybe he hadn't been able to endure the shame, but she felt no shame.

She loved her name. Loved what her father had accomplished. And just because he wasn't around to fight for himself anymore that didn't mean she wouldn't continue the fight herself.

"A sin. A wrong. A tragedy." She met Tristano's narrowed gaze and lifted her chin in outright defiance. "You can arrest me. You can throw me in jail. Take me to court. But I won't cease and desist. I won't. I will fight you forever. Understand? I will not give up. I will not forget."

"Fighting words," Tristano said softly, watching her face every bit as intently as she'd watched his.

She saw the curiosity in his expression, the blatant interest, and it wasn't innocent, either. He looked very male just now, very much engaged in the hunt.

What on earth was this anyway? What had brought them on this collision course?

They'd once played together as children, behaved like brother and sister...cousins...

Hadn't they?

Or had there always been this edge of anger? This vein of emotion that went deep, so much deeper than anything Emily had ever felt for anyone else?

"Marry me and this stress—this fear—will disappear." Tristano's voice sounded soft, persuasive.

His soft, smooth voice had temptation buried in it, its deep tone compelling, soothing, as if he had a power greater than she knew—as if he could put everything right, as if he were the answer to all her problems...

But he had created all her problems.

"*Marry?*" She said the word just as softly, but there

was no give in her voice, no persuasion. She was angry, deeply angry. "Marry you? Never. Ever."

"Aren't you tired of worrying so much? Tired of the pressure? The weight of caring for your mother?"

Her head lifted and her hot gaze met his. "I love my mother. It's a joy to care for her." A lump filled her throat. The pain of his betrayal was fresh all over again. "And if we have worries, if we're bowed by pressure—"

She broke off, pressed a knuckled fist to her mouth to contain the sound of heartbreak. She fought for control. "You were supposed to be the good guy," she said finally, and the words were wrenched from her, practically a confession.

He laughed once, a low, mocking sound that made their differences all the more obvious. "But, Emily, I was never the hero. Maybe that's what you wanted, but I've never wanted to be the good guy, and you shouldn't have been surprised. We were once close...at least close enough that you should have seen the truth. You should have known that my family would come first, that the business would always be important. Essential."

But I didn't think you'd put the business before me.

There—the truth. Only she hadn't admitted it to him, just herself, and that was bad enough.

Hours later, lying in bed, with the windows open to let in the fresh air and the dull roar of the sea, Emily tried to sleep. But the day played like an endless movie in her weary mind, scene after scene, discussion after discussion, every nuance and inflection slowed, repeated, her life on rewind.

The arrest on Anguilla.

The never-ending confrontations with Tristano.

Dinner and his absurd proposal, the realization that she still responded to him, that she didn't know how not to respond to him...

She shouldn't be here. She should have stayed home, celebrated Christmas with Mum like she always did, instead of making this crazy trip with Annelise. Well, Annelise was gone, and she was trapped here on St. Matt's—her former home—under house arrest.

The only small mercy was the fact that her mother didn't know. Her mother would be protected from the chaos and indignity of it all.

Another hour passed, and Emily flipped from her back onto her stomach and back again. The sheets were hot, the Egyptian cotton clinging limply to her skin. She couldn't stop thinking, couldn't shut off her mind. But it wasn't just being here. She simply couldn't sleep anymore. For the past couple years she'd take forever to fall asleep, and then once asleep would wake repeatedly in the night, thoughts racing, muscles twitching, her body unable to shut down long enough to let her rest.

She'd gone to her doctor about it, asked for help so she could start sleeping properly again, and though the doctor had said he could prescribe pills, he'd thought she needed more than pills. She needed a change of lifestyle. Too much stress, he'd said. If she wasn't careful, he'd added, not knowing the details of her father's death, Emily would end up just like him...

Emily had left the doctor's without getting a prescription for sleeping pills and returned to work, to her small office, and the stress had continued—just as had her sleepless nights. But her sleep deprivation was getting worse. Soon she'd have to do something about the insomnia. Soon she'd have to give her body a break, before her body broke her.

Hopelessly wide awake, Emily left her bed, put on shorts and a cotton top and headed outside, away from the plantation house, down the worn stone steps to the cove.

It was late, well past midnight, but the night air wasn't cold. She walked along the edge of the surf, her feet wet, waves splashing and breaking against her calves. The water was warmer than the night air.

The heaviness on her chest didn't ease, and the heaviness in her gut just grew worse, as if she'd taken to eating bricks.

When had everything gotten so hard? She looked up at the sky, at the nearly full moon obscured by a silver-plated cloud. When had she'd become this tired, flat version of herself?

She didn't need to ask the question. She already knew the answer, knew exactly how and when. So the issue wasn't what was wrong, but how to deal with it. How to fix it—because something had to give. Something had to go. But what?

And somewhere from inside her she heard the answer.

Let go of Father.

Let him go.

And Emily's eyes, which never watered, never felt anything, burned again, burned for the second time in one day. Before she could fall apart, dissolve into tears, she stripped her shirt off, pulled off her shorts and dove naked into the water, swimming out, swimming far, as far as she could. Then, turning onto her back, she floated, looking up at the sky. In the clouds that slowly covered and uncovered the moon she felt her tiredness, felt the endless weight of battle, the fatigue of never being able to rest, never being able to find peace.

But how to let go of her father?

She flipped over, began swimming again, parallel to the cove, trying somehow to outrun her thoughts. And yet before she'd swum far she understood why Tristano had brought her here, trapped her on St. Matt's alone with him. He was going to force a confrontation with the past even if it killed her...him... them.

Feeling a prickle of awareness, the same awareness she'd felt earlier at the pool, she knew she wasn't alone in the cove anymore. Tristano had arrived. She couldn't see him, but she knew he was on the sand somewhere. Watching.

Slowly she swam back to the shore. As she neared the beach Emily lifted her head and caught sight of him. He stood close to the surf, dressed in faded jeans and a dark T-shirt. He was watching her, waiting for her, and she let herself sink deeper into the water, trepidation weighting her limbs. She couldn't do this again. Couldn't argue so soon, not when their confrontation at dinner still troubled her so much.

It wasn't fun fighting with Tristano. At least there was no fun in it now, when she was close enough to see his face, feel his warmth and intense energy. She'd once been part of his inner circle, and yet now she stood on the outside, bayonet in hand.

As she walked out of the water she kept her chin high, making no apology for her nudity. Tristano dropped

a towel around her shoulders, lightly buffed her skin. "You shouldn't swim alone at night," he said.

She took the towel away and wrapped it around her torso, cinching it tightly over her breasts. "I've always swum at night."

"That doesn't make it right. It's dangerous—"

"My career is dangerous," she interrupted impatiently, wringing water from her hair.

Shipping merchandise from China into the States wasn't without traps. She'd learned all the different methods for avoiding customs—trans-shipping, selling the goods first to a country not associated with counterfeiting and then importing from there, or smuggling the merchandise in containers filled with legal goods— but the pressure was intense, the fear of being caught always there at the back of her mind.

He looked away, muttered something unintelligible, then glanced back down at her. "What happened to you?"

Even in the dark she could see his face clearly and she held his gaze. "I learned from you."

"Oh, *cara*—"

"It's true." She reached up to comb wet hair back from her forehead. "You were my role model. Whatever you did, I wanted to do." The corners of her mouth tipped. "Just better."

"I don't recall stooping so low as to make cheap, knock-off merchandise."

"My handbags and suitcases aren't cheap, and they're not knock-offs. They're exact Pelosi design. And maybe you don't have to go to Asia to get your merchandise made, but I vow if you can make a thousand bags, I can make ten thousand. If you can produce a gorgeous leather, I can do it one better. And that's been my goal—not to just match you, but beat you."

"Beat me?"

"Yes."

"What a terrible waste of your life."

"I've no regrets."

When he said nothing, she smiled, but she hated how she felt on the inside—so cold, so tired. It felt as if she'd been carrying this enormous burden on her shoulders forever, and she felt exhausted by the weight of it—the weight of worrying, the weight of hating. She'd vowed to make the Ferres pay, and yet she saw now she'd been the one who just continued to suffer.

She could have sworn he knew, that he was thinking the same thing, and he shook his head, his jaw pulling.

"You would have been better off focusing your considerable energy into making Ferre Designs succeed."

"I would never help Ferre Designs."

"Not even if it benefited you?" he asked softly.

"The only way I could benefit is if Ferre Designs fails."

"That won't happen."

"You sound awfully confident."

"I am. I know our revenue." The corner of his mouth lifted in a faint smile. "You're the one backed into a corner, *carissima*. You're facing not just jail time but financial ruin."

Furious, she squeezed her wet hair again. "I'm prepared."

"Are you?"

Her chin inched higher. "Yes."

His gaze never left her face, his blue eyes searching hers intently. "And your mother? Is she prepared?"

For a moment Emily heard—saw—felt nothing, and then the implication of his words hit. "You wouldn't go after Mum."

His blue eyes were hard, cool. "I already have."

Emily let his words seep through her, let the stunning pain go on and on, until she was certain she could speak without her voice betraying her. "What have you done?"

Tristano tipped his head. His expression appeared to gentle, but it was deceptive—nothing about him had gentled. She knew him too well for that.

"Tristano." She said his name, low and sharp.

YOUR OPINION POLL
THANK-YOU FREE GIFTS INCLUDE

▶ **2 ROMANCE OR 2 SUSPENSE BOOKS**

▶ **A LOVELY SURPRISE GIFT**

OFFICIAL OPINION POLL

YOUR OPINION COUNTS!

Please check TRUE or FALSE below to express your opinion about the following statements:

Q1 Do you believe in "true love"?

"TRUE LOVE HAPPENS ONLY ONCE IN A LIFETIME."
○ TRUE
○ FALSE

Q2 Do you think marriage has any value in today's world?

"YOU CAN BE TOTALLY COMMITTED TO SOMEONE WITHOUT BEING MARRIED."
○ TRUE
○ FALSE

Q3 What kind of books do you enjoy?

"A GREAT NOVEL MUST HAVE A HAPPY ENDING."
○ TRUE
○ FALSE

Place the sticker next to one of the selections below to receive your 2 FREE BOOKS and FREE GIFT. I understand that I am under no obligation to purchase anything as explained on the back of this card.

Romance

193 MDL EE4P

393 MDL EE5D

Suspense

192 MDL EE4Z

392 MDL EE5P

0074823 ‖‖‖‖‖‖‖ ‖‖‖‖ ‖‖‖‖   **FREE GIFT CLAIM #** 3622

FIRST NAME	LAST NAME

ADDRESS

APT.#	CITY

STATE/PROV.	ZIP/POSTAL CODE

(TF-SS-06)

The Reader Service — Here's How It Works:

Accepting your 2 free books and gift places you under no obligation to buy anything. You may keep the books and gift and return the shipping statement marked "cancel." If you do not cancel, about a month later we'll send you 3 additional books and bill you just $5.24 each in the U.S., or $5.74 each in Canada, plus 25¢ shipping & handling per book and applicable taxes if any.* That's the complete price, and — compared to cover prices of $5.99 or more each in the U.S. and $6.99 or more each in Canada — it's quite a bargain! You may cancel at any time, but if you choose to continue, every month we'll send you 3 more books, which you may either purchase at the discount price...or return to us and cancel your subscription.

*Terms and prices subject to change without notice. Sales tax applicable in N.Y.
Canadian residents will be charged applicable provincial taxes and GST.

His lips curved. His blue eyes flashed. He intended to destroy her. "You weren't the only one arrested."

Her jaw dropped, eyes widening in horror. "You didn't?"

"*Cara*, you don't listen. You didn't heed my warnings. I tried—"

"Not Mum."

"She's a Pelosi, too."

Emily felt wild on the inside. She couldn't breathe, couldn't seem to get air inside her despite the fact that her head had begun to swim.

Mum didn't deserve this. She hadn't been well. She hadn't been well for years. But it was worse now...her arthritis so crippling she needed help doing the most basic things, like bathing and dressing. Emily had hired a nurse to stay with her mother so she could make this trip.

"Mum's not well," she said quietly, unable to even look at Tristano.

"The officers told me."

Panic welled fresh. "Officers?"

"The two that arrested her."

Emily's legs nearly went out beneath her, and she sank slowly down into the sand, chilled. "You've had my mother arrested?"

"She's on the company letterhead."

"That's just paper."

"And she shares ownership in your company stock."

"Where is she now?"

"Being looked after."

Her fingers curled into her palms.

Silence stretched, lengthening, and Emily felt as though the sweeping indigo night sky was smothering her, suffocating her. She'd come to St. Matt's and left her mother at home, helpless and vulnerable. She should never have left at all, but Mum had insisted...had agreed with Annelise that Emily needed a break... Oh, no...

"This isn't that difficult." Tristano broke the silence. "You should count yourself lucky—"

"Lucky?" Emily scrambled to her feet, sand flying. She marched on Tristano, trembling with shock and anger. "You killed my father. You killed him, and you think I should feel lucky? That I should welcome marriage because it will what? Stop me from infringing on your copyrighted designs?"

She was poking him in the chest, each furious word accompanied by a stab of her finger, and Tristano gazed down into her flushed face. The moon was reflected in her green eyes, lit with flecks of blue, bright and intense, like the Caribbean waters surrounding the island.

He took her anger, let her fury wash over him. He could handle it. He'd been her first lover, and in some ways he knew her better than himself.

"I want my mother home for Christmas," she said, her finger still jabbing against his sternum. "She should be home—"

"Marry me, and she will be."

Emily gasped, fell back a step. "You didn't just say that."

"I did. Marry me and we'll start over. A fresh start—"

"For Ferre Design!"

"For both of us. Correction, for all three of us. Because your mother will benefit, too. As the mother of my wife, I'd make sure she was surrounded by every comfort conceivable."

Emily took another step backward. Her expression was stricken. "That's blackmail."

"If you look at it like that."

He moved toward her, settled his hands on her bare damp shoulders and felt a shiver race through her. Her shiver should have moved him, but it didn't. He felt cold and hard on the inside, and he wasn't going to back off. He knew exactly what he was going to do. Make Emily his. Make her a Ferre, make her family— his family—and nullify the threat to his business and his sanity.

She tried to squirm away. "And how do *you* look at it, Tristano?"

"Business."

Her eyes flashed daggers. She hated him. He knew she hated him. But she was still attracted to him, still responded when he touched her, and for now it was enough.

"Merger and acquisition," he said lightly, carelessly, his fingers tightening against her shoulders. He was rewarded with fresh fire in her eyes, the blue-green irises hot, stormy, like the sea churned by wind and rain.

"I don't want to be merged or acquired."

Her voice sounded like brittle bits of glass, and he smiled—because he knew what this was costing her—

knew she was fighting for control, for calm—knew that Emily loved a good fight. But he'd taken all her weapons away and she was virtually cornered. Trapped. His favorite place for his favorite Pelosi.

"You should have thought of that before you devoted the last five years of your life to counterfeiting Ferre Designs."

"They aren't your designs—"

"Legally they are."

"Morally they're not."

"But law isn't about morality, is it?" One hand stroked upward, along her neck, to cup her cheek while the other tangled in her long wet hair, keeping her still so she couldn't escape. "Which is why I can make you mine without any pangs of conscience."

He forced her head up, forced her to see the desire, the determination in his eyes. "But it's not as if you've no choice, Em. You don't *have* to become Signora Ferre."

"No, I can just let my mother rot in jail."

"I'm certain the courts would be lenient with her."

He saw the fury sweep through her, and as she opened her lips to speak he covered her mouth with his and drank her breath and warmth and anger into him.

His lips moved across hers and he could taste salt water, taste the cool ocean on her tongue, and as he sucked the tip of her tongue into his mouth she shuddered, this time with pleasure.

Tristano reached between their bodies, grasped the towel and tugged it off Emily, drawing her naked body into his arms. She arched as she came into contact with his hips, her body instinctively pressing against his.

He loved how her breasts felt crushed to his chest, her nipples peaking hard and tight, and as he pressed a hand to her bottom she moaned deep in her throat.

He was hard, and his jeans barely restrained him. It would be so easy to lay her down on the sand here, so easy to put his hand between her legs and feel her softness and warmth. But he kept his desire in check, concentrating instead on the satin texture of her skin and the sweet gentle curve of hip and breast.

She was so responsive to his touch, her slender body rippling with pleasure, and he parted her mouth wider, his tongue teasing her inner lip. Emily tasted of honey and spice. He wanted her, all of her, loved the feel of her body against his, the cool, damp taste of her mouth.

He remembered how sweet she'd tasted when he'd kissed her years ago. As her first lover, he'd taught her his favorite pleasures, showed her how exciting, how erotic lovemaking could be with the right partner. He'd been with plenty of women since that summer, but he'd never forgotten the way she'd felt in his arms, beneath his body. Nor had he forgotten kissing her intimately, tasting her wetness, feeling her shudder against him as she broke in waves of sensation.

He'd discovered everything he could about her that August, discovered she was curious and open, trusting, sensitive. He'd discovered she welcomed his hands, his mouth, his body, his touch. He'd discovered she enjoyed lovemaking—sex—as much as he did, and they'd spent hours alone—hours wrapped in nothing but each other's skin.

Tristano had waited a long time to reclaim her, but he'd known all along that eventually he would. She didn't even know that the lawsuits, the counterfeiting, had just played into his hands, giving him power over her.

His hands shaped her hips, held her firmly against him, and she quivered when he curved his palms across the firm contours of her bare bottom, molding her even more closely to him.

"Tristano…" She choked against his mouth and she shook, her whole body trembling.

He lifted his head and gazed down, uncertain what he'd find in her eyes. They were wide, wet with tears.

"You will make me hate you," she said, her voice breaking, her control smashed.

"But you already do," he reminded her, stroking her soft, warm cheek before tracing the swollen contours of her mouth.

Blindly Emily pushed against his chest, pushing to be free, and his arms fell away. He was the one who stepped back and retrieved her towel, draping her body again.

Emily clutched the edges of the towel. "I'm not afraid of you, Tristano."

"No, you're just afraid of yourself."

Sick with self-loathing, Emily stumbled back to her bedroom. She headed straight for the bathroom and turned on the shower.

What had she done?

But she didn't have to try hard to remember…didn't have to try at all to see herself in Tristano's arms, her body fitted to his, her desire spiraling higher and hotter, threatening to spiral right out of control.

Despite it being three-thirty in the morning, she was desperate to get clean, to rinse the sea and sand and

Tristano's touch away. But even after scrubbing, even after toweling off and climbing back into bed, she still felt his hands, his mouth, his hard body against hers. In his arms she'd lost all control. She'd been completely gone—reason and rationality swept away in the face of her tremendous physical need.

Maybe that was what made her feel so sick right now. The fact that she'd wanted him so much. The fact that she'd turned her conscience off, turned down the volume on her voice of self-respect and given herself over to Tristano's touch, given in to hedonistic pleasure.

Worse, she still wanted his touch. Wanted more of what they'd started. But it wasn't right. She knew who he was, what he represented…how could she just hand herself over to Tristano like that?

Yet thinking back to the beach, remembering the feel of him against her body, the shape of him, the strength and hard warmth of him, she knew it had been natural.

The attraction hadn't died over the years. If anything, it was stronger, more real than ever before. Desire had just flared, shooting to life, superseding everything else. Including self-preservation.

Marry Tristano? She might as well put her head on the chopping block.

CHAPTER FIVE

"WE'RE heading out for the day," Tristano said the next morning, appearing on the terrace, lazily ruffling his still damp hair. He'd obviously just showered, for his jaw was freshly shaven and his shirt hadn't been buttoned yet, the linen fabric hanging open over tanned, honed muscle.

He looked too good, Emily thought resentfully, not knowing where to look—at his clean, smooth jaw or the lean hard muscle of his torso.

Her gaze skimmed his face—the intense blue eyes, the deep groves etched on either side of his mouth, his mouth itself. She'd always loved Tristano's mouth. He had lips that were real. Firm. Full. Wide enough to smile, sensitive enough to kiss properly. But then her gaze dropped down, to the sinewy plane of his chest, and then lower still, lingering appreciatively on his flat stomach with its tight, rippling abs.

It wasn't right that a man in love with his company, a man married to his work, should have a body like this. Tristano's large frame, with its abundance of smooth, hard muscle made her crave skin. His skin.

"I didn't think I could leave the island," she said, feeling absurdly primal.

"We're just going out on the water. We won't be heading ashore."

She pictured a day of sunbathing in skimpy swimsuits. A day of bare, gleaming skin. A day of heated bodies fragrant with coconut oil. It wasn't what she needed right now. "I'm to spend all day on a boat with you?"

The corners of his mouth lifted in a faint, challenging smile. "You make it sound miserable."

"It will be. If I'm trapped with you."

"Trapped." His smile grew fractionally. "Trapped. Hunted. Bagged. Caught." He said each word slowly, as if savoring the syllables. "Interesting words. Particularly when applied to you. And, yes, *cara*, I suppose you're right. You are trapped. At least until after the holidays. And then…"

She knew what he meant. "Jail."

"It's up to you."

"And I wouldn't go to jail if I married you?" The muscles between her shoulderblades tightened. He was treating her as someone very dangerous…a threat to be eliminated. Permanently.

"There are worse things."

"I can't think of any."

"You've clearly led a sheltered life."

Emily shot him a poisonous glance. She shouldn't have come back to St. Matt's—should have stayed away. Mum had stayed away, and Mum was the smart one. Good. Sensible. But then Emily was neither good nor sensible. She'd thought she could handle the return, thought she was ready to face the ghosts of Christmas past. But the ghosts were bigger than she'd thought.

The ghosts of the past owned her. Body and soul.

Tristano leaned over, brushed hair from her eyes before straightening. "You need me."

"I don't."

"You do. You need someone to watch over you, keep you from harm, keep you from ruining your life."

A lump filled her throat, and as she looked up into Tristano's face the lump grew bigger.

He regarded her steadily, and as he gazed at her she felt a current of energy, a sizzle of light, and for a moment all she saw was possibility. For a moment she thought life could be anything she wanted it to be, that not everything had been predetermined. Her father's failure and shame had run its course; the future could hold something good and beautiful for her after all.

For a moment she could feel Tristano's warmth, feel it deep inside her, where she'd once kept everything she held dear. She could focus on all the good things again. Think about that which gave meaning, contentment, pleasure.

No more feuding, no more anger, no more conflict and no more revenge.

She could let go the burden, the dead weight she'd been dragging around, and she'd be free.

Then she glanced past his shoulder to the beach, and she saw the girl she'd once been running down the sand, laughing. And then she saw the woman she'd become, bent over her father, battling to pump air into lungs that had stopped working.

She'd grown up that Christmas on St. Matt's, and

she might want to be young and innocent again but she knew who she was. Knew who Tristano was. The realist in her took over.

She couldn't kid herself. Tristano might find her physically attractive—might desire her body and be willing to bed her—but the attraction would end there. She'd be a temporary distraction, a woman to bed, but once the challenge was gone...so would she be.

"So full of mistrust," he said softly.

She turned back to him. It was on the tip of her tongue to say that he didn't know what she was thinking, that he didn't know her, but he probably knew her just as well as she knew him. "Too deeply engrained now."

He said nothing for a moment, just studied her, and Emily felt the heat between them grow. His eyes said all the things he wasn't speaking aloud: he wanted her. And the attraction was mutual.

They'd always had something raw and physical between them, a slow simmer on a low heat, with the potential to boil over. The heat wasn't definable, wasn't entirely physical, and wasn't based on externals, either. They'd always had this peculiar competition between them, sparked by admiration and a hunger for challenge. They'd spent years dueling in unwritten one-upmanship. Who could best the other?

And yet this wasn't a contest. This was real life, serious life, and there were unholy consequences.

She tried to break the hold he had over her, reminding herself about the past. Hell had broken loose once. He'd broken it open, too. How could she forget?

How could she ever let him close after what had happened?

Life was hard. Savage. She had to be hard and savage, too.

"Why can't you let the past be the past?" he asked.

She could never tell him what she'd given up to exact her revenge, never admit that she'd given up her own life, her own dreams, to bring justice to her father's name.

Tristano, standing so close, his body strong, hard, taut with honed muscle, was nothing short of sexual—physical, gorgeous. And his maleness did something to her. It made her see the world as suddenly bigger, made her realize how small and puny she was. She could fight for her father all she wanted, but his time had come and gone and now she was taking her life, taking her energy and her heart and her hope, and pouring it all into something that would never truly reap a just reward.

Because nothing she did, nothing she could ever do, would bring her father back.

And no matter how hard she fought, how long she battled, he would always have died the way he did.

By his own hand. Broken by his own despair.

So he'd never be truly avenged and she'd be—what? Alone and bitter? Bitterly lonely?

As it was, she'd given up love. Companionship. Nearly all her friendships. There'd been no time or energy for relationships, no emotion for love or even a love affair.

How could she love when she was so angry, so hard, so intent on destroying the Ferres?

All this time she'd thought she was breaking down the Ferres peace of mind, and yet it had been her own.

She'd destroyed herself, crushed what she'd needed, and for what?

She didn't like the answer—didn't want to face it. She knew herself well enough to see that if she admitted the futility of her pursuit it would negate everything she'd done these past five years. And then what would her life mean? What about all the grief? All the heartache?

"Nothing in life will ever be fair," Tristano said, and he reached for her, took her by the arm and pulled her against his bare chest, into the circle of his arms.

She resisted the tug, but he was stronger, and he was determined. She knew she couldn't want this, but at the same time she needed his arms and his mouth and his kiss.

She needed someone who would hold her, keep her. Someone who knew her and still...loved her.

But Tristano wasn't talking love. He was talking conquest. Ownership. Possession.

Entirely different than love.

She shivered at the press of his body, suddenly sensitive all over, aware of him from the hardness of his thighs to the muscular planes of his chest. He felt even better than he had down on the beach, and she was beginning to want this contact, crave the closeness.

"Stop fighting me, *carissima*," he said, and he tipped her head up and kissed the corner of her mouth so lightly that her nape tingled. "It's a useless fight," he added, and she knew he was speaking on several levels.

He wanted her to stop attacking Ferre with her counterfeit goods, and he wanted her to stop fighting the physical attraction between them. But in all honesty it would be easier for her to drop her attack on Ferre than it would be to drop her defenses with regard to him.

Tristano had been the bad guy for so long she didn't know how to think of him otherwise. And even if she stopped manufacturing her leather goods she'd still remember how Tristano had buried her father with so many legal threats that he'd had no choice but to leave the company with nothing but the shirt on his back.

She'd always remember. She had to remember. Because if Tristano could do that to her father, he could do that to her. Maybe not now, maybe not this year or next. But sooner or later he'd harden whatever it was inside him—and it wasn't a heart, she knew that much: he had no heart—and she'd be lost.

Twice broken.

Twice stricken.

And she couldn't do it. She was too proud, had too much self-respect. You could play her for a fool once, but you couldn't twice.

"Don't," she whispered, her voice tremulous as he widened his stance and drew her into even more intimate contact with his body. He was touching her everywhere, his hips cradling hers, his arms encircling her waist, hands resting low on her back, shaping her firmly against him.

"Why not?" he asked, kissing the side of her neck.

She burned at his touch, nerves tightening, skin prickling, her heart leaping to her throat. She wanted him, so wanted him, but she couldn't give in to the desire. Desire was passing, fleeting—oh, hell, desire would just complicate an already impossible situation.

"Because I haven't said I'd marry you and I don't want a cheap fling."

"It wouldn't be a cheap fling, and you *will* marry me. You're mine already. You just haven't admitted it."

Heat flooded her, heat and hunger, weakening her limbs. "Not yours."

He lowered his head, whispered against her cheekbone. "Yes, mine. And mine for the taking."

Emily closed her eyes, felt her heart race, felt everything collide. He was tormenting her, creating twin strands of excitement and fear. She couldn't allow this to happen. She couldn't seem to stop this—him— much less her response, because she wanted his touch, felt positively frantic for more him, more power, more of everything.

"Where's the protest?" he murmured, his breath warm against her heated skin.

Her lips parted to answer, but before she could speak his hands encircled her waist, his fingers splayed, spanning the width of her, fingers touching from hipbone to lower ribs. He seemed to know the right way to hold her, to silence the stream of words, the empty, frantic thoughts. She had felt lost—yes, lost—and suddenly she was found.

He was big and hard and powerful. He was strong. He was everything she wasn't.

She repeated the last words in her head, repeating them so this time she heard, understood. He was everything she wasn't.

He was Ferre. She Pelosi. He was brain. She was heart. He was strong. She soft.

This would never work, never do.

One of his hands brushed the swell of her breast and she shuddered. "Tristano…" She'd meant to sound a warning but instead his name had come out a husky whisper.

His hands wrapped beneath her ribs, his fingers brushing the undersides of her breasts, and sensation rushed through her, nipples peaking, hardening, her body responding.

"Not going to let you go," he said, his head dropping lower, his mouth nearing hers, and she froze, waiting, heart hammering. And when his lips finally covered hers she exhaled, tension dissolving, her body sinking into him.

He tasted like the sun and the sea, like life and intensity, and as his lips moved across hers she wanted to feel more, wanted to capture what had been lost between them.

His mouth firmed, his lips parting hers, and what had been light, teasing, quickly became searching. Insistent. He demanded a response from her, his lips drawing so much more than she wanted to give—but hadn't that always been the way?

He won. He had to win because he was the conqueror. The victor. And she, despite all, gave in to him.

His thumbs stroked the outer swell of her breasts and she stiffened, sensation, fierce sensation, running rampant through her. He stroked again and, arching against him, she groaned.

He seized advantage, finding her tongue with his, using everything he knew, everything he could, to destroy, to ravish her senses. His hands caressed. His lips sucked and nipped. His body heated hers all the way through, warming her, melting the last of her resistance. She clung to him, resistance gone, thoughts silenced, leaving her warm and willing.

Tristano's lips briefly left hers and he whispered at her ear. "I told you that you were mine. And if you stopped thinking about yourself for a moment you'd realize that your mother doesn't need a nasty trial."

It was like ice water being thrown in her face. Emily jerked, hands rising to cover herself. "What?"

"Your mother doesn't need your father's problems—or his poor decisions—made public knowledge—"

"My father did nothing wrong." Her head still spun, her senses reeling, and it was a struggle to put together an argument.

"If this goes to court, there will be endless public scrutiny," he continued, as if she'd never spoken. "The media will follow the trial closely. You'll be besieged by snooping reporters, sleazy photographers, trying to get close, to get unflattering photos of your mother as she enters and exits court.''

"That's enough." Her voice shook. She felt sick all the way through.

Tristano's dark blue eyes narrowed, gleamed dangerously. "*Cara*, the pressure hasn't even begun."

She took an unsteady step backwards. "How can you do this? You know Mum. You *know* her. She's not part of the business—never has been, never will be. How can you punish her like this?''

"You're the one punishing her. You're punishing her because you can't let go of the past.''

Trapped. Hunted. Caught. The words circled wildly inside her head. She did feel trapped. Caught. "I can't let go of the past because my father died tragically and yours is alive and well.''

"Quite well, yes," he agreed.

"Rich, too.''

"That's true. My father was able to retire comfortably. But we are not our fathers—''

"No. We're not. I don't have a father anymore. I don't have his love or his advice. I don't have his laughter or his sense of humor. I just have pain." Her hands balled, fingernails digging into her palms. "And that's why I can't let go of the past. Because the hurt, the suffering, makes me desperate for justice.''

"Justice?''

"Revenge," she clarified. "It's all I think about. Making you suffer." She closed her eyes, pressed a hand to her eyes, seeing red—all red—the red of heart-break, the red of heartache.

After a moment she looked at him, numb, exhausted. "I've lived to destroy you." Ice-cold adrenaline shot through her and her voice sounded faint, eerily disjointed. "I've wanted to destroy you just the way you destroyed my father. An eye for an eye, a tooth for a tooth."

"One life for another?"

Tears filled her eyes. "Yes."

"And you'll be satisfied when you've taken my life from me?"

"I hope so. Because you're right. I hate living this way. I hate who I've become. But it's too late to go back. I am who I am, and I don't know how to change."

"Em—"

"No." She moved away from his outstretched hand, needing to keep her distance, needing to keep her heart surrounded in thick, impenetrable ice. "I'm not your Em. And you're not my Tristano. We're nothing to each other— understand?"

His expression didn't change. "I don't accept it."

"You'll have to."

"No, I don't. And as long as you're here, under my roof, I'm not going to give up on you. You need more, even if you say you don't."

Wearily she stared at him, her words used up. He didn't understand. He'd never truly understand.

"We might be nothing to each other," Tristano continued calmly, "but that doesn't change our plans.

We're still heading out for the day. So pack a bag with your swimsuit, a change of clothes, and something for the evening. I'll meet you at the dock in a half-hour.''

Emily threw her swimsuit and clothes into a small travel bag and headed down to the dock with time to spare. The yacht was already moored, waiting for them, and as she approached she drew a deep, rough breath, her emotions wildly chaotic.

Tristano was confusing her, knocking her off-balance with his arguments, his lovemaking, his not-so-subtle pressure and persuasion. She hated Tristano. She did.

So why did she want the old days back? Why did she want everything the way it had once been between them, before the families had split apart, before Tristano had fallen off his pedestal?

Standing on the dock, Emily breathed in the tangy salt air and looked out across the shimmering ocean. The turquoise and lapis waters sparkled beneath the incandescent Caribbean sun. It had looked this way on the Christmas morning she'd found Father, too. Stunning. Beautiful. Unforgettable. That Hollywood kind of lovely, where the beaches are all smooth white sand, blooming hibiscus and fragrant orchid blossoms.

Tristano was late. Nearly a half-hour late. And when he arrived down on the dock he looked tense. Distracted. Not at all Tristano's usual unflappable calm.

"Sorry to make you wait," he apologized, giving

her a hand and assisting her onto the sleek white yacht.
"I had a call come in. It was important I took it."

She felt the warmth of his fingers around hers as
she stepped onto the yacht, caught a whiff of his co-
logne as she moved past him. Her skin prickled with
awareness, her nerves stretched taut. You hate him,
she told herself harshly. Don't lose focus.

"It's fine."

He joined her on the deck. "Another offer from
Tony Viders came in just as I was leaving, and it was
a good offer. Clean. I couldn't ignore it."

And just like that her icy reserve shattered. "An
offer for St. Matt's?"

"A very good offer."

"You accepted?"

"We'll probably counter."

Emily gripped her travel bag by the handles. "What
does your estate agent think?

"That it's an incredibly generous offer. She thinks
we should accept and sign today."

Sign today. *Today.* Her stomach rose up, high in her
throat, and she nearly gagged. The island could be
gone by the end of today. "Don't sell," she choked.
"Please don't sell."

"I don't need it, Em."

No, but I do.

The yacht was pulling away from the pier in a slow,
steady hum of sound and motion. But Emily couldn't
feel the engine's hum—not when everything inside her
was squeezing tight, choking her. Battling tears, she
turned to look at the island, the green slopes emerald

in the sun, the beach a blinding white. Home, she thought. This was home. Not London. Not China.

Her gaze fixed on the plantation house, nestled among lush palms. The history of St. Matt's was nearly as colorful and violent as that of the bloodthirsty pirates who'd once taken shelter in and among the islands. As a child she'd made up stories about pirates and life on the old sugar plantation. Her stories had been dramatic, rich, and her father had used to pinch her cheek and tease her—"My baby has an imagination, *si*?"

It had made him proud, her imagination. "You'll be the next generation," he'd say, pinching her cheek again. "You'll make us all so proud."

Half-laughing, half-crying, she'd beg him to stop pinching so hard, beg him to leave her alone, give her space. And now she had all the space in the world.

"You don't really want to turn St. Matt's into a tourist destination, do you?" The anguish in her voice was palpable. "You don't."

He shifted his weight, looked at her. "I can't take care of the island anymore. It takes a lot of time— time I don't have now, between managing the Altagamma and trying to control the damage you're inflicting on my business."

"So this is *my* fault?"

"It's been war, Em. You've turned my life into a living hell and it's got to stop."

He was right. But stop how? Just let him—the Ferres—win? *Again?*

"Marry me and the island is yours." His voice

reached her, deep, placating. "Marry me and you'll have St. Matt's in the family forever."

He knew she'd spent every important holiday here on St. Matt's, knew all her early family memories were here. Even her favorite gifts had been given to her here. Like the shiny aqua-green bike she'd been given when she was seven. Her father had hand-painted flowers on the shiny frame, added a straw basket to the handlebars, and she'd loved the bike, ridden it everywhere. The white Vespa scooter when she was sixteen...

Her lips curved in a small, painful smile. "Marry you. How? I don't even like you."

"You could like me again. If you wanted to."

He was right. She could like him. She could like him a great deal. In fact, if she carved away the hate and anger, she'd find the love she'd felt for him all those years ago...

But there was Father, and there was pride. There was fear and problems of faith. As well as trust.

Or maybe it was just pride.

She reached up, pressed a knuckle to her brow bone, trying to ease the pressure building. "There's got to be another way to make this work, Tristano. What if we merge companies—?"

"I don't need or want your company."

"Then hire me. Put me on your staff. Let me prove that I'm valuable, that I can help Ferre's bottom line."

"I want a wife, not a business partner. And it's children I need, not another member on my board."

His bluntness sent blood rushing to her cheeks, her

skin burning with shame. "Ironically, I don't need a husband. Now, I wouldn't mind sex, but I don't need someone checking up on me and asking me where I'm going and what I'm going to do."

"So what do you suggest? That I make you my mistress instead of my wife?"

The thought hadn't crossed her mind, but now that he'd mention it, yes. Being his mistress would be a whole lot more palatable. "It's an arrangement I could live with."

He made a rude sound in his throat. "I couldn't."

She relished his expression. He looked like a dog about to lose his steak bone. "I could get an apartment in Milan. We could...*see*...each other regularly. You'd have access to me, you'd know what I was doing, and you wouldn't worry about my activities."

"What about children? How do you raise children in different households?"

"But we're not talking children—"

"I am." He caught her chin in his hand and lifted her face to his, his blue gaze hot. Possessive. "I'm Italian. And traditional. I want family, a wife. I want *you*. In my home. In my bed. Not in some apartment across town."

"You'd sleep better if I were across town."

"Probably. But the children wouldn't—"

"I don't want children."

"You always wanted children. You used to say you'd have two or three—"

"That was before." She wrenched away, moved as

far from him as possible, her skin scalded from his touch, her pulse racing like mad.

"Before?" And then his expression cleared. "Before everything," he added quietly, and those two words did indeed say everything. She'd been a different person once. "But you'd be a wonderful mother."

"I'm sure I could get them fed and dressed." She smiled, but her eyes felt dry, cold, like her heart, which had been on ice ever since Father had taken his life. "But the rest? No. Can't protect them, Tristano. They'd be hurt, they'd feel things they should never have to feel, and I can't do it...can't bring children into the world and let them be hurt like that."

"Everyone gets hurt."

"Some less than others."

"But that's life."

"Exactly my point."

She felt his hard gaze, felt his disapproval. "It's not right. You're Italian."

"Half."

"And one hundred percent devoted to your family."

She couldn't argue that. Look at how she'd spent the past five years. Look at how she'd picked up her father's cross and followed him into battle.

"I do love Mum," she said after a moment, walking away from him, moving to the other side of the deck. "But..." Emily shook her head, long hair rippling. "Can't have more. Can't risk more. There's not enough of me left." She smiled almost wistfully. "I'm sorry, Tristano. I'm sorry I've turned out the way I have. But I am what I am, and you can't change me.''

His expression was surprisingly gentle as he stared back at her. ''No, I don't suppose I can.''

A little later the yacht slowed, circled once in the middle of the ocean, and then dropped anchor. ''Where are we?'' Emily asked, emerging from one of the guest bedrooms where she'd changed into her two-piece black swimsuit.

''Fifteen miles off the coast of St. Bart's.''

She smoothed the straps of her suit flat. ''Hassel Ledge?'' she guessed, naming a famous diving spot— a ledge nearly seventy feet down—home to some of the most unusual coral in the Caribbean.

''You've been here before?'' he asked.

''Long time ago.'' She'd only dove here once before, and it had been years ago. She'd been considerably younger—probably sixteen, maybe seventeen— and the seas had been rough that day, the water cloudy. Today the sea was calm, the sky a gorgeous blue, with not even a cloud overhead. But even with the calm seas they'd want wetsuits since they were going down so deep.

They tugged on neoprene suits, Emily drawing hers snug over the shoulder and zipping the front closed. The suit fit tightly, which was good.

Once dressed, Tristano and Emily crouched on deck, checking their equipment—the air, the gauges on the tank, the tubes. The procedures were both familiar and discomfiting. She'd gone diving with Tristano before, when there'd been a group of them one holiday, but her usual dive partner had been her father. She hadn't been down since.

Emily felt the weight of Tristano's gaze. "You okay?" he asked.

His concern felt genuine, and for the first time since arriving she felt a flicker of their old friendship, the deep ties that had once made her love Tristano more than anyone.

"I'll be fine."

They hit the water slowly, leisurely swam down. Despite the depth they were going to, the clarity of the water was stunning. The world was so still beneath the surface of the ocean, and Emily relaxed, her tension leaving her.

For awhile they swam together, and then, as Tristano slowed to inspect a crevice harboring an eel, Emily swam on, following the intricate beds of coral, fascinated by the vivid schools of tropical fish.

Gradually she became aware of the time—she'd been under nearly thirty minutes, and she'd swum a considerable distance, following the exquisite coral reef.

She checked her gauges. She still had oxygen. Enough for another ten, fifteen minutes, but she ought to head back—return to the boat. The last thing she needed now was Tristano worrying. He already thought she didn't know how to manage her own life.

She took her time surfacing, aware of the dangers of rising too fast, and as she broke the surface of the water lifted her mask, removing her mouthpiece and swimming to the side of the boat.

One of the stewards was standing on the deck of the yacht. "Signor Ferre?" she asked, gesturing to the deck, assuming Tristano had already gone aboard.

The steward shook his head. "No. He hasn't returned yet."

Emily trod water. "He hasn't surfaced at all?"

"No. Haven't seen him since you both went down."

She glanced at her watch again. Thirty-five minutes since she and Tristano dove deep. Tristano didn't have that much in his tank. He shouldn't push it this close.

He never pushed it this close.

Emily felt a knot in her chest. Her belly did an icy flip. She didn't like this. She'd used to be a really good diver, but it had been years since she'd spent a lot of time in the water and her skills were rusty. Tristano was the more experienced scuba diver now, and he ought to be here at the moment. On the surface. At the boat. His tank was nearly empty.

So where the hell was he?

CHAPTER SIX

STILL treading water, fighting the curl of icy panic in the pit of her stomach, Emily glanced at her own gauges. Not much air left.

"I need another tank," she said to the steward. "Quickly."

"I'll get the captain."

"Where is he?"

"I'm not certain."

Time had come alive. Emily felt it breathing down her neck, showing teeth. She couldn't afford to wait for the steward to hunt down the captain, or locate another tank. Time was precious now. Fleeting.

"I'm going back down." Filled with resolve, Emily knew it was now a matter of doing what needed to be done. There'd be no fruitless discussion, no worrying. "Let the captain know there could be a problem."

"Mademoiselle—"

Emily barely heard the steward's protest. She was already swimming away from the yacht, popping the mouthpiece back between her lips and pulling the mask over her eyes.

Everything was fine, she told herself. Stay calm. Panicking will only use up more oxygen and more energy.

This time as she submerged she could hear her heart

pounding in her head, hear the frantic beating of her heart echo in her ears. The water now seemed too still. The ocean less clear.

It's your imagination, she told herself, swimming deep, knowing she was a strong swimmer, capable, knowing that if anyone could help Tristano she could.

Emily knew she had just minutes left on her own tank. The pressure gauge had dropped to nothing. She had to swim fast, be smart, and not give in to fear.

Reaching Hassel Ledge, she was confronted by the immense size of the coral reef. When they'd first begun to explore the reef earlier she'd been thrilled to be under water again, and she hadn't felt anything but excitement.

But now, facing the huge, delicate reef, she realized she'd forgotten the numerous nooks and crannies, the hollows where the coral formed beautiful caves large enough for a person to swim through. Where to even start looking for Tristano?

Emily did her best to retrace her path even as her gaze swept the coral, side to side, searching for a glimpse of Tristano's midnight-blue wetsuit, or a flipper. Near the edge of the ledge she peered over and down. The sea shelf gave way to nothing but deep, bottomless ocean.

Her heart contracted. What if something had happened and he'd fallen down there?

No. Not possible. Tristano wasn't a risk-taker. Not like that. She was the risk-taker. Tristano played according to the rules.

And the rules meant he'd stay on the ledge, he'd swim close to the coral, he'd—

And then she saw him. Floating face-down above the coral, his body oddly twisted.

Bullets of ice shot through her, one after the other, until she felt nothing. Why was he floating like that? Why wasn't he moving?

She swam to Tristano's side, tried to lift him—couldn't budge him. He was stuck. She looked into his face. His eyes were closed, and yet as she touched him his lashes fluttered open and he looked at her, recognition briefly darkening his eyes before his lashes dropped again.

Propping him up she checked his gauges. Empty. The tank was empty.

How long had his tank been empty?

She removed her mouthpiece, put it to his lips and pressed an arm around him, gratified when he took a short, rough breath. Good. She slipped her tank off her shoulders, put it on his. There wasn't much left in her tank, a minute maybe, and she had to get him dislodged before it ran out.

Holding her breath, Emily ran her hands down his legs and discovered his right flipper deeply wedged in a coral crevice. She tugged on his foot. It wouldn't move.

Swimming lower, she took a closer look at his flipper. He'd obviously been struggling to free himself. His ankle looked shredded, his flipper punctured near the instep. She couldn't reach his toes.

Slipping her hands into a different crevice, Emily

felt around the bottom, trying to discover what was holding Tristano prisoner. Her fingers scraped sharp rock, traced it until it ended at Tristano's flipper.

The coral rock had broken, a piece caving in on his foot.

Without tools she wasn't going to be able to get him out. And she didn't have enough air to reach the top and get the necessary tools.

Hot emotion filled her, tears burning at the backs of her eyes. This was bad. So bad. She didn't know what to do.

And then she heard her father's voice in her head. *Be calm, Emily. Stay calm. Everything's okay.*

The fear lessened—just enough. Just enough to know she needed a breath, air, time to figure this out.

She could do this. She'd find a way. She always did.

Emily swam up a little, took the mouthpiece from Tristano and drew a breath, before replacing it between his lips. The gauges had fallen. The tank had to be virtually empty. That would be her last breath, she knew. Whatever was left was Tristano's.

As she replaced the mouthpiece between Tristano's lips his lashes fluttered open again and he looked at her, his expression puzzled, and then he shook his head, once. He tried to lift his arm, point, but he was too weak.

She put her hands on his chest. I'm not leaving you, she answered silently, defiantly. I'm going to get you out.

She could do it, she told herself. Her father believed

in her. Her mother believed in her. Tristano had to believe in her, too.

With air bottled in her lungs, she dug around in the coral again, jamming her hands into the rock, pounding away with another piece of broken coral. Her head grew light. Specks drifted before her eyes. She shook her head, trying to focus. She had to free him. She *had* to.

Her father's voice whispered in her head again. *A life for a life...*

No, she answered, uncertain now if it was her father's voice or her own. *Not Tristano's life. I don't want his life. I want him happy.*

But you said...

She knew what she had said, knew far too well, and remorse washed over her. Remorse, regret, sorrow. What had she done? To him? To them? Everything about the past five years was wrong.

The sea seemed to rush at her, enclose her, and in turn she reached for Tristano. She didn't feel strong anymore. Didn't think she could hold on.

At least she was with him. She was scared, but she wouldn't want Tristano to be alone.

She loved him.

Her arms wrapped around his chest, she held tight, exhaled—and then suddenly Tristano was free. Moving. They were both moving—floating up.

Emily's lungs burned, bursting for air. Her head bobbed forward against Tristano's chest. She needed air, needed air, needed—

A mouthpiece was roughly shoved into her mouth.

She gasped, gulping in air and then spluttering at her greediness. She breathed deeply, desperately, and arms wrested Tristano from her grip. She tried to protest, didn't want to let him go, and then lifting her head, she realized that help—members of Tristano's crew—had arrived.

Tristano was safe.

Two days later Tristano was home from the hospital after observation, and he was fine. At least physically. Mentally, emotionally...that was another story.

He burst through Emily's bedroom door, stalked across the room to where she sat at the writing desk.

"Don't you ever do anything so stupid again," he said roughly, his throat raw, his voice hoarse. "What you did was stupid—stupid, stupid."

She'd jumped when the door flew open, but the moment she realized it was Tristano, home safe from the hospital on St. Thomas, she smiled. "Welcome home."

His brow darkened. He practically growled at her. "Don't you dare smile, Emily Pelosi. What you did on Hassel Ledge was insane."

"*Stupidaggine!*" Emily flashed in Italian, rising from the desk to face him.

She'd spent two days worried sick about Tristano—unable to now sleep despite the fact the doctors had assured her that Tristano was fine—and now finally she had proof he was well. He must be well. He was certainly in a foul enough temper.

"That's rubbish," she repeated, switching to

English. "I was not going to let you die, or drown. Besides, you're always taught to share oxygen during certification—"

"We weren't sharing," he interrupted grimly. "You gave up your oxygen for me. You had nothing."

"I was fine."

"*Emily!*" He tried to roar a protest, but it came out a guttural groan. "You don't do things like that. You can't."

"I do." She jammed her hands on her hips and attempted to stare him down, but she couldn't quite keep a straight face. He was back. He was safe. He was fine. He might be madder than hell, but this was her Tristano. Tough. Arrogant. Opinionated. "I can't help it. I am who I am. I fight for my family and I fight for those I—" She broke off and blood surged to her cheeks.

Tristano's gaze narrowed. "For those you…?" he demanded softly.

Her face burned. She felt exposed. It was one thing to try and protect Tristano. It was another to declare love. "For those I am loyal to," she concluded awkwardly.

"Loyal?"

"Yes."

"And that's why you'd die for me? Because of your *loyalty*?"

She said nothing, her lips compressing, and Tristano took another step closer. "Two days ago," he said quietly, leaning toward her, his tone conversational, "you hated me."

She swallowed, picked her words with care. "I didn't actually *hate* you."

"No?" One black eyebrow lifted. He seemed to wait in anticipation of what she'd say next.

"No."

"But your feeling now has to be pretty strong if you'd be willing to give up your oxygen for me."

"You're making a big deal out of nothing." She gestured breezily, attempting bravado. "You're fine. I'm fine. Can we just move on to other issues?"

Tristano made a hoarse sound before grinding his teeth. "You can't escape me forever."

"I'm not trying to escape. I'm trying to put a nearly tragic situation behind us and concentrate on what's before us."

"Like…?"

"Dinner."

"And…?"

"Christmas."

"Ah." He studied her face for a long moment, his gaze resting on her eyes and then her lips. "It is Christmas, isn't it?" He suddenly reached out, stroked her cheek with the pad of his thumb. "Doesn't feel much like Christmas. We've no tree, no ornaments, no tinsel—nothing festive."

Her eyes burned and she swallowed hard, hating the lump filling her throat. "I don't need ornaments and tinsel. You're safe. You're healthy. And now you're back home. That's all I wanted this year, all I asked for."

His jaw pulled, a muscle working. "I think the lack of oxygen down there did something to you."

He was right. It had scared her witless, made her realize everything she was about to lose—time, life, love. Tristano.

Emily tried to smile but her chest constricted, the muscles tight. Her emotions were hot and painfully chaotic. "It just brought me to my senses. I realized I was everything you said I was—bitter, hard, selfish—"

Tristano abruptly leaned forward, pulling her into his arms, firmly against his body, and silenced her words with a long kiss.

"I never said that," he said much later, when he finally lifted his head. "I know you're not hard or bitter. You just miss your father. And I don't blame you. I never have."

"You hated him."

"I didn't. As you said, we were practically family. Nothing about this situation has been easy." Gently he smoothed a tendril of hair from her cheek and then lightly caressed the curve of her cheekbone with the tip of his finger. "And losing your father the way you did would tear anyone's heart to pieces."

The lump in her throat seemed to swell. She gulped air, dizzy, feeling submerged all over again.

"I know," Tristano added, tracing the shape of her mouth. "I know how he died. I've known for years. I just never knew what to say or do."

She couldn't speak. She tried to smile, but she couldn't do that either.

"Emily, an eye for an eye—"

"No." She shook her head fiercely.

"A tooth for a tooth."

"No, Tristano. I don't want your life. I don't want this to continue. I can't anymore. It's wrong. Wrong of me. I'm ashamed. Ashamed that I wanted to hurt you that way—"

He touched her mouth with the tip of his finger to silence the stream of words. "But you have my life. I give you myself. Completely. Freely."

"No," she whispered against his finger, even as her emotions rioted inside her. She wanted to say yes, wanted to throw her arms around him, hold him, feel his warmth and strength all the way through. But she was scared.

"Emily, everything's changing—and you better get used to it."

Everything's changing…

Tristano's words echoed in her head as Emily dressed for dinner. Everything *was* changing, and she wasn't sure where the changes would lead…or what the changes would entail. Setting her hairbrush down, she turned toward the bathroom window, gazed out over the turquoise ocean. The sun had begun to drop in the sky, painting the horizon bronze and orange.

She wanted a different life, was ready for more out of life. And if Tristano proposed again would she accept?

She cared for Tristano—cared deeply, passionately—but in her mind marriage could never be a business relationship. Marriage wasn't about contracts or deals, terms or power. It was love. Plain and simple.

Finished dressing, Emily checked her reflection in the mirror twice, nervous. She was wearing all black tonight—a black lace halter top by one of Italy's top designers paired with slim black silk pants and black leather criss-cross wooden mules. At the last moment she'd swept her hair up, pinning it in a loose chignon, and the only jewelry she wore was a wide sterling silver bangle on her wrist.

Now or never, she told herself, leaving her room to meet Tristano.

He stood on the terrace, facing the ocean, waiting for her. The sun's orange rays cast long golden fingers of light in every direction. He looked amazing. So strong, so male, so important in her world.

His head turned and he looked at her. The reddish-gold light played off his striking cheekbones, bronzing his dark hair. *"Bella,"* he murmured. "You look beautiful."

"Grazie."

Dinner was served in the formal dining room with the expansive windows overlooking the ocean. The table had been covered in a red linen cloth, the flowers were white orchids with dark green, and the red linen napkins had been tied scroll-like, with a pearly sea-shell on a white satin ribbon.

But seated at the table, directly opposite Tristano, Emily could barely get the appetizer down. Food was the last thing on her mind. Her appetite wanted something entirely different from what the chef was preparing in the shiny stainless steel kitchen.

Tristano knew, too. She looked up from her little plate of canapés and her gaze locked with his. He was smiling, but his expression was intense, his dark blue eyes hiding nothing, and she knew something was going to happen soon.

She'd been waiting for that something ever since she'd arrived. She wanted him. Wanted to be seduced. Loved.

"Let's go somewhere a little more private," he said, pushing away from the table.

She could only nod. She wanted to go somewhere more private. She wanted him to strip off her clothes—the black lace halter, the silk trousers, the heels. She wanted his mouth where her lace and silk had been. She wanted his hands everywhere.

Wordlessly she followed him from the dining room, through the mahogany great room to Tristano's bedroom suite. She'd never been there, and when he pushed open the door she knew it was most definitely his room. The walls were painted a rich chocolate, the cream raw silk drapes were drawn for the night, and the large iron lamps had been turned down low. The bed was covered in the same rich silk as the windows and the top cover had been pulled back to reveal paler ivory sheets.

Tristano stood in the middle of the bedroom. "Close the door," he commanded quietly, and she did.

"Lock it," he directed.

She locked it.

"Look at me."

Heart racing, she forced herself to turn and meet Tristano's gaze. He looked hard, determined, fire blazing in his dark blue eyes. His navy shirt was open at the throat, exposing the upper planes of his bronze chest where the muscle was dense and smooth.

As she watched he began unbuttoning his shirt, one button at a time. His shirt unbuttoned, he held out a hand. "Come to me."

She suddenly felt fear.

"I'm afraid," she confessed, skin heating, blushing.

"Of me?"

"No. Of…this." She could see he didn't understand. She wasn't sure she could explain, but she tried. "I think I've forgotten how."

His brow knit. "Has it been that long since you've made love?"

Years, she thought. Her desire had been killed along with her dreams. But the desire was returning, and she wanted Tristano so much she didn't know if she could handle the fierceness of her emotions. "Yes."

"Nervous?"

"Very." That much she could admit.

"I'll come to you, then." His gaze was possessive as he walked toward her. At her side, he drew her against him, cupped the back of her head and kissed her.

She felt his fingers in her hair, felt the press of his hand against her head, felt her mouth quiver beneath his.

He deepened the kiss, and as he kissed her he slid

a hand up her ribcage, beneath her flimsy lace halter top, to cup one breast. She gasped as he brushed the fullness of her breast, his fingers catching, tugging on her hardening nipple.

She couldn't silence her husky groan of pleasure, couldn't keep from pressing closer to him. She needed more from him, needed all of him.

Funny how she could go years without contact and yet just one touch from Tristano and she couldn't survive twenty-four hours without more. Without everything.

She felt his hands at her neck as he unhooked the top, peeling the delicate black lace down over her bare breasts. "Stand still," he said, stepping back to better appreciate the fullness of her breasts, the taut tips aching to be touched. "I want to look at you."

But she didn't want to be looked at. She wanted touch, and she wanted it now. Emily reached for Tristano, clasped his arms, pulled him back to her. "You can look at me later. Now I want you. I want us."

Her clothes seemed to fall away as he laid her on the bed, his hands caressing her skin, his mouth following the path of his hands, sucking, kissing, tasting her breast, her hip, her inner thigh. Emily shifted impatiently against Tristano's body. She loved the feel of his hands and mouth on her heated skin, but she wanted more of him—the more that could only be answered with him inside her.

He moved between her knees, poised between her thighs, and she reached out, stroked the hard length of him. His erection strained against her, and her body was very warm and willing.

Gazing up at Tristano's face, she thought he'd never looked more gorgeous or sensual as he lightly stroked between her thighs, his fingers finding every sensitive nerve. She felt the warm slickness of his finger against her, slick because of her, and it aroused her even more, her readiness for him. He'd been her first lover and no one had ever replaced him in her heart or her affections.

She trembled as he stroked her again, the pad of his finger teasing the delicate hooded nub, and she lifted her hips, trying to find satisfaction. And then he was on his knees, between her thighs, and she felt him press against her. Her body was tight, she was nervous as well as excited, and Tristano leaned over her, kissed her, teasing her with his lips and tongue.

He slid in slowly, deeply filling her. The moment he'd buried himself all the way inside her she dug her fingers into his shoulders, overwhelmed by the incredible sensation of him with her, of him in her. He was warm and hard and her body gripped his, holding fast. For the first time in years Emily felt safe, secure. It was as if she'd stumbled her way home.

And then he moved, a long, slow thrust that made her hold him tighter, closer, as helpless tears burned the back of her eyes. She was here, with Tristano, and she knew even if he'd never said the words that he loved her. He had to love her. No one else had ever touched her like this, held her so.

As he thrust again she rose up to meet him, overwhelmed by an emotion she'd never thought she'd feel again. Tristano was supposed to be the enemy, but he actually was the hero. He'd rescued her, saved her from herself.

His body filled her, pressing more deeply, and she opened her arms, opened her heart, needing him, needing to give herself over to him. There had been so much anger, so much hurt and resentment, and suddenly she needed only that which was good, that which was life-giving.

Together they made love, their bodies moving smoothly, seamlessly, both silent, needing no words at this time. But his thrusts were stronger, deeper, and she felt the muscles deep in her belly begin to tighten. Hot emotion rose, waves of love and waves of need.

Her father had left, but Tristano remained. An eye for an eye, a tooth for a tooth, a life for a life. She would have given her life for Tristano's. She loved him more than she could ever say. Her lips found his, clung, trying to tell him that he was right, she needed him—needed him not just now but always, forever. She needed his love and his strength, his courage, his stability. But most of all she needed him to spend her life with.

Suddenly the pleasure was too hot, too bright, the sensation too intense. She reached for his hands, found his wrists and gripped him tightly as the pleasure surged to a blinding peak.

''Tristano,'' she whispered urgently, her nails biting into his skin, his body both familiar and tantalizingly new. It was like being hit by a tidal wave, a rush of brilliant green and blue. The sun seemed to glint whitely in her eyes and she was gone, sucked under, pulled in, her body rippling beneath his.

He sucked her breath from her as his orgasm hit hard, strong.

"Bella," he murmured against her mouth as his body emptied into her. "I want children," he said, kissing her. "Many, many children—with you."

CHAPTER SEVEN

LATE the next morning Tristano stood in his silk boxers on the balcony overlooking the water, knowing things were about to get exciting.

He wasn't sure how Emily would react to what he had to tell her, and, lifting the small porcelain cup, he took another sip of strong black coffee. It had been an incredible night, a night stretching into morning, the morning stretching into midday.

Just remembering the hours of lovemaking, the erotic pleasure he'd found in Emily's smooth, satin skin, in her softness, in her willingness to meet him where he was made him hard all over again.

It had been years since he'd felt desire like that—years since ardor hadn't been just an idea but a tangible thing. And desire...hunger...made him feel young, alive, strong.

The corner of his mouth lifted in a small self-mocking smile. Rather ironic that the two best lovers he'd ever known had been Emily the Innocent and Emily the Woman. There was just something about the way she felt...about the way she fit his body, fit his life.

She belonged in his life. Maybe it was fairness, justice, or maybe it was the fact that he loved her, understood her. He knew she belonged with him.

Now if he could only convince her of the fact before the wedding began...

He returned to the bedroom where Emily still slept the deep sleep of one who has earned her rest. Her long brown hair was a silky gloss against the pale ivory cotton pillowcases. Beautiful Emily.

He leaned over and kissed her cheek, near her ear, smelling the hint of perfumed bodywash from their shower some hours before, when they'd wandered from bed to shower and back to bed again. They'd been like teenagers...insatiable...the night had been unforgettable.

"Wake up, *carissima*," he whispered, brushing his lips across her cheek a second time. "Time to get up."

Emily's lashes fluttered. She stretched and rolled over onto her back to get a look at Tristano. Her blue-green eyes were still cloudy with the unfocused gaze of lingering sleep. "What time is it?"

He lifted a long tendril of hair from her cheek, smoothing it back. "Time to wake up and dress."

"Why?"

"Your mother will be here in an hour."

She struggled into a sitting position, sheet haphazardly clutched to her breasts. "*My* mother?"

"The very one."

Emily blinked up at Tristano and dragged a hand through her tangled hair, trying to clear her head. "Why is Mum coming here?"

"It's Christmas."

Recognition dawned. "It is! Oh, Tristano, lovely.

Really—that's lovely of you. I'll be with Mum for Christmas.''

"Annelise, too.''

She was blinking again, her brow wrinkled anew. "Annelise?''

"Yes. They're arriving quite soon.''

"But why Annelise?''

Tristano kept his expression carefully neutral. "She didn't want to miss the wedding, and I thought you'd want her as a witness—''

"Wedding?'' Emily interrupted, the sheet creasing in her fists. "Is that what you just said?''

"Yes.''

Emily's mouth dried. Frowning, she touched her tongue to her upper lip. Her mouth was like cotton, her lips chapped from a night of kissing.

Tristano glanced down at her, his expression kind, considerate. "Should I send for coffee, *cara*? Might help clear the head a little.''

"Yes.'' Her head definitely needed clearing, because she could have sworn that Tristano had said Mum was on her way to St. Matt's for their wedding and Annelise would be a witness. "I don't remember any plans for a wedding,'' she said, leaving the bed, accepting the white silk robe Tristano was holding out to her.

"We've discussed it many times these past few days.''

Emily cinched the silky sash tightly around her waist. "And I always said no.''

"But you didn't mean no.''

She couldn't believe it. She'd only spent one night in his bed and he was already making decisions for her, acting as if she didn't have a mind of her own.

"Tristano, I'm not marrying you." She crossed her arms over her chest, the cool silk fabric shaping her full, firm breasts. "It may be Christmas, and you may have my mother flying in, but there's no wedding today and no wedding tomorrow. We're lovers. Nothing more."

He grimaced. "You explain that to your mother."

"I will."

"Because she's thrilled. She's like a kid at Christmas—" He broke off. "An English cliché, but you get the picture."

Unfortunately Emily did. She headed for the bathroom, then turned in a circle, faced Tristano again, her head spinning. "I'm not a puppet or a doll—some little plaything you can manipulate."

"I know."

She couldn't believe he was doing this—couldn't believe he was controlling her like this, shifting her as if she had strings attached to her arms. Little wooden marionette girl.

There was a discreet knock on the door and Tristano opened it. One of the young French Caribbean housemaids carried a silver tray into the bedroom, setting up the coffee service on the round mahogany table— an antique piece sent over as a wedding gift to the daughter of the original plantation owners from England.

Emily waited for the young maid to leave, doors

quietly closing behind her, before facing Tristano. Heart hammering, her eyes searched his. She needed to understand, needed the truth. "Why would you tell my mother we're getting married?"

"Because I thought it'd make her happy—"

"You don't tell people things like that... You don't get their hopes up..."

"And I love you."

Emily's lips parted and then closed. She stared at Tristano, not knowing what to say now.

"We're meant to be together, Emily. Ferre & Pelosi. It's the way it always was. It's the way it should always be."

"But you don't want a business associate."

"No, I want a lover. A best friend. A wife." He reached out, stroked her cheek, smiled down into her eyes clouding with tears. "And I do want you back in the business. I want you on my side, working with me, to make Ferre & Pelosi the best it can be."

"Your father doesn't want Ferre & Pelosi—"

"But he does." Tristano's voice dropped and his expression grew sober. "My father and I have discussed the mistakes we made—both then and now. We were both wrong. We acted rashly, my father and I. My father was angry, and I was determined to do what was right. But what I did wasn't right. And I ask you to forgive us...forgive me..."

"I forgive you. But your father..." Her voice drifted away and she gazed across the bedroom, seeing not the painted walls or the view of the water but the morning she had discovered her father, the anguish of

losing so much so quickly. "Your father prospered
while my father died."

"But my father didn't prosper. My father went to
hell, too." He crouched before her, his hands on her
thighs. "You don't know how he suffered, Emily.
How your father's death broke him. My father loved
your father. As you said, they were like brothers. It's
been a nightmare for the Ferres, too."

But her father's name had been blackened; her father's shame had crushed them.

Turning her head, she looked at Tristano, and her
self-righteous anger died. Because she saw now the
suffering in Tristano's face, saw the haunted expression in his eyes. Tristano had hurt, too. And Tristano
was a man of his word. If he said his father, Briano,
had suffered, regretted his actions, then Emily believed
him.

Reaching up, she touched Tristano's face, his hard
cheekbone, the square cut of his jaw. "My father was
just borrowing that money," she said softly, needing
to clear his name one last time. "It was a loan…he'd
written a letter, had it notarized. He was going to pay
the money back." She blinked, looked into Tristano's
eyes. "Father wasn't a thief."

"I know. My father knows." He hesitated. "My
father isn't the way you remember him. He's quite ill,
Emily. Very frail. He's grieved terribly…and I don't
think he'll ever recover. But know this: my father did
love your father. We all did."

Emily blinked again and a tear slipped free, sliding

from the corner of her eye. "What now? How do we move forward?"

"We just do." Tristano's lips curved but his smile was hard, fierce. "We learn from our mistakes, we accept what we've lost and we decide we deserve happiness. We make a new life, together."

"Again," she whispered.

"Ferre & Pelosi."

"Ferre & Pelosi," she echoed, before biting her lower lip to keep the tears from falling.

The corner of his mouth lifted. "Has a nice ring to it."

"Yes."

His eyes searched hers. "So you'll marry me? You'll come live with me, share a life with me, my own Emily?"

She couldn't look away from his lovely blue eyes— the blue of the sky before midnight, blue like the sapphire waters surrounding St. Matt's, blue she loved better than any shade in the world. St. Matt's was like a precious emerald surrounded by sapphire and gold, and yet it was nothing…meant nothing…compared to the love she felt for him. Tristano. Her treasure.

"Yes." She smiled at him, heart full, aching. "I'll marry you, live with you, share a life with you."

He kissed her, her lips trembling beneath his. She reached for him, hanging on to his forearms, needing his strength. The kiss stole her breath, weakened her knees, and warmed her soul all the way through.

She moved even closer to him, slipping into his arms, and the strength of his body comforted and teased. They'd made love for hours last night, and yet she hungered for him again.

"Make love to me," she urged, shuddering as his hands slid beneath her robe, settling on her naked satin skin.

It was too sweet an invitation for him to resist.

Later, sated, their bodies still warm and damp, Tristano cupped her face in his hands and kissed her again, more lightly but no less tenderly.

"Merry Christmas, Em," he murmured, his voice still husky. "I hope we can spend every Christmas here."

"Together, you mean," she corrected lazily, her palm pressed to his abdomen, loving the feel of sleek sinewy muscle beneath golden skin.

"Together, yes, but specifically here."

"Here?"

"St. Matt's."

It took her a moment to understand, her mind as languid as her limbs, and then with a prickle of heat and another prickle of joy she pushed up on her elbow to gaze down at him. "You're not selling the island?"

"I can't." He reached up, drew her down to him, kissed her deeply.

She could hardly breathe. "Why not?"

His eyes glinted at her for a moment and then, tossing back the covers, he leaned out of bed, opened a drawer on the nightstand and pulled out an envelope. "Open it," he said.

Hands shaking, she tore the back of the rich cream envelope open and drew out a Christmas card. She read the sentiment on the front, opened the card and read the verse printed inside. It was romantic, emotional, but it was what he'd written below, in his own strong, firm handwriting that brought tears to her eyes.

To commemorate our first Christmas together, I deed the island of St. Matthew's to you, Emily Pelosi.

She looked up at him, eyes burning, tears not far off. But she'd had enough tears, didn't want to cry.

She shook her head, struggled to speak, words nearly impossible. "You're giving the island back to me?"

"It should be yours. No one will ever love St. Matt's like you do."

And despite her best efforts the tears fell. It was impossible to hold such fierce, hot emotion in.

Wrapping her arms around Tristano, Emily held him tightly, afraid to let go. This wasn't a dream, was it? This wasn't a wonderful dream that would disappear when she woke?

"Tell me you're real."

"I'm real."

"Tell me I'm awake."

"You're awake."

But it wasn't enough. Her heart burned, bursting, and she needed him more than she could ever say. "I love you, Tristano," she whispered against his neck, where his skin was warm and fragrant and everything she loved best. "You've no idea how much I love you."

He reached up to cup the back of her head. "But I do. That's just it, Em. I do." His deep voice broke and he drew her even closer, holding her within his arms, holding tight, as if to protect her from every gust of wind and storm. "A life for a life, Emily, and you have mine."

THE SULTAN'S SEDUCTION

Susan Stephens

CHAPTER ONE

'WHEN you walk through those doors you leave your world behind and enter mine.'

Was that a threat? Lizzie Palmer wondered, drawing herself up as she followed Kemal Volkan's gaze across the vast palace courtyard.

'Who told you where I live?' he demanded as she walked past him through the gilded gates.

Wisely, Lizzie kept her own counsel, but she caught the glint of something in Kemal Volkan's eyes that made the tiny hairs stand up on the back of her neck. In spite of her resolve, she suddenly felt apprehensive. And then he laughed. It was a harsh, masculine sound that bounced off the damp black cobbles between them.

'You've got some cheek,' he said.

Determination? Definitely. Cheek? Perhaps, Lizzie reflected, moving ahead of the man they called *The Sultan*, making for the entrance to his home. But it couldn't be helped.

There were just two things in life that mattered to Lizzie: her work as a lawyer, and her brother Hugo. And her brother always came first. She only had to remember Kemal Volkan was holding Hugo somewhere in Turkey to know she was right to be forcing her way into his home.

After the static-fuzzed call from her brother, Lizzie had caught the next flight to Istanbul. What she had learned about Kemal Volkan had only increased her level of concern. It seemed he lived like a feudal warlord, surrounded by a wall of silence. She'd had to use all her legal expertise and connections to dig a little deeper into his affairs, and as she had done so, she'd discovered that his acquired name was no exaggeration. *The Sultan* was an immensely powerful man, and accustomed to ruthlessly wielding that power.

When she had turned to the embassy for help, they'd said she was on her own. This was a commercial matter, rather than political or criminal, and the Foreign Office couldn't get involved in the legal process of another country. So she had tracked down a local lawyer who specialised in commercial work, and Sami Gulsan had told her the really bad news: the company Hugo had been working for during his gap year was in trouble.

The passports of company employees were being withheld until parts missing from the machinery Hugo had helped to install arrived on site. Volkan intended to barter the men's freedom for those parts, and heaven knew where he was holding them in the meantime. Even Sami Gulsan couldn't tell her that. And with the company in financial difficulties, Lizzie knew that the parts would be almost impossible to obtain.

She stole a glance at her adversary, knowing she had to make him see sense. It was almost Christmas; surely he didn't plan to keep the men over the holidays?

'Thank you for seeing me,' she said, in an attempt to build a bridge between them. 'I can assure you I would not have troubled you at home had I not considered this a matter of the utmost urgency.'

He dipped his head briefly without shortening his stride. She couldn't tell if he had softened towards her or not. But he was right about one thing, Lizzie realised as they reached the grand entrance to the palace building—his world was very different from her own. Even the air felt different. It had the peculiar stillness only the extremely rich seemed to gather round them. And there was a faint scent too—sandalwood, she guessed—worn by Kemal Volkan. Normally she reacted violently to any strong perfume, but somehow this was different.

Hearing the gates close behind them, Lizzie knew it was too late to turn back now even had she wanted to, which she didn't. A tip-off from Sami Gulsan had got her this far, and she had no intention of wasting the opportunity.

It might have been better to introduce herself more sedately, but she had not anticipated arriving at the palace in a beat-up old taxi at precisely the same moment as Kemal Volkan in his chauffeur-driven Bentley. On her instruction, the taxi had slewed across the entrance, blocking his way. Volkan had sprung out ahead of his driver and ordered the cab to move on, and she had almost fallen at his feet in her rush to waylay him. She could still feel the imprint of his hand on her arm from when he'd reached out to steady her, waving his bodyguards away...

Jolted out of her thoughts by the sight of men in jewelled, vividly coloured robes opening the splendid entrance doors for them, Lizzie was suddenly acutely aware of where she was—and of the man at her side. She hesitated briefly as he stood back to allow her to precede him, and then, raising her head high, she stepped over the threshold into the palace. She had allowed for Kemal Volkan wearing the mantle of power that came with immense wealth, had even allowed for his looks being different—more exotic, perhaps, than the people she was accustomed to dealing with. But nothing could have prepared her for a meeting with a man who possessed such a forceful aura.

It would take every ounce of her adversarial skill to bring her brother home in time for Christmas, Lizzie realised, mentally preparing herself for the confrontation that lay ahead.

'Welcome to my home, Ms Palmer,' he said, forcing her to turn and look at him.

'Thank you. It is spectacular,' Lizzie said frankly, gazing around. 'I don't think I've ever seen anywhere quite so beautiful.' And he was stunning too, Lizzie conceded, glancing back at her host.

Kemal Volkan was tall, powerfully built, and rugged, so that in spite of his formal business suit he looked more like a buccaneer returning home from his latest expedition than the billionaire businessman she knew him to be. She could just imagine that by the time most people got over the sight of Kemal Volkan he would have tied them up in knots. But that could not happen to her. She had to ignore the way the blood was rushing through her veins, and stifle her growing sense of apprehension. She would somehow negotiate the release of the men—and she wasn't going to leave until she did.

'Won't you come in, Ms Palmer?' he said, gate-crashing her thoughts.

Glancing up, Lizzie saw that he had paused and turned to her on his way towards some inner door. Hearing her name roll off his lips with just the trace of an accent sucked a response from deep inside her. His deep, husky voice was every bit as disturbing as his striking appearance, she realised, wishing time had allowed for the anonymity of legal letters passing to and fro between them.

'Ms Palmer?'

For the first time he could remember Kemal wished he could free himself from centuries of tradition. He wanted nothing more than to be alone and to relax after his long and particularly demanding business trip, but the code of Turkish hospitality had been hung around his neck at birth. However inconvenient it might be, custom decreed he must grant her a wel-come. And he would—before sending her on her way as fast as possible.

She wouldn't even have got this far if she hadn't announced she was Hugo Palmer's sister. And how had that happened? She and her brother were as dif-ferent as could be. A repressed female on a mission was the very last thing he needed right now...

Repressed? Kemal's eyes narrowed as he turned the word over in his mind. Ms Lizzie Palmer was certainly wound up as tight as a spring, but... His brow furrowed as he inhaled appreciatively. What was that? Lavender? And there was something more...amber, perhaps? Very English—with just a hint of the East. Maybe there was hope for her after all, he conceded, feeling his senses stir.

Lizzie's face burned as she sensed Kemal Volkan's very masculine interest. She avoided his glance, affecting interest in her surroundings instead, and found she was genuinely captivated. The roofed entrance vestibule they were crossing was exquisite. Stretching the whole length of the palace, it was subtly lit, and awash with colour thanks to the moonlight streaming through glass panes as brightly coloured as jewels in the vaulted roof. Semi-precious stones glinted darkly beneath her feet, and there was a fountain playing in a raised central pool. There were even songbirds fluttering through the flower-strewn foliage cloaking the walls.

It was all very beautiful, but so foreign, and so dangerously beguiling. And she was here on business, not a pleasure jaunt. She could only be relieved that she had dressed the part. There was nothing remotely frivolous in her appearance. A plain black overcoat covered an austere Armani suit, and her soft blonde curls were tied back severely. She wore very little make-up, and neat designer spectacles provided the shield she always worked behind.

Before studying law she had longed to become an actress, but the precariousness of life on stage had ruled that out. Hugo's security had always come first.

She had embraced the responsibility for him gladly at eighteen, and since then her life had been geared to taking care of him. Over time her dreams of a life on the stage had faded, and now she found an amusing irony in the many similarities between that career path and her current profession: she still wore a gown and a wig—a costume, of sorts—to act as a barrister, and still fine-tuned her performance each day in court.

She understood only too well the importance of the visual message she sent out to men in the course of her work, and was glad of that knowledge now. It gave her the confidence to deal with a man like Kemal Volkan. She needed to treat him like an adversary, rather than waste time lapping up his masculinity like some gullible adolescent.

But the deeper they ventured into the palace, the greater grew Lizzie's sense of foreboding. She looked round anxiously as another set of heavy doors closed behind them. Her own world was growing more distant—just as Kemal Volkan had promised it would.

Finally they came to an elegant square hallway that seemed to belong to a slightly cosier and perhaps even private living space within the vast formal structure of the palace. The floor was white marble, and antique hangings in muted shades of burnt sienna, rose madder and topaz covered the walls. There was a large Turkish rug on the floor: it was undoubtedly priceless, Lizzie thought, pausing alongside Volkan who had drawn to a halt.

The surroundings were breathtaking, but where was Hugo? Where was her nineteen-year-old brother? How could she secure his freedom? The best alternative, Lizzie realised, was to avoid confrontation and appeal to Kemal Volkan's better nature—though she doubted he had one. And if he had hurt one hair on her brother's head…

Lizzie blinked at the look Kemal flared down at her. It was almost as if he had read her mind and issued a lightning response to the challenge. It made her wonder what price he might exact in return for her brother's freedom.

A servant distracted her, coming to kneel by the edge of the fabulous carpet at his master's feet. Loosening the laces on Kemal Volkan's highly polished shoes, he slipped them off, replacing them with a pair of lavishly embroidered Turkish slippers.

Seeing Volkan indulged in this way only fuelled Lizzie's anger. Wherever Hugo was incarcerated, she was quite certain he would not be enjoying luxury such as this. And now the manservant was kneeling beside her, with a second pair of slippers in his hand.

'Don't looked so shocked, Ms Palmer.'

The low drawl seemed to resonate at a frequency that made her whole body thrum in response, Lizzie noticed with resentment. But she could see the sense of protecting the priceless rug. 'I don't need slippers. I'll just slip my shoes off—'

'Indulge me,' Kemal Volkan murmured.

Lizzie's first instinct was to be bloody-minded. She couldn't remember feeling such passion outside the courtroom. Her childhood had left her with an overwhelming urge to control every aspect of her adult life, and up to now she had always succeeded. But the fact was she couldn't be rude to the elderly retainer who was even now trying to ease up her foot. Round one to Kemal Volkan. She would have to yield to his wishes on this occasion.

'Thank you,' she said politely to his manservant.

'Seni sevdim,' the old man replied. Slanting a shy smile at Lizzie, he hurried away.

'What did he say?' Lizzie asked.

'Mehmet likes you,' Volkan said dryly. 'The phrase is freely offered here in Turkey—unless of course you do something drastic to prevent it.'

Something drastic? Lizzie thought. She would do something drastic if that was what it took to set her brother free.

'In Turkey, East and West meet seamlessly,' Kemal Volkan continued. 'Hence the slippers. It is a very small concession for me to make to someone who has served my family all his life. Those of us who are fortunate enough to live in Istanbul enjoy the very best of both worlds—'

'I am well aware of the geographical significance of the Bosphorus, Mr Volkan,' Lizzie cut across him, 'but right now my only concern is for my brother.'

She dared to interrupt him? Kemal kept his thoughts behind a mask of indifference as he ushered Lizzie towards his study. 'My time is yours, Ms Palmer,' he murmured politely.

They could only have been sitting down in his study for a few minutes, but Lizzie felt as if she had been

talking for ever. Her neck was aching, and all the time
Kemal Volkan just sat watching her, without saying a
word. In the end, his remorselessly neutral expression
pushed her into an uncharacteristic display of passion.

'I won't leave until I know exactly where Hugo is,
what's happened to him, and how soon he can return
home.'

She waited tensely, fairly sure that her argument
was persuasive In her view there was no reason why
a satisfactory compromise could not be reached. She
was even prepared to act as intermediary between
Volkan and the receivers for the bankrupt company, if
he thought that would help to expedite the men's return home.

This was turning into a novel encounter, Kemal reflected. He doubted he had ever met a woman so full
of determination, and so unswervingly set on defiance.
He felt some admiration for her. It took nerve to confront him on his home territory, and she had certainly
researched everything thoroughly...a little too thoroughly, he decided, feeling anger start to take the place
of his grudging admiration.

She presumed to have an understanding of his complex business dealings in no time flat, and had invaded
his privacy to a degree he had never experienced before. But he would not get into a debate with her. She
might have found out plenty, but now she was facing
a brick wall. And that was how it was going to stay
until he decided otherwise. He would tell her absolutely nothing, and wait like a hunter stalking his prey,
using silence as a weapon, feigning uninterest, until
he was ready to strike.

CHAPTER TWO

DID nothing provoke a response from this man? Lizzie wondered, as they sat across the desk from each other. Her frustration was growing by the minute as she stared at Volkan's watchful face. Did nothing unzip that firm, sensuous mouth?

The more he exercised control, the more she found herself determined to elicit a response from him. The only curb on that determination was the fact that she had to be careful: she couldn't risk antagonising him. She had the sense of a powerful engine idling, waiting for her to make the next move, reveal her hand. But she did have one slight advantage. She was a guest in a very traditional home where custom insisted that Volkan at least listen before he threw her out—an unfair advantage, perhaps, but where her brother's welfare was concerned she had no scruples.

Lizzie averted her gaze from the wide sweep of his shoulders, clad in the finest wool tailoring. The ink-dark suit was almost certainly from Savile Row, and both his grooming and his smooth bronze tan bore the unmistakable stamp of the super-rich. But that didn't exclude him from the human race, she mused angrily. He must have some feelings. Surely he could understand her concern for her brother?

'Ms Palmer?'

As Volkan unexpectedly broke the silence Lizzie's focus became acute. She straightened up expectantly. 'Yes?'

'Shall we have tea?'

Tea? To choke him with, perhaps! Where were the answers to her questions? He still hadn't even told her where her brother was!

Viewing his imperious profile as he turned to call one of the hovering servants forward, Lizzie decided angrily that it wasn't too great a stretch of the imagination to picture him as a sensual, pleasure-loving sultan. It was quite possible one of his forebears had been some self-indulgent pasha. Kemal Volkan was certainly above all normal human feeling. In fact, nothing about him was usual, from the luxuriant black hair he wore a little long, to the dusky shadows cast by his sharply etched cheekbones. And his eyes, she noticed, were the colour of a smoky-grey wolf pelt...

He was staring at her. She quickly looked away, pretending interest in her surroundings. It was hard to remain insensitive to the beauty around her when everything in the room had been designed to please the senses. The wood panelling insulated the study against outside noise, and there was a log fire blazing in the over-sized grate that under other circumstances might have made her feel relaxed enough to grow sleepy. A mellow light was cast by twin table lamps, and aside from the noise of her own heart hammering in her ears there was no sound other than a faint trickle of classical music coming from surround speakers.

It was all quite different from the small modern

apartment she shared with Hugo. But then she suspected Kemal Volkan must have inherited many of the beautiful artefacts, whereas she had inherited nothing at the age of eighteen but a bewildered nine-year-old brother, when their hippie parents had taken the ultimate trip late one Christmas Eve.

Lizzie tensed anxiously as she thought about Hugo. She wasn't doing much for him now—and never would if she allowed those childhood memories to get in the way. And she had been so sure they were all banished to the deepest archives in her mind. One day she would deal with them properly. But not now. She couldn't afford any distractions now.

Determinedly, Lizzie closed her mind to the past. She never allowed the past to rule the present. Dwelling on things she couldn't change was a destructive pursuit, and she chose to look forward. Hugo was nineteen now, and had secured a place at a good university where, after his gap year, he would follow in her own footsteps and read law. They had made it through together; that was all that mattered. And no one, especially not an arrogant individual like Kemal Volkan, was ever going to come between them.

'Do you have anything more you would like to say to me?' he said.

Plenty! Lizzie took a moment before resuming, heeding the warnings she had been given about Kemal Volkan, that like the wolf he was a predator—strong and cunning, a hunting beast. But if he thought for one moment that he could frighten her off, or play the 'men rule here' card, he was about to discover how very wrong he was. She was often forced to take on lawyers of the old school, and that experience had given her the mental armoury necessary to do battle with dinosaurs of any nationality—even Turkish entrepreneurs who thought she was a pushover.

Her argument might be couched in the most polite terms, but her hostility was all too evident. Her attitude offended him, and called for a response. He would master her, Kemal decided as Lizzie's soft, insistent voice washed over him. It was a challenge too rich to be ignored, and he would even be doing her a favour. Intellectual jousting was all very well, but there was another, unawakened side to Lizzie Palmer. All her fires were directed at her work, and her sisterly concern for Hugh Palmer. Commendable. But if she did not find something else to spend her passions on Hugo would only shake her off, as all young men must shake off any feminine influence in the home. And work was a poor companion through the night.

He affected close attention as she talked on. She was certainly a formidable opponent where words were concerned, but he had other weapons in his armoury—weapons he would enjoy using on Lizzie Palmer.

It never ceased to amaze him how one sibling could be so different from another. Hugo was so gregarious, so carefree and fun-loving, whilst his sister was none of those things. But apparently Lizzie had brought him up single-handedly, so Hugo was what she had made him. She had done a good job as far as that was concerned, Kemal conceded thoughtfully. Another plus: it had obviously been some time since she last brushed her long blonde hair, and it was escaping in soft tendrils that curled around her face—a face that in spite of the fact that her eyes were spitting fire at him still managed somehow to appeal.

Kemal shifted position impatiently. The world was full of beautiful women, all melting to order like sickly-sweet ice cream. He was tired of them all. His palate was hopelessly jaded, and business was his mistress now. It had been a long day, a difficult trip, a protracted business negotiation. On the drive back from the airport he had dreamed of the many indulgences awaiting him at the palace: a shower, a massage, a Turkish bath, all of which he could enjoy in the luxury of his own home. Or he might have swum a few lengths in the indoor pool first, and then taken his ease later.

Instead, for some reason, he was giving this intense and surprising young woman more of his time than even good manners demanded. So what was it about her that appealed? The answer, of course, was that she was ice and fire—perhaps a perfect combination of the two. He would listen to what she had to say, and then decide what to do with her.

Lizzie's precise movements as she organised the papers in her briefcase distracted Kemal. He was attracted to her. In fact, he wanted her to stay. The physical reaction that followed took him completely by surprise—control was normally his middle name—and it was all he could do to suppress a very masculine smile as he continued to gaze at the extremely uptight, and immensely proper Ms Lizzie Palmer. If she knew the effect she was having on him now, she would run for her life.

Relishing the opportunity to study Lizzie in some detail, Kemal settled back in his chair. Her trim ankles and shapely calves gave some clue as to the rest of the package, though she was pretty well trussed up in her drab business clothes. Still, there were agreeable curves in all the right places, and the way her hair was beginning to wave softly where it had escaped from the tightly drawn ponytail made him want to wind his fingers through the wrist-thick fall and bring those full red lips a little closer.

There was certainly passion contained in that outwardly respectable frame, but all of it was channelled in entirely the wrong direction. And her impertinence intrigued him—she dared to challenge his code of honour, making it clear she thought he had Hugo locked up somewhere. She was without question a most contentious woman, as well as the most contained he had ever encountered. And that made him curious to know if she might succumb to temptation of a more erotic nature. He shifted position again, barely able to contain his pent-up energy. He was restless now, dangerously restless. His hunting instinct was in full spate, Kemal realised, as he gazed at Lizzie through half-shut eyes.

Lizzie's voice caught in her throat as she started to summarise her thoughts on ways of securing Hugo's speedy release. She wondered suddenly if Kemal Volkan was actually listening to her, and tensed, seeing the slight tug at one corner of his mouth. It wouldn't do to encourage the very masculine interest she could see brewing beneath the surface of his harsh exterior. There was too much sensuality in his face for her to risk relaxing in his presence, and far too much confidence radiating from him in hot, compelling waves.

The idea that he might find her attractive came as a complete shock. She had never imagined herself to be overly attractive; she was too pale, too reserved. And she didn't exude the necessary *vibes*, according to her friends. Which was how she liked it. The idea of sex with a man like Kemal Volkan was a terrifying prospect. She had about as much experience as a gnat, whereas he was sure to have a harem stocked with sophisticated temptresses. Better not to think about it, Lizzie decided. She had expected to wrest her brother from the clutches of a jailer, or argue for his release in the safe and sterile confines of a lawyer's office, but this was definitely the worst-case scenario.

'Are you cold?' Kemal said, as she shivered with apprehension. 'Let me hurry up the tea and send for some food as well.' Without troubling to wait for her reply, he stood up and pulled a velvet cord hanging from the wall.

Freed from Kemal's penetrative gaze, Lizzie battled to regain focus. This was not what she wanted—this ease, this familiarity. She had believed herself ready for anything, but she had not factored a man like Kemal Volkan into her thinking. His phenomenal level of success had led her to assume that he would be a much older man, and she had learned that once they recovered from the initial shock of having to deal with a woman, older men's fatherly instincts usually kicked in, making them easier to handle. There would be no such concessions with this man, Lizzie thought tensely. Her only hope was to get their discussion back on track as fast as possible, and this time nail him to the mast.

'I really would prefer to talk than to eat,' she said when he turned back to her.

'Is there any reason why we can't do both?' Kemal said easily, dipping to stir the blazing logs with a long steel poker.

'Well, no, but—'

'Then we eat,' he said with a shrug.

What harm could eating together do? Lizzie thought. After all, he was as much sinned against as sinner—

What was she thinking of? The circumstances in which he was holding the men made fairness irrelevant. She had come to free Hugo and his colleagues— not to defend their jailer!

'It's really very warm,' Kemal commented as he moved away from the fire. 'Why don't you let me take your coat? You're still cold,' he said with surprise, when Lizzie failed to stop the quiver of awareness that rippled across her shoulders at his touch. 'We will eat soon, and then you will feel much better.'

She doubted that somehow.

As he swung Lizzie's coat across the back of a chair Kemal realised that he liked the way she had felt beneath his hands, and the way she'd responded to his touch. Her skin had felt warm and soft, not cold.

The thought that it might be good to tutor her in all those things that her education had so obviously neglected to teach her was growing. Too often women were like hothouse flowers: too ripe, too blowsy, hardly recognisable one from the other. But Lizzie Palmer was different. She was fresh and unspoiled—though, like any difficult mount, she would have to be mastered before she could be enjoyed...

She would have to leave soon, Lizzie thought, picking up on Kemal's brooding interest. She had always thought herself a hard-bitten professional, but Kemal Volkan was really beginning to frighten her.

She was distracted by a gentle tap on the door, and when the servants returned with food and drink she realised she was very hungry. Seeing the same elderly servant smiling encouragement at her as he brought over some delicacies for her to sample, Lizzie felt a little reassured. She would stay long enough to eat, and then she would pin Volkan down over Hugo's release. Once that was done she would take the greatest pleasure in putting as much distance between them as possible.

A few nibbles were brought to them, as well as Turkish tea served in tiny vase-like glasses and accompanied by slices of lemon and white sugar cubes.

'Try some,' Kemal insisted. 'The tea is very refreshing.'

Lizzie hesitated. Taking anything from Volkan's hands seemed like a betrayal. His voice might be neutral, but his steel-grey gaze was shrewd and watchful, and she felt guilty indulging her own needs whilst her brother was still being held. But the key to Hugo's release, she reminded herself, was Kemal Volkan. And while she was under his roof she at least had a chance of getting Hugo home in time for Christmas.

'Where have you been staying?' Kemal asked her as they sipped the tea.

'At the Hotel Turkoman,' Lizzie said distractedly. The last thing she wanted was to allow him to steer the conversation away from Hugo and towards her.

'Ah, yes,' he murmured thoughtfully. 'Close to the law courts, and with an excellent view of the Blue Mosque.'

'I'm really not interested in the view, and I don't plan to stay,' Lizzie informed him. Maybe she wouldn't even need a hotel room, she thought tensely. She was quite prepared to take Hugo's place in a far more primitive location than the Hotel Turkoman. 'Look, I don't feel we're getting anywhere. Let me get to the point. Hugo must be released—'

'Released?' Kemal echoed with a hint of impatience. 'What are you talking about?'

'I think you know,' Lizzie countered. 'My brother must be released in time for Christmas,' she repeated impatiently, meeting his steely look head-on.

Did she think he was a barbarian? Kemal wondered as he held Lizzie's gaze. Did she really believe he had the men locked up in a dank cell somewhere?

And was this emotional blackmail now? Her eyes had grown misty at the mention of Christmas. It suggested a change of tactics on her part. All the more reason for him not to be drawn. He would keep his own counsel, just as he had planned to do when they first met.

Kemal leaned forward across the desk that divided them and passed her a card. 'It's very busy in Istanbul at Christmas,' he said. 'There can be confusion. Take my business card. If you have any difficulties at the hotel, just ask them to call me.'

Didn't he get the message? She wasn't going to be around at Christmas if she could help it, Lizzie thought tensely. And neither was Hugo. It was on the tip of her tongue to say that she could manage very well without his help, but when he dropped the card on the desk in front of her for some reason she picked it up.

'Thank you,' she said briefly, slipping it into the front pocket of her briefcase.

'Today is Tuesday,' Kemal murmured thoughtfully. 'You haven't left yourself much time if you want to have your brother home by Christmas Day, on Saturday.'

Was he goading her? Or was this an unexpected moment of concern? Highly unlikely, Lizzie decided. 'Hugo *will* be home in time for Christmas,' she said pointedly.

Her stubbornness should have infuriated him, but instead he was forced to admire her cool. Nothing he could say fazed her at all—except for any mention of Christmas, which for some reason really got under her skin. But that was his curse, Kemal reflected. He noticed everything, and sometimes wished that he didn't.

He turned to murmur an instruction to one of the servants in his own language, asking for some food to be prepared and brought to the sunken lounge for them. Then he turned again to Lizzie. 'I do recommend you confirm and perhaps extend your hotel booking. Every bed is likely to be taken in the city over Christmas.'

'I will be staying in Istanbul until my brother and all the other men are released,' Lizzie assured him. 'And I can see no possible excuse for reasonable and honourable people not to achieve that satisfactory conclusion before Christmas.'

A muscle worked in Kemal's jaw as he curbed the angry words that flew to his lips. She questioned his honour and she constantly rejected his help. She had arrived in Istanbul assuming the worst, taking a tough line with his office, refusing to accept local protocol, refusing to talk to anyone but him—even turning up on his doorstep believing she could bend him to her will! She chose to assume he was a barbarian—so maybe it was time Lizzie Palmer learned that no one bent Kemal Volkan to their will.

'Mr Volkan!' Lizzie exclaimed with concern as he stood up. 'You're not leaving? We haven't finished our discussions—'

'I have finished.' And now she dared to question his intentions! Kemal's gaze blazed down on Lizzie. *Masallah!* But she was beautiful. If only she could have been a little looser, a little more self-indulgent, like her brother. She would certainly have to learn to be a lot more biddable if she stayed around for much longer! 'Ring the hotel, just to make sure you have somewhere to stay tonight,' he instructed, hardly trusting himself to stay in the room with her a moment longer.

'Thank you, but no,' Lizzie said flatly, also standing up.

'Why not?' Kemal said, his eyes narrowing with mistrust as they confronted each other.

'I won't make the call because I don't need to,' Lizzie said confidently.

'You don't need to?' Kemal repeated suspiciously.

'No. If I have a problem at the hotel I will simply find another,' Lizzie said firmly. 'Look, I know this has been hard for you—'

'Hard for me?' Kemal repeated incredulously.

'I do understand the damage caused to your business because of those missing parts,' Lizzie pressed on.

'You understand? You understand nothing!' Kemal said, his voice like a whiplash.

The look in his eyes made Lizzie's spine go cold. She didn't think she had ever seen anyone so suddenly in a fury, or anyone control it quite so well. She had overstepped the mark. She had attacked his pride once too often. She had refused his offer of help. She had defied him. And for a man like Kemal Volkan such behaviour was incomprehensible

'How dare you come here and lecture me?' he erupted. 'I paid millions up front in good faith, only to be let down very badly by your brother's employer. You see this as a personal problem affecting your brother. I see it as a setback in trading—in trust between our two countries.'

'Don't you think that's a bit extreme?'

'Extreme?' Kemal said icily. 'You talk of your concerns for Christmas, whilst I have to consider the possible long-term consequences for my business and my employees. I have invested a fortune in this project, and *I will not allow it to fail*.'

His final words flew at Lizzie like shot from a gun. She was in no doubt that he meant every one of them. Tension rose between them as he held her stare. This was a far more dangerous situation than anything she had encountered in court. Kemal was a leader of men, unaccustomed to failure, a man to whom nothing was ever denied. And in his eyes she was merely a woman...

Lizzie's mounting anger overtook her caution. The day would never come when a man could intimidate her, and Kemal Volkan would never browbeat her into submission.

'This is not just another case for you to win, Ms Palmer,' he was informing her as Lizzie drew herself up. 'And I resent the fact that you imply I have acted dishonestly, or illegally, when all I ask is that people honour their obligations. The fact that your brother is one of those people does not alter the situation one bit.'

Now she would demand to be returned to her hotel, Kemal thought, as he waited for Lizzie's response. But for some crazy reason that was the very last thing he wanted. He almost laughed out loud with relief when she levelled an unflinching gaze on his face. He should have known she would have more guts than that.

'In spite of what you think of me,' Lizzie said coldly, 'I can assure you I do understand the problems you've had. I know what honour means to you, and you have every right to feel let down. But I have my own agenda, and you must understand that I will not be swayed by anything you—'

'I *must*?' Kemal interrupted her softly.

'I am determined to stay,' Lizzie told him, 'until I know that Hugo and all the other men will be home in time for Christmas.'

'What do you want me to say, Ms Palmer?'

Lizzie's thoughts were in confusion as silence fell between them. Reason could never prevail when they were poles apart in culture, in thinking—in everything. Her head was throbbing with concern for Hugo, and she was so keenly aware of the influence Volkan wielded she could scarcely think straight at all. And then there was the passion that had so unexpectedly slipped through his guard...

Kemal Volkan was a force on a level she had never encountered before. She had no cards left to play. Her mind raced as she considered the alternatives. She had to make one last big gesture. Something even he could not dismiss. *She should have left everything ready so that Hugo could enjoy Christmas without her, but she had thought of nothing beyond coming to Turkey to negotiate his freedom...*

'Ms Palmer?'

'Consider this proposal—'

'When I know what it is,' he agreed.

Lizzie drew a deep breath. Honour was her code too, and she would stop at nothing to protect her brother. 'Call the authorities,' she said calmly. 'I'm going to take the place of my brother and his colleagues.'

CHAPTER THREE

LIZZIE'S brave speech took Kemal by surprise. Keeping her close a little longer had been plucking at the edges of his mind. He'd been ready to engage in a battle of words and wits—at which he excelled—to keep her there. Instead of which she had elected to stay—and of her own free will. What a battle for his conscience! A beautiful and intelligent woman had just agreed to become his hostage. He should refuse, of course. But, what the hell? For him, Christmas had come early!

'Sit. Sit down again, please, Ms Palmer,' he said, wanting to give them both time to digest this turn of events.

'I still hope to be free in time for Christmas.'

Kemal looked up. His focus had sharpened as she spoke. Could she tune in to his thoughts? And what was this fixation she had with Christmas? Foolish sentiment? Or a poor attempt at working on his emotions? He stared at Lizzie. She seemed so young, almost vulnerable. But that was a trick of the light—or wishful thinking, perhaps. She was at least mid to late twenties, and there was nothing the least bit vulnerable about her. This harping on Christmas was simply a lever to make him release her brother.

'It may not be possible for you to be free for Christmas,' he said coldly. 'We shall have to see.'

He looked again and saw her eyes briefly close against her fate. No doubt she was imagining all the horrors awaiting her. He turned his face with some irritation. Her suspicions insulted him. They made him want to grab hold of the virtuous Ms Lizzie Palmer and shake some sense into her. And that only made him angrier still, Kemal realised. He wouldn't have believed any woman could rouse such passion in him.

But he would never allow such a base emotion to master him. He would retain control of this situation— and of Ms Lizzie Palmer.

'Will you arrange the exchange for me?' she asked, reclaiming his attention.

'That's quite an offer—one woman in exchange for five men?'

'I would have thought it a good bargain,' Lizzie countered.

The challenge on her face made him glad; made the blood race in his veins. He had never met a woman like this before. They locked gazes like two protagonists in the ring, and in that moment she had never appeared more attractive to him. If a man was to have children, wasn't this tigress the mother he would choose for them?

Was he going completely mad? Kemal wondered, launching himself from his seat in front of the desk to pace the room. Tiredness, he realised with relief, swiping a hand across the back of his neck. Only extreme exhaustion could have allowed such a crazy thought to enter his head!

He relaxed briefly, and then tensed again, seeing Lizzie was still staring at him, still doggedly pursuing her crusade to rescue her brother. Would she never give up? He had never met anyone so unshakeably determined to defy him. His feelings were swinging wildly between anger and desire. All he could think of now was that her stamina had better match her determination. But first, he remembered, there was that sheath of steel she was cloaked in to dispose of.

'Do you accept?' Lizzie demanded quietly.

A muscle flexed in Kemal's jaw. Was she daring to put pressure on him? Whatever the consequences, he knew now that he would never rest until he had mastered her. This was no longer an impersonal negotiation for him—if it had ever been. She had made it deeply personal. 'I accept,' he said. 'Now we will eat. We will discuss the detail later.'

His arrogance was outrageous, Lizzie thought angrily as he turned away from her. It was obvious no one had ever challenged his right to impose his will wherever he chose. *Well, prepare yourself, mister, because I won't stand for it!*

For a moment Lizzie indulged herself with wild thoughts of springing out of her seat to beat her fists against the wide expanse of his back. But she remembered how close she was to achieving her aim. Hugo might be free that very night if she could keep her cool just a little bit longer.

Taking his seat across the desk from her again,

Kemal leaned back. It was time for the gloves to come off. 'Don't you mind missing out on Christmas?'

As far as Lizzie was concerned, only four words registered: Missing out on Christmas. 'I would hope that as a man of honour and influence you would not take advantage of this situation,' she said shakily. 'I expect you to help me find a solution before then.'

Would the need to mark Christmas never leave her? It was like a great black hole she had brought with her from her childhood, a hole that had to be filled—with festive food, dainty ornaments, fat crackers stuffed with plastic gifts and silly jokes and paper crowns...a tree, and presents—there had to be presents...

'Ms Palmer?'

Lizzie's eyes cleared and focused again as she looked up at Kemal.

'I will do whatever I can to help you,' he said, with an impatient gesture.

Wounding her had brought him no pleasure. And how could he enjoy a woman whose eyes brimmed with tears every time he mentioned Christmas, even if it was just a case of foolish sentiment? Though he still suspected emotional blackmail, there was a haunted look in her eyes that might have been genuine, or might have been some leftover from her acting days. Hadn't Hugo told him his sister had once dreamed of a life on the stage?

Lizzie's jaw firmed visibly. 'If you refuse me, Mr Volkan, I'll make sure you never do business with my country again.'

Was she threatening him? He almost laughed in her

face. 'Enough, Ms Palmer,' he snapped, raising one hand to silence her. But the flash of desperation in her eyes made him rein back. He remained still for a moment, until he could see she had become receptive once more, and then added softly, 'There is no reason for us to become enemies. My name is Kemal. You will use it. And I will call you Lizzie.'

Oh, no, she wasn't going to fall for the 'good cop, bad cop' routine, even played by the same man. 'I'd like to make the exchange tonight,' Lizzie said, as if he hadn't spoken.

'You are a very demanding woman.'

'My brother must be home in time for Christmas.'

Kemal held up both hands in a show of surrender to try and slow her down. 'I realise Christmas is important to you, but who's to say you might not enjoy Christmas here in Turkey?'

While I'm locked up, presumably? Lizzie thought, her lips tightening.

'Why not make this Christmas truly memorable?'

Thanks to him, it already was, Lizzie thought, breaking eye contact when she saw the look in Kemal's eyes. She could not risk offending him by admitting that Christmas in Turkey was the last thing she wanted. 'I didn't think you would celebrate the day.'

'Turkey is predominantly a Muslim country, but my mother was Christian.' Lizzie was surprised, Kemal noticed, and he seized the moment to explain. 'Many of the people who work for me celebrate Christmas. I honour every custom wherever I do business.' What

was this? Was he trying to win her favour? It had to
be a first for him, Kemal reflected dryly.

'I see,' Lizzie said, colour flooding back into her
face. 'Then you do understand—'

No, Kemal thought, I do not. But he would find out.
Something troubled him—something behind Lizzie's
eyes. His glance dropped to her lips. The thought of
mastering her had been replaced by another, more
pressing need: the need to awaken her, to steal away
the shadows in her eyes.

Kemal's senses leapt when he heard Lizzie's sharp
intake of breath, but he saw that his interest was making her tense.

'Mr Volkan—'

'Kemal,' he reminded her.

'Kemal.' The name felt strange on Lizzie's lips, and
yet it rolled off her tongue like melted chocolate, so
that she wanted to say it again, and again.

'You are exhausted,' he observed, in a softer voice
than she had ever heard him use before.

Lizzie was instantly on guard. But she was too slow
to resist when Kemal leaned across the desk, and she
gasped to see that her own small hand was completely
swallowed up in his fist. She snatched it away, but not
before she had a chance to be aware of his incredible
physical strength.

'I would like to leave tonight,' Lizzie said, hoping
she sounded calm. *Now! Right now!* Every sensation
she had ever known was concentrated in the hand she
was nursing in her lap. It was as if Kemal Volkan had

scorched her. 'I must see my brother before I am locked up—'

'Locked up? What on earth are you talking about? You will stay here, of course.'

'Here?' Lizzie's gaze darted around the room. She was ready to take Hugo's place in a cell, in a dungeon—anywhere. Staying here at the palace, under the same roof as Kemal, seemed a far worse fate.

'This is a very large residence,' he said, as if reading her mind. 'The palace is every bit as large as the Hotel Turkoman, where you would have been staying. And here you will have your own suite of rooms, complete independence from me. And before you ask, you will not be inconveniencing me in the slightest. In addition you will have the freedom of the palace gardens, the spa, the swimming pool…'

'I can't possibly agree—'

'Why not?' Kemal said impatiently. 'As my guest you will be free to do as you wish. It will not alter the outcome of any discussions between us. You have my word on that.' He sat back, satisfied that she would stay. It was a *fait accompli*.

Still she hesitated. He had not expected indecision. 'It has been a long day,' he said at last. 'You *will* stay here.' He made a decisive gesture.

'As another hostage?' she said tensely.

'No one forced you to take your brother's place,' Kemal pointed out.

'And I still intend to do so,' Lizzie said. 'But I will not stay here with you.' She got up.

Planting his knuckles on the desk, Kemal leaned

across. 'You will stay here—because you have no alternative.'

His angry words seemed to vibrate in the air between them, and after a few tense moments Lizzie sat down again. Kemal was right. She could not do anything that might jeopardise her brother's release. *The Sultan* has spoken, she reflected tensely. Kemal Volkan's sobriquet was well earned, but he was not, and never would be, *her* master.

CHAPTER FOUR

'Ms PALMER will be staying tonight,' Kemal told Mehmet. 'Make guest quarters ready for her.'

Bowing, the elderly man gave Lizzie a gentle smile. 'This is excellent news,' he said in heavily accented English. 'Welcome to the palace, Ms Palmer.'

Lizzie felt a shiver of apprehension run down her spine. What had she agreed to?

'Perhaps I should put your mind at rest?'

'Yes, perhaps you better had,' Lizzie agreed tensely, levelling a stony gaze on her host.

'The palace is huge. You will sleep in one wing while I will sleep in the other—in *The Sultan's* bedroom.'

Of course! Lizzie thought cynically. Where else would Kemal Volkan deign to lay his head? But she was tired, and she was hungry, and common sense overruled any inclination she had left to defy him.

'Are you reassured?' he demanded sardonically.

Lizzie held his stare. 'Reassured? I am reconciled, for now,' she said, hoping she wasn't about to make the biggest mistake of her life.

Meeting Lizzie's gaze in those few seconds, Kemal learned many things: she was certainly strong, but however hard she tried to hide it there was sadness behind her eyes. And those eyes, as he had just discovered, were a very attractive shade of aquamarine. But why should he care what the hell he saw behind her eyes? What was so different about her?

He did care, however much he tried to pretend otherwise, and that irritated him. It was doubtless down to curiosity, which was a great driver. The puzzle surrounding Lizzie intrigued him. And, whatever she was trying to hide from him, he would find out.

'I hope I can rely on your complete co-operation tomorrow morning,' Lizzie said as Kemal showed her to the door. 'Whatever the conditions might be where my brother is, I insist on seeing him.'

Kemal maintained a diplomatic silence, knowing Lizzie was in no position to issue commands. She was like a tigress in defence of her cub where her younger brother was concerned, and he could only approve of that. There were certainly qualities to admire in Lizzie Palmer. But Hugo was old enough to make his own decisions. It was time for Lizzie Palmer to let go—in more ways than one.

'First thing tomorrow morning, we will move this matter on,' he promised. He viewed Lizzie's tense features with a very masculine mix of self-interest and desire. The attraction of channelling her fire and honing it in his own direction was keen—and he would only be doing her a service, after all. Someone had to release the pressure building up inside her.

Kemal saw Lizzie's eyes glittering like green ice as she stared back at him. Even when she had every reason to be reassured he could still feel her defiance flying at him. But it only fuelled his appetite. Had her beauty and her bravery derailed his pride? Certainly they made him long for the tussle of words between them to end, and for the combat to begin in earnest.

It would have to be conducted somewhere a lot more comfortable than his study, though, he reflected wryly, and it was still a little soon for the bedroom. She would need maximum reassurance, maximum preparation, maximum foreplay. Any haste on his part would only consign her to a life of repression, of inhibition—and, anyway, it pleased him to make her wait.

'Shall we go somewhere we can relax and talk?' he suggested, when she made to follow Mehmet. 'Now that you are reassured about your brother, the business part of our meeting is concluded.'

'There is no other part to our meeting,' Lizzie pointed out. 'This isn't a social call. I would prefer to be shown to my room.'

'Ah, yes, the dungeon,' Kemal murmured sardonically. 'But may I suggest you take some refreshment before your confinement begins?'

'No, I don't think so,' Lizzie said, heading for the door.

As she reached it, Kemal was forced to lunge forward and snatch her to safety, before it swung open to admit a servant coming to inform him that food was ready to be served in the sunken lounge. Shaking herself free, Lizzie dislodged her spectacles.

'Let me help you—'

'No!'

'I insist.' Taking hold of the delicate gold arms between his lean, tanned fingers, Kemal held them up to the light as if to check for damage. It was just as he had suspected. 'Well, well,' he murmured. 'Why do you hide behind these?'

Lizzie was conscious of the servant still hovering. This was not the moment to make a scene. 'I don't hide behind them,' she said tensely. 'I choose to wear them.' She held out a stiff hand for their return and after a moment Kemal gave them to her.

But she didn't need to wear them, he thought, puzzling over the spectacles as Lizzie put them back on. Both lenses were clear glass. The clues were piling up. She couldn't leave now until he had solved every one of them.

'We will eat in the sunken lounge,' he said, refusing her the chance to object.

'I'm really not hungry,' Lizzie said, reddening with embarrassment when her stomach growled in disagreement.

'Well, I am going to eat,' Kemal informed her. 'You may do as you please.'

She couldn't remain in his study alone, Lizzie realised as the servant silently pivoted on his heels and left them.

Kemal stood back to let her pass, and then led the way into another sumptuous room. A richly padded seating area was sunk into a floor of snowy white travertine marble, and torches in high brackets on the walls cast a discreet light over the intimate space. The servants had arranged the food on a long, low table set between two plump banks of cushions.

It was a set for seduction, not a business meeting, Lizzie decided, holding back. But it did look incredibly comfortable—and she *was* incredibly hungry.

It was also incredibly decadent, she discovered, struggling to keep her pencil skirt below her knees as she sat down. Kemal had no trouble adapting his powerful frame to the exotic relaxation area. Where he was concerned East and West were one and the same, Lizzie realised as he shrugged off his jacket. Loosening his tie, he tossed that aside too, and a tremor tiptoed down her spine when she suddenly realised that they were quite alone. There wasn't a sound now, other than water splashing rhythmically over tiles somewhere far in the distance.

'Relax,' he said, mind-reading again. Stretching powerful arms along the back of his bank of cushions, he viewed her with amusement. 'Or I promise you will get indigestion when you start to eat. *Borek*?'

Lizzie stared at him. It was hard to believe this was the same man who had ordered the detention of her brother and his co-workers. But then it was a struggle to impose clear thinking of any sort on a mind churning with such unexpected thoughts. She should never have agreed to move into such sultry surroundings, Lizzie realised, checking her skirt. At least in his study there had been the huge expanse of mahogany desk separating them. Here, on silken cushions, their knees were almost touching.

Kemal's gaze was disconcertingly direct as he gestured towards a platter loaded with crisp golden pastries. 'I think you will find *borek* quite delicious…'

His eyes never left hers for a moment, and Lizzie felt a treacherous heat start to invade her veins as he continued to explain the food to her. His low, gravelly voice seemed to be telling her something very different from the ingredients he was listing.

'Or perhaps you would care for a ripe plum?' he suggested finally, in a matter-of-fact tone.

The change in his voice was as good as an alarm bell. It was as if she had been in an erotic trance—a trance into which he had placed her, Lizzie realised, recovering herself fast. 'The food does look delicious,' she admitted coolly, 'but there are other things to talk about. I'm really not interested in taking a culinary safari,' she added in a tone of mild apology, 'but thank you all the same.'

'Then perhaps you won't mind if I do,' Kemal said, refusing to be put off. And, taking his time to select the plumpest fig, he used a small pearl-handled knife to skilfully expose the moist fruit.

Lizzie found she could not look away as he devoured the succulent flesh. His lips, his tongue, the nip of his teeth—the very thorough way in which he went about the task—made the breath catch in her throat.

She shifted position awkwardly on the unusual seating, hoping Kemal's mind-reading skills were taking a break. He had the ability to make her long for pleasure, for self-indulgence, to be the fruit beneath his mouth, the object of his very thorough attention. And there was nothing more dangerous to her cause than that, Lizzie thought, looking at him. Not unless she turned the tables on him…

The idea of seducing *The Sultan*, bending him to her will, played in Lizzie's mind for a moment, until reason won through and she looked away, knowing she had neither the inclination to allow fantasy into her life, nor the talent for putting her wandering thoughts into practice.

'You must excuse me for being so greedy,' Kemal murmured, 'but when the fruit is sweet and full of juice it requires my fullest attention.'

Lizzie's stomach lurched. There was something very dangerous in his eyes. She looked away quickly, feeling her cheeks burn. It was such a human look, rather than the cold and very calculating expression she had come to expect. But even when she looked away the image of Kemal—his lips, his tongue working rhythmically and so very thoroughly on the fruit—took root in her mind and refused to go away.

Kemal watched the transition in Lizzie as she sank a little deeper into the cushions, and he allowed the moment to hang long enough for her full lips to part and her small pink tongue to sneak out to moisten them. Then, reaching for another plump fig, he said, 'Would you like me to prepare this one for you?'

'Thank you—'

'And feed you?'

Lizzie realised some minutes must have passed while she was in a daze. Now he was holding out a plate of prepared fruit. 'That won't be necessary, thank you,' she assured him quickly.

But Kemal brought a piece up to her mouth before she could stop him, and, brushing the warm sweet flesh against the full swell of her bottom lip, he murmured, 'Open wide.'

Lizzie's gaze slid away from the disturbing look in his eyes to the even more worrying strength in his hands. She noticed that he had unbuttoned his cuffs and rolled his shirtsleeves back to reveal powerful forearms shaded with dark hair. There was hard muscle and sinew showing clearly beneath the tanned flesh, and he was so close she could feel his body warmth reaching out to envelop her. Sandalwood invaded her senses and his warm minty breath mingled with her own.

'I'm really not hungry,' she said faintly.

'Of course you are,' Kemal insisted, placing the fruit between her lips. 'And anyway, you don't have to be hungry to enjoy this.'

Well, that was true at least, Lizzie thought, closing her eyes as she drew the fruit slowly into her mouth.

It pleased Kemal to see the faint flush on Lizzie's cheeks, and to hear the raised pitch of her breathing. Her full lips parted again when she had swallowed, as if she was waiting for him to fill them once more. Obliging her, he watched as she tested the next piece of fruit delicately with her tongue. He hardened instantly, and when she drew the firm flesh into her mouth he almost groaned out loud.

Now they were both slaves to erotic thoughts, he mused as his senses soared to a new level. 'This fruit is so ripe,' he murmured, feeding Lizzie another mouthful, 'it is practically begging to be eaten.'

Another sharp intake of breath mingled with his

words, and when their fingers brushed, trying to dab at some escaping juice on her lips, their eyes met too.

It was enough for now, Kemal brooded with satisfaction. She was firmly secured upon his erotic hook, and very soon he would reel her in.

'My brother—'

As she spoke she frowned and drew away. She was so sensitive to his thoughts, to his slightest change in mood—he would have to be more careful in future, Kemal realised at Lizzie's soft and unexpected exclamation. She was a far more complex creature than he could ever have imagined, more intriguing than he could ever have wished. He liked it that way.

Lizzie forced herself back into an upright position on the cushions, and, seizing a large linen napkin, wiped every trace of juice from her lips. 'Do you give me your word that Hugo is all right?' she said, fixing a determined expression back on her face. She would not be led astray, or distracted from the only reason she found herself in this position.

'I have given you my word,' Kemal said, straightening up too.

'When can I see him? Tomorrow?'

'Before Christmas.'

Christmas… Christmas… Lizzie swallowed hard, determined that nothing she was feeling inside would show. But as she watched Kemal fastidiously clean each one of his strong, tanned fingers on a square of linen, she knew, just from the slight emphasis he put on the word, that he had already begun to understand the power that even the mention of Christmas allowed him to wield over her. It was as if he could see where others had been blind, and his intuition frightened her more than anything else. The ugliness in her past was not for public view.

The shadow flitted across her face so fleetingly Kemal might have missed it had he not been watching for precisely that reaction. It confirmed all his suspicions about Lizzie Palmer, and supplied a framework into which he could place the pieces of the jigsaw. When the puzzle was completed he would know all there was to know about her. Already he knew that Christmas was the source of some deep-rooted pain. But there was more.

'Shouldn't you ring your parents to let them know where you are?'

Up to that point it had been just a game for him. But instantly Kemal regretted his graceless probe. From the look on her face he might have hit her.

'They're dead,' she said flatly.

The light that had burned so brightly in her eyes was completely extinguished, he noticed. 'I'm sorry,' he said after a while.

'Don't be,' Lizzie said. And the way she compressed her lips warned him not to push her any harder. 'If all the holiday flights are full, how will the men get home?' she asked.

For a moment Kemal was surprised by Lizzie's change of tack, her swift recovery. 'That's my problem,' he said. 'Once everything is resolved to my complete satisfaction we will talk about the men.'

'But I'm here. Why can't they go now? Shouldn't you at least be trying to book their flights?'

Irritation rose inside him. No one pressed him. *Ever.*

Maybe it was time. Maybe it might be more fun this way. Maybe he should try it for a change...

A shiver ran down Lizzie's spine as she tried to gauge Kemal's reaction. His eyes were so changeable—one moment silver-grey, and hard like steel, the next dark and unreadable. The sooner Hugo could get back home, the sooner he could stir up a hornets' nest of lawyers to get her out of this mess. She had to have some sort of goal to work towards. Or did he mean to keep them all as hostages? Had her offer been in vain?

'I must have something to work towards,' she said. 'The least you owe me is a proper answer.'

'I owe you nothing,' Kemal said, his gaze sharpening as he looked at her. 'I accepted your offer, freely made. You will stay here. Your brother and the other men will return home when I say.'

Tension between them was suddenly snapping again, like an electric current along a wire, and there was an edge to Kemal's voice Lizzie hadn't heard before. There was something primal and fierce at work, and it should have warned her off. But instead it only redoubled her determination.

'Sit down. We haven't finished,' she said sharply when he moved to get up.

Kemal froze in position and slowly turned to look at her. For a moment the air hummed with his incredulity. 'Oh, yes, we have,' he told Lizzie in a dangerously soft voice. 'And now I will have someone show you to your room. We will meet again tomorrow, at nine o'clock prompt.'

'Just wait—please—' Lizzie struggled up from the cloying embrace of the soft silk cushions and managed to catch up with Kemal at the door, grabbing his wrist.

Kemal gazed down, noticing how quickly she snatched her hand away from his naked arm. They were an explosive combination. There was nothing about her he would not find out at a time of his own choosing. 'Yes?' he said.

'Where am I to sleep?' Lizzie asked.

'Didn't I tell you?' Kemal said.

'No, you did not,' Lizzie informed him. 'Other than to assure me that it would be in a wing well away from you.'

'And so it shall be,' he assured her.

'So where—where, exactly?' Lizzie pressed.

'Don't concern yourself,' he said. 'I'm quite certain you will be delighted with your suite of rooms.'

'Which is where?' Lizzie asked, glancing around at a number of archways leading to different areas of the palace.

Kemal took a moment, and she didn't like the look on his face one bit.

'In the harem,' he said at last.

'You're asking me to sleep in your harem?' Lizzie demanded, her heart pounding with indignation.

Leaning back against the door, Kemal folded his arms and granted her a long, considering look. 'Don't flatter yourself, Ms Palmer,' he said.

CHAPTER FIVE

DAZED and exhausted, Lizzie woke with a start, disorientated by her nightmare, her surroundings, but most of all by her confused memories of the previous evening's events. Staring blearily at an ornate clock on the marble mantelpiece, she felt as if a bucket of cold water had just been dashed in her face. She was more than an hour late for her nine o'clock meeting with Kemal!

After showering briskly, she dragged on her clothes and raced out of the room. She ran down endless corridors and across acres of marble floor, only slowing when she saw some servants looking at her curiously. Emerging through the archway that led from the sumptuous quarters where she was being housed into the main hall, she stopped dead. Kemal, dressed in full business uniform, was waiting for her outside the door to his study.

He dipped his head in greeting. 'I trust you slept well?'

'Very well, thank you,' Lizzie lied. 'I'm sorry I'm late—'

'I'm also sorry you are late—because you're too late,' Kemal murmured, snatching a look at his wristwatch. 'I have another meeting.'

'Another meeting?' Lizzie echoed. 'But I thought I was seeing my brother this morning.'

'Unfortunately that will not be possible.'

'Not possible!' Firming her mouth, Lizzie blazed a stare up at Kemal. 'So your word means nothing?'

'I do not recall giving you my word that you would see your brother. I merely said we would meet again at nine o'clock. Had you arrived on time—'

'How can I believe anything you say? How do I know you will allow Hugo and the men to go now I am here in their place?' Lizzie demanded angrily, watching with annoyance as Kemal checked his watch a second time.

'You have my word,' he said coolly. 'Had you arrived at nine, as we arranged, I could have given you about fifteen minutes of my time—'

'Fifteen minutes? You could have spared me as long as that?'

This made a change from the cool, prim professional who had turned up on his doorstep the day before, Kemal reflected. He should have known when she lurched out of the taxi-cab that there was a wildcat inside Lizzie Palmer, just waiting to be set free. 'Why, Lizzie,' he said, 'I do believe you're angry.'

'Damn right I'm angry! You rant about honour— now I see how much honour really means to you—'

She broke off abruptly when, seizing her arm, Kemal brought their faces very close. 'Don't push me too far, Lizzie—unless you're ready to take the consequences.'

'Then explain yourself. If you can—which I doubt.'

Kemal lifted his hands away while Lizzie was still reeling from the close contact.

'Very well,' he agreed. 'I will tell you this much. There has been a complication I could not have foreseen—'

'Hugo's all right?' Lizzie said quickly.

'Your brother is well. I'm afraid the weather is causing problems. All flights to and from Ankara have been cancelled.'

'Ankara?' Lizzie said anxiously. 'Is that where he is?'

A muscle flexed in Kemal's jaw. He didn't have the heart to deny her the truth. 'Yes, Hugo's there—with the other men.'

'But you said I could see him. Is it far?'

'Conditions are forecast to improve tomorrow—'

'Tomorrow?' Lizzie exclaimed. 'But that's Thursday. Christmas Day is on Saturday!'

'I had not forgotten,' Kemal said more gently, hearing the rising note of panic in her voice.

'Hugo will be so worried,' Lizzie murmured distractedly. 'He knew I was coming to Turkey to sort this out—'

'Hugo is a grown man,' Kemal intervened. 'He understands the position.'

'How can he?' Lizzie said. 'When he doesn't even know where I am?'

'He knows.'

'You've been in contact with him?' Lizzie's mouth firmed into an angry line. She could see the truth in Kemal's eyes. 'Why didn't you let me speak to him?

No—' She held out her hands as if to ward him off. 'Don't. I don't want to hear it. Just get him out of there. The sooner he leaves the country, the sooner I can follow him.'

'We will share the same relief when that happens,' Kemal assured her. 'And now, if you will excuse me—'

'That's it?'

'Should there be something more?'

'There's a little matter of my liberty, and when you think I'm likely to be free. Let me remind you, I am not on holiday. And I haven't come all the way to Istanbul to be fobbed off with five minutes of your time!'

'Ten,' Kemal murmured, checking his watch. 'And your time's up.'

Lizzie's lips parted with sheer disbelief. 'But what am I supposed to do all day?' she said at last.

'I have no idea,' Kemal said with a shrug.

Lizzie gasped as he took hold of her upper arms and firmly moved her to one side.

'But please don't get in the way of the servants,' he said.

Flinging all the papers she had gathered for their meeting down on a chair in her bedroom, Lizzie tugged her jacket off and tossed it after them. She might have spent the night in his harem, but if Kemal Volkan thought she was a suitable candidate for assertiveness reversal therapy he was sadly mistaken! And if he thought she was going to sit around all day, doing nothing to secure her freedom, he was wrong about that too.

She still had one card up her sleeve, Lizzie remembered—Sami Gulsan, the local lawyer. And this was the perfect moment to call him. Going to her briefcase, Lizzie retrieved his card and her mobile phone.

Keying in the number, Lizzie was disappointed to be put through to the lawyer's voicemail. But, with time running out if she was to get the men home before Christmas, anything was better than nothing, she reasoned. She explained the position in which she found herself, and the outrageous manner in which her brother and his colleagues were still being held in Turkey against their will, and then for good measure added her suspicions that Kemal could not be trusted to let the men go, even though she had offered to stay in their place.

When she cut the line, Lizzie felt that at least she had done something positive. But until she heard from the lawyer, or Kemal came back and she could talk to him, she was powerless to move things on.

Wondering how she was going to pass the day, Lizzie's glance fastened on a collection of small brass ornaments displayed on a low table. As she picked one up, it was as if the cause for her late arrival at the meeting with Kemal became suddenly obvious. Running her fingertip over the pierced brass surface, Lizzie remembered all too clearly the nightmare that had kept her tossing and turning all night.

There had been many similar ornaments at home when she was little. Of course her parents' drug-warped attempts to recreate the mystical East had been a sham, whereas everything here in Kemal's palace was an expensive original, but the two worlds had become hopelessly entangled as she slept. The incense and the curios from her childhood had been a stage set for a tragedy, and they could never be compared to the beautiful works of art and fragrances with which Kemal Volkan filled his home. But the Eastern ambience, the ever-present scent of sandalwood and spice had trespassed on her dreams, transporting her to a different time. That was why she had suffered one of her worst nightmares for years—and why she had been late for the crucial meeting. She could never allow it to happen again.

Walking slowly around the perimeter of the room, Lizzie made a point of handling and examining everything she believed might have stirred her memories. On close inspection she realised that nothing bore the slightest resemblance to the cheap imitations that had littered the squat where she had been raised.

Satisfied that she had laid the ghosts to rest, her thoughts veered off again in the direction of all the other women who must have waited here for their sultan to return. Had their future been any more secure than her own? Had they been happy to wait in the harem? Or had they felt as she did—trapped and uncertain—birds in a gilded cage? How had they prepared themselves for the moment when the gilded doors opened and they were summoned into the Sultan's presence?

Wandering over to the window, where sunlight filtered in through magnificent stained glass panes, Lizzie opened it and peered out. The courtyard was deserted. She was quite alone. Or was she? She turned back to face the room. How many spyholes existed in these richly decorated walls? How many places where a discreet listener could press an ear? This was the harem—after all, a place of intrigue and voluptuous secrets.

Hugging herself, Lizzie stared properly at the scenes depicted on the wall hangings, and then up at the fabulously painted ceiling arching high above her head. The illustrations on the hangings showed scenes of a gentle and romantic nature, but the paintings on the ceiling were quite different. They were unashamedly erotic. Her pulse began to race as she guessed at their purpose, and the position from which they might best be viewed. And then her mouth firmed angrily at the thought that Kemal must have found it infinitely amusing to house her in the harem.

But a quiver of excitement took hold when she gazed at the silk-draped bed. It had been eighteen months since her last relationship—eighteen long months of celibacy. And she couldn't help wondering how long it might take to view every one of the highly descriptive scenes on the ceiling properly. Dragging her gaze away, she surveyed the plump cushions arranged in shady mirrored alcoves furnished with low tables bearing dishes of fresh fruit. Everything in the harem was designed to delight and seduce the senses. But she would not succumb by so much as a single grape, Lizzie decided, turning away.

Kemal had mentioned a pool, and a spa. Perhaps it was time to make the most of her stay in this gilded cage...

Lizzie made a sound of impatience, remembering she had no casual clothes—they were all at the hotel—then a knock on the door made her start.

It was so timely she should have been pleased, but Lizzie felt a chill run through her as a manservant entered carrying her suitcase. Kemal had clearly given instructions that her belongings were to be removed from the Hotel Turkoman.

'Who told you to bring my things here?' she asked, but the man only bowed low and then left the room as quietly as he had arrived.

'Oh, no— I didn't order anything,' she said, when a maid entered next, with a number of exclusive-looking carrier bags. But she might not have been there at all, Lizzie realised with exasperation, for all the heed the woman paid to her. The maid deposited the bags in a neat line beside the bed, and then walked away from her on silent feet across the cool marble floor.

Lizzie's heart stalled when she saw what she was about to do next. 'No!' she cried out, and raced across the room. But the wicks on the scented candles were already burning strongly. And now the maid was moving on to light a large incense burner.

'No. No! Please—don't!' Lizzie fought to keep her voice steady, but the sweet and pervasive scent was already curling around her nostrils, stealing away every bit of breathable air...

Kemal had always believed it was gut instinct that had brought him success. And it was gut instinct that had made him cancel his meeting and brought him back to the palace. Now he knew why, he realised as he strode across the room. One look at Lizzie was enough to tell him he had been absolutely right to return.

'Leave us,' he commanded the serving woman, his focus never wavering from Lizzie's face. Quickly extinguishing the flame of the incense burner between his thumb and forefinger, he removed it to a window ledge far away from her, beneath an open window. Then, returning to Lizzie, he dragged her into his arms just before she hit the floor.

Lizzie could hardly understand what was happening. She was having trouble breathing. She was confused, bewildered, knew only that for some reason Kemal was holding her up, and that she should push him away. For a moment something new took over, and she felt safe...protected. But that was dangerous. It was a false impression, Lizzie realised, pulling back.

'I don't know what came over me,' she said with a half-laugh, trying to make light of what had happened. But her voice sounded brittle even in her own ears and she could see he wasn't convinced. 'I have always been sensitive to perfume,' she added. 'I have a rather highly developed sense of smell.' She gave another short, dismissive laugh.

'And a highly developed aversion to incense?' Kemal commented lightly.

It gave him no pleasure to see Lizzie hugging herself now, in an instinctive gesture of defence. And a report from one of his servants was still playing on his mind. Mehmet had heard her crying out in the night. Nightmares, he'd thought. That would explain why Lizzie had missed their meeting, and it also explained why he had felt compelled to turn the car around today. Could he possibly be developing a conscience? Kemal wondered dryly. Or had feelings more physical than cerebral brought him racing back to Lizzie's side?

'Would you feel happier in another suite?' he suggested, looking around. 'I have more modern accommodation than this available if you would prefer?'

'This is absolutely fine,' Lizzie assured him, still regretting the fact that she had shown her Achilles' heel to him. 'As prisons go, this is definitely at the better end of the market.'

'Prison?' Kemal murmured, cocking his head as he stared at her.

Meeting Lizzie's gaze, he tried to read her thoughts, but a veil had come down over her extraordinary eyes and it was beyond him. At least she was calm again. He was careful not to show his amusement when she settled the most important part of her armoury back on her nose. Instead, he took the couple of steps necessary to reach her and take them off.

'Why are you still hiding behind these?' he said. 'Why don't I just lose them somewhere?'

Lizzie took them out of his hands again and gave him a look as she put them back on. 'Maybe I like wearing them. What's wrong with that?'

'Or maybe you're frightened of something, or someone, and like hiding behind them,' Kemal suggested softly.

'I am certainly not frightened of you,' Lizzie assured him without breaking her stare. 'You are bigger than me physically, and that is all.'

Kemal's eyes flared with passion. Her defiance amused him, and it aroused him too. No one had ever defied him as she did; they were always too frightened of overstepping the mark, of losing his interest. But Lizzie Palmer was different. She was a woman of fierce contradictions—vulnerable, combative, contained—and passionate? Yes, passionate. He was sure of it. Even though she was staring at him now in that cool and very English way. But one day those fires burning beneath her frosty exterior might just erupt. And he would be there when they did.

Her skin was so fine and pale it was almost translucent, but there was a blush about her cheeks that betrayed a matching interest in him, whether she cared to admit it or not. Just a few minutes ago, when she had been at her lowest ebb, vulnerable, weak and exposed, he could never have touched her, but now...

Lizzie's heart refused to stop racing as she stared up at Kemal. She struggled to ignore the excitement building inside her, and fought hard to dismiss the way her flesh sang where his arms had briefly held her. She could not banish the memory of his drugging warmth, his clean, masculine scent. But at the same time she knew that finding sanctuary and a kind of peace in his embrace would be a huge mistake—fool's gold.

She made a little sound of surprise and refusal deep in her throat when he reached out to take hold of her.

'Yes,' Kemal insisted. And his voice was so soft, so caressing, that just for a moment Lizzie knew he was going to kiss her. 'Are you all right now?' he asked instead, dipping his head to stare straight into her eyes.

'Fine,' Lizzie said, trying not to show how disappointed she was.

'You will find some leisure clothes in those carrier bags. Dress for lunch out. I am going to change, and then we will relax.'

She looked at him.

'Don't pretend surprise,' he said practically. 'You surely don't mean to live in that one black suit for the whole time you are here?'

'I meant to go back to the hotel and change,' she said, tensing again as she remembered the arrival of her luggage.

'You wanted to talk,' Kemal reminded Lizzie. 'So I have cleared my diary for you.'

Lizzie's hand flew to her face as in one deft move he removed her glasses.

'And you won't be needing these,' he said, placing them in the breast pocket of his jacket. 'There will be nothing between us now, Lizzie, but the truth.'

CHAPTER SIX

REMOVING the beautiful designer clothes from the stiff, expensive-looking carrier bags was heaven. Lizzie never indulged herself, and certainly never accepted gifts from someone like Kemal, who was practically a stranger. But these were different—these she would pay for.

Soon the circular fur rug where she was sitting was completely covered in tissue paper and clothes. Everything had been carefully packed, and the rainbow-hued packages neatly sealed with a label from each exclusive store. Her heart was thundering with excitement at each new discovery, and she flushed red as she held up a set of cobweb-fine underwear in delicate flesh tones. She had seen something very similar in England, but it had been so expensive she had just smiled and walked on. But she wasn't about to resist temptation now, and she put them to one side with the other clothes she had chosen to wear that day.

Kemal hadn't meant to stand and watch, but found it impossible to resist. As Lizzie had suspected, the harem had many secret places from where the occupants might be discreetly observed. He had slept badly the previous night, disturbed by the fact that she was sleeping so close by. He had also felt some guilt, knowing he had exploited her anxieties as well as her loyalty to her brother by accepting the audacious offer she had made to take his place.

This was a unique situation, he had reflected. There were no rules dictating how he should or shouldn't behave. He was far from sure how he wanted it to end with Lizzie—or if he wanted it to end at all yet. Whatever the final outcome between them, instinct had told him he must soften the situation quickly—hence the glamorous clothes he had ordered for her. Her lack of luggage had provided him with the perfect excuse.

But he shouldn't be hanging around here. He had pressing commitments, little time to spare for Lizzie Palmer, however beautiful she might be…but he was interested to see how she would look dressed in something other than formal business attire.

Kemal's eyes hardened as he watched her obvious glee and remembered how easily some women could be bought. He had thought Lizzie Palmer was different. But no matter—he had no thought of creating a permanent space for her in his life, and no inclination to sort out her problems. He pulled back from the fretwork screen as Lizzie stood up. She had an armful of things and was heading for the bathroom. Her modesty touched him. Briefly. She was lodged in the harem for one reason only as far as he was concerned—and modesty wasn't part of his plan.

'I trust everything is to your liking?' he said coolly when Lizzie finally emerged from her suite and crossed the hall towards him.

She looked fabulous. And it was hardly surprising.

Her natural beauty needed little adornment, so his instructions to the personal shopper had specified elegant simplicity rather than a selection of blatantly fashionable clothes. The slim-fitting navy trousers, Gucci loafers and tan leather blouson suited her to perfection. The jacket had felt like silk beneath his hands when it had been brought for him to approve. He liked everything to feel good—just like Lizzie, he mused as she walked up to him.

He noticed she was wearing hardly any make-up—something else he approved of—and her thick, glossy blonde hair was secured on top of her head with a couple of the tortoiseshell pins he had ordered with her long hair in mind. One quick movement and the whole shimmering cape would cascade down around her shoulders—but that was for later.

'It's all very nice. Thank you,' she said politely.

Kemal's cynical thoughts were confirmed—even Lizzie Palmer could be bought with a few trifles.

But, breaking into his thoughts, she added, 'Naturally I will pay you back for everything.'

'Of course,' he agreed dryly. 'Whenever you are ready.'

However he tried to harden his heart against Lizzie Palmer, she managed to surprise him, Kemal acknowledged. He didn't know if that was a good thing or not—he only knew that he wanted her in the most pleasurable way.

'A quick lunch, and then we discuss the detail of my departure to take the place of the men?' she was saying optimistically.

She was nervous. He guessed she was untutored—not vulnerable, as he had first supposed—and that made anything possible. He would soon teach her to relax, in a way he hoped she would find dangerously addictive. There was a vacancy on his staff for a short-term mistress, and Lizzie Palmer satisfied his list of requirements perfectly.

'A relaxed, informal lunch,' he corrected her, 'and then we talk.' On his terms, as always, Kemal determined, amused to think that Lizzie might imagine it could be any other way.

Lizzie stared at Kemal. Freedom for Hugo and herself meant she must comply with his every wish. But he was trying to make it easier for her, and this wasn't so hard, she conceded as she linked her arm through his.

Catching sight of them in one of the huge gilt-framed mirrors, she was stunned to see what a striking couple they made. It hardly seemed possible—or even likely. Kemal was so glamorous, in a hard-driven, masculine way, and she had never considered herself particularly attractive. The glamorous clothes certainly helped, but she couldn't help suspecting he had dressed her for a part, and began to wonder exactly what role he expected her to play.

'I've changed my mind,' Lizzie said at the door. 'I'd rather eat here—something quick and simple—and then we can talk while we eat—like we did last night,' she pointed out hopefully. 'Look,' she said, when she saw Kemal's expression harden, 'why don't you arrange for a phone and an Internet connection in my room? Then I can help you to track down the parts for your machinery before I leave—'

'Please leave business matters to me,' he said. 'I need you to help me with something else.'

'Oh?' Lizzie said, surprised. 'What's that?'

'Christmas shopping.'

'Christmas shopping?' She frowned. It seemed so out of context. 'Can't that wait?'

'I'm afraid not,' Kemal said. 'As you are always reminding me, Lizzie, time is running out where Christmas is concerned.'

'But surely you have people to do that for you?'

'This is different,' Kemal said. 'This is something special. I had hoped you might help me.'

Tit for tat? A shopping expedition in exchange for her speedy departure to take Hugo's place? She couldn't refuse, Lizzie realised.

'I have to buy presents for my nieces. And I never know what to buy,' Kemal said impatiently, while she was still deliberating whether or not to agree to his request.

Lizzie studied his face. He certainly looked convincing enough. Perhaps this was an opportunity to rebalance their relationship. 'All right,' she agreed. 'But only on condition that the moment we get back you help me with this exchange so Hugo and the other men can go home.'

'That seems fair enough,' he agreed. 'And if it makes it any easier for you, let's say that you are helping me out in return for your bed and board.'

'One night's bed and board,' Lizzie reminded him,

only to have Kemal shrug and give her another in-
scrutable look.

'Surely you don't have a problem with such a simple request?' he said.

'No, of course not,' Lizzie said.

If they only knew it, Kemal's nieces were in for the
best Christmas they'd ever had!

'I want you to consider my three nieces very carefully,' Kemal said as they halted first outside an exclusive clothes store.

Everything in the window was displayed beautifully
beneath carefully angled lighting, with spotlights picking out the choicest pieces in each range, and Lizzie
was dazzled by the array of handbags, costume jewellery, gloves and silk scarves. The colour scheme was
a stylish mix of winter white and tan, with highlights
of a soft chalky red, and her eyes widened when she
recognised a tan jacket that looked very similar to her
own. It would take her an age to pay Kemal back for
that item alone, she realised with concern.

'My first niece, Anya,' Kemal said, reclaiming her
attention, 'does not indulge herself as I believe she
should. I've seen her looking in this window, and
judging by her face we're sure to find something just
right for her here.'

'These had better really be your nieces,' Lizzie said,
as a pang of suspicion caught her unawares.

'Why, Ms Palmer,' Kemal retorted mildly, 'what
sort of man do you take me for?'

'I wouldn't like to say,' Lizzie admitted truthfully, walking past him into the shop.

Kemal didn't bat an eyelid as the sales assistant, under Lizzie's direction, wrapped up the most expensive handbag, gloves and silk scarf in the shop.

'My second niece—'

'Her name?' Lizzie prompted as they walked further down the fashionable shopping arcade.

'Kerola.'

'Tell me something about her, so I can get a picture of her in my mind,' Lizzie suggested.

'Feminine, and rather studious. She likes to read, and I guess she likes to write long letters to her friends.'

'You guess?'

'She's the type,' he said with a shrug.

Kerola didn't sound like mistress material Lizzie concluded, reassured. And now it was her turn to lead the way into a small, wood-panelled shop she'd spotted, specialising in writing materials. Picking out a beautiful fountain pen in sapphire blue lacquer, she held it up to the light admiringly. There was a gem inset at the top of the cap, and the nib was pure gold. She tested it thoughtfully between her fingers, before trying out a few words on a clean vellum sheet presented to her by the sales assistant.

'Do you like it?' Kemal asked.

'It is perfectly balanced, and quite beautiful,' Lizzie said. And very, very expensive, she thought. Apart from wreaking a very female type of vengeance on her tormentor, she couldn't help but smile when she imagined the look of pleasure on Kerola's face when she opened this package on Christmas morning.

'We'll take it,' Kemal told the shop assistant. Turning to Lizzie, he added, 'Don't you think Kerola would like this five-year diary too? She could confide all her secrets inside and then lock them away.'

Lizzie had to move very close to peer over Kemal's shoulder as he stared into a glass display cabinet, and it was a struggle to concentrate when she was inhaling the by now familiar scent of sandalwood and clean, warm man. She saw that the diary was covered in fuchsia suede, and there was a tiny gold lock complete with miniature key. 'Perfect,' she agreed.

'I was hoping you would think so,' Kemal murmured, turning his face up to look at her.

Their faces were very close now, and as he smiled Lizzie's heart lurched.

'Only one more niece to go,' he announced, straightening up abruptly. 'And then lunch,' he added, offering Lizzie his arm.

Lizzie hesitated a beat, but then linked her arm through his. It was better for everyone if they stayed on friendly terms.

As they walked along her mind strayed back to the sight of him, his arms locked around the sides of the display cabinet in the shop. The wide spread of his shoulders, and the waves of thick, glossy black hair licking over the collar of his casual jacket. There was so much strength contained in his hands it was almost impossible to believe how gentle he could be. But she had seen him peel a fig with the utmost delicacy, and the careful way in which he had handled each of the precious items they had bought reflected a very different side to Kemal's character from the tyrant she had imagined him to be. He was a powerful man, but he was a connoisseur too.

These were very dangerous thoughts, Lizzie reminded herself. 'Don't bother with lunch,' she said suddenly, determined to keep her thoughts under control. 'We still have to find a gift for your third niece, and we have to talk—'

'I'm sure we can find time to do both and have lunch,' Kemal told her calmly.

There was nothing for it, she would just have to curb her impatience, Lizzie realised. 'So, what do you think we should be looking for?'

'Jewellery.'

'Real jewellery?'

'Is there any other kind?'

Seeing the quality of the jewellers in the arcade down which they were strolling, Lizzie became suspicious. This gift was surely for someone other than a niece. But if it was, why should she care? She would be just as objective about selecting this Christmas present as she had been with all the others.

But then Kemal said unexpectedly, 'Do your best. She's been having a really hard time.'

Lizzie looked at him in surprise as they stopped in front of another exclusive store. She would leave her cynical self outside the shop, she vowed, and try her best to choose something special.

Lizzie knew the moment they walked in that this

was the hushed and reverent showroom of a serious gem dealer. She felt anxious suddenly. She knew nothing about good jewellery. 'At least tell me your niece's name,' she said while they were being escorted to a discreet booth to view the gems. 'I need help here.'

'You don't need help,' Kemal assured her. 'Just go with your gut instinct.'

'That's quite a responsibility,' Lizzie murmured.

'I'm sure you're up to it,' Kemal countered, turning away from her to speak to the assistant. 'Aquamarine?' he suggested. 'Something special, unique—a necklace, perhaps?'

'Certainly, sir.' Excusing himself, the man hurried away.

'You're very generous,' Lizzie said.

'I can be.'

Lizzie was relieved when the jeweller returned. For a few moments no one spoke. The collection of fabulous gems took her breath away.

'This is our most exclusive range,' the jeweller explained. 'Each item is fashioned by our finest craftsmen, and each piece has its own story to tell.'

'Pick out whatever you like,' Kemal said, turning to Lizzie.

For an instant Lizzie almost envied the young woman who was to receive such a fabulous gift, but then she made herself concentrate on choosing something special, as she had promised to do.

It was like dipping into the most fantastic dressing-up box in the world—there was so much choice—but finally she settled on two pieces upon which she hoped

Kemal would make a final decision: a large oval aqua-marine ring, set with diamonds, and a fine aquamarine drop hanging from a white gold chain. The drop was particularly pretty, as it hung from a tiny bow studded with brilliant white diamonds.

The jeweller applauded her choice.

'These pieces are from one of my favourite design-ers,' he said. 'I like the necklace in particular—if you look you can see the drop here represents a tear, and the bow represents the love that prevents that tear from falling.'

'Why, that's beautiful,' Lizzie murmured, entranced by the jeweller's romantic description. Looking in the mirror, she held the necklace up to her neck and sighed.

'It suits you,' Kemal observed dryly. 'I'm quite sure my niece will be very pleased with your choice.'

He was right—it wouldn't do to get too fond of it! Lizzie thought, quickly replacing the beautiful neck-lace on the velvet tray.

'I'll take it,' Kemal informed the assistant. 'Please have it gift-wrapped and delivered to the palace.'

Bowing, the jeweller escorted them both to the door. 'It has been a pleasure doing business with you,' he said, including Lizzie in the pleasantry.

'Oh, no—it's nothing to do with me.' Lizzie blushed red.

Her determination to exact a penalty from Kemal had been well and truly scuppered by his incredible generosity, she realised. And now she felt deeply guilty, thinking of the amount of money she had forced him to part with.

'Come along,' Kemal said briskly, apparently unconcerned by the huge sums of money involved, 'or we will be late for lunch.'

Lizzie became so relaxed over lunch she hardly realised she was talking non-stop about her brother.

It had almost taken the edge off his appetite, Kemal thought ruefully, but not quite. 'What would you like to do now?' he said, after calling for the bill.

'Chase those parts you need for your machinery, sort out flights for Hugo and the other men, and get the exchange underway,' Lizzie suggested.

'Quite a shopping list.'

'I'm sorry,' Lizzie said, seeing Kemal's face had darkened. 'But you're right—there is a lot to do, and not much time left.'

Was leaving all she thought about? Kemal wondered. He had thought she was becoming more relaxed—big mistake.

'I would at least like to make a flight reservation for Friday—Christmas Eve—if that's possible,' Lizzie said. 'If I don't make it, so be it.'

'You are not in a position to book your flight yet.'

'Just a reservation,' Lizzie reminded him. 'I can't imagine what I'll do for Christmas if I'm still here.'

He would not allow those wide-set eyes to soften his resolve, Kemal determined, or those tremulous lips to do anything other than his bidding. 'Well, I shall be very busy,' he said crisply. 'Irrespective of Christmas,

I have matters that must be attended to. What you choose to do is, of course, entirely your affair.'

'That's if I'm still here…'

Kemal shrugged, and Lizzie could be in no doubt that her options were limited to whatever suited him.

Maybe she could just close her eyes and sleep through the whole thing, Lizzie reflected tensely. She had no intention of weakening now, allowing him to see how badly she needed to be home for Christmas. She had nothing to barter for her freedom. Taking in Kemal's firm, sensuous mouth, with the shading of rough stubble already showing on his jaw, Lizzie knew she had nothing to offer that he could possibly want. Seducing the Sultan and making him give in to her demands might have been easy for some women, but she didn't have a cat in hell's chance—

'The lady's jacket, please,' Kemal demanded, cutting brutally into her thoughts. 'We're leaving now.'

CHAPTER SEVEN

SEATED an arm's length away from Kemal in his sleek black limousine, Lizzie felt as if she had tumbled down Alice's rabbit hole and woken up in someone else's shoes. In a matter of hours it seemed as if her whole life had been transformed. She had been swept up into Kemal's glamorous and very addictive world. His reality was most people's fantasy, and it was dangerously beguiling.

Was this how it felt to be a rich man's mistress? Kemal's mistress? she wondered, and her throat dried as she pictured that bird in the gilded cage, being brought out for the occasional treat—a resource to be dipped into at will. The pun tugged at her lips until she had to smile.

'It's good to see you smile.'

Not if you knew what I was thinking about, Lizzie thought, knowing she would have to be more careful in future. She was going home as soon as she could. She didn't belong here. She didn't belong with Kemal.

But still her pulse speeded up just from stealing a glance at him. He was staring out of his window, clearly preoccupied with something or someone else, while her thighs were tingling at the thought of possible contact between them—not that that was very likely, unless the limousine picked up speed and swerved around a corner.

She reddened guiltily when Kemal swung around to face her, as if he knew exactly which route her thoughts were taking.

'When we get back, you will join me in the spa.'

'I will?' Lizzie queried, collecting her wits. Half-naked bodies? Cocoon-like warmth? Clouds of hazy steam? No way!

She had to think up with some reason why she couldn't. No, in fact she didn't have to make excuses, Lizzie determined. She would just refuse—

'I bought you swimsuits, didn't I?' Kemal said, in the manner of a man who knew very well that he had. Gym clothes, swimsuits, trainers…the list went on and on. 'Do you have a problem?' Kemal pressed. 'They do fit?' he added dryly.

'Yes,' Lizzie admitted. 'Perfectly.'

OK—truce. She couldn't let Kemal think he could intimidate her to the point where she wouldn't even share a swimming pool with him. What chance would Hugo stand then? And, after pounding the pavements all afternoon, she really did feel like a cooling swim.

'All right,' she said. 'Why not? The spa sounds great.'

What harm could a swim do? She didn't imagine icebergs were his type.

Kemal's idea of a spa was having the most sumptuous health club imaginable installed at home for his own private use. And when your home was a palace, that allowed for something on rather a splendid scale.

He was waiting for Lizzie at the foot of a wide sweep of marble steps: bare feet, black jogging pants, tight-fitting black vest. *Amazing.* She pretended not to notice.

'We will take a Turkish bath before we enter the pool,' he said, heading off.

'We?' Lizzie demanded coolly, staying exactly where she was. Apart from the fact that she was determined to set the rules here, she needed a moment to deal with the sight of a bronzed male body blatantly made for sin.

'You will see,' Kemal murmured, pausing to look at her, his arm resting on a heavy arched door. 'Well, are you coming?'

Thankful her every erogenous zone was concealed beneath a baggy tracksuit, Lizzie went past him through the arch into a vast, echoing, marble-tiled room.

'The changing rooms are over there,' he said, pointing them out to her. 'And you will need these,' he added, swooping down to pick up what looked like a pair of wooden clogs.

Not exactly what she would have chosen to go with her outfit, but...

'The floor gets slippery with soapsuds,' he warned. 'These *nalin* will keep you safe.'

It would take more than a pair of wooden clogs, Lizzie mused, levelling a cool glance on Kemal's fiercely arrogant face. 'Soapsuds?' she queried evenly.

'Lots of them,' he promised.

She didn't like the look on his face one bit. She felt like a very small mouse that had lost its way in the wolf's den.

'Oh, and by the way,' he added, easing away from the door, 'strip naked, will you?'

'I'll do no such thing,' Lizzie assured him.

'There are plenty of towels in the changing cubicles,' Kemal said, as if she hadn't spoken a word. 'Help yourself to as many as you want.'

He was enjoying her discomfort just a little too much, Lizzie thought as she tilted her chin at a rebellious angle and moved past him towards the changing cabin.

Her heart was pounding nineteen to the dozen when she stepped out again. Every inch of her body was concealed under towels, apart from her head. She had redressed her hair, using the tortoiseshell clips to keep it off her shoulders, and was wearing the wooden clogs as Kemal had advised...but where was he? she wondered, looking around.

'I'm in here.'

She followed the sound of his voice through an archway into another room. Slipping off the clogs, Lizzie looked around. It was a wet room, with a huge hot tub in the centre of the tiled floor. A series of raised platforms ran around the tub like giant steps, and there was a domed ceiling above the water towards which steam was billowing in dense white clouds.

Kemal was already in the tub—and naked, she

guessed, certainly from the waist up. If a man could be called beautiful, then he was beautiful. His wet torso gleamed like polished bronze, every muscle perfectly delineated. The wide sweep of his shoulders reminded her of an etching she had seen of naked gladiators, and there was an unconscious grace to his movements as he lazily slicked soapy water across his powerful chest.

'I'm quite happy to join you,' Lizzie said briskly. 'But as a man of honour, I take it you will respect my modesty.'

This *was* novel, Kemal mused, sinking a little lower down into the suds. After a moment of wry consideration he averted his face.

As soon as Kemal turned, Lizzie sprinted up the steps, dropped her towels, climbed in, and sank beneath the bubbles. Quickly lowering the straps of the swimsuit she was prudently wearing, she kept just her face above the foaming water. 'OK,' she announced. 'You can turn around now.'

Kemal's dark slanting stare held just enough humour to make Lizzie feel gauche. Doubtless his more sophisticated female companions would have taken a very different line, perhaps stripping off and parading themselves in front of him. She had neither the confidence nor the inclination. And she was in a unique position—neither companion nor guest; she was merely the bird in his gilded cage.

Hearing Kemal speak in his own language, Lizzie turned to see an older woman who must have come silently into the room. Dressed neatly in a white uniform, she stood discreetly in the shadows, obviously awaiting instruction. Before Lizzie could question Kemal, he relaxed back against the side of the tub, arms widespread, and closed his eyes. The next minute the woman was standing next to Lizzie, and gesturing with a smile that she should climb out.

Lizzie couldn't get out fast enough. Kemal might look harmless enough, with the warm bubbles frothing around him, but his stillness seemed deceptive somehow.

The attendant quickly fashioned a comfortable bed with clean towels on one of the wide lower steps at the base of the hot tub. When she picked up soap and a sponge Lizzie supposed she must lie down, but as she went to position herself the woman gave a cluck of disapproval and a smile, and mimed that she should take off her swimming costume.

Glancing back to the tub, Lizzie realised that Kemal couldn't see, so after a moment's hesitation she did as the woman had suggested.

After the soaping came an abrasive mitt, and finally, when she was glowing like a beacon, the woman walked away to turn on the drench shower, leaving Lizzie gazing at the tantalising stack of fluffy white towels she had left just out of reach.

'Do you intend to lie there all day covered in foam?'

Lizzie tensed as she looked back up at the tub. 'Are you speaking to me?'

'Who else?' Kemal said. 'Well? What are you waiting for?'

Not for you to get your ounce of fun out of me,

that's for sure, Lizzie thought as she got to her feet. A naked back view was regrettable, but unavoidable. She held her head high as she stalked across the soap-covered tiles towards the shower.

'*Nalin,*' Kemal reminded her dryly, sweeping her up into his arms moments before she hit the floor.

'Let me go!' Lizzie insisted, struggling to escape.

'Not a chance,' Kemal informed her. 'I guess we'll have to miss the steam bath…'

'Put me down!' Lizzie warned, painfully aware that she was completely naked and in his arms.

'And the massage…' Kemal complained, as if he still hadn't heard her.

'Please!' Lizzie gasped throatily, kicking her legs. Kemal's warm, hard body seemed to be making embarrassing contact with every single part of her.

'Shall I drop you here?' he said.

'No!'

She turned her face away from him, shutting out his mock-innocent expression. Worst of all, he must have registered the tremors scorching through her…and he must know as surely as she did that they had nothing whatever to do with her fall.

'Say please,' Kemal prompted, settling Lizzie more comfortably in his arms, 'and then I might let you go.'

Lizzie's lips compressed as she considered her options. 'Please,' she said at last, grudgingly.

At least he had the good grace to ask if she was all right, she thought mutinously, testing first one foot and then the other on the ground. 'I'm fine,' she said. 'No

harm done... Thank you,' she muttered somewhat be-
latedly, crossing her arms over her chest.

She watched Kemal cock his head to one side, and
knew he was trying hard not to smile. The towels were
still out of reach. But that didn't stop her making a
lunge for them.

'Not so fast!' Kemal said, stopping her. 'Towels are
for *after* the shower, not before—didn't you know
that?'

Lizzie shook herself free angrily, her skin burning
where he had touched her, her temper rising when she
saw the laughter in his eyes. Her hands balled into
fists, but she dropped them back to her sides again.
Wouldn't he love that? A slippery, soapy tussle in the
nude? A tussle she couldn't hope to win!

And then she saw that the hunt had sparked fire in
his dark gaze, and there was a confident twist to his
hard, sensuous mouth. There was no escape route
available to her and he knew it. For some crazy reason
Lizzie realised she was incredibly aroused. And he
knew that too. She made one last desperate attempt to
reach for a towel.

But Kemal caught hold of both of her arms and
brought her round in front of him. 'Now what are you
going to do?' he demanded huskily.

'I would hope you are a gentleman,' Lizzie challenged, staring him straight in the eyes.

'Would you really?' Kemal murmured, as if he
didn't believe a word of it. He gave a short, virile
laugh, and then there was silence.

Lizzie's breathing sounded loud in her ears. She was

intensely conscious of Kemal's naked body, only inches from her own, and then he reached up, freeing the tortoiseshell clips from her hair so that it tumbled around her shoulders like a shimmering golden cape.

'Beautiful,' he murmured, sifting it through his fingers.

As Lizzie opened her mouth to protest he kissed her hard on the lips.

The shock made her sway towards him, and before she could pull away he tightened his grip. And then she stayed because she wanted to—because she had to. The kiss was long and perfect, the sensation streaming through her intense. He could kiss away her heart, kiss away her soul—but what to do about it? How to hold back? How to distance herself from him? She had no answers, only wordless sounds that spoke of need and pleasure until finally, responding to her wishes, Kemal deepened the kiss.

At last he broke away, leaving her breathless. 'Shower,' he suggested.

'Good,' Lizzie blurted half with relief, thinking it a sign that the kiss was out of his system.

'Excellent,' Kemal murmured. 'Because now I want to wash every part of you, taste every inch of you.'

A small cry leapt from Lizzie's throat as her veins were infused with sensation. It was as if every nerve-ending was naked and exposed, awaiting Kemal's attention. And then, cupping the back of her head in one hand and using the other to drag her close, he kissed her again.

Kemal tested the stream of water and made sure that

it was warm before allowing Lizzie to stand beneath it. Then he joined her, throwing his head back so that the whole of his beautiful body was exposed for her enjoyment.

And now she did look, her gaze lingering on every perfect inch of him: the long powerful column of his neck, the hard chest tanned to the shade of nutmeg, the shading of black hair that narrowed to a vee as it tracked down below his waist. She quickly looked up again and slicked back her hair self-consciously, and as she did so she became aware of the effect her innocent action was having on Kemal: her breasts were fully exposed for his perusal, the pert nipples taut and outthrust, damp pink peaks, provoking him, tempting him—

She jumped when he hit the switch that turned off the shower.

'I'm taking you to bed.'

'Just like that? No, *Please may I?* Or, *How do you feel about it?*'

'I know how you feel about it,' he assured her.

His confidence was compelling, the look in his eyes irresistible. Sensation was already pooling in sharp insistent pulses between her legs by the time Kemal wrapped her in towels and swung her into his arms.

'This is *The Sultan's* palace, and you are my captive,' he teased her provocatively.

'Will you tie me down with ribbons of silk and tantalise me with feathers?' Lizzie demanded, responding in kind to his wicked mood.

'You have been indulging in far too many fantasies,' Kemal observed as he shouldered open the door. 'I have something far more fulfilling in mind for both of us.'

She didn't doubt him for a minute. But, as for fantasies, she had never indulged in them before coming to Turkey. Happily, it seemed all that was about to change.

CHAPTER EIGHT

KEMAL took Lizzie in the opposite direction from her own rooms. He stopped outside some fabulously carved doors in a grand hallway, where everything was the same exotic mix of exuberant ornamentation and vibrant colour. But the moment they walked through the doors they might have been in another world.

Kemal's private kingdom was a triumph of ice-cool minimalism. The chocolate-brown leather chairs and sofas would be from Italy, Lizzie guessed, and the rest of the furniture looked as if it might have come from Scandinavia. Huge rugs in neutral shades provided pools of contrast on a stark white marble floor, and on the pure white walls just two large, colourful modern paintings were expertly displayed.

The totally unexpected decor, and the realisation that it must reflect Kemal's inner self, fascinated Lizzie. Like him, this apartment was powerful and controlled, with a touch of the audacious—the perfect mix in any man.

Laying her down on the bed, Kemal stretched his length against her so that Lizzie felt at once extremely dainty by comparison. She started to tremble when he lightly ran the fingertips of one hand very slowly down from her slightly parted lips to the apex of her thighs, and then she gasped, wanting more…wanting much, much more.

'Not yet,' he whispered reluctantly, kissing her lips with frustrating restraint.

But his mouth was a channel from which pleasure poured, and her limbs were running with molten honey. Lizzie groaned with impatience as she shamelessly angled herself towards him.

The cool and oh, so contained Ms Lizzie Palmer was a volcano waiting to erupt, Kemal realised. That vacancy on his staff for a mistress had just been filled.

And now he would take the greatest pleasure in spinning everything out, taking even longer than he had planned over her seduction. She was beautiful, and ripe like the figs they had both enjoyed. She needed release and he would give it to her—but her defiance must be curbed. Everything would happen at a time of his own choosing. He would tease and tantalise until she was in a realm beyond reason. He was a master of the art, and she would be a most responsive pupil.

He watched in fascination as Lizzie cupped her breasts, to taunt him with the sight of her extended nipples. It was as if she was seeking his approval—and he did approve, Kemal allowed with a groan of contentment. Dipping his head to suckle, he felt her arch towards him, and, reaching down, he cupped her buttocks with his hand, spreading his fingers and using his thumb to caress her—just enough. It pleased him to hear her cry out—a short, sharp cry of need. But he would never accede to her will in such matters, and instead pinned her beneath him, holding her still while he pleasured her at his own pace.

'You're very greedy,' he observed softly with satisfaction. 'But greedy must wait.'

He smiled again, hearing her small cry of disappointment. And, looking down, he saw that her nipples were pink and taut, stretching out to him as if begging for his attention. With a growl of triumph he rasped the rough stubble of his chin across the tender peaks, and revelled in the sound of her whimpers of desire.

Kemal recognised that he was just as hungry as Lizzie, but he was eager to find out just how high he could push her capacity for pleasure. And that quest, he realised with surprise, was even more important to him right now than his own pleasure.

Reaching down, he eased her thighs apart and gently parted her swollen lips with one skilled and searching finger.

'Oh, Kemal, please—'

'Not yet,' he murmured, pretending regret. He held her firm as she bucked beneath him. 'You must stay very still,' he instructed softly, whispering against her lips.

'I will—I promise…anything,' Lizzie cried hoarsely. 'But don't make me wait too long.'

'You will wait as long as I think is necessary,' Kemal said quietly. 'You must learn to pace yourself.'

'Will you teach me?' Lizzie challenged, trying to stop herself moving beneath him.

'I said still,' he reminded her. 'Or I won't touch you

at all. In fact,' he said, moving away, 'I don't think I will touch you more tonight—'

'What?' Lizzie lashed out at him furiously. 'Where do you think you're going? Don't you dare!' she warned, when he threatened to get off the bed.

Kemal whirled around. In that moment Lizzie saw the warrior he might have been centuries before, his face so harsh and fierce…but his eyes, she noticed as they held her glance, were still warm, still full of passion, and glinting now with a very potent mix of humour and desire.

'You drive me to the limits,' he confessed huskily.

'And my penalty is?' Lizzie demanded, holding his gaze.

'You will touch yourself,' he instructed her steadily. 'I think that would please me.'

'What?' Lizzie's eyes widened with surprise.

'You seem to think that we Turks have a monopoly on erotic practices; I don't want to disappoint you.'

'Brute!' Lizzie exclaimed, knowing he was teasing her. 'Monster!'

'Anything but, I can assure you,' Kemal said steadily. Seizing one of her hands, he slowly dragged it to his mouth, and, keeping his gaze locked on Lizzie's face, took each finger into his mouth and began to suckle her fingertips in turn until they turned pink.

Lizzie felt faint with pleasure and surprise when he brought her own hand down between her legs. It was so unexpected…forbidden, and so very, very good. Closing her eyes, she groaned as Kemal guided her. It was intensely erotic—the most erotic moment of her life.

She exceeded all his expectations, Kemal realised, relishing every nuance in Lizzie's expression as she climbed to a plateau so high even he hardly knew how she sustained her hold upon it without tumbling off. She had been so very cool, ice-cool, and now he watched as her face flushed pink with arousal. Only he could have guessed what lay beneath the frigid façade.

'Stop, stop... No, I mustn't—' she protested huskily, trying not to lose control; it seemed so very wrong.

'Why? Why mustn't you?' Kemal demanded softly, giving her all his attention again. And then he decided to tantalise her a little more, by holding her arm above her head and kissing her breasts, before finally transferring his kisses to bring her the release she craved.

She cried and moaned in his arms for ages afterwards, while he held her close, stroking her until at last she was calm. 'Didn't I tell you it would be good for you?' he murmured wryly when finally Lizzie grew quiet. And when she said nothing Kemal pulled back to look at her, and saw she was asleep.

'Lizzie...Lizzie...'

The voice came from far away, down a long, dark tunnel of sleep.

It wasn't an angry voice, or muffled, like her parents when they were locked in their den. No, Lizzie realised with surprise, it was Mrs McConnell from next door.

'Lizzie, dear, what are you doing?'

The little girl looked up, worried because she knew she was doing something wrong, but still eager to share her plans. Mrs McConnell was always kind to her, always smelled so good. 'I'm sorry, Mrs McConnell, but we don't have holly on our side of the fence. And yours has got such lovely bright red berries.'

'Look at your hands.' Mary McConnell made a sound of concern as she bent low to take hold of two grubby fists in her own workworn hands. 'You're all scratched and bleeding, Lizzie. No need to ask whether your mother has any antiseptic, I suppose?'

'She has magic mushrooms. Maybe those—'

'Heaven protect you, child!' Mary McConnell exclaimed with alarm.

And then later, when they were in the food-scented haven of Mrs McConnell's kitchen, she asked, 'And what were you going to do with my holly, Lizzie?'

'I wanted it for Christmas,' Lizzie explained, forcing in a last bite of mince pie even before she had swallowed the first. 'I saw your decorations and so I knew it must be time—'

'No need to hurry, Lizzie,' Mrs McConnell said, in that soft voice of hers, which made Lizzie painfully aware of how hungry she was, and how hard she must try not to seem so. 'I'll send you home with a batch of mince pies, and then you can share them with your brother and your parents—when they wake up,' she added under her breath.

She wasn't supposed to have heard that, Lizzie realised, watching Mrs McConnell bite her lip to stop the flow of words. Now she had swallowed down the last delicious crumb, Lizzie's attention was drawn back to the kitchen table, loaded with freshly baked pies. 'Couldn't I stay here with you for Christmas, Mrs McConnell?' she asked, already anticipating the refusal that was sure to come. 'The baby too... I could bring Hugo with me. Mum would never notice—'

'No, dear,' Mrs McConnell said softly. 'I'm afraid that's just not possible.'

'Please!'

Of course she hadn't begged, Lizzie recalled, tossing restlessly in the half-world between sleeping and wakefulness. She had just slipped down from the kitchen stool, placed her hand in Mrs McConnell's and, with the box of mince pies tucked safely beneath her arm, walked dutifully back with her kindly neighbour to her own house. But she had so wanted to stay with Mrs McConnell. She would have loved nothing better than to stay and help her put up the last of the decorations, finish the tree...

Lizzie groaned as she snapped her face away from the reflection of her younger self's pale, resigned face in the hall mirror at Mrs McConnell's home. It was like seeing someone else altogether—a stranger—someone she wanted to reach out to and help, but couldn't. She started thrashing about in angry frustration on the bed.

'Wake up, Lizzie…wake up.'

The low voice grew more insistent. A man's voice—one the child didn't recognise. But the woman Lizzie did.

'You've had a bad dream, Lizzie,' Kemal said, bringing her into his arms. 'But it's all over now. You're safe here with me,' he said, murmuring against her hair. 'You'll be all right now.'

Would she? Lizzie wondered, dashing the tears from her eyes. Would she ever be all right?

CHAPTER NINE

BACK in her own fabulous suite of rooms at the palace, Lizzie sat on the bed with her head in her hands. Had she lost every semblance of self-respect and control? No wonder the nightmares had returned. She had allowed herself to be seduced by a cold-blooded man who meant nothing but harm to her family. And Hugo *was* her family—her only family; Hugo, her brother—had she forgotten him?

And she hadn't even been properly seduced. A contemptuous sob escaped Lizzie's lips at she remembered her behaviour. She was a freak, a bumbling, unsophisticated idiot where sex was concerned. And she had let Kemal humiliate her. How could she have allowed it to happen?

Kemal Volkan. She need search for no other answer. A wave of panic rose in Lizzie's chest as she thought about him. Just the image of his face in her mind sent shock waves racing through her. Kemal had stirred fires she had never guessed might be inside her. But they were destructive fires. She came. He saw. He conquered. Some stand she'd made! And when she'd finally woken up this morning, after suffering one of her worst nightmares for years, he'd already left her. Too much trouble for too little return, she suspected.

Lizzie buried her head in her hands, wondering

what she might have called out during her nightmare. She knew that by revealing the demons she lived with to Kemal she had made herself look like a victim— something she had always refused to be.

Kemal Volkan was one of nature's predators, and she had rolled over for him in every way that a woman could roll over for a man. What an outstanding victory! She would have to be sure to try those tactics in court some day. She had certainly learned some bitter lessons in Istanbul, Lizzie reflected. And Hugo still wasn't home. But she would get him home for Christmas, whatever it took. Firming her lips, she went to find her phone.

For once the lawyer she had found in Istanbul, Sami Gulsan, answered immediately. He advised Lizzie to sit tight, stay calm and do nothing other than leave her phone on until she heard from him again. The situation had been dealt with, he said reassuringly. But Lizzie refused to be reassured. It was about time someone knew exactly what kind of man Kemal Volkan was.

She was forced to cut the conversation short when she heard the door open.

'Kemal!' Springing up, Lizzie backed away instinctively. There was a look on his face that frightened her.

'Don't end your call on my account,' he said.

Putting the phone down on the table beside her, Lizzie stood tensely—waiting.

Kemal stopped a few feet away from her and Lizzie saw that he had a sheet of paper tightly clutched in his hand; so tight, in fact, his knuckles had turned white.

'What's that?' Lizzie said.

'Honour,' Kemal told her. 'A shining example of your idea of honour.'

Lizzie flinched as he flung the paper at her feet. Swooping down, she picked it up and read quickly, backing away at the same time to put some urgently needed space between them. It was a hand-delivered document written in English from Lizzie's lawyer, Sami Gulsan, questioning Kemal about her illegal imprisonment. Gulsan demanded her immediate release, and added that a claim for damages would shortly follow.

'There is nothing in this letter that I am ashamed of,' Lizzie said, looking up. 'Far from impugning my honour, it shows yours in a poor light, don't you think?'

'Did you really imagine you could make money out of this situation?' Kemal demanded contemptuously, when she had finished.

'Money?' Lizzie exclaimed. 'What are you talking about?'

'If it wasn't the money, then what—what made you stoop to this?' Kemal said icily.

'It has nothing to do with money,' Lizzie said. 'I'm perfectly within my rights to consult a lawyer if I choose—'

'Your rights!' Kemal turned away, as if he couldn't bear to look at her a moment longer.

'I consulted a lawyer regarding my position,' Lizzie

said, addressing his back. 'So what? Are you telling me you wouldn't have done the same?'

'I might have chosen my lawyer with a little more care,' Kemal replied, turning back to face her again. 'I might have exercised diplomacy, for instance.'

'What do you mean?'

'Just this,' he bit out. 'You went behind my back and consulted with a lawyer who represents my strongest competitor.'

'But how could I know?'

'That's the point,' he said icily. 'You don't know anything, but you continue to meddle in things you know nothing about. What do you think Gulsan will do with this information? He's no friend of mine. Another thing you don't know is that as one of the major creditors I was given first option to buy the company Hugo works for. Now Gulsan has pushed my competitors into submitting a counter-bid.'

'But I couldn't possibly have known that—'

'Fortunately,' Kemal continued, ignoring her, 'they were too late. My deal was too far down the line. But, had it not been, you could have spoiled it for me.'

Lizzie looked at Kemal, shaking her head slightly in bewilderment.

'Yes,' he said with satisfaction. 'In spite of your best efforts, I agreed terms some time earlier.'

'Agreed terms?' Lizzie repeated in a dry voice. She wanted to stop up her ears. She wanted to stop him speaking. But he went on relentlessly.

'I agreed terms to buy the company Hugo was

working for out of receivership the morning after you arrived.'

'You...did...what?' Lizzie stared at him open-mouthed. Ice streamed through her veins and into her heart as she realised everything this information meant to her.

'That meeting I had to postpone when I came back to the palace to see you?' Kemal reminded her brusquely. 'Luckily I was able to hold it by conference phone. And just as well I did. But I had no idea until I received this letter from Gulsan that it was you who had betrayed me.'

Lizzie stared at him in disbelief, barely hearing his last words. 'Why didn't you tell me you had bought the company?' she asked hoarsely.

'I am not in the habit of discussing my business decisions with anyone. I make them; I execute them. It's that simple.'

Lizzie felt each of his statements as a physical blow. She couldn't believe anyone could be so callous. She had to be sure. 'You knew all along that the situation was resolved,' she said, 'and yet you allowed me to make a fool of myself. You used a situation you knew didn't exist any longer to force me to stay—'

'Force?' Kemal cut across her harshly. 'You were in no hurry to leave, as I remember.'

'You used me,' Lizzie accused him bitterly, 'and you abused my trust. What kind of person are you?' Her mind was in turmoil as Kemal went on listing her supposed offences. Finally, Lizzie could stand no more of it. 'How dare you accuse me of ruining your plans?

If you had told me the truth in the first place this would never have happened!'

'I am not in the habit of discussing my plans. My business is my affair.'

'And me?' Lizzie demanded tensely. 'What about me, Kemal? What about us?'

'Us?' he said, stiffening.

'Oh, I see,' Lizzie said bitterly, determined at all costs to maintain her composure. 'There is no *us*. There is only Kemal Volkan, *The Sultan*: the man who uses everyone for his own ends. You manipulated me, Kemal. You led me to think that you were as much a victim in all of this as my brother, when all the time you were controlling the situation. You seduced me—'

Kemal's contemptuous laugh, short and harsh, cut her off. 'You were eager to be seduced.'

Lizzie cheeks flared red and she grimaced with disbelief. 'Where is Hugo?' she demanded furiously. 'What have you done with him, Kemal? Tell me where he is,' she warned, 'or never mind calling a lawyer, I'm calling the police.'

'Oh, no, you're not,' he said, catching hold of her wrist as she went for her phone.

'Get off me!'

He ignored her.

'You disgust me!' Lizzie raged, trying to shake him off.

'That's not what you said last night,' Kemal reminded her roughly.

'You're contemptible! You made love to me, knowing how things were. I demand to see my brother.'

'And so you shall,' Kemal assured her in a low, fierce voice.

Lizzie whipped her face to one side so that she would not have to stare any longer into his wolf-grey eyes. 'Will I share Hugo's cell?' she challenged him derisively.

At once she felt Kemal tense, felt it in every tissue by which they were connected.

It was as if every inch of him was balled up, ready to spring to the defence of his honour, Kemal realised. There was not a single insult left for her to throw at him.

His grip on Lizzie's arm tightened as he brought her closer still, but rather than keeping her face averted as he expected, she snapped around to blaze a look of defiance straight into his eyes. She was more than a match for any man. For him?

Kemal wasn't sure if that thought pleased him or not, he was still too busy deflecting her insults.

'Hugo isn't in a cell,' he said. 'He has never been in a cell—he was in a camp out in the wilds, where my new factory is being set up, yes. But now, as you never allow me to forget, it's almost Christmas, so he's due to land with his workmates at Heathrow round about—now.' As he released her to check his watch, Lizzie lurched back and away from him.

'You bastard!'

Kemal stared at her in shock.

'You knew all along that my brother was in no danger!'

'Danger! What kind of man do you take me for?'

'The worst—the very worst,' Lizzie assured him.

'Then why are you still here?'

Lizzie stared at him, speechless with disbelief. 'Because you kept me here.'

'I have never tried to stop you leaving,' Kemal said. 'Do you want to go so badly?'

'Damn right!' Lizzie agreed. 'And I want transport out of here—'

'No problem!' Kemal cut across her with an angry gesture. 'My private jet is standing on the tarmac in Istanbul. Why don't you use that?'

As the executive jet soared high above Istanbul, Lizzie felt her emotions might overwhelm her. It was a battle to keep the expression on her face neutral for the sake of the flight attendants.

Her time in Turkey had been an absolute disaster. Instead of returning home with her mission successfully accomplished, she was returning home as the villain of the piece. And her brief affair with Kemal Volkan had left a wound so deep she knew it would never heal.

Kemal was right about one thing, Lizzie conceded wryly. She would never forget this Christmas. *And what about Christmas Day?* She still felt numb. Maybe it would be better to sleep through it—let this one be the Christmas she never had.

'Hugo? Can you hear me?' Kemal demanded. 'Isn't it about time you got yourself a decent mobile phone?'

'Kemal! Is that you? How can I help you?'

'This isn't about business. It's personal,' Kemal said tersely.

'Personal?'

Kemal heard the wariness in Hugo's voice in that one word, but he had to press on. 'It's not about you,' he said. 'It's your sister.'

'Lizzie?'

Hugo's anxiety proved how much he loved his sister, Kemal realised. 'Yes, Lizzie,' he said.

'What do you want to know?'

'She's been here with me in Istanbul...'

'I should have known she would jump on the next flight,' Hugo said. 'I should never have called her. The line was so bad—'

'It's too late to worry about that now,' Kemal said, cutting across him. 'I couldn't get hold of you at the camp, otherwise we could have talked sooner—I could have reassured you. If the weather hadn't been so bad, and communications so poor, I would have let you know that she was here. But she's OK, Hugo. She's on her way back to England right now in my jet. Will you be there?'

'Yeah—sure. But I'm not at the flat.'

'I gathered that,' Kemal said, hearing a girl in the background. 'Can you go somewhere private to talk?'

'It's important, I assume?'

Kemal heard the subtle change in his voice. 'Yes, it's important,' he said.

'Give me a minute.'

Kemal pulled the receiver away from his ear and waited until Hugo came back on the line. 'I'm afraid

I have to talk to you about your past,' he said. 'And I need answers, Hugo.'

'OK,' Hugo said, but Kemal sensed his reluctance.

'I'd like to start with your childhood,' he said.

'Not much to tell,' Hugo said evasively. 'What do you want to know?'

How to get the most out of him? Why should Hugo put the family skeletons on show for him? Kemal wondered, his mind racing. 'Tell me about Christmas,' he said, choosing the direct approach.

'Any bar will do,' the younger man said flippantly.

'Hugo, this is serious,' Kemal said quietly. 'Why does Christmas mean so much to Lizzie?'

'Does it?'

'Don't stonewall me, Hugo,' Kemal warned. 'Why does she wear those damned glasses? Why does she have nightmares? Why does she call out in her sleep? What happened to her, Hugo?'

'I'm sorry, Kemal, I don't want to talk about it.'

Kemal forced himself to wait. He had to give him space. 'Did you often see Lizzie upset when you were younger?' he said at last. 'Did she ever tell you why she was crying?' There was a long silence, and every moment he expected Hugo to cut the line. But he didn't.

'No one cries when it's really bad, do they?' Hugo said at last. 'They just hold it all in.'

Kemal sat back, and then he said carefully, 'Can you tell me about it, Hugo?'

'Lizzie didn't tell you?'

'No,' Kemal admitted.

'Then I can't. Sorry,' Hugo said gruffly.

Kemal let the silence hang. The line rang with silent tears and he had no wish to trample on Hugo's memories. 'I need this information, Hugo' he said at last, 'for Lizzie's sake. She can't go on like this. You must know that.'

For a few seconds that seemed a lot longer there was nothing. And then: 'Lizzie found our parents dead,' Hugo said, talking in a fast monotone. 'There was incense everywhere in the house. It nearly choked her—nearly choked me. I was only nine. I was hiding in my bedroom with the window open. When I heard Lizzie scream I ran out. She was downstairs, looking through the glass door that led into the kitchen— She'd been bringing stuff in for Christmas decorations: holly, red berries. She did it every year—it was sort of a tradition—'

'Stop there,' Kemal interjected softly. 'Go slowly, Hugo. I need to understand.'

'They OD'd,' Hugo told him. 'Lizzie was standing outside the glass door, looking in at Mum and Dad slumped dead on the floor.'

'And she's worn glasses since then?'

'How did you know that?'

'It's not important,' Kemal said. 'She doesn't wear them any more.'

'Does that help?' Hugo said, clearly uncomfortable that he had betrayed some long held secret.

'It helps a lot,' Kemal assured him. 'And now I want you to forget about business for a while, Hugo. I need you to do something else for me.'

* * *

The flat seemed smaller than Lizzie had remembered, and it was cold—very cold. She tried to get hold of Hugo on the phone the moment she got in, but he was staying round at a friend's. A girlfriend's, Lizzie guessed, judging by the muffled giggles in the background.

'Thank God you're safe!' she exclaimed with relief.

'Safe?' Hugo demanded. 'The only danger here is a couple of girls from uni, and I seem to be coping!'

'Er, thank you, Hugo. That's far too much information,' Lizzie said, dragging her coat a little closer. 'Don't you ever put the heat on at the flat?'

'When I'm there.'

'OK, so tomorrow's Christmas Eve. Will I see you?'

'I have to go on somewhere from here,' Hugo said. 'What about if I come round to the flat tomorrow morning?'

'I promised to go into Chambers in the morning,' Lizzie said, thinking out loud, 'and then I expect there will be drinks, Christmas lunch—that sort of thing—'

'I could come round really early in the morning?' Hugo offered.

Lizzie smiled, knowing that was quite some sacrifice. 'Thanks, Hugo. I'd appreciate it. I want to talk to you about Istanbul.'

'No problem. Look, I'm a bit tied up right now...'

I bet you are, Lizzie thought. Kemal was right again—her kid brother was all grown up.

Pacing around the small flat, Lizzie tried hard not to think about Kemal. His chauffeur had taken her to the airport. There had been no sign of anyone else from the palace. Kemal had made his feelings towards her crystal-clear before they parted, so why should she have expected things to be different?

But for some reason a stubborn kernel of hope kept on refusing to give up—even though she knew it could never have worked out between them. They were like twin tornados, cancelling each other out. They were both in the wrong, both too passionate, too intense to give an inch. It was time to get on with the rest of her life, Lizzie told herself, and file *The Sultan* away, along with her other memories.

Flicking open the well-used diary on her desk, Lizzie saw that, just as she had told Hugo, Christmas Eve was going to be hectic. There would be barely enough time to dash round the shops to try and gather up some last-minute seasonal goodies. She looked around the cold, modern flat. She would have to make time. It was all so drab. Wandering across to the window, she pushed the curtain aside and looked out. Under the street lamp she could see the holly bush flourishing beneath her window. It was covered in red berries.

Lizzie woke early on Christmas Eve morning. Bouncing out of bed, she hurried about the flat, barefoot in her pyjamas. Munching toast, and slurping coffee out of her oversized mug, she backed into the tiny sitting room to check over the simple Christmas arrangements she had fashioned late the previous night.

But her gaze flew instinctively to the telephone. Her

heart gave a lonely thud. There was no winking light. No message. Stuffing the last piece of toast in her mouth, she crossed over to her desk and logged on to her computer to check her e-mails. Nothing. There was nothing—no voicemail, no text, no recorded message—nothing.

'So, that's it,' she informed the empty room.

Unless…

All she had to lose was her pride, Lizzie thought, remembering the business card Kemal had insisted she keep. She still had his private number…

For a moment Lizzie was surprised to hear a woman's voice. Then she realised that of course Kemal would have a PA. She wished she hadn't made the call. Kemal might have said to call him if she needed help—but the only help she needed was in getting over him! Giving a false name to the woman, Lizzie said she worked for one of the Financials, and then casually dropped into the conversation the name of the company Hugo had been working for.

It was now part of the Volkan group, the woman said economically, before asking if there was anything else she could help Lizzie with.

'No. No, nothing else, thank you,' Lizzie said, cutting the line.

Hugo's visit lasted about five minutes. He was clearly in a hurry to get somewhere else, Lizzie realised when he joined her for some coffee. Any detailed chat about Istanbul would have to wait—not enough time now, he explained. But enough time to request a new mobile phone for Christmas, Lizzie thought with a wry smile. Typical brother!

And then later in the day she just couldn't say no to her colleagues when they insisted she join them for Christmas lunch. They all arrived together at the luxury hotel in a fleet of taxis, but, quite suddenly, she was on her own. How could seven people simply melt away? Lizzie wondered, looking with bemusement around the brilliantly lit entrance foyer.

She tensed as the elevator doors slid open. But in spite of the frisson that tracked down her spine it was just a young mother, laughing as she struggled to manage two excited children and the pile of presents in her arms. Lizzie looked away quickly, but then, drawn to the sound of happy laughter again, she turned back and smiled at the family.

It was then Kemal saw her.

After speaking to Hugo he had to come and find her. He couldn't allow them to part on a wave of acrimony and recriminations. His business was under control—always had been, in spite of Lizzie Palmer's best endeavours. But his personal life was not under control, Kemal realised as his heart lurched at the sight of Lizzie.

She was even more beautiful than he remembered. But now she was relaxed and smiling, and he had failed there. He had never succeeded in bringing Lizzie that type of uncomplicated happiness, because they had spent all their time fighting—almost all their time, he amended with a faint smile. But they only fought because no one had ever stood up to him as she did, and he had come to admire her for that. That was why he had come to London. He could not draw a line beneath their relationship yet.

CHAPTER TEN

'KEMAL!'

Lizzie froze when she spotted him. In spite of everything that had happened, when he walked towards her she thought she might faint.

'Lizzie.'

He stopped a few feet away, giving her that half-smile that always knocked her off balance. And even after despatching her from Turkey with all speed, his voice was low, even intimate, as if they were lovers.

'Kemal,' Lizzie said coolly, regrouping fast. He was so self-possessed, so confident of his reception. The same very masculine humour shaped his gaze. She held out her hand to him politely. 'You're the last person I expected to see.'

Did she seriously expect him to shake her hand? Kemal thought, ignoring it as he moved to kiss her on both cheeks, continental-style. Her face was ice-cold, he noticed, but she still trembled at his touch.

'I'm glad to see you,' he said with matching formality. 'I know how busy you must be so close to Christmas—'

'How did you know I would be here?' Lizzie said. 'This isn't a coincidence, is it, Kemal?'

'I followed you,' he said casually. 'And your colleagues were most helpful.'

'My colleagues told you—'

'They're not at fault,' he cut in. 'I wanted to find you. But, look, if I'm keeping you…'

For a moment she was so shocked she couldn't speak, and she saw Kemal's gaze turn cool.

'I mustn't keep you from your friends,' he said, moving as if to go.

'No. Wait.' Self-consciously Lizzie drew her hand back from touching him. 'We could have a drink first, maybe?'

'Won't your friends be waiting for you in the restaurant?'

'Perhaps, but…'

'But?' he demanded quizzically.

'For old times' sake?' Lizzie suggested, finding she was unable to meet his gaze.

'Have we known each other that long?' he said, affecting a weary tone, but as she looked up she saw the spark of humour in his eyes.

'It feels like it sometimes,' Lizzie admitted, smiling a little 'Aren't you going to eat lunch somewhere?'

'Perhaps. I hadn't thought about it, to be honest.'

'Why don't you join us?' Lizzie suggested on impulse. It would be a safe environment inside the restaurant, with her colleagues around to chaperone them. There was no reason for her to part from Kemal on bad terms.

'I don't want to intrude,' he said. 'And afterwards there'll be things you want to do. You'll be too busy—'

'Oh, no—that's fine,' Lizzie heard herself say. 'There's loads of time.'

She looked up at him. She didn't want him to go. Not yet.

She didn't want him to leave. It was a shock, and a pleasant one, Kemal discovered. He took every woman on earth for granted, but not Lizzie—never Lizzie.

'OK, so I give in,' he said softly.

Lizzie flushed red. The tone of his voice was everything she had ever hoped for—more than she could possibly have expected. She loved everything about him, she realised as Kemal linked her arm through his: the power radiating from him, his amazing build, his intoxicating scent, the thick black hair that always escaped so wilfully from his careful grooming. She even loved the piercing gaze that could strip her to the core in an instant. But most of all she loved the harsh mouth that had kissed her so very thoroughly, and that even now was tugging up in a smile.

She was quite sure that every one of her X-rated thoughts was printed in large type across her forehead. But this was nothing more than two people parting as friends, she reminded herself. It was the civilised way to behave.

'Oh, that's a shame,' Kemal murmured, looking round the dining room. 'Your friends seem to have gone. They must have decided to move on.'

'But where—'

'Does it matter? We can eat here—unless, of course,

you want to try and find them?' Kemal offered, un-linking her arm and standing back.

'No,' Lizzie said quickly, 'that's fine. I'm quite hun-gry now, aren't you?'

'Very,' Kemal agreed, smiling into her eyes.

Was the secluded table at Kemal's request? Or was the *maître d'* particularly sensitive to his client's re-quirements? Lizzie wondered, as she handed over her coat. She was becoming neurotic, she decided. Glancing in the mirror, she wished there'd been time to change. Dressed all in black for work, she looked as pale as a wraith. Whereas Kemal dressed in black—Italian tailoring, she guessed—seemed more vibrant than ever. Black looked fabulous against his tan.

As he held the chair for her Lizzie felt Kemal's forcefield pulsing behind her. And when he settled himself across the table and she glimpsed the hard, bronzed torso beneath his open-necked shirt she could taste his warmth on her tongue again, feel the silky texture of his hard, muscled frame beneath her hands.

Drawing a deep breath, Lizzie closed her eyes, rev-elling in the warm, musky man scent, laced with san-dalwood. Suddenly aware that he was staring at her, she accepted the menu from a waiter with relief, and quickly buried her head in it. But she had chosen to wear the fragile silk and lace underwear Kemal had bought for her in Istanbul beneath the severely cut suit. And she felt as if he knew. If ever there had been an occasion for wearing blue serge gym knickers, this was it!

'Don't I owe you some money?' she said quickly, to distract herself, looking up.

'For what?' Kemal asked, leaning back comfortably in his chair.

'For the clothes you bought for me while I was in Istanbul.'

'It was nothing—just some underwear, wasn't it?'

He *did* know! And in case he was in any doubt, her cheeks were on fire.

'Won't you accept it as a gift?'

'I don't accept gifts from anyone.'

'That's a pity.'

'You'll send me the bill?' she pressed.

'I hear the food is very good here, and the waiter is waiting for our order,' Kemal pointed out. 'Won't you choose something?'

'Don't change the subject,' Lizzie warned. 'You have to give in.'

'Do I?' he murmured. 'Perhaps later.' And then he turned to concentrate on his own menu.

Lizzie was so flustered she asked for the first thing that came into her head. And very soon after that the hors d'oeuvres arrived.

'Just tell me how much I owe you,' Lizzie said again.

'I'll let you know when I've worked it out,' Kemal said. 'But now we eat.' He dipped an asparagus spear into thick, buttery sauce. 'This has come all the way from Peru, just for our enjoyment,' he pointed out, offering one to Lizzie. 'It would be churlish of us to let it go to waste.'

Lizzie drew the succulent stalk slowly into her mouth, trying not to look at Kemal. But her face was burning beneath his steady gaze.

'Would you like to taste the wine, sir? Sir...?'

'No. Thank you,' Kemal said politely, wiping his lips on a large linen napkin. 'I'm afraid we have been called away—some urgent business.'

'I quite understand, sir.'

Lizzie sincerely hoped he didn't. But then she was on her feet, her hand in Kemal's. 'My coat!' she exclaimed, when they were almost at the door.

'Someone will return it,' Kemal said, pulling her behind him.

Lizzie pressed back against her own side of the elevator. Kemal was leaning against his. They didn't speak. They didn't need to. The space in between them was a forcefield crackling with energy and intention. Maybe she was mistaken, Lizzie thought wildly. Maybe she was going crazy—maybe her imagination was running away with her. Yes, that must be it, she decided. Kemal was so calm—too calm.

'We're here,' he said at last, standing aside to let Lizzie pass him when the lift doors opened.

The same silent retainers she had seen in Turkey opened double doors for them, and Lizzie walked past them into a sitting room the size of a small ballroom. The cream carpet was so thick it felt like a mattress, and the air was filled with the subtle scent of roses.

'Do you like them?' Kemal asked conversationally, as he waited for the servants to leave.

'I love roses,' Lizzie admitted, touching one of the

velvet petals with her fingertip. 'Especially cream roses. They are so delicate.'

'I had them flown in especially for you.'

'For me?' Lizzie said incredulously, looking up. 'Why?'

'You don't know?'

'Should I?' Lizzie said, turning to him.

'You are without question the most surprising woman I have ever met.'

'Good surprise or bad surprise?'

'That depends on the moment,' he said. 'Fortunately, I like a challenge.'

As the door closed on the last of the servants Kemal dragged her to him. Pushing her jacket off her shoulders, he turned impatiently to the tiny pearl buttons on her blouse.

Placing her palms firmly against the wall of his chest, Lizzie pushed weakly at him. 'Kemal…'

The word was little more than a sigh, but he stopped it with a kiss. 'We've talked enough,' he said at last, releasing her to watch her reaction as he moved to trace the swell of her breasts very lightly with his fingertips.

Lizzie's lips parted to drag in air as Kemal used the firm pads of his thumbs to chafe impatiently against her fine lawn blouse. She didn't want subtlety, or foreplay. They had explored that particularly frustrating activity to the limits.

Soon they were tearing the clothes off each other and flinging them aside, dropping them and kicking them away. And Kemal was lifting her, entering her

even as he lowered her down onto the nearest surface—which, fortunately for Lizzie, was a heavy sofa
that held her securely as Kemal moved above her,
thrusting deep.

They were greedy for each other. Ravenous. They
had waited too long, and Lizzie was every bit as demanding and as forceful as Kemal. Her hands grabbed
for him, her fingers mercilessly pushed and pressed,
forced him on while she cried out repeatedly, wondering if she could ever get enough of him filling her,
stretching her, pounding her. There was only one
thought in her mind now—one goal, one driving, overwhelming need. And finally, crying out to him in triumph, she brought him with her in a series of shud-
deringly intense, pleasure-filled waves.

They made love in every room in the plush apartment—every room and every corner—until finally
they made it to the bed. There was no conversation,
no need for speech; they could communicate very well
without it. And the longer they were together the more
perfectly they understood each other.

'Tomorrow is Christmas Day,' Kemal reminded
Lizzie, when she was drifting off to sleep at last in his
arms. 'Do you have any last-minute preparations to
make?'

Remembering Hugo's request for a new mobile
phone, Lizzie was instantly alert. Glancing at her
wristwatch, she exclaimed, 'Oh, my goodness!' And
then she swung out of bed. 'I'm so sorry—I feel terrible about this—but I have to make the shops before
they close. I promised Hugo—'

'I understand,' said Kemal, lazily stretching out his length on the bed. 'You'd better get going if you want to catch the shops.'

'Will I see you again?' Lizzie asked, pausing with her hand on the bathroom door.

'I'd say there's a very good chance,' Kemal promised, slanting her a grin. 'But hurry up, Lizzie, or you will be too late.'

CHAPTER ELEVEN

'HUGO? Yes, I'm here. Of course I'm at the flat. You're speaking to me, aren't you?' Lizzie said, breaking off to suck hard on the thumb she had just pricked with the last of the holly. 'You are still coming here for Christmas lunch tomorrow? Bring friends, if you want.'

There had been no call from Kemal since she had returned home from the shops, and Lizzie was beginning to wonder if there ever would be. He had surely made his own plans for Christmas Day by now. She didn't want to think about it, because each time she did the words 'used and abused' sprang to the forefront of her mind.

'You don't have to come, if you have other things to do,' she said, remembering that Hugo had a new girlfriend.

'Don't be an ass, Lizzie. Look, sis, I have to go— people are waiting for me.'

'OK, have a good time—but just be careful,' Lizzie said, smiling down the phone. She stared thoughtfully at the receiver after the line was cut. This was a new phase in her life. Hugo didn't need her as he'd used to. That was good. It was what she wanted for him.

And she was not going to spend Christmas feeling sorry for herself. She had a brilliant career, a fantastic brother, and was still throbbing from the attentions of her billionaire ex-lover—not bad for someone raised in a squat.

From then on Lizzie concentrated on the bare flat, making it look the best she could, with candles and a home-made holly wreath on the front door. She had kept plenty of baubles over the years, and she hung those on a small fake tree. There was no way she could get a real one up two flights of stairs, which was a pity, but it couldn't be helped. When she was finished, she went to her small refrigerator and took out a bottle of champagne. But champagne was for sharing...

She was just about to put it away again when Hugo burst in through the front door like a tornado.

'Where did you come from?' Lizzie exclaimed delightedly, hugging him.

'We have to go now. *Now!* Right this minute,' Hugo said, breaking away from her.

'Where are you talking about? Hang on—where are you taking me?' Lizzie asked, as he started dragging her towards the door.

'Don't ask so many questions.'

'I have to,' Lizzie pointed out. 'Do I change into a tracksuit? Are you taking me down the pub for a drink? Or is this an outing to one of your crazy parties? Just tell me if it is, so I can put something washable on—'

'We don't do that sort of thing now,' Hugo informed her, adopting a pious expression. 'I'm all grown up,' he added ironically. 'Or hadn't you noticed yet?'

'I've noticed,' Lizzie said dryly. 'So. What do I wear?'

'Something pretty,' Hugo said, giving it a moment's thought. 'Something really special.'

'All right,' Lizzie said. 'I'll see what I can do. Give me half an hour?'

'Five minutes.'

'Fifteen,' Lizzie bartered, flashing him a smile; Hugo's enthusiasm was infectious.

The Carlton Towers?' Lizzie grimaced when she heard Hugo instructing their taxi driver. 'Do we have to?'

'You can't change your mind now; it's already booked,' Hugo informed her grandly.

'You shouldn't have,' Lizzie said, squeezing his arm. 'A meal there costs a fortune. And look at you—you can't go like that. You've got glitter dust on your jacket. How did that happen?'

'It's nothing,' Hugo said, quickly brushing it off. 'There's glitter dust everywhere at this time of year.'

'I'll come with you to the Carlton Towers if you promise me we'll go halves,' Lizzie said, looking at her brother.

'You should have a treat for a change,' Hugo insisted. 'You've done so much for me. I only wish—'

'Hugo,' Lizzie broke in. She had never seen her brother in sentimental mode before. 'This Christmas is going to be really special,' she promised softly. 'Just knowing you're safe makes it special for me.'

'It had better be special,' he muttered tensely.

They were both locked in their own thoughts as the

taxi wove in and out of traffic on the busy streets. When it finally drew to a halt outside the brightly lit hotel Lizzie got cold feet, and hung back as Hugo leapt out.

'Come on,' he insisted, poking his head back into the taxi. 'We can't leave the doorman holding the door for ever.'

Lizzie shook her head. 'You don't understand,' she said. 'Kemal's staying here. I know you and I never got the chance to talk properly about Istanbul—but honestly, Hugo, he's the last person I want to see—'

'That's good to hear.'

'Kemal?' Suddenly Hugo was nowhere to be seen, and Kemal was standing in his place.

'Shall we move inside out of the cold?' he suggested, extending his hand to help her out.

'This is crazy,' Lizzie murmured with shock, sitting back in her seat.

'Crazy is one way of describing it,' Kemal conceded. Leaning into the taxi, he drew her out onto the pavement beside him.

'I'm with my brother...' she said faintly, already wondering if that was strictly true.

'You're with me now,' Kemal said.

'Basimin ustunde yereniz var.'
It was the same old gentleman who had welcomed her to *The Sultan's* palace, Lizzie remembered, smiling with pleasure when she saw him again. 'What did he say?' she asked Kemal as they walked past him into the presidential suite.

'You're sure you want a literal translation?'

'I'm prepared to risk it,' Lizzie said, laughing with happiness.

'OK,' Kemal agreed, trying not to smile. 'He said, you can even sit on my head if you want to! It means you pass the test; he really likes you. In fact, he will do pretty much anything for you.' As I will, he wanted to add, but it was too soon for that.

His old friend Mehmet had done him better service than he knew, Kemal thought, seeing Lizzie so happy. 'Have you eaten yet?' he asked, pausing at the door to the main room.

'I think Hugo has arranged dinner for me here at the hotel,' she said uncertainly.

'And so he has,' Kemal assured her softly. 'Happy Christmas, Lizzie.'

As the door swung open Lizzie gasped. The sumptuous room was lit by hundreds of candles, and there was a Yule log blazing in the modern open fireplace. There were even Christmas stockings hanging above it, bulging with gifts, Lizzie noticed, her eyes widening with amazement.

'And look at this,' Kemal said, drawing her attention to another part of the room.

As Lizzie turned she saw the Christmas tree. Stretching almost to the ceiling, it had the faintest tang of pine. 'It's real!' she exclaimed, moving straight towards it.

Hung with dozens of baubles in red and gold, and strung with glittering bands of tinsel, it was the best tree she had ever seen in all her life. 'You did all this for me?' she murmured incredulously, running her fingertips lightly over the supple spines.

He could not remember the last time he had felt so much emotion, Kemal realised. He wanted to do this every day for her—make it Christmas every day for Lizzie, for the rest of her life.

'And look!' Lizzie said, hands clasped with excitement as she moved away to examine something else. 'There's a sleigh, and Father Christmas with all the reindeer, and presents—' Whirling her hands around, she laughed delightedly. 'I just can't believe it.'

Her voice was breaking now, but her expression…her expression…

Kemal crossed the room in a couple of strides and brought her into his arms.

'You've got glitter dust on your jumper,' Lizzie accused softly, looking up into Kemal's eyes. 'Just like Hugo—' She stopped as understanding dawned.

'I wonder how that could be?' Kemal murmured dryly, staring down into her eyes as if he could never get enough of looking at her. 'Why don't you go back to that sleigh and see if Santa has brought anything for you?' he said at last.

'For me?'

'Go on,' Kemal chivvied her, pushing Lizzie in the direction of the sleigh full of presents he had arranged on a side table.

'Do you mean this?' Lizzie said, hugging a box wrapped in silver paper.

'Why don't you take a look and find out?' he said, walking over to her.

Lizzie's eyes widened as Kemal took the velvet case from her hand and removed the aquamarine and diamond pendant she had chosen for his 'niece'.

'For me? It's far too much,' she breathed.

'No, it isn't,' Kemal assured her as he fastened it around her neck. 'And it goes perfectly with your lovely dress.'

The dress he had bought for her in Istanbul, Lizzie realised, smoothing down the soft chiffon folds. When Hugo had said to choose something special it had been the first thing she thought of when she opened her wardrobe. Had Kemal planned this all along?

'I'm not sure what to believe any more,' she said out loud.

'Do you like it?' Kemal said, turning her round to face him.

'I love it,' Lizzie breathed against his lips.

'Then that's all that matters. But there is one condition.'

'What's that?'

'You have to stay with me. Always.'

She wanted to, Lizzie thought, fingering the fabulous jewel on her neck. She wanted nothing more in all the world than to be with Kemal. But she was too independent to make a very good mistress, and there were too many ghosts in her past...

'I know, Lizzie,' Kemal murmured, tipping up her chin. 'I know all about the past.'

'You know?' Lizzie repeated softly, seeing understanding in his eyes.

'Hugo told me—don't be angry with him,' Kemal

said quickly, holding her a little way in front of him. 'I asked the questions. I made him answer.' With a sigh he brought her close when she started to pull away. 'It's over,' he whispered fiercely. 'The nightmares are over, Lizzie.'

Kemal's heart ached for her when she looked up at him. There was so much hope in her eyes. 'I promise you, they're over,' he said steadily.

When he released her, Lizzie looked around at everything Kemal had done for her...the candles, the Yule log blazing, every type of delicious food she could think of laid out on the table, champagne chilling in an ice bucket. And there were crackers, and chocolates, and candied fruit for nibbling...

'So, you and Hugo...'

'Hugo played a critical role in my plan,' Kemal assured her, giving credit where it was due. 'Without Hugo I could never have got all this done in time— What?' he asked, seeing the expression on Lizzie's face.

'But where *is* Hugo?' Lizzie exclaimed anxiously. 'How will he spend Christmas if I'm here with you?'

Kemal's lips tugged up in a wry smile.

'I know what you're thinking,' Lizzie said, putting her hand on his chest as if that could stop his thoughts. 'You think he's far too old for me to be worrying about him.'

'I think you'll always worry about each other,' Kemal said. 'You are brother and sister, after all. But you can stop worrying now,' he said, dipping his head so he could look directly into Lizzie's eyes. 'I've invited Hugo and his new girlfriend to join us for lunch tomorrow—if that suits you?' But he could already see that it did. Lizzie's face was radiant.

'You've thought of everything,' she said.

'I hope so,' Kemal agreed. 'What about looking on the tree for something now?'

'Another present?' Lizzie exclaimed. 'I can't—'

'Why not?' Kemal demanded softly.

'Because your gift is back at the flat.' She had intended to send it to him—a small silver fruit knife to remind them both of the famous figs.

'There will be time for you to get that later—when you return to the flat to pack up your things,' Kemal pointed out.

'Pack up my things?'

'I'm sure there will be some things you want when you come to live with me.'

'You're very confident.'

'Isn't that what you like about me?' Kemal said softly.

'But I can't be your mistress,' Lizzie said, as Kemal started backing her towards a convenient sofa.

'I realised some time ago that having Lizzie Palmer as my short-term mistress would never work,' he admitted wryly, holding her still.

'What do you mean?' Lizzie said, feeling all her new-found happiness draining away.

'I have a much longer arrangement in mind.'

'What are you saying, Kemal?'

'I'm saying that I love you, Lizzie,' he murmured, dropping kisses on her lips, her eyelids and her brow.

'More deeply and more intensely than I would ever have believed possible. We are equal partners, you and I. You're so courageous, so tender, and I want to be the one to cherish you, to make you happy every day of your life. My life is nothing without you, Lizzie. I am nothing without you.'

Reaching up, Lizzie touched Kemal's lips with her fingertips. 'And I love you too,' she said softly. 'More than life itself.' And it was true, she realised. Whatever the consequences might be for her future.

By the time the backs of Lizzie's legs touched the sofa Kemal had freed the zip on her dress, and the catch on her bra, and was already pushing her tiny lace thong down over her hips.

'You are incredible,' she breathed, reaching for his belt.

'I certainly hope you think so,' Kemal agreed, dark humour flashing in his eyes.

And he was, Lizzie realised, closing her eyes as he sank deep inside her. She was hungry for him, starving, as if they had never been together in this way. And as if he was infected by her sense of urgency, Kemal went purposefully about his task—no teasing, no delays.

'More,' Lizzie cried out greedily, moments after he had tipped her over into fulfilment. 'I need more,' she exclaimed, wriggling out from under him. 'There,' she cried with satisfaction, straddling him and throwing her head back in ecstasy as he bucked beneath her to bring her satisfaction. 'I can never get enough of you,' she confessed, collapsing on him at last, only to feel that Kemal was still ready to give her more.

'I'm pleased to hear it,' he said. 'I've a pretty healthy appetite myself.'

And with that he swung her beneath him and took her again, firmly. 'But now we take it a little more slowly,' he said, controlling the pace.

'Anything you say,' Lizzie agreed, breathless from an overload of sensation.

Kemal paused momentarily to look at her. 'Is this the key to mastering you?' he demanded, slanting her a look.

'Could be,' Lizzie agreed wickedly, urging him on.

'Presents?' Kemal murmured later, when they were dozing together, exhausted.

'I've had my present,' Lizzie managed, too drugged by all their lovemaking to even form the words properly.

'More presents,' Kemal said, easing her off him. 'Remember the tree? Here,' he said, 'wrap yourself in this.' He tossed a silk throw from the sofa over to her.

'This is all very mysterious,' Lizzie said, as Kemal led her across to the Christmas tree.

'Is it?' Kemal asked, reaching for a small package.

'Shouldn't you get dressed first?' Lizzie murmured, hardly able to keep her hands off him.

'Not much point in my getting dressed, is there?' he pointed out. 'But I would like you to have this before we return to bed.'

'What is it?'

'Open it and see.'

Lizzie turned the small box over in her hand, and, flashing a glance at Kemal, responded to his nod of encouragement. Tearing off the paper, she opened the case and gasped. The aquamarine and diamond ring matching the teardrop pendant she was wearing flashed spectacularly from a nest of deep blue velvet.

'Would you like to put it on?' Kemal said.

'Are you serious?'

Taking it from her, Kemal placed it on the third finger of her left hand. 'I'm extremely serious,' he said, staring deep into Lizzie's eyes. 'In fact, I've never been more serious in my life. I want to marry you, Lizzie Palmer. There's no one else on earth I want to be my wife and bear my children. Will you marry me?' he asked. There was an edge of tension in his voice as he waited for her answer. 'Will you agree to become my wife?'

'If you will be my husband,' Lizzie challenged softly, holding her face up for his kiss.

'Let battle commence,' Kemal murmured wryly. 'Or in this case, let it continue for ever.'

And then he kissed her.

Silhouette Desire

Don't miss
DAKOTA FORTUNES,
**a six-book continuing series following
the Fortune family of South Dakota—
oil is in their blood and privilege
is their birthright.**

This series kicks off with
USA TODAY **bestselling author**
PEGGY MORELAND'S
Merger of Fortunes
(SD #1771)
this January.

In February, expect MORE
from

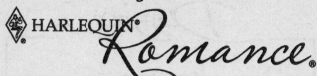

as it increases to six titles per month.

What's to come...

Rancher and Protector

Part of the
Western Weddings
miniseries

BY JUDY CHRISTENBERRY

The Boss's
Pregnancy Proposal

BY RAYE MORGAN

Don't miss February's
incredible line up of authors!

nocturne™

JEWEL SMITH HAS LOST THE MOST IMPORTANT PART OF HER BEING...

Her ability to shape-shift into a wolf. On the run now from the dangerous mobster who destroyed her special gift, Jewel faces even deadlier stakes. Her urge to shift awakens burning carnal desires, forcing Jewel to put everything on the line.

CRY OF THE WOLF

KAREN WHIDDON

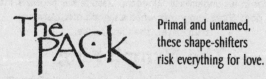

Primal and untamed, these shape-shifters risk everything for love.

SNCWJ07

REQUEST YOUR
FREE BOOKS!

2 FREE NOVELS
FROM THE ROMANCE/SUSPENSE
COLLECTION PLUS 2 FREE GIFTS!

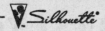

SPECIAL EDITION™

Silhouette Special Edition brings you a
heartwarming new story from the *New York Times*
bestselling author of *McKettrick's Choice*

LINDA LAEL MILLER

Sierra's Homecoming

Sierra's Homecoming
follows the parallel lives
of two McKettrick women,
living their lives in the
same house but
generations apart,
each with a special son
and an unlikely new
romance.

December 2006